MY
DARLING
DUKE

MY
DARLING
DUKE

STACY REID

Entangled Publishing, LLC
2614 South Timberline Road
Suite 105, PMB 159
Fort Collins, CO 80525
rights@entangledpublishing.com

Amara is an imprint of Entangled Publishing, LLC.

Edited by Stacy Abrams
Cover design by Erin Dameron-Hill, EDH Graphics
Cover art by VJ Dunraven/PeriodImages.com
and Shama/123rf.com
Interior design by Toni Kerr

MMP ISBN 978-1-64063-745-0
ebook ISBN 978-1-64063-746-7

Manufactured in the United States of America

First Edition January 2020

AMARA

ALSO BY STACY REID

Du'Sean, always and forever.

CHAPTER ONE

Brampton Manor
Hertfordshire

"We will have to be wicked, improper, and terribly scandalous."

Those words fell trembling from the lips of Lady Maryann Fitzwilliam, a young lady who wouldn't know what it meant to be scandalous if it slapped her across the face at the crest of each dawn.

It was a concept wholly improbable to the Honourable Katherine Iphigenia Danvers—Kitty to her friends and family—but nevertheless she felt effortlessly captivated. Or perhaps the sinful plan burning within her heart—the one she had prayed for, asking for a sign—was being validated.

It has to be. Ladies who were regulated to the status of wallflowers and spinsters were never wicked... and most assuredly *never* terribly scandalous.

"Wicked!" all four other young ladies present at their intrepid meeting chorused.

There was a breathless pause, the only sound in the drawing room the strains of the orchestra filtering through the closed doors as they played from the grand ballroom several doors away.

"Yes," replied Maryann empathically, her gaze piercing her audience with its bright resolve. She stood and sauntered to the center of the room, the hem of her elegantly draped icy blue gown swishing over the Aubusson carpet. How delightful Maryann appeared this evening, yet Kitty knew she had not yet been asked to the dance floor.

Maryann folded her arms beneath her bosom and captured all their attention with a steely gaze. "I am not content with my lot. I cannot believe *any* of you is happy with your situation. We must be daring and take what we need instead of waiting, wasting away on the shelves our family and society have placed us on. We are all over two and twenty, we're not getting any younger, and our prospects grow dimmer each year. What have we to lose?"

"I daresay you may be correct, Maryann," chimed in Lady Ophelia Darby, another member of their society, jokingly named the Sinful Wallflowers. Only they hadn't done anything sinful, except for the time they had emptied a bottle of Ophelia's father's finest whiskey among them, giggling and hiccupping like loons in the night. Ophelia was their most illustrious member, being the daughter of a marquess, albeit without a dowry. Her deep golden-brown eyes were filled with trepidation—and a glimmer of excitement, if Kitty was not mistaken.

"I've been out since I was eighteen, and each season is growing more painful than the last," Ophelia said.

There were several nods, which seemingly granted Maryann more courage, for her shoulders squared, a sparkle lit in her hazel eyes, and determination settled across every line of her willowy frame. "We *all* want to experience something other than the humdrum that is our lives."

More enthusiastic nods followed.

"We all want families," continued Maryann. "Don't

we? Or even just a moment where we are more than what society tells us to be?"

There was another aching, breathless pause as all six members of their private club sat on the edge of their padded chairs, a charged excitement and the sense of something different happening at tonight's impromptu meeting enveloping the room.

"We want love," murmured Miss Charlotte Nelson, a flush rising in her cheeks. Everyone knew she was painfully, desperately in love with the Marquess of Sands, and he had not deigned to notice her.

They were all overlooked, of course. Kitty and her friends were rarely asked to dance at balls, or called upon by gentlemen, or asked to ride in Hyde Park, or even to afternoon teas by the diamonds of each season.

"We want love, even passion, and we've all endured a few seasons. We are wallflowers with little prospect of ever attaining a well-connected match," Maryann said fiercely.

The nods turned into longing sighs.

Impatience burned along Kitty's nerves, and a sense of something new and wonderful hovered, if only she could reach for it.

Kitty and her friends had been withering away in the *ton*, season by season, with no chances of improving their prospects. They were all fairly attractive but could not be considered great beauties, nor were they especially accomplished, having little useful connections and less dowries to inspire any real serious matrimonial attachments. They were generally ignored by those young gentlemen in society who were looking for a bride.

Yet a lingering desire to wed and have their own families resided in each of their hearts. Or perhaps, they wanted only to feel what it was like to drop their handkerchief in front of a gentleman who would pick it up, ask them to dance, and send them flowers the next day.

"How marvelous if we should *all* be guilty of doing something wicked, just for once," Kitty said softly, drawing five pairs of eyes to settle on her person. A wild idea had overtaken her good sense, borne of desperation. It was dredged from a place beyond logic or reason.

Kitty knew who the desires in her heart were for, though they were not traditional desires—Alexander Masters, the reclusive Duke of Thornton. He was the solution to turning around her family fortunes...

Well, Kitty thought convincing society she was the fiancée of a man she had never met was the solution.

In their world, success depended on who one knew, how powerful and prestigious those connections were. Vouchers for Almacks, invitations to balls, the opera, and the theater were all provided on the strength of how well known in society one was. And Kitty desperately needed that power to secure suitable matches for her sisters.

She couldn't abide the notion of her three darling sisters—Anna, Henrietta, and Judith—withering away as Kitty had done because of their poor connections and nonexistent wealth.

The patronage of a duke would undoubtedly open the most eminent doors to her family. Their desperate plight had already seen Anna working as a lady's companion and having to fend off the unwanted advances of a lecherous scoundrel. The country cottage they had been relegated to after Papa's heir had claimed his estate was in dire need of repairs. Mama's widow's portion allowed only for the hiring of a cook and the barest appearance of gentility—and Kitty, being the eldest, was expected to secure a well-connected match.

Kitty stood, smoothing away the imaginary wrinkles of her rose-colored gown. Tonight, she had worn her most elegant dress, and not one gentleman had been kind enough to ask her to dance. There were too many more ladies with appealing dowries in attendance at Countess Musgrove's ball. "It is time for us to do more than wait for someone to gain the courage and ask to court us. Not when we are so inferior in our connections and ranks."

Her friends' curious eyes rested on Kitty's face, capturing every nuance of her expression, perhaps analyzing the fierce determination in her tone.

"We can no longer afford to fade into the ballroom walls. We need to be *more* than wallflowers."

Thank heavens. This meeting had revealed itself to be a validation of her prayers. Kitty had honestly thought she'd have to hide the wicked leanings in her heart, the only solution she had envisioned for getting out of the genteel poverty in which she, her three younger sisters, and her mother lived.

Miss Emma Prendergast wrinkled her nose, her dark gray eyes unusually somber, quite at odds with her cheerful mannerisms and humorous charm. "I am three and twenty and have had four seasons because of the generosity of my godmother. I have never been thought of as more than a wallflower," she said wistfully, the ache for more evident on her face.

"We have been biddable and dutiful daughters and sisters. And that has gotten us nowhere," Maryann continued.

Everyone stood, and the excitement that filled the air was electric. "We must commit to pool our resources together and help one another to be more. We have never...none of us, ever been sinful, have we?"

Wicked...sinful...and not at all proper.

Those murmurs slipped from her friends' lips, and a breathless, tense silence blanketed the private parlor.

After that, everything became a blur as Kitty and her friends laughed and plotted. How delightfully improper it all was, and she ardently prayed they would have the courage to act upon their hearts' desires and not falter.

Sometime later, her friends dispersed back into the ballroom, anticipating that perhaps tonight would be the night their fortunes started to change. Tonight, they would all start being wicked...and bold.

Kitty turned to face Maryann, her dearest friend. "You never mentioned when we rode in the park earlier that we would have such a rousing conversation."

Maryann smiled, the prettiness of her features rendered beautiful with that curve of her lips. If only the *beaux* of society could see beyond the spectacles perched atop her elegant nose and her intelligent humor. It did not bode well for the young bucks of the *ton* if they were not attracted to her wit and vivacity.

"Papa has accepted an offer from Lord Stamford. He informed me this morning, and I cannot bear the notion."

Kitty gasped and hurried to her friend, clasping her hands between her own. "Say it isn't so! Why, he is older than your papa!"

Maryann's eyes twinkled with surprising humor. "I know...but I have a plan."

Kitty stilled. "A wicked one?"

"Oh, Kitty, a most diabolically wicked plan, and it involves Nicolas Ives."

Shock tore through her. "The earl everyone calls London's most notorious scoundrel for his unforgivable debaucheries?"

Some undefinable emotion pierced Maryann's eyes before she lowered her lids. "The very one," she murmured, a flush coloring her cheeks.

Kitty stepped back, picked up her reticule, opened it, and withdrew a clipping of a newspaper article. She cleared her throat nervously. "I have a plan, too."

The wicked notion was so audacious, so scandalous, she hadn't the heart to put it into words until now. "One I am mad and reckless to even think of. I prayed, Maryann... I prayed for days, wondering if I am on the right path, and then tonight you confirmed everything I have been thinking. There is more to life, isn't there? And we cannot let society, our fathers, or our brothers decide it all for us."

Maryann hurried to the door and turned the lock, ensuring no one could come upon them. "What mad plans do you have?"

Kitty thrust the paper at her. "I believe I've found a solution to my family's problems."

Pushing her glasses atop her nose, her friend scanned the gossip sheet. "What is it?"

"My father always said everything in the world, every tier to climb, is not about how skilled one is but about who you know." Familiar grief welled in her heart, and she pushed it aside. Her papa had died four years past, and the sting of losing him was ever present, especially given how much harder life had become.

"Papa always said connections are the currency of our world and are the only way to survive." She lifted her chin. "Maryann, please read the passage I've circled."

Her friend cleared her throat delicately, squinted, and read silently.

Kitty knew every word to the article that had been burning a hole in her reticule these past three weeks.

Rumors abound that the enigmatic and reclusive Duke of Thornton is on the hunt for a bride. At one point the duke, dubbed the "mad, bad, and dangerous" catch of the season, left a trail of broken and hopeful hearts in society, and we cannot help speculating who the lucky lady may be. Of course, The Scrutineer *is unable to confirm, for no one in society has seen Thornton in several years. Is it all another piece of fantasy surrounding our favorite absent duke? Or is there some veracity to this delectable tale? Anyone with news is welcome to share with us, of course; we protect the identities of our sources.*

Maryann glanced up. "How does this connect to your plans?"

Taking a deep, steadying breath, Kitty withdrew a folded paper. "This is my reply…which I mean to post."

Maryann plucked it from Kitty's trembling fingers and started reading aloud.

"Dear Lady Gamble, it is with great delight I inform you that I, the Honourable Katherine Danvers of Hertfordshire, am honored to be the fiancée of His Grace, the Duke of Thornton. After giving the matter some thought, I decided to pen a reply to satisfy society's interest. The duke spends most if not all his time in Scotland, where he intends for us to reside after marriage. Because this will see us from London's society for a while, he has agreed to a lengthy engagement to give two of my younger sisters the opportunity to secure matches for themselves before we wed. I am confident you can publish my news and will be elated to be the first to break such a delightful tidbit.

Sincerely, Miss Kitty Danvers."

Maryann's expression of shock would have been comical if Kitty wasn't so anxious.

"You know the duke?"

"Of course not," she whispered. "But I mean to use society's fascination with the man and the power of his name to my family's advantage."

"Oh, Kitty…this is almost as naughty as my plans." Then Maryann laughed, and it wasn't Kitty's imagination that there was a touch of hysteria there.

"Maybe too wicked?" Kitty whispered, wings of indecision fluttering in her stomach. "I do not expect my plan to work in *my* favor at all, as if I am discovered, I would be a ruined spinster forever! But I *must* do something to help my sisters. The connections we will foster by using the duke's name will be enough to see Anna and perhaps even Judith settled comfortably."

A piercing disquiet settled in Maryann's eyes. "His Grace is not a man to be taken lightly. Kitty... The newspapers call him 'the puppet master.' He is influential with the lords, and his power is far reaching even if he does live at a remote estate. Don't you read the political tracts?"

A knot formed in Kitty's stomach. Excitement or fear? She didn't know.

Perusing political news and cartoons had never been an interest of hers. The duke was an enigma to both the press and society. Kitty was relying on exactly the air of mystery that surrounded him to enhance her popularity.

Why had he driven himself from society? Some vague whispers said that he was scarred, others said he was malformed, and yet others said he was merely a hermit hiding a broken heart.

Kitty had no notion of what to believe and had tried subtly prying from her mother what she could about the duke, but the viscountess had not been keen on granting her a proper response. The only thing Kitty had been certain of was that society had not seen the Duke of Thornton in years, and he was not liable to re-enter the glittering whirl of the *ton*.

Once she revealed their fake attachment, the fickleness of the *ton* and their insatiable need for gossip would result in some invitations being quickly delivered. They would be hungry to know the lady who had snagged the attention of the elusive Thornton.

Nerves rioted dreadfully inside her, but her family depended on her, and she had been failing them for the past two seasons. Kitty was at her wits' end to see them settled in a modicum of comfort and security. She believed at long last she had found the way to rescue her family, leaving at least their dignities intact.

Except…*she* would surely burn in purgatory for the deception she was about to orchestrate.

A passing reference of a few notable names would not do. She must *become*. Kitty believed her aunt Harriet, who had scandalized the family by taking to the stage, would burst with pride.

It was all such a delicate situation that could lead to the worst sort of ruin.

As ladies, they were expected by their families and society to *conduct themselves with* good sense and temperance, always. Anything else could lead to scandal and ruination. But what must one do when desperate straits for her family loomed?

The deception she would weave on society at times filled her with terrible nerves, and in the dark of her chambers, she had questioned her sanity. Was this the kind of person she wanted to be?

She'd told herself she had no choice, but was that the truth? One always had a choice. And Kitty was willing to do *anything* to save her family.

"You know Lady Gamble will publish your response using her artful words. What if the duke should see this?"

Oddly, that was the least of her worries. "Oh, Maryann, no one has seen or spoken to him in almost seven years, according to my mamma. She did not share the details of his last appearance in society, and I did not want to arouse her overly inquisitive nature with my probing. As for the duke, I daresay if that man read or cared to read scandal sheets, he would have responded to the ones that speculated last year that he had died, and his cousin Mr. Eugene Collins would be summoned to court and a declaration that he was the new duke would be made. Then, how about that rumor that said he had ruthlessly seduced Lady Wescott's niece and absconded with her? Last season *that* furor was rabid, and the duke hasn't even demanded a retraction or an apology. No one has heard from him. I promise you he will not see this. I would be astonished if he did."

"And if he does?"

"He won't," Kitty stubbornly insisted. "But…even if he did, surely he would think it another baseless speculation of the press to be added to the many over the years. And my ruse won't be forever, only for the few weeks remaining in the season. After my sisters have secured important matches, I will cry off the engagement."

Maryann's face softened with sympathy. "You'll be ruined after."

Kitty lifted a shoulder in an indifferent shrug. "Oh, you know I am without expectation of contracting an eligible alliance."

Her friend considered, and Kitty schooled her expression into what she hoped was a neutral mask. She'd already cried over what the damage to her reputation at the end of it all would mean.

A possibility of no marriage and children of her own.

Even without the damage to her reputation, no gentleman had shown an interest to court a young lady like her. The past two seasons testified to that distressing knowledge. She was three and twenty. It had been remarked more than once how agreeable and sweet-natured she was. No one used epithets such as "pretty" or "sought-after." A young man had once said she had "interesting eyes."

Kitty thought that was the most particular compliment she'd ever received.

"I am not worried about my future. I have long seen that a family of my own is not in the cards for me."

Her family's lack of wealth and connections had cemented that for the last few seasons. Now her ruse would be the proverbial final nail in the coffin. On the other hand, if she succeeded in taking advantage of the duke's connections, at the end she would have to pretend the engagement had been called off. Whispers would abound that the duke had jilted her. Either outcome would see her reputation in tatters at the end.

It is a risk I must take…for Mamma and my sisters. And I must not think the worst!

"I worry that you do not think of your own happiness," Maryann said with a sigh.

A frightening surge of longing and an ache traveled through Kitty's heart, and she forcibly suppressed the need for something more. "My sisters are so charming and uncomplaining. They deserve some happiness. Our papa is gone, and Mamma is still stricken with grief over our lamentable prospects and dire futures. It is up to me to secure alliances for them. We will become sought-after once it is known we are related to a duke."

Maryann hugged her, and with a watery laugh, Kitty returned her embrace.

"We are really doing this," Maryann vowed. "We are going to be sinful wallflowers."

Yes, we are... And Kitty prayed she wasn't making the most dangerous mistake of her life.

CHAPTER TWO

Two weeks later...
Cheapside, London

"Have you seen this?" Annabelle demanded, slapping the newssheet onto the old scarred satinwood table in the center of the small and barely furnished parlor. It pained Kitty to see another tear in the side of the blue muslin spring gown her sister wore. It was only a few days past she had repaired the hems and pockets.

"I haven't had a chance to read the papers," Kitty murmured, popping a tart into her mouth and chewing thoughtfully.

"This outrageous *on-dit* says *you* are betrothed to the Duke of Thornton. A *duke*, Kitty. It reads 'Lady Gamble has learned from the most unimpeachable source that His Grace, the Duke of Thornton, is betrothed to the Honourable Katherine Danvers of Hertfordshire.' That is *you*," her sister ended on an incredulous gasp.

A shock of pure fear and exhilaration tore through Kitty's heart.

Finally, a response.

Their younger sister Judith lowered the gothic novel *The Devil's Elixir*, which she'd been reading in the dim light of the single lit candle, glancing back and forth between her elder siblings. "Kitty, could this be true?"

Kitty had her sisters' undivided attention. Even their youngest sibling, Henrietta, who had been practicing her music on a pianoforte in desperate need of a tuning, had faltered. Their mother stirred, shifted from beside the lone window in the room to perch on the arm of the sole, bedraggled armchair present in the parlor to settle her pale blue eyes on her eldest daughter. She indicated for the newssheet and it was pressed into her hands.

Her mother was visibly distressed and struggling not to cry. Lifting her shoulders, she met Kitty's stare. The vacant, hopeless look disappeared from her eyes to be replaced by a hope so bright and painful, a lump grew in Kitty's throat.

"Katherine, is there any veracity to Lady Gamble's claim?"

She had prepared for this, yet there was a moment's hesitation in her heart. For this decisive step in her deception felt more profound, more frightening than anything else. Now she was offering her family a hope that could be crushed if Kitty was not clever and resourceful. There was also a heavy fear, deep inside, that disappointing her mother would crush the remaining life from her. The very notion was unbearable, and an odd sort of pain clutched at Kitty.

"Yes, Mamma," she said softly.

A peculiar stillness settled over the parlor, as if they dared not breathe for fear the promise of a different future would burn away like ashes in the wind.

Mamma favored her with a long, probing stare. "I am astonished you never told us you met a duke, let alone one as powerful as Thornton. I met him years ago via your father. A most charming and handsome young man, I recall, though there were whispers of an accident that left him hurt. He has been missing from society for a number of years, and there has been much speculation as to if he would ever return. I cannot fathom how such news was not imparted to me. What is going on, my dear?"

A rather large lump formed in Kitty's throat. She hated very much to lie to her sisters and mother, but she did not want them to be a part of her mad scheme. If she was ever found out, Kitty wished for all the recriminations to be laid at *her* feet. Once again, her heart trembled, and her resolve wavered. If her ruse were uncovered, the scandal would be far-reaching, destroying all her sisters' chances, as little as they were.

"Our correspondence has been through letters. I…I did not wish to give false hope, but we have formed an attachment." Tears burned in her eyes that she had to deceive them so, and she almost crumbled and confessed all.

Except with a gasp, her mother lifted trembling hands to her lips and said, "We might be saved?"

Yes, I promise it, Mamma.

"I cannot perceive it to be true," Anna cried. "Why would he choose you, Kitty?"

Her sister's astonishment hurt Kitty when it shouldn't have. "I do not pretend to any extraordinary beauty, but why shouldn't a duke offer for me? I am pretty, my eyes are fine, I am quick in thinking, and I am educated. I am not a spendthrift, and I daresay I can manage a large household. I am also the daughter of a viscount, even if he had been an impoverished one. We do have some connections, Anna."

"Oh, of course, anyone would appreciate your fine qualities. It is all so extraordinary. What will this mean for us?" Anna intoned.

And for the first time in a very long while, hope shone in their eyes, and the cold knot of doubt in Kitty's stomach loosened.

"It means our family may be saved," Mamma said fiercely. "It means we will have coal this winter. It means I will no longer have to swallow my pride and pen letters to your father's heir, begging for scraps. It means you will not have to return to that dreadful house, Annabelle, and good heavens, it means my girls may have a chance for a better life."

Judith clasped her hands together. "I may have a season?"

Kitty smiled at her sixteen-year-old sister, who spent most of her days dreaming of balls and courtship. She was already quite decided about her future and possessed too much of a romantic nature. "I daresay in a couple more years it may be possible. A coming-out at eighteen is acceptable. And we may be able to hire a governess for you, Henrietta."

As it were, Kitty was responsible for her eleven-year-old sister's education, and she had taken rich pleasure in teaching her varied subjects.

She faced Annabelle. "This season will be yours. As the fiancée of His Grace, I will be better positioned to introduce you to those who wish to be in his good favor. You will not be going back to *that* house, as you were suggesting."

Her sister cast a furtive glance at her mother before lifting her chin and nodding firmly. Anna was one and twenty and wasn't out in society as Kitty was. All their fragile hopes had been hung on Kitty finding a good match. After it had been evident Kitty was to be a failure, Anna had accepted a position as lady's companion to Lady Shrewsbury, and her son had frightened Anna greatly with his brutish advances. Anna's arms had been badly bruised, and the imprint of the viscount's fingers on her sister's inner thigh would haunt Kitty forever.

How Kitty wished it had been her, and not her sweet, gentle sister. Not that she had wanted to be defiled or frightened, but she was made of sterner stuff and not as fragile as dearest Anna.

Kitty was grateful her sister had confided in her; how she wished she could call out the blackguard to defend her sister's honor, but instead the knowledge had been the additional spur Kitty needed to conjure up her daring scheme. The weight of her sister's pain and shame felt like evidence of Kitty's failure to see them all safe, as she had promised her papa on his deathbed.

Kitty hadn't hesitated to confront the bounder with her papa's pistol and warn him to stay away from Anna. Of course, the scoundrel had been more amused than afraid, but she had gotten her sister away from that dreadful place. A life like that wasn't to be Anna's, Judith's, or Henrietta's future— Kitty would ensure it.

Anna nodded, clearly still dazed. "But when will we meet him?"

I pray, never. She had only this season to get

things right.

While the duke was a recluse, Kitty did not believe she could fool society for more than that time. Everyone would wonder where the duke was during this farce. They would wonder at the wedding never taking place, and they would rabidly speculate why he was not by her side. She had to move quickly and smartly to secure her sisters' futures in one season.

It felt impossible. It felt hopeless. It felt terrifying.

Kitty wetted lips that had gone dry. For several nights she had lain in bed unable to sleep, planning for all eventualities. Taking a bracing breath, she spun tales of hopes for them, of an eventual meeting when he returned from Scotland, and how they would take the last of their money and order three new daring ball gowns for herself, two for Anna, dancing slippers, and assorted fripperies. It was such a gamble to spend the last of Mamma's portion, but she also had to look the part of a duke's fiancée, and Anna had to be out in society for the plan to bear fruit.

Now that the news had been announced, the wave of interest and curiosity into their lives would move unchecked.

Her mother stared at her for quite a while, and a lump grew in Kitty's throat at the emotions she spied in her mother's eyes.

"Sometimes it steals my breath and crumples something in me when I think of the weight of the responsibility on your shoulders, my dear," her mother said softly, an odd sort of knowledge in her eyes. "You've always been a lively and daring spirit,

Katherine, and for so long I've worried the onus of taking care of us would dim your charming light. You've not flinched from everything required of you and have taken on a burden to see this family well, a responsibility that should belong only to your father and me. My Artie would be so very proud of you, my dear."

Kitty swallowed and nodded, offering her mother a watery smile.

While they sipped tea and ate sandwiches that had the cheapest fillings, she gave them hope, and in return, her family bestowed on her the brightest smiles she had seen since before her papa had died.

And it was in that moment the last kernel of doubt died.

I'll not fail you.

• • •

Two weeks later
Dear God in heaven…. I've really done it.

Kitty had remade herself into the fiancée of the reclusive Duke of Thornton, was declared by the scandal sheets as incomparable, and was toasted for snagging the elusive duke. The eager reception in society of the news of her betrothal to a man of rank and fortune had sent her mother into swift recovery, pleasing Kitty, for she had been dreadfully worried she would lose her mamma to melancholia.

Only this morning, her dear friend Maryann had sent a footman to deliver over a dozen invitations to balls, musicales, soirees, and even an invitation to a scandalous house party that had arrived at

Maryann's parents' elegant town house in Berkeley Square for Kitty. They had thought it wise to drop hints here and there that Kitty resided with the earl and countess of Musgrove for the season. The small house her mother had managed to rent in Cheapside must not be discovered by the *ton* as her place of dwelling during the season.

Kitty glanced down at the small packet of invitations in her hands. *Oh dear.*

This one was for the Marchioness of Sanderson's ball a couple of weeks from now. She had never been invited to that auspicious and most sought-after event before. It was all absurd, of course, as she was the same person who had been among society for the last three seasons. But the almost daily articles published by Lady Gamble had wrought changes Kitty and her family hardly knew what to do with.

The articles had rambled on about the idea of such a match, assessing if it was imprudent or the society pairing of the season. The wave of interest that followed had been more than she had allowed possible. The solicitor who had executed Papa's will approached her and suggested letting a town house in Mayfair. Kitty had nearly expired from shock and embarrassment, for Mr. Walker had politely suggested he would send the bill to the duke's lawyers.

At first, she had been confused, and then awareness had dawned. Financial avenues had also been opened to her family because of her fake engagement. She had denied Mr. Walker, of course. That night before bed, she had prayed twice as hard for her eternal soul.

And now one of those startling changes was seated on the sofa by the fire, seemingly both nervous and self-assured—Mr. Adolphus Pryce. Kitty was pretending to quickly read the stack of invitations in her hands while they awaited refreshments so that she could take the measure of the man. He was thin and carefully but plainly dressed. Pryce had high coloring on his cheekbones, and his curly hair was trying to escape from his pomade into pretty kiss-curls at his forehead. This was a very curious contradiction, and Kitty wondered how he had found her. The card he had presented said he was a lawyer from a prominent law firm.

The door to the parlor remained ajar to lend the correct air of respectability to their meeting. Anna brought in a tea tray and shot Kitty a questioning look. She lifted her shoulder in an elegant shrug, for she had no idea why a young solicitor from Smith and Fielding's had called upon her. The painful cramps in her stomach suspected that the duke had seen the article, and perhaps she was being sued for misrepresentation and fraud.

Nevertheless, tea and cakes were served, and her sister departed, leaving her alone with Mr. Pryce.

"How may I be of assistance, Mr. Pryce?"

He hurriedly gulped down his tea and settled the teacup and saucer atop a small scraped walnut tablet. His apparent discomfiture relaxed her.

"Miss Danvers," he started, tugging at his cravat, which truly seemed as if it were choking the man. "I am a part of the team that handles His Grace the Duke of Thornton's affairs." At that pronouncement, his chest puffed with pride, and he sat a bit straighter on the sofa. She dearly hoped it wasn't the lumpy cushions affecting his posture.

Kitty clasped her cup, the warmth soothing to the chill forming in her heart. She had to cleverly handle him without his awareness. A hysterical laugh bubbled in her throat, and she swallowed it down. How complicated her ruse got day by day. "Yes?"

"Ah…my superior has tasked me to…ah… We recently became aware our client is betrothed to you."

She pinned him with an unflinching stare. "Yes?"

"The team has tasked me to, ah…" He blushed, and her throat went tight. "I'm to make discreet inquiries… Ah, that is to say we were not aware the duke had intended to take a duchess."

The team wanted to find out if the engagement was real. *Of course.*

But why had they approached *her* and not the duke directly? Could it be that he was reclusive even with the people who managed his estates?

"Has Alexander not informed everyone of the happy news?" she asked with a small smile, desperate to portray a serene countenance, hoping her probing was on point. Kitty was very deliberate with the intimate use of the duke's name, and Mr. Pryce stiffened. "Why haven't you written to him? I am sure he will respond. He did promise it."

"He did?"

She took a sip of her tea and then responded graciously. "Of course."

Mr. Pryce's shoulders relaxed. "My superior Mr. Fielding did send an inquiry to the duke, but we've received no reply."

"How odd, and perhaps not so unlike His Grace."

Kitty hoped the duke was an indifferent correspondent and she hadn't just blundered. Her pause was deliberate. "But how may I help your office?"

He glanced around, his gaze landing on the worn-out sofas and the threadbare peach carpet. "It took some time to find you, and I did not expect to see the fiancée of the duke residing in Cheapside." The man was now watchful, his light blue eyes calm and calculating.

Her composure was rattled, and she took a delicate sip of her tea, her thoughts churning furiously. "My father's solicitor's office is currently seeking a more suitable establishment at the duke's behest. Mr. Walker of the Dunn and Robinson firm…you are familiar with them?"

"I am," he said tightly.

"Yes, Mr. Walker found the most delightful town house in Mayfair, but I am afraid Alexander was not at all pleased with the selection. I believe his words were that only the very best was suitable for his betrothed." There, that would explain why she still resided in Cheapside, and yet the terrible sense of unease lingered. There were days she hated the depth of deception she weaved, and today was such a day. Why did this man have to show up here?

Still, better him than the duke…

Adolphus Pryce blanched, and he sat straighter on the lumpy sofa. "His Grace…His Grace went to another firm to handle this matter?"

The man's shock had alarm flipping in her belly and a realization dawning. They had been concerned because the duke hadn't used their offices to draft up any sort of agreement, or even an offer of the marriage contract. They were worried the duke may not be satisfied. Of course they had thought it prudent to investigate these new rumors. It occurred to her then they must have investigated the other past rumors as well.

Drat. She frowned, tapping her chin thoughtfully. "It was my suggestion to go with that firm, for they dealt with my papa's estates. Alexander does indulge me, shamelessly." She paused in the act of selecting a cake. "Do you believe your firm is capable of finding a house that would please His Grace?"

Relief lit the man's eyes, and he nodded eagerly. "Of course, of course, Smith and Fielding is always honored to cater to His Grace's needs. We will get on the matter right away. By the end of the week, I'll find a town house in Piccadilly or Grosvenor Square and open a line of credit for you, Miss Danvers, at various shops. You may assure His Grace you will want for nothing, and the offices of Smith and Fielding will gladly serve *all* your needs."

A line of credit? Dear God. This was going too far.

But who would genuinely believe she was the fiancée of a duke as powerful as Thornton if she lived in Cheapside and wore last season's modes? Or only the three new ball gowns recently procured?

If she refused this offer, would they then write to the duke? Vast holdings such as the Duke of Thornton's had several stewards and solicitors dancing attendant to his orders. Minuscule affairs were not brought to his notice. If she rejected this offer and insisted her father's solicitor would deal with the matter of a town house, the office of Smith and Fielding would feel compelled to bring the matter to the duke, for fear of losing even a bit of his patronage.

Doubts once again rose in her. But would they not also alert the duke that they had found her suitable apartments? "I cannot credit that Alexander did not respond to your office's queries. I will speak with him."

Another grateful sigh issued from the man. So their client was an ogre, was he?

"That would be very satisfactory, Miss Danvers."

Mr. Pryce then opened a slim black leather case and retrieved a sheaf of paper, a small inkwell, and a pen, then got down to business. He was quite thorough, even demanding to know the type of drapes she desired to frame the windows, the furniture required for each room, and if a seven-roomed town house would be sufficient for her needs. They discussed how many servants she would need to staff the house and the shops she would need for the lines of credit. An hour later, Mr. Pryce departed with a confident spring to his steps.

She dropped the faded damask silk curtains as the hackney rolled away down the street with Mr. Pryce. The web she had woven had just gotten so frightfully tangled, Kitty doubted she would ever be free.

She hugged an arm around her waist. There was a ball to prepare for, and she must not dawdle.

When the news had appeared in *The Scruntineer*, she had found the gumption to visit one of London's reigning modistes and ordered three new ball gowns and most delightful riding habits for herself and Anna. Then she'd suddenly been offered a considerable discount on the bill and found that they were able to add some new day outfits as well.

Being the duke's fiancée had more than one advantage.

That night she had cried in her pillows, for her heart had been heavy with uncertainty at using the last of the monies Papa had left. Come winter, they wouldn't have two shillings to rub together.

Now a line of credit was being opened at the most famous shops in London. She would have to be very careful not to make any purchases, even if the situation became dire. While she would borrow the man's reputation and connections, taking money felt sordid and far too nefarious. But what was she to do about the town house? Kitty fretted as she made her way from the parlor, down the small hallway, and up the stairs to her bedroom.

I will pay him back every penny, she vowed.

• • •

Several days later, Kitty strolled through Hyde Park with Ophelia. The day was quite dreary for a spring afternoon. The morning had dawned cold; intermittent rain had fallen in a listless, icy drizzle. That had not prevented numerous callers from descending on her newly occupied town house. Her mother had been beside herself at the duke's generosity, even though such a gesture stretched... more like shattered the bounds of propriety.

Her mother had sniffed and declared that it was not as if the duke intended to reside under the same roof. And he was the soul of kindness and gentlemanly honor to be so concerned with their welfare. "Of course, no man of his stature would have his fiancée's family living in Cheapside!" her mother had declared, marshaling them to pack their few belongings like a general.

Still, Kitty had not expected the bevy of nosy bodies who had descended a few hours ago. Her mother had basked in the attention and had taken to her role as hostess quite effortlessly, managing cakes and refreshments adroitly and keeping the conversation surrounding the mundane and light gossips, skillfully deflecting all questions pertaining to the duke.

A suffocating dread had risen inside her. The success had felt too surreal, too alarming, with un-alterable consequences stalking her, promising ruin and scandal. Kitty had mumbled some nonsense and had escaped as if the devil had been nipping at her heels.

Grabbing her bonnet and parasol after donning sensible walking shoes, she had made her way from the house. A carriage had paused by her several minutes later; she had been quite glad to spy Ophelia, and her dear friend, sensing her turmoil, had suggested a stroll through the park despite the inclement weather.

They walked along a winding path, and Kitty was grateful the park was not overly crowded. Dear Ophelia appeared resplendent in a fetching dark green pelisse and a walking dress a shade lighter, but there was a bit of forlornness about her eyes.

"Are you well, Ophelia?" Kitty asked softly. "It

has been several days since we last spoke." And it made her wonder if Ophelia was perhaps hatching her own daring plan.

"I believe we should call a meeting of our group soon. Perhaps a saloon of sorts? There is much I would like to discuss with everyone, and I can sense that you are troubled."

"Oh, we shall," Kitty declared, truly wondering how everyone fared. "There is much to discuss."

Ophelia slid her a considering glance. "And can your troubles wait until then?"

Kitty sighed. "I never imagined such success with my ruse. It is frightening."

A wide smile lit her friend's face and her eyes glinted with mysterious allure. "But it is wonderful to be so daring, yes?"

"I daresay it is. There are times I thrill in being so positively wicked and bold. Only a couple days ago, I rode your horse astride in Hyde Park. I declare I am not the first lady to do so, but the scandal sheets were agog with my daring, and Mamma almost had the vapors." She laughed, delighted with the reminder of how indecent and free it had felt. "Kitty Danvers must be *very* devilish to keep the interest of the papers and society. I want them hungry to know me, to be shocked by *and* attracted to my audacity. Invitations to even the most exclusive balls and events will come in more."

"Then I declare that is where you should direct your attention wholeheartedly, Kitty. I assure you, if you let only the doubts and fear in, you will falter and possibly miss something wonderful, and quite different than the humdrum that can be the expected life of a lady," Ophelia said with aching sincerity.

Kitty had always thought that of all her friends, Ophelia could have been married if she wished for a union. She was terribly pretty with a small, determined month, a button of a nose, and sweetly curved lips, and she had the most beautifully haunting singing voice Kitty had ever had the privilege to hear. Despite being the daughter of a marquess who was lauded in parliament for his reforming efforts, for the last few seasons only one man had made an offer for her—Peter Warwick, the Earl of Langdon. And Olivia had rejected him, for she had an artistic temperance and sensibility...*and* a secret identity no one could ever discover.

She was Lady Starlight, revered and worshipped as a masked and bewigged songbird.

"How glad I am we ran into each other," Kitty said with a light laugh, brushing aside all feelings of misgiving. "I shall not falter in my thoughts anymore."

A faint shout had them pausing and turning around. A man in a dark tweed coat hurried toward them, a notebook clutched in his hand, a briefcase dangling in the other. They shifted to the side of the path to allow him to pass, but quite alarmingly, he stopped in front of them. Kitty narrowed her eyes and gripped her parasol, not in the least afraid to slap him with it should he accost them.

Not that they had too much to worry about with Ophelia's footmen within shouting distance.

Intelligent brown eyes landed on them. "The Honourable Katherine Danvers, I presume?" he gasped out.

"And who is asking?"

"I'm Robert Dawson, a reporter from *The Morning Chronicles*. I have some inquiries about your engagement to His Grace, the Duke of Thornton. May I be permitted a few questions, Miss Danvers?"

Mr. Dawson's eyes were watchful, curious with a hint of slyness.

Kitty glanced at Ophelia and saw the message in her golden gaze. *Be daring. Be bold. And be more wicked.*

So she did.

CHAPTER THREE

Perthshire, Scotland, McMullen Castle

"I hope I am not overstepping, Your Grace, when I offer my sincerest felicitations on your upcoming nuptials."

Those murmured words from Thomas Biddleton, Alexander Masters's most trusted steward, arrested him as nothing had ever done. Well, except for the sight of his sister chasing a pig through the woods only a week ago, screaming for it to run and be free.

The pig had been recaptured later that day, but he knew better than to tell her so.

The memory pulled a ghost of a smile to his lips, and the other men gathered in his study shared a speaking glance. Except he did not understand its language. Did they ponder the nature of his smile or the beastly mien that must have been highlighted in stark silhouette with that small movement of his lips?

As it were, the taut skin marring his left cheek down to his neck ached at the movement. There had been little reason to exercise those scarred muscles of late. Even his sister's wild antics rarely managed to bring levity to his heart, when before a simple hug from her had made him feel whole. The echoing emptiness had become somewhat of an enigma to Alexander, for he did not perceive its purpose. He'd long accepted his fate and no longer roared his anguish at his misfortunes, yet he was also inexplicably aware of the heart of darkness that lingered within him.

He was lonely.

The stark reality of it had been a crack in the belief that all he needed was his sister, Penny. But he'd decided to send her to England for the necessary social polish and a season. She would not like it, but he would not allow her to bury herself in the wild moors of Scotland forever when the possibility of happiness might await her.

"Please forgive my impertinence, Your Grace," the man hurriedly said at his lack of response.

Positioned in a high wingback chair by the fire, Alexander swallowed the last of his brandy, schooling his expression into impassivity. "My nuptials? To whom?"

Startled owlish eyes cut into his, and Mr. Biddleton seemed lost for words. "Miss Katherine Danvers, I believe she prefers to be called Kitty...is she not your betrothed? Everyone has said so."

"Then it must be true," Alexander said caustically, dismissing yet another intrusive rumor into his life. In the ten years since he had withdrawn from society, he had heard it all—the exotic French mistress he had to throw off a cliff, that he had perished in the fall that had broken his body, then damn his black heart, he had done away with his heir presumptive. Those were the rumors that had reached him in his cold corner of Scotland.

Mr. Biddleton's furtive glance cut to the three solicitors seated around a massive oak table. They were meticulously packing up reports in the proper order for his perusal later. From the stiff manner in how they held themselves, he surmised they were discomfited. Perhaps they dreaded the invitation for dinner he would extend, as was his custom. They were too afraid to refuse him, and they were aware he knew their discomfiture.

Something ugly scuttled across his thoughts, a black awareness that he was lonely and had only these retainers resembling obsequious cockroaches who sat without spine, bowing to all his whims because he was the duke.

Mr. Pryce, a new addition to the law offices, and who was aiming to leave his mark on the world, cleared his throat. "I had the privilege of finding a suitable town house for Miss Danvers when her late father's lawyer was unable to do so, Your Grace. Miss Danvers was quite pleased with the house in Portman Square."

Alexander was momentarily transfixed. A member of his team had seen and spoken to this creature?

Then a peculiar stillness settled over his mind. It seemed this was more than gossip crafted from the silver tongues of boredom and spiteful pettiness. It was quite astonishing. He took a few minutes to assess the strangeness of not having his mind darting in several directions, calculating profits, or penning some inflammatory letter to Britain's parliament.

"Was she?" he murmured in a deliberately disinterested tone.

The pup, evidently eager to please, and dismissing the cautioning look from his superiors, hurried to extrapolate. "Miss Danvers has been declared incomparable, Your Grace, and the story of your courtship is splashed in every newspaper and scandal sheet. They do admire her for her charm and kindness. The story of your meeting and secret courtship has become a sensation. You…you've become the rage…"

Mr. Pryce's voice left him as he became aware of the heavy disapproval beating down on him from his two senior lawyers.

None of that mattered to Alexander, as for the first time in years, a pulse of raw, vibrant emotion stirred beneath the controlled surface he presented to the world. A young lady had deliberately claimed to be his fiancée; she had either been struck with madness or ingenuity.

He felt an unfamiliar twist of curiosity.

He turned the crystal brandy glass slowly between his hands, absently tracing the puckered scars dissecting his thumb. "This meeting is over, and I will see you all next month."

Mr. Pryce and his senior lawyers stood, bowed, and made their way from the study.

"Not you."

Somehow sensing that it was he, the young buck faltered. "M-me, Your Grace?"

"Yes."

Everyone else shuffled out, the last one closing the door to the study quietly.

"Tell me, Mr.…."

"Adolphus Richard Pryce, Your Grace," the young man hurriedly answered.

Alexander could feel his uncertainty and did nothing to put him at ease. "You've personally met Miss Danvers."

The man hurriedly explained how he had found the town house for her and had tried to open a line of credit with the best dressmakers and milliners, but she had refused.

How interesting. A charlatan who was not interested in his money? *Who are you and what do you want?*

The lawyer's voice droned on in his eagerness to please. Certain phrases caught at the sharp edges of Alexander's mind; others he dismissed as he stared into the flickering flames. The scarred half of his face throbbed, as it always did whenever he looked upon the force of nature that had caused his greatest pain.

The ton *is fascinated…*

Everyone is amazed at how indulgent you are…

It is a love match…

A winter wedding…

A duchess at last…

It was simply too outrageous to be believed.

"I task you to ensure that every newssheet that has mentioned Miss Danvers is delivered to me immediately, and all that mention her moving forward should be sent to me posthaste with no expenses spared."

"Yes, Your Grace," Mr. Pryce murmured, pleasure rich in his tone. "I am happy to serve."

"You are dismissed."

The man bowed, a spring in his step as he made his departure.

Silence once more blanketed the massive study like a shroud. He stood, gripping the head of his cane, absorbing the pain winding across his back. The doctors recommended he try to operate without his wheeled chair for at least an hour each day. Alexander had ignored them, and no less than three hours was spent on his legs every day, despite the agonizing discomfort.

He made his way along the hallway, which was redolent with the scent of lemon wax and flowers. The large hall echoed with memories of a life long forgotten, a time when his sister had shrieked without decorum as she ran down these hallways, the servants smiling at the unlikely picture of his mother, a duchess, chasing her child. His sister's presence had never allowed him the luxury of being overly maudlin.

She'd needed him more than he'd needed darkness to hide away in.

Each step jarred him, the pain at times making his steps falter. But he did not call for his bath chair or his manservant. He made his way down the winding stairs, past the drawing room and the grand ballroom, to a private room that had been designed solely for his use. Gripping the handle, he opened the door and entered the only paradise he allowed himself—his library.

A room where shelved walls of books and scrolls and stone tablets rose in three stories of splendor. It was decorated in antique gold and blue, with six soaring windows facing the rolling expanse of the green castle grounds. It was a room fit for a *pasha*, overflowing with antiques and unique items he had collected before his accident.

There had always been a deep-seated need inside him to study human culture and the different civilizations. He had toured the continents, locating precious gems and stones, revered scrolls, miniature sphinxes and statues of exotic animals, rare vases from the Ming dynasty, and books; he had hoarded them like a dragon protecting his lair of treasure.

During his recovery, he'd hired a team of archaeologists, lawyers, and hunters of exceptional and unique things, and each year something more precious, more unique had been brought to him. He felt as if he collected the great beauties and wonders of the world, yet he had never been fulfilled. He touched his latest acquisition: Emperor Kublai of the Mongol Empire immortalized in the cold jade of the statue.

It brought him no pleasure.

The void was not filled; there was no rioting need to immerse himself in the rare books that accompanied this and each acquisition. His mind did not reach toward the abyss where he could submerge himself in another exotic world and be free. For his desire to collect suddenly burned with a furious need to add another object to his growing trove of treasure.

Miss Katherine "Kitty" Danvers.

But once they came behind these massive oak doors, his treasures did not leave. An unusual interest pulsed through him at the notion of this daring creature in his castle.

"Finally, your meeting is over!" a muffled voice filled with annoyance exclaimed.

He smiled, moving farther into the grand library and around a wall of bookcases to another open area to see his sister sprawled indecorously on the dark green oriental carpet, her peach day dress already showing signs of smudges. She had been in one of his crates.

"I surmise you have been waiting long?"

"At least two hours." She shot him a quick smile, her turquoise eyes filled with excitement. "Look what has arrived, Alexander. A sacramental vessel from the Temple of Seti. Isn't it glorious? I believe Mr. Cook has outdone himself with his latest acquisition. There is a book of hieroglyphic—" Penny pushed to her feet and fisted her hands on her slim hips. "You seem out of sorts! Should I summon Dr.—"

He waved aside her concern. "I'm quite well. I simply got a bit of unexpected news."

She shot him a birdlike look of inquiry. "Is it news from the doctors?"

"No."

Relief lit in her eyes. "Is it good or bad news?"

"It depends on your outlook on—"

"Please spare me any more philosophical lectures and tell me," she cried with endearing frankness.

Alexander chuckled, recalling their spirited debate this morning as they had rowed on the frigid loch waters. "It appears I am engaged."

She gasped and sank into the well-padded cushion of the sofa. "You are to be married?"

"So it seems," he said with droll amusement.

"But how? I cannot credit it or perceive if I should be delighted or pity the poor lady who will have to withstand your eccentricities," breathed Penny, looking eagerly up at him.

He scowled.

"Though they are delightful ones," she added

hurriedly with an impish grin. "But truly, how did this happen?"

"As I understand it, it was announced in the papers by Miss Kitty Danvers. I do admit, I have yet to meet this lady."

The import of his words reached his sister, and she straightened. "Oh dear. I wonder what circumstances would embolden someone to announce such a falsehood? Are you considerably angry?"

Letting his finger trail over the cold marble statue of Hera, Alexander moved with his jerky gait over to the wall of windows overlooking the palatial lawns and gardens of his estate. "I'm…surprisingly not angry," he murmured, testing the emotions behind the words.

What he *was* was curious.

The moon struggled to appear, the clouds covering it like a thin veil. It was then he felt the press of silence. It swarmed through him and burrowed beneath his skin. An almost overpowering restlessness came over Alexander.

Who are you, Miss Kitty Danvers?

Intemperate and reckless, that much he knew. There would be no other reason to summon a beast into her life. Why would anyone say they were engaged to him? What charade was she playing— and why?

He was no longer society's brightest diamond, the mad, bad, and most elusive catch all the beauties had yearned for. He'd become their scarred, reclusive monster. He remained an influential voice in British politics through his pen. No woman wanted him, and he desired none, for his cock was an empty husk that would never rise again. Yet somehow, he had himself a fiancée...one who was taking the *ton* by storm.

A rustle behind him indicated his sister had returned to the mound of scrolls on the floor. She was quite used to his lengthy introspections and always knew when to leave him be with his ruminations.

He was intrigued. The hovering loneliness with its jagged and sharp edges, which pierced him when he least expected it, flickered as if it sensed something different on the periphery of his soul and thoughts. Instead of icy darkness settling over his emotions, instead of a muted fury of loss, instead of a sense of nothingness, a curious sort of anticipation blanketed his mind.

• • •

A couple of weeks later, another set of newspaper articles had been delivered to Alexander. Mr. Pryce had executed his commission exceptionally well. Before Alexander, laid out in an organized sprawl on his oak desk, were five stacks of articles, all from various newspapers. *The Morning Chronicle*, *Times*, the *Gazette*, *The Morning Herald*, and a *Lady Goodie's Scandals and Secrets*, a paper he was unfamiliar with but one that promised all the juicy gossip for those avid devourers of scandals.

They were just as silly as himself, it seemed, for they followed Miss Danvers's outings relentlessly.

Alexander plucked up the sheet taken from *The Morning Chronicle*. It was an interview. Incredulous amusement filled him as his gaze devoured her brazen words.

The reporter: *"Society has not seen the duke for a number of years. What can you tell us about that?"*

Miss Danvers: *"That the duke likes and values his privacy."*

Alexander tried to envisage the expression that could have possibly accompanied that sassy remark. An arched eyebrow, a sweetly deceptive curl of her lips?

The reporter: *"Will the duke travel to town for this season?"*

Miss Danvers: *"Dear me, no. The duke much prefers the quiet comfort and fresh air of the countryside. But he does write me quite often. Such delightful letters."*

The reporter: *"And where in the country does the duke reside?"*

Alexander imagined that she had laughed before responding. Was it low and husky or bright and thrilling?

Miss Danvers: *"Come now, Mr. Dawson, surely you do not expect me to own to it. My dearest Alexander surely would not forgive me. I must keep his confidence."*

Now Alexander imagined the reporter shifting closer, entirely charmed by the deceptive vixen.

The reporter: *"And what does he write you?"*

Miss Danvers: *"Oh, the most charming letters and poems."*

Such breathtaking insolence. Had she blushed prettily when she told that lie? Or fluttered her lashes?

The reporter: *"Does the duke send you more gifts?"*

Miss Danvers: *"Very charming and acceptable*

*gifts between an engaged pair. Alexander spoils
me endlessly with books of poetries and the most
eloquent verses of his creation. He dotes on me and I,
too, dote on him."*

The reporter: *"Is your attachment a love match,
then?"*

Miss Danvers: *"I do declare it to be so! He indulges
me shamelessly."*

Impudent wench! He indulged her, did he? And
not just the regular kind…but *shamelessly*.

The reporter: *"Will the duke return to the House
of Lords anytime soon? He's a powerful voice of
reason, his pen an instrument for change."*

Miss Danvers: *"We do not discuss anything as
droll as politics, Mr. Dawson. We speak on matters of
the heart."*

Somehow, Alexander did not think her as vague
as she implied. No, this woman was as cunning as
they came.

With an impatient sigh, he moved on to the mention in the scandal sheets.

*Lady Goodie has spied the most daring lady of the
season walking to Hyde Park several times, her lady's
maid a few paces behind. Discreet inquiries indicate
Miss Kitty Danvers is without a phaeton or a carriage
of her own.*

Whoever this Lady Goodie character was, she
made it her duty to inform society in each of her
weekly columns how lacking Miss Danvers was in
appearance and gentility to become a duchess. Last
week's scandal sheet had mentioned how vibrantly
Miss Danvers laughed, and that her riding boots had
seen better days.

Why the charade, Miss Danvers? And how exactly does it benefit you? he silently mused. She hadn't used her deception to gain anything for herself, beyond the town house his lawyer had insisted on securing for the lady. He felt an odd compulsion stirring inside him to understand this stranger's drive and complexities.

Flipping the newssheet, he carefully read several mentions of her. While the other papers' articles were done in admiring tones, Lady Goodie seemed of a mind to vilify Miss Danvers with biting, sarcastic remarks that poked at Miss Danvers truly being the fiancée of the Duke of Thornton.

Lady Goodie has it on the highest authority that the captivating and almost scandalous Miss Danvers was once again seen riding a horse astride in Hyde Park! Shocking, of course, and the last lady to titillate society in such an audacious manner was our darling Lady Caroline Lamb. This author wonders: What does the duke have to say about his fiancée's outrageous and speculative manner?

Alexander picked up another paper, which referred to the same incident but defended her action as courageous and defying conventions of the biddies of the *ton*. In fact, this article thought the duke should be proud to have such an intrepid duchess-to-be.

It seemed one set of society was liable to believe the lying wretch, but the other half was wary and cutting. How was she maneuvering the dark and treacherous waters she'd willingly dived into?

With deft aplomb…or are you afraid, Miss Danvers?

His lips curled, and he reached for the inkwell

and feather. Pulling a sheaf of paper from his top drawer, he started his composition. He was too enthralled by the unconventionality of Miss Danvers to ignore her any longer.

Dear Miss Danvers…

Alexander paused, assessing the impulse to write to her. And say what? Demand an explanation? Alert the bold vixen that he was aware of her scheme?

Blast his heart for being so perplexed, so intrigued by her subterfuge. She was a puzzle…and he liked puzzles for how they occupied the mind and allowed for the passage of time with some modicum of enjoyment.

Damnable nonsense to be so captivated by a female he knew to be a lying wretch.

His heart jerked and he blew out a slow, audible breath. Yet…he was enchanted. And she'd achieved this without Alexander ever meeting her.

Instead of sending her a letter, he quickly scrawled:

Mr. Pryce,

You will see that Miss Danvers is fitted with a phaeton and a matching pair. You'll arrange for the horses to be stabled and cared for. At no time must you make Miss Danvers aware that you and I have discussed her. You must convince her to take these items as befitting the fiancée of a duke. She must not be told that I had anything to do with the command.

The Duke of Thornton.

His letter would perplex the young lawyer, but Alexander knew he would obey him without questions.

A quick knock on his study had him lowering the

quill. The door was flung open with exuberance, and his sister fairly skipped into his sanctuary, a small pink bundle squished lovingly between her arms.

She'd found the pig.

Even more surprising, the cook had left the animal for her. Clutched in her other arm was a newspaper.

"Dear brother, have you seen this one?" his sister cried out with a choked laugh. "I daresay I've won our wager. Our Miss Danvers is beautiful."

A quick jerk of his heart, a primal slither of interest. In one of his earlier ruminations, he'd imagined Miss Danvers was unattractive and unmarriageable, and this ruse was a desperate bid to make herself more appealing to suitors. He'd dismissed that assumption almost immediately, but he'd still wagered with his sister that Miss Danvers was unattractive.

"Is she?" he murmured.

"Oh yes," Penny gushed, her eyes dancing with merriment and admiration.

With a grunt, Alexander took the paper, which showed a cartoon drawing of a small-boned lady, a hat with several plumes of decorative feathers perched rakishly atop her head, a gloved hand pressing to her lips in apparent delight. And a man who was supposedly him, lowered to one knee, holding up a bouquet of flowers and what appeared to be letters spilling from every conceivable pocket, looking every inch a besotted fool.

Alexander blinked; then he chuckled.

His sister sucked in a harsh breath and he glanced up.

"You laugh," she said with wonderment.

A peculiar jolt went through his heart. "Do not act as if the action is strange for me."

"I dare not wish such genuine amusement, or is your fascination growing for this strange creature?"

"Perhaps I should not have shared the newspaper mentions."

His sister rolled her eyes. "You did not take me into your confidence. I fettered the truth."

He'd been so engrossed in reading about Miss Danvers last week, he hadn't heard Penny creep up on him. A voice too close had simply drawled, "I never knew you read the scandal sheets, Alexander. And how curious you read only the sections that mention Miss Danvers. How I wish to know her."

He'd swiveled to meet Penny's broad, heartwarming grin. Then a wager of sorts had started between them.

Was she comely with blond hair and a buxom figure as he had preferred women in the past? Or was she plain with hardly any rousing attributes? Was Miss Danvers plump or petite? He'd said it was neither here nor there in his estimation; Penny had said a woman with such a large and bold personality must have the body and attitude to match.

His gaze lowered again to the small-boned woman in the garish cartoon.

Another wager had been: Was she blond or dark haired?

He'd put up fair, Penny dark haired. The cartoon shed no light there.

When would she outrageously set a wedding date? Alexander had wagered never. Penny had said a December wedding.

"I just finished reading about the first time you met her," Penny said, her eyes wide with amusement. "How I wish I could meet Miss Danvers! She must be so very brave and original. I wonder what out-landish tale we will read of next?"

Alexander grunted, trying to bury that flare of interest for a damnable stranger who was quite shameless and unorthodox in her manners.

"I am persuaded that when you have made her acquaintance, you shall love her!" Penny declared.

He smiled at his sister's naïveté. *Love?* A notion he hadn't thought or dreamed of in years.

And for this unusual creature? *Unlikely.*

But why was he humoring her wild and improper antics? He could hardly find the answer.

He had been reading all the mentions of her in the newspapers, his curiosity growing in leaps at her unchecked audacity. He could not help being intrigued by her daring. His haven of treasure and books that fed his intellect and entranced him so much could not push away the stark, raw loneliness of his existence. And this Miss Danvers served as a distraction from that disquieting awareness.

A part of him that had been dead and buried whispered through his soul. *What would you do should I come for you, Miss Danvers? Retreat and hide? Or would you face me...challenge me...compel me?*

And inexplicably, Alexander knew that before the season was over, he would find out.

CHAPTER FOUR

Several days later, Alexander sat beside a table outside in the eastern gardens with his sister; his godmother Countess Darling, a dear friend of his mother; and one of his most trusted friends, George Hampstead, the Marquess of Argyle. Lady Darling and George had arrived unexpectedly, and Alexander suspected it was the news of his mysterious lady that had compelled them to his castle.

They had been obliged to seek him out in the gardens, for he had refused to attend them in the drawing room. Here in the gardens was where he stayed when that hunger for something more—a wife, children, impossible dreams and hopes—clawed inside. Whenever he inhaled the scent of spring— roses and jasmine—into his lungs, basking in the cries of the meadowlark, and felt the heat of the sun on his face, the memories of sitting atop his father's shoulders and the soft laugh from his mother were most vivid.

"Alexander, my dear, the news circulating about town has forced me to travel up to this dreadfully cold place you call home. Tell me, is it true you are engaged to Miss Kitty Danvers? I could not credit the news when I heard it, nor the outlandish story of your courtship."

"It seems we met a few months ago when her carriage lost a wheel traveling to this godforsaken part of the kingdom. It was love at first sight," he murmured. "We spent hours discussing the arts and poetry."

Lady Darling gasped, her hand fluttering to her throat, the blue turban on her head bobbing. "Oh, Alexander, how wonderful! I positively had to come when I heard the news, and you know how I loathe traveling."

He had some notion. His godmother had always complained of her dreadful journey whenever she visited and how she dreaded being accosted by highwaymen. With some amusement, he noted that had not prevented her from dressing in the height of fashion in a high-waist empire gown with a string of pearls and earbobs, effortlessly displaying her wealth.

"I'm so very pleased for you, but why aren't you in London?" she asked tentatively, dark blue eyes that reminded him so of his mother's softening with concern. "I had no idea you had expectations ever to marry."

His expectations of marrying and starting a family had been real and attainable ten years ago, but his godmother undoubtedly wondered who would marry a scarred cripple now. "Perhaps my title and wealth are the appeal," he said mildly and without any true sting.

She flushed. "I did not mean to imply—"

"Think nothing of it," he said with a small smile.

Her eyes flashed to the scarred skin on his cheek and traced his blemishes to where they continued below his neck cloth, then dipped to his wheeled chair. The countess looked away, visibly composing herself, before settling her regard on him once more.

"I do pray she will not cry off." There was a hope in her eyes that was painful to see.

Of course, everyone could recall that he had once been engaged to the diamond of the season, the Earl of Danford's exquisite daughter. She had fainted the first time she saw him after the accident. When he had given her the doctors' report that he would never walk again, nor would he function as a man, she had wept piteously.

Her overwrought tears had left him feeling hollow, for he had sensed it was the loss of being a duchess that had pierced her. It would be easy to cast blame on Lady Daphne for running from his estate and never looking back, but he hadn't had the heart to do so…

Or perhaps he hadn't loved her as much as he had thought.

Alexander had acknowledged it would take a rare soul to accept his limitations, and he would be a damned fool even to try to find such a woman.

The memories twisted through him, dark and ugly, a persistent specter he had never tried to close the door on. One did not flee from memories but faced them with resolute tenacity. He had come too far to flinch away from his thoughts, for that was where he resided most, in the deep labyrinth of his mind.

Flames licked along his mind, burning away the good memories like ashes in the wind. His stomach twisted into tight knots, but he did not shy away from them, as that suppression would lead only to haunting nightmares. He'd learned that in the first few years while he had battled for sanity and survival. He let the waking dream come, baring his teeth in a mocking grin.

As it were, he often woke up drenched in sweat, his heart pounding, pain twisting his gut into knots. Those early days and the present memory of losing his parents in the fire had been endless, a sea of torment, his brain often reminding him of it while he slumbered.

In this very house, a fire had raged in the east wing, claiming the lives of his parents, several staff members, and his youth. The one good that had come from it all was that he had saved his sister, Penny, who had been only seven years old at the time.

The slithering memory, the horror of the smoke stealing his breath, the rancid smell of his own flesh sizzling, the burning of his skin, the smoke in his eyes and throat as he searched for a way to escape the inferno with Penny were always with him. To save their lives, he had leaped through the windows of his bedchamber with her tucked as securely as possible in his arms.

It had been a miracle, the doctors said, that his sister had escaped unscathed. And as if mocked by the heavens, the sky had opened with lightning and thunder and a great deluge. If only it had fallen even ten minutes earlier.

It seemed God had a twisted sense of humor— one Alexander hadn't appreciated.

"Yes…why aren't you making the social whirl with your fiancée?" George asked, his eyes watchful and curious. "I had to leave the delightful charms of a most accomplished actress—"

His lips flattened when Alexander lifted his chin

toward his sister, who was busily cutting roses to place in the vase on their table. George at times forgot to mind his tongue when he spoke of his conquests.

The butler brought Alexander a pressed scandal sheet and departed.

Penny laughed as she placed the freshly cut flowers in the vase. "I fear Alexander is of a mind to occupy himself with newspaper clippings of his daring fiancée. He's not yet realized he'd found a new treasure for his horde," she said with far too much wisdom. "I'm quite eager for when the dragon in him will roar and hunt for this peculiar treasure."

George shot her a puzzled frown, and she had the gall to wink. With a frown, Alexander realized it was truly time to send Penny to London for her polish. She was becoming too impertinent in her thoughts and manners and lacked that refinement of ladies of the *ton*.

Yet…he loved her as she was and would never want to see her different.

"I thought it odd you would engage yourself to a woman with little connections or fortune. Her father, Viscount Marlow, left them with little money, and his heir does not support them. Miss Danvers's family is beneath your notice," George muttered. "I cannot credit it is *her* you would choose to be your duchess."

Alexander smiled. Who gave a damn? He was interested.

How long had it been since he had thought of or desired the company of a woman? *Years.*

The marquess sighed and crossed his legs, seemingly admiring the new boots that encased his calves. "I will give it to her— she is nothing if not inventive and original. I hear tell you *indulge* her shamelessly." The marquess grabbed the newssheet, a frown puckering his brow as he read the latest *on-dits* on Miss Danvers. "The hell you say! I cannot credit the romantic nonsense she claims you do. *You* write poetry? Sing ballads to her? Come, man!"

Pretty little liar.

Alexander reached for the newssheet, snapped the paper twice, and lowered his attention to the article. The sheer outrageousness of it awakened his curiosity to an astonishing degree. A perverse enchantment with her gall scythed through him. Unable to temper the need, he kept reading, baffled at the romantic compliments she attributed to him.

His godmother made another stab at eliciting a reaction. "Please tell me, is it true, Alexander? Are you really to be married to this creature?"

He did not want to lie to his godmother but found that he did not want to reveal how clever and deceptive Miss Danvers truly was. "There is a slight misunderstanding between Miss Danvers and me. When it has been cleared up, I will inform you all of the state of our relationship."

He chuckled at Georgie's expression of disbelief.

The man straightened in his chair. "Good God, man, what does that mean? Are you to go to *town*?"

Alexander had not ventured into the *ton* for years, not since the last time he had attended the House of Lords over six years past. The ugly memory of his legs giving out while he stood debating the Bank of England's planned return to the gold standard rushed through him. He almost flinched from it, but he allowed himself to absorb the remembered whispers from his peers who had filled parliament.

Dear God, his scars are hideous.

He is a cripple…

Not the duke he could be…

He had retreated to the country without any attempt to partake in the frivolities of the season. The newspapers had already had a field day with his loss of dignity on the floor of parliament, and he hadn't cared for the fainting of young ladies or the *ton*'s endless speculation.

He had worked to strengthen his legs, slowly moving from being able to be out of his bath chair for more than a few minutes until he could stand unassisted for hours. There hadn't been anything pulling him to the heart of London, for he had good friends to read his arguments and to ensure his will directed the lords in parliament when he wanted a vital bill passed.

But now…Alexander's growing interest in meeting his little schemer was undeterred by reason or common sense. What he would do with the fair intriguer when he saw her was another question altogether.

• • •

Pride burst in Kitty's heart at the radiance of her sister. Anna's smile seemed to be lit from within as she dipped into an elegant curtsy and stepped into the arms of Baron Lynton. Her emerald ball gown and silver dancing slippers glowed iridescently under the candlelight of the crystal chandeliers in the glittering ballroom. The baron twirled her sister with effortless grace, and to Kitty, they appeared the most charming couple. This was the second time they had danced this evening, and his marked attention to her sister was rather pleasing.

Kitty had ensured Anna attended most of the balls she'd been invited to over the course of the last three weeks, and the first night the gentlemen had crowded around her sister, begging for dances. The plan was working. The only disadvantage was the rakes and dandies seemed to now believe Kitty herself was a conquest.

At first, the attention had flummoxed her; then she'd been amused at their fickleness. She had drawn on a mask of amused indifference, refusing all offers of dancing and riding in the park. Kitty still grappled with the fact she had her own personal carriage pulled by a team of matching bays. It seemed Mr. Pryce had thought of everything, and the little notepad she used to keep track of the sum she would need to secretly pay back the duke held an astronomical figure.

"Annabelle and Baron Lynton are delightful together," murmured Miss Fanny Morton, another dear friend of Kitty's and a member of their wallflowers club.

Fanny wasn't celebrated as a beauty, but there was nothing in the least objectionable in her fair countenance. She had short dark red hair cut in the height of fashion and the most beguiling pair of gray eyes—deep and unfathomable. She'd had the misfortune a few years ago to believe herself in love with a young baronet. After the banns had been called, he'd jilted her in favor of an heiress who commanded fifty thousand pounds a year, and somehow society hadn't forgiven *her* for the baronet's terrible conduct.

"Wouldn't it be grand if he should offer for her?" Ophelia whispered over the strains of the waltz as she approached with a glass of punch. "He seems halfway in love with her already."

"I dare hope she waits until after an offer has been secured…or better, *after* the marriage to declare her own affections," Fanny said softly, throwing up her hands in affected dismay, shadows of remembered pain in her eyes. "It would not serve her to be too obvious in her affections and then…" She shrugged inelegantly and sipped her champagne.

"I can tell they are a well-matched couple with genuine attachment. Oh, Kitty, your plan is working brilliantly," Ophelia said with a happy but surprisingly envious sigh.

"And let's not forget, most marvelous of all, Baron Lynton has ten thousand a year and no less than two estates," Maryann said, moving toward them, appearing far too breathless. Or was she frightened? Her cheeks were flushed, and her lips appeared bee-stung.

Had she been kissed?

"Your walk onto the terrace seemed invigorating," Ophelia said, her eyes wide with speculation and wonder. "Were you for once being *wicked*, Maryann, darling?"

"Of course not," she said with a smile that belied her denial, pushing her round, golden spectacles up her nose.

While Kitty had shared her wicked plan with all her friends, Maryann had disclosed only the barest details of her sinful musings of London's most dangerous libertine and had stubbornly insisted she would inform them when she was confident of her path forward.

The waltz ended, and the baron escorted Anna over to their small gathering. He bowed gracefully after greeting them, his eyes twinkling with good-natured fun. Kitty liked him and thought him perfect for her gentle sister. If only he would move to secure her faster.

It had been only a few weeks since she had assumed the mantle of Kitty Danvers, fiancée of the reclusive duke, and she had started to anticipate that she might be uncovered. Kitty could no longer take any comfort that the rumors said he'd not been seen in town in years. The mentions of her in the newssheets had grown completely out of her control, all keen to remind society their most reclusive duke was engaged to the dauntless Kitty Danvers.

Surely the duke would hear of her at any moment. If the baron was to offer soon, then the end of this nerve-destroying charade would be in sight.

"May I ask you for the next dance, Miss Morton?" he asked graciously.

Fanny gasped, her eyes widening. Sadness pierced Kitty, for this was the first time a gentleman had asked Fanny to the dance floor in two seasons. Her lower lip trembled with her smile. "I would be honored, Lord Lynton."

She dipped into a curtsy and allowed him to lead her away. If Kitty hadn't been satisfied before that the baron was her sister's match, his wonderful action had just cemented her belief.

Anna turned to her, her blue eyes burning with excitement, her color a trifle heightened. "Oh, Kitty, isn't he the most amiable and good-natured gentleman you've ever met?"

She smiled, her sister's joy and hope contagious. "I daresay he is."

"Oh, dear sister, I love him. I am certain of it." Anna clasped her hands to her front, evidently trying to be ladylike with her joy.

"Do be careful," Kitty said. "You've only just met him, and while his attentions are noteworthy, he has not declared himself!"

Anna's expression became dreamy. "I daresay when two souls connect, it hardly signifies if they've met only two weeks past. He is a very eligible connection. He has the most wonderful, amiable qualities, most distinguished manners, and he loves poetry as much as I do. Oh, Kitty, I feel he will offer for my hand."

Before she could make a reply, a booming voice announced, "The Duke of Thornton!"

Shock blossomed through Kitty.

The room swirled around her and then resettled, her corset suddenly too tight.

The air was cold, as if all the blood had drained from her body, leaving her shivering. Her only sign of life was her thundering, dread-filled heart.

A slap was what she required to wake her from this horrid dream, but her friends had frozen. Anna turned anticipatory eyes atop the landing of the staircase. Murmurs of astonishment and speculation crested through the ballroom like a fiery wave. Then for a single, breathless moment, a startled hush fell over the throng as the import of the majordomo's announcement settled.

Alexander Masters, the Duke of Thornton, had arrived at *this* ball.

Several seconds passed, and the ballroom remained unexpectedly silent, as if everyone was collectively holding their breath. The emotions pouring through Kitty were like water flowing through fingers—impossible to control or shape into any semblance of tangibility.

I'm going to faint.

Kitty had spent weeks learning everything she possibly could about the duke before she had dared to masquerade herself to Society as his fiancée. The press painted him as a recluse, an enigma, a man who did not acknowledge or respond to the gossip in scandal sheets, and society had no hope of ever seeing him again. He was an intensely private man since his rumored accident.

So why was he *here*?

A disaster of the scandalous and unrecoverable type loomed. The humiliating truth of her desperate scheme would be aired for public consumption. A spasm of anguish snaked through Kitty. She had ruined her family and Anna's chance at a love match with her desperate ruse.

There could be only one reason for his presence—to unmask and repudiate her.

In that moment, Kitty was obliged to master the impulse to retreat and flee as if the devil nipped at her heels.

Then the man himself appeared on the landing. A ripple of shock went through the room, along with a few furious whispers.

"Is it he?"

"No one has seen him in seven years or more, I've been told!"

"Upon my word, what made her consent to marry such a man?"

"His fortune, of course, why else?"

He was bound to a wheelchair.

And his face…

She could hardly breathe. A smooth white mask covered half his face like white porcelain. The effect was eerie and powerful.

Dear God, this could not be the duke.

Broad shoulders moved as his hands turned the wheels of his contraption, which took him to the very top of the stairs.

The champagne glass slipped from Kitty's nerveless fingers and crashed onto the parquet floor. The horrifying sound reverberated through the stillness of the ballroom and, as if by some unseen command, the crowd parted. Her loyal friends pressed closer, and Kitty could feel their alarm. They knew the intimate details of her sinful plan and correctly perceived how calamitous the duke's presence was to her. A few ladies lifted their fans to their faces, and sly whispers reached her.

"Look how pale she is!"

"Oh dear, why is she so shocked to see her fiancé?"

"Well, look at him!"

It struck her forcibly how momentous this occasion was. All her research indicated he had not stepped foot into a ballroom in years.

"You must go to him," Ophelia said softly. "You must do everything to persuade him against ruin. *Please*, Kitty, do not run. The scandal would be unceasing if you do."

Panic closed her throat, and fear threatened to steal her sanity. Her feet, as if they had a will of their own, crept forward, then faltered. Of course he could not descend. Instead, his gaze scanned the massive ballroom, his expression impossible to read even with the flawless male beauty not hidden by the white mask.

He was a king, surveying his domain, and she had the inexplicable awareness she had unwittingly invited a most dangerous man into society's limelight.

Why else would he resurface now, after years of shunning the glittering world of society? Never in her wildest fantasy had she dreamed her outlandish prank would succeed on such a monumental level. For she'd had real success, if she had dragged him from the cave where he had buried himself for so long.

Dear God, what am I to do?

Taking a few bracing breaths, she squared her shoulders. There was only one thing she could do. Face him...this, whatever *this* was...head-on and never allow him to see how she quaked. Surely he could have her arrested and charged with fraud. Ruination and a far worse fate for her and her sisters danced into her vision.

Weaving through the still-paralyzed crowd who seemed trapped by the sheer magnetism pouring from the man on the landing, Kitty walked to the bottom of the steps, then made her way up on trembling legs. He watched her, that half mask making it impossible to ascertain the emotions that painted his expression.

The elegantly dressed manservant who stood behind the duke, his hand on the edges of the wheeled contraption the duke was sitting up straight in, seemed just as fascinated with her ascent.

She reached the top of the stairs, and the dreadful, ogling eyes of the *ton* were upon them.

The gaze behind the mask was dark, cold, and steady. His eyes were a brilliant, striking blue, and she couldn't break the power of his stare. She felt like a terrified field mouse beneath the piercing regard of a hawk. Kitty's heart pounded, and her knees trembled. She managed to dip into an elegant curtsy without pitching onto her face.

"Your Grace," she said. "How delightful that you made it. How…pleased I am to see you."

Surprise flared in his eyes, then curiosity…then admiration. Before his gaze was once more rendered inscrutable.

In the stillness of the ballroom, her voice carried, and a ripple of whispers began as her words were passed in a chain to those who did not hear. Kitty desperately prayed he did not publicly repudiate her. Certainly that could not be his purpose at Lady Sanderson's ball?

She chose her words carefully. "Should we take a turn in the gardens?" she asked softly, needing privacy to explain her madness.

She could feel the kiss of his eyes as they traced over her features, her décolletage, her hollows and curves. The intensity of his stare encompassed her entire body. Anxiety cramped her gut. Being the sole recipient of his unflinching regard was thrilling and frightening at once. Though she feared his words, she began to wish he would speak, for the silence was dreadful.

Power and arrogance radiated from the duke, and Kitty fought against a wave of pure panic. She was out of her depth in every way, and she had no notion of how to deal with the man before her. Wings of indecision fluttered in her stomach, her thoughts frantically skipping along the avenues of escape, discarding one idea after the other.

The silence felt thick, charged. Then finally, he stirred.

"Miss Katherine Danvers, I presume?"

CHAPTER FIVE

The duke's low tone was darkness and sin and something wickedly delightful. And she heard the threat of challenge and warning in his soft, contemplative question.

Before she could formulate a proper response, the sound of the hostess ordering the orchestra to play pierced the air. Too slowly for comfort, the strains of the waltz leaped to life, and those who found the scandalous dance more rousing than Kitty and, presumably, the duke swept themselves away onto the floor.

Suddenly, Lady Sanderson herself was by their side.

"Your Grace, you honor me," the marchioness breathed, dipping into a curtsy, her eyes glowing with her pleasure. What a coup it was for her to be the first to declare the Duke of Thornton had been under her roof. "I've summoned my lord from the card rooms, and he shall be here momentarily."

Her gaze lingered too long on the porcelain mask before flickering to the bath chair. The marchioness wrung her hands, her fluster spiking the nervous tension inside Kitty.

It was imperative she find a way to escape the ball, rush home, pack her belongings, and disappear.

As if the duke sensed her silly, panicked thoughts, he spoke. "I will meet with Sanderson before I depart. As it stands, I must confer with my...*beloved* immediately."

Dear God.

He had read the scandal sheets.

The marchioness dipped into a curtsy and hurried away.

"If I recall correctly," the duke continued, turning back to her, "Sanderson has a small drawing room this way, which would offer us privacy, Miss Danvers."

Away from the ball, and safety, and her friends, and possibly flight? Most certainly not.

Yet her tongue would not loosen. A mocking smile ghosted across the half lips not covered by the mask, and Kitty narrowed her eyes, not liking that he perceived her dreadful anxiety.

"Certainly, Your Grace. If you'll lead the way," she said staunchly.

They turned away from the ballroom, and the weighted speculation of the *ton* felt like a boulder pressed on top of her shoulders. As her fiancé, he could converse with her in relative privacy without undue conjecture, and Kitty would still ensure she left the door ajar.

The manservant spoke to him in Greek as he pushed him in the wheeled contraption down the empty hallway.

Why was she merely following like a lamb to the slaughter?

"I believe this to be the drawing room," the duke said smoothly.

His manservant opened the door, and she cheered up slightly to see it was a small study. That, however, did not deter him. There was a fire burning low in the grate, and the room was cast in more shadow than light.

"This is adequate," he said, then addressed the servant once more in the same language.

His servant bowed, and then a silver-handled walking cane seemed to materialize in the hands of the manservant. The duke gripped it and stood.

Oh. He could walk.

The duke was taller than she imagined, and though he had a cane, his posture was impeccable. Her forehead barely cleared his chin, bringing the masculine breadth of his chest into stark review. He was dressed in formal trousers and jacket, complemented by a blue waistcoat and an expertly tied silken cravat.

His body was lean, lithe, powerful, with no trace of softness anywhere. That she did not expect from a man in a bath chair.

How had he ended up this way? While the gossip had hinted of an accident, no details had been revealed. The question hovered on her lips, and she forcibly swallowed it back.

He waved for her to precede him inside, and she sauntered into the room with affected calm. She jolted when he closed the door behind him with a decisive *snick*. "I believe, Your Grace, the door should be ajar. For propriety's sake," she hurriedly added.

It was important to her he did not think her afraid or witless.

"Do you?"

Kitty felt an odd sense of shock at that bland remark. "Yes, of course."

His unswerving gaze made her uneasy. "I cannot

credit you would want anyone from society over-hearing the conversation we are about to have."

Oh dear. This was a disaster.

He considered her in the silence that followed. The duke stood perfectly still, rigidly erect with the aid of his walking cane, and aristocratic. Kitty found his quality of stillness so unnerving.

Then he asked, his tone soft and lethal, "How do you dare?"

Ice lodged in her stomach, and her entire body trembled for precious seconds. She gathered herself. Straightened her spine and took a hard, deep breath. "I was desperate and foolish," she said with fearful honesty.

He angled his sleek, dark head to one side and studied her with unflinching intensity. A flare of restlessness blossomed through Kitty, and for a moment she could hear only the pounding of her own heart. She barely managed to maintain her calm composure.

"Why are you pretending to be my fiancée, Miss Danvers?"

Lie, her instincts screamed, but she could not. Her sins were already too great against this man. Kitty began to feel the weight of his stare, and it took an inordinate amount of will not to flinch. "Your Grace, when I consider how dreadfully I have imposed upon you, I am stricken with mortification."

A barely-there smile touched his lips, then vanished so quickly she wondered if it was her over-wrought nerves encouraging her imagination.

"I truly doubt a woman of your ingenuity might be mortified in any situation."

Kitty took a deep breath and tried to be quick in her explanation as to why her pretensions had been needed. "It was ill judged of me to concoct a plan that shamelessly importuned upon your good name and reputation. My intention was to save my sisters and mother from a life of poverty and unhappiness. I promise I will repay every penny spent on letting the town house and the monies and the carriages. I have planned to secure employment as a governess after my sisters are settled comfortably, and by my calculation, I shall be able to repay your unmatched generosity in about…ten years or so."

He smiled. And it was her turn to simply stare. Why was he smiling? The man must be addled.

"You…you are not angry?"

He seemed to consider this. "No."

Something brilliant and cunning glowed in the depths of his eyes. Then the fireplace flickered, the light shifted, and only the most arresting cerulean blue pinned her beneath its piercing stare. His entire body, his very demeanor spoke of strength. A duke secured in his elevated position, the embodiment of privilege.

Who is this man?

"May I ask why, Your Grace?"

"You wish me to be angry with you, Miss Danvers?" he murmured.

"Of course not. I have imagined every scenario in which you confronted me, Your Grace, and none resembles this. I…I fear I am failing to understand what is happening."

There was a disconcerting hint of sensuality in his slight smile. *Oh, what do I know?* She was fighting to keep her wits about her; nothing was making sense. For all she knew, he could be withholding flatulence. Gentlemen tended to do that in a lady's presence.

Heat bloomed through her at her unladylike thoughts, and his piercing gaze sharpened. "Would you like to share more of your thoughts, Miss Danvers?"

"No." Her blush got hotter, and she turned away, lifting her face to the fresh night air coming through the slightly open windows. She walked away to the fire, and after a struggle to regain her composure, she said, "I fear you've lost all good opinion of me before we've had a chance even to converse. Not that I flatter myself to think we would have ever met or that you would find me favorable."

She flushed at her panicked ramblings, took a deep breath to steady her nerves. Kitty lifted her chin, looking beyond his shoulder, finding his mask disconcerting. *Do not be a silly miss*, she chided herself, then leveled her gaze to his face cast in shadows.

She wondered how he had placed himself so well in the ominous shadow cast from the fire. Habit perhaps? Did he feel more comfortable in the arms of darkness? She was being morbid when she desperately wanted the circumstances to be anything but. "May I ask…what is to be done about our situation, Your Grace?"

"I believe these unorthodox circumstances call for informality, Katherine. Please call me Alexander."

Why did he sound so reasonable and unruffled? Certainly the entire affair was beyond remarkable. *Alexander.* Though he had invited the familiarity, she could not be so intimate with a man who made her feel so desperately unsure of her position. Worse, why did his request sound like an invitation to sin and debauchery? Surely it was her overwrought nerves.

"You are awfully silent, Your Grace."

"I am content with observation."

"Of?"

They fell into a striking silence, which was distinctly uncomfortable. A few moments later, it struck her that perhaps he was not a man at ease with conversation. The rumors did say he was a recluse and had been without the proper company of society for many years. Why, she had never imagined anyone could be so unflappable in such a potentially ruinous situation.

"Observation of what, Your Grace?" she asked again, not certain what to do or say anymore. It was simply all too surreal.

"You invite study, Miss Danvers. I've been following your conquests of the *ton* most carefully."

Her heart jolted. "My conquests?"

"The newspaper articles and scandal sheets of your many outings and escapades. Reporters seem fit to compare your laugh with that of a nightingale, your smile to that of sunshine. Quite riveting, I'm sure you would agree. The *ton* declared themselves scandalized by our courtship, but we know they are secretly fascinated and hunger for more. I am not quite certain what to make of you."

The reporters had been merciless in their pursuits for quotes from her about the reclusive duke. It shattered her to think he might have read all the ridiculous flattery she'd claimed he showered upon her. He might have thought her a woman desperate for artful compliments and love.

A flush worked its way over Kitty's body as humiliation crawled through every crevice of her heart.

"I spent most of my journey here wondering what kind of woman you are," the duke said. "I imagined Kitty Danvers in numerous scenarios. A hardened fraudster? A con artist fleecing the merchants on my good name? A jewel thief using my connections to enter the best houses? A bored lady simply stirring mischief and mayhem? I wondered how to best dispose of you."

Her heart lurched, and a shiver went through her entire body. "Your Grace, I—I fear 'dispose' may not be the right word to use in this situation. I daresay it rings too ominously."

Nothing warm lit in his eyes at her miserable attempt at humor. Dratted man.

Still, a reassuring remark would not be misplaced, yet he offered none. The duke merely stared, as if she were an unusual creature that invited the most intense speculation. She could hear the faint din of laughter and clinking of glasses from the ballroom, and she concentrated on those muted signs of frivolity, slowing her heart to normalcy. Her entire family depended on her to be unflappable and courageous in the face of such ruinous uncertainty.

She dipped into a quick, elegant curtsy before lifting her chin and squaring her shoulders. "I never meant you any harm, Your Grace. I truly only wanted to borrow your connections for a few months. If I had dreamed for even a second it would reach your ears, I would *never* have done it. Pray believe that I am sincere."

He took a step forward, and she shifted back. Their slight dance had the visible side of his face cloaked entirely.

"And does that excuse validate your outrageous deception, Miss Danvers?"

The mask staring at her was at once cold and removed, then glowed with sinister intent. A strange roaring thundered in her ears, and she felt a moment's unwilling fascination.

"Of course not, but I pray it may temperate your disgust and anger and allow me the chance to make amends."

A slow, fascinating smile curved his mouth. She began to think that he was a very strange man, and one with whom it was going to be more difficult to deal than she had foreseen.

Kitty glanced away, hurrying over to the far left corner, and lit a candle atop the oak desk. *There.* Fewer shadows and, indeed, less anxiety on her part. She faced him, frowning her displeasure to see that the candlelight had served only to throw more shadows into the small study, and the wretched man seemed to be…amused? Discerning with that dreadful porcelain mask was hard.

"I have the greatest apprehension my family will never recover from the scandal exposure will bring. I must know, Your Grace. I believe you are too honorable to willfully subject me to the anxiety I currently feel. Will you please inform me how we are to proceed?"

She prayed he wouldn't send notices to the papers of her deception. Poor Anna would be wretched for certain. She would lose whatever admiration the baron possessed. The implication of everything else was simply too frightful to consider. This man could have Kitty jailed or committed.

"Without knowledge of my character, you presume me to be honorable? How naive you reveal yourself to be. Or are you being artful in your flattery for an advantage? You are a beguiling complexity, Miss Danvers."

The dark indulgence in his tone rattled her equanimity as nothing else had done that night. A message throbbed in his voice, one she was unable to decipher, but a ripple of awareness scythed through her. The duke was a man who stood in the gray area of morality. Perhaps that was the reason he'd not exuded disgust at her charade, the reason he hadn't penned a letter to the newspapers denouncing her... and maybe the reason he had traveled to see her.

The very implication of *that* being the reason he stood before her left her breathless with a bewildering clash of fear and anticipation.

"May I ask what you will do, Your Grace?" How odd she sounded so calm when she wanted to scream her fear at his slow response.

A tense silence blanketed the room for gut-wrenching moments. *Say something*, she wanted to snap. But she worked to be temperate and bury the panic.

"Ah," he said with that odd, fleeting smile. "I believe I shall do nothing."

Kitty laughed and then sobered instantly. In fact,

she tugged the glove from her right hand and placed the back of her palm against her forehead. Her skin was surprisingly cool. She understood nothing, and she was uncertain that she wanted clarity anymore.

"Are you well, Miss Danvers?"

The cool mockery in his tone suggested the wretched man knew he toyed with her composure.

"Yesterday I was caught in the rain. I had a mild fever when I went to bed. I am not altogether certain I did wake this morning. There is a very strong possibility I might still be in bed dreaming."

He tilted his head. "You are also peculiar. I like that."

Kitty was even more confident she was stuck in some delirious nightmare. There was a trace of amusement in the odd warmth of his voice. Nothing was clear, and she glared at the mask obscuring the nuances of his features. She wanted to flee from the madness of this encounter, and perplexingly she wanted to stay...to converse with him, to find out why he had truly come for her, what path she needed to traverse to avoid scandal and ruin.

"Why do you wear a mask?" she asked. "The speculation of your peculiarity will be on the lips of everyone within society."

He faltered into such complete stillness, she wondered if he breathed.

"My face is scarred," the duke finally replied.

She had not heard that rumor or even a mention in the newspapers she'd dug up on him. And Kitty was glad there hadn't been rabid speculation that fed his pain to the *ton* as fodder for gossips.

"Show me," she whispered, mildly shocked that

she would dare be so familiar and improper. What madness had overtaken her? She could not credit it. Though her reaction was unpardonable, Kitty lifted her chin, an evidently defiant gesture, and waited.

"Ah…not only are you peculiar but also daringly impudent. My interest soars, Miss Danvers, infinitely so. I wonder, is this your diabolical design?"

She sucked in a breath at that bit of provoking cynicism.

He took one step closer, and the room shrank. How did he do it?

"I thought only to look upon the features of Your Grace. It is decidedly odd to converse with you so masked, as I am ignorant of your full appearance. There was nothing else behind my request."

The hand not gripping the cane pressed against his heart, and two fingers tapped twice. "How disappointing, truly."

He was the peculiar one, and Kitty felt like a leaf floating on the vast waters of the ocean, being churned about in its frothy waves. The duke was a man of consequence, and she sensed the force of the crafty and intelligent personality surrounding her.

While it pained her to admit it…she was intimidated.

Every instinct warned her that it would not do to appear frightened or witless, that he would not mind that she was in possession of an unruly tongue, as her mother often lamented. Yet why should it matter that he would like her oddity? The only thing of import was that her family escaped unscathed, even if she were sacrificed upon the altar of her desperate recklessness.

"Your Grace seems to want me to have another reason for my request; I would not dare disappoint you." She canted her head left, assessing him. "Perhaps you are not the Duke of Thornton…and a charlatan out to deceive me."

He smiled, and her heart beat faster.

"Is that the best you can do?" He *tsk*ed, as if disappointed. "Do you really think I'm not Thornton?"

"I believe you are the duke," she admitted. It was too preposterous to consider another scenario. Only the real duke would know she pretended.

"Why do you think I came for you?"

"Am *I* the only reason you are here?"

"Yes."

Dear God. It was so odd, Kitty could not dismiss him from any part of her awareness, and she so desperately wanted to. "I…am not sure, Your Grace. You are not angry or outraged. Your intentions are elusive to me, and I dearly wish they were not."

The hand gripping the silver-handled walking cane tightened. "Did you think it was mere rumors, wicked gossips, which I'm long used to, that pushed me with the force of a battering storm from my estate in Scotland to mingle with these vipers of society? Did you think I traveled for days and nights unceasingly to be faced with pretense from your lips, Miss Danvers?"

She stared at him helplessly, her mouth dry and alarm flipping through her belly with the speed of a racehorse at Aston. It touched his lips again—that unfathomable half smile that hinted at a secret or forces at play only he understood.

"You are different, Miss Danvers. In the cold

silence of my chamber, my thoughts were consumed with meeting you. I fancifully wondered if you had bewitched me; then I wondered if I had become so desperate in my emptiness that a prick of light in the form of deception could rouse me so. Different is always good, welcome, something bright, wonderful, and exquisite from the ordinary drudgery, don't you agree?" he asked with surprising frankness.

What was he saying? Her skin felt sensitized, and her heartbeat was impossible to control. "Your Grace…"

The hollowness in his tone as he referred to his desperate emptiness struck her forcibly. And the notion that her mad scheme had inspired him somehow was too remarkable. She was something bright…and *exquisite*? Her mouth went even drier.

The duke had come for something from her, and she wanted to cry her frustration, for she still could not perceive it. "What do you require of me?"

"Honesty, Miss Danvers." His voice was like a slow stroke of flames across her sensitive skin. "Going forward…let it be honesty that binds us."

She took a quick breath of utter astonishment. "Your words imply a state of future entanglement for us, Your Grace. I question such a possibility. I will, however, at this moment endeavor to be honest…always," she whispered.

He deserved it from her, considering how she had used his reputation without shame or regret.

The cold brilliant blue of the eyes behind the mask glittered with something fierce before his lashes fluttered down. When they lifted, only curious indifference stared at her.

"Tell me, why do you wish to see the face behind the mask?"

"I…" She laced her fingers before her stomach and considered the man who stared at her with such penetrating regard. As if he wanted to strip her of all facade and see the heart of the woman in front of him. *Honesty*… "Perhaps I want to see the face of the man who inspires such vexatious impetus inside me."

A quick flash of intrigue and expectation before he canted his head left and said, "Oh?"

As their eyes met, she felt a shock of some undefinable sensation dart through her. Awareness flowered inside Kitty. He enjoyed the notion she was not cowering before him.

"My heart beats, my palms are sweaty, a thousand questions swirl in my mind, yet I feel more alive than I've been in longer than I can remember. I feel fear but also anticipate something I do not understand."

Pleasure lit in the cold blue beauty of his eyes. "Ahh."

Such satisfaction in his soft exhalation.

Stupidly, shockingly, she stepped closer to the man. "Your Grace. Let me see your face."

Kitty knew she would never be able to look back and know in what moment of this intimate encounter she had decided to abandon all sense of propriety and expectations of her position in society and all the gentle admonishments of her dear mamma over the years. The excuse of honesty felt like the reason she used to reveal the wanton and improper lady who had always existed within.

Silence lingered. Yet she sensed he was inordinately pleased with her. Was it her turn to be fanciful?

Embers sparked from a log in the fireplace. Un-expectedly, he reached up and removed the mask. The revelation was abrupt, the ensnarement of her complete regard immediate.

The twisted skin of his face was so macabre, yet the man so beautiful.

The release of her breath trembled on her lips and settled in the room.

The skin across his left cheek and down to his chin and neck was indeed roped with brutal scars. Kitty wondered how a man who seemed so self-assured and powerful could be wounded in such a manner. It was unsettling to see such imperfection in an otherwise stunningly masculine face.

Without the mask obscuring his features, the bold, arrogant slash of his cheekbones hinted at restrained power. Lips that had seemed full and sensual before now had a ruthless curve. And his eyes without the sunken shadow cast by the white mask…were exquisite in their dark blue brilliance and piercing intelligence. The unscarred side of his face was smooth, wrinkle free, clear of laugh lines or frown lines. As if he meandered through life expressionless, his heart reserved with no outward emotion to show.

This time when he moved closer, she stood her ground. They stared at each other. He had a quality of stillness that hinted at unfathomable depth. And helpless curiosity roiled through her, feeling as if invisible strings reached from him to her…

And pulled them closer.

Kitty tried to recall how many glasses of champagne she'd consumed.

He measured her with a cool, appraising glance.

"The last ball I attended and showed my face at, at least nine ladies fainted. I believe I can still hear their shrieks of horror."

How had she not uncovered that bit of gossip in her research on the duke? She lifted a shoulder in an inelegant shrug. "That must have been some time ago."

"Seven years if I recall correctly."

"I must say I know no one with such delicate nerves."

The duke gave her an arresting stare. "So you are not frightened, Miss Danvers?"

"I would be the worst sort of lady to be frightened by someone hurt by misfortune, wouldn't you agree?"

He remained silent, studying her with uncomfortable intensity, and she returned his regard with unabashed curiosity. It was then she observed grooves of discomfort bracketing his mouth. *He's in pain.* His posture had also altered, and though now he leaned heavily on his cane, he did not seem less. The duke was the most virile and arresting person she had ever met, and her face heated for having such improper thoughts.

Kitty swallowed her alarm when his hand tightened on his walking stick, and he slowly ambled closer. He stumbled, and with a gasp, she lunged toward him.

He slapped her outstretched hand, but she did not recoil, gripping his upper arm to steady him. "Your Grace!"

His impossibly beautiful eyes iced over. Slowly she released him but didn't step back. Kitty suspected she had offended him with her instinctive reaction, as fierce pride and a guarded watchfulness burned in the gaze that settled upon her.

This was not a man who relied on others for help, and even now with the grooves of pain deepening the frown on his lips, he did not unbend. There was a stillness in his gaze that spoke of suffering, an unfathomable strength, and something elusive that she might never touch or comprehend. Suddenly her heart ached, and her throat burned, sensing the depth of pain he must have endured to be this indomitable.

Finally, he reached for her hand and she allowed it, though she could not say why.

"Forgive me, Miss Danvers. I confess I am not used to being touched by anyone other than Penny."

His lover? Why did the notion make her heart squeeze?

His thumb made a slow stroke down her wrist. "My sister."

Oh. She took a long, ragged breath. "I didn't wonder at it."

"Liar," he whispered with soft amusement. "Your eyes are very expressive. It is a wonder you were able to fool anyone."

He lowered his head, and Kitty stared up at him uncomprehendingly. Then nothing else mattered, for his lips pressed against hers, and her senses caught fire. She gasped at the soft featherlike pressure as his mouth gently molded over hers. With a quiet sound of surprise, she parted her lips and stiffened as shock poured through her veins when he touched his tongue to her bottom lip.

"You are truly an innocent. I wouldn't have

thought it," he murmured against her lips.

Kitty stumbled back, staring at him helplessly. "Whyever did you kiss me?"

Inexplicably, Kitty's heart pounded, and something long dormant inside her stretched and hummed to life. The ripple of interest to know this man burned through her, igniting a need that was at once terrifying and exhilarating. She was not the fanciful sort. Papa had always praised her for being sensible. This surge of interest felt irresponsible and silly. Yet it was there, roiling through her in confusing waves.

Finally, he said, "You are my betrothed."

Dear Lord. His tone was mocking, and worldly, and thrummed with a tension she hardly understood. The fierce intensity of his gaze sent her pulse into a gallop. "You *are* angry, and you have every right to be so, but I pray you will oblige me to make amends."

"I am not out of sorts in the least. I've already mentioned you invite in-depth study. I am fascinated and curious about our engagement."

Our engagement? Hope stirred in her breast. "Do you mean you will permit me the charade of being your fiancée?"

His dark, arrogant head lifted. Many indefinable emotions tumbled through Kitty. It seemed improbable that he would go along with this. What would be the benefit of this arrangement to a man such as himself? It was astonishingly generous of him to allow her the farce.

"Why?" she demanded, then stiffened as a notion occurred to her. "I'll not be your mistress." That disgusting proposition had been placed to her once, and it had infuriated her that gentlemen truly had no tender, respectful regards for a woman without fortune or connections. "If that is why you took liberties and kissed me, I assure you—"

"You'll not have to worry about ravishment. I am not interested in you in a carnal manner and will never be. Disabuse yourself of the notion."

The force of his reply struck her speechless with mortification. "You kissed me, and I—"

"I am impotent, Miss Danvers. I assure you, ravishment will never be your fear."

The low words settled between them, both icy and heated. The chilling finality in his tone warred with the fiery rage that burned briefly in the dark depths of his eyes before his expression shuttered.

"I…I am dreadfully sorry," she muttered, trying to understand the full implication of this impotence and what it had to do with ravishment. Cleary there was some connection, not that she would reveal her ignorance and naïveté. This man was so coldly self-assured, so effortlessly commanding despite his infirmity and scars that she must not falter in their negotiations. Or what she hoped would be the start of a negotiation. "Then, please be explicit with whatever you want from me, Your Grace."

He smiled, and it rendered him charming. "Perhaps we shall be friends."

"Friends?"

"Yes," he smoothly affirmed.

"Surely you did not leave your home to meet me to suggest we be *friends*?" Suddenly Kitty felt frightened. That assessment felt too simplistic to be rooted in reality. The duke must be in possession of a motive he was not ready to share.

The shrewdest of gazes leveled on her. "Perhaps kissing friends," he murmured, his eyes alight with amusement and interest.

Kitty felt a rush of heat, a fiery ache. She was increasingly, unwillingly captivated. She and a duke… friends. *How laughable.*

He wanted something else from her—what, she couldn't perceive, but she was sure of it. "There will be no more kissing," she whispered, because clearly his lips were not impotent. "Unless you are proposing to make our engagement a reality. I am a respectable lady, Your Grace."

She had no notion of why she said that, but icy civility replaced the provoking amusement in his eyes.

"Never that, Miss Danvers," he murmured. "I will never marry."

CHAPTER SIX

Miss Danvers's eyes were exotically slanted, her orbs the golden brown of whiskey fringed in thick ebony lashes. *Cat eyes*. A man could drown in her eyes. Slowly, inch by inch.

"Never? You'll never marry?" she whispered, her gaze skimming over his face and down the length of his body in a caress he felt as if she'd touched him.

"Correct," Alexander murmured, his interest growing in shocking leaps and bounds. "Nor will it be a topic of discourse between us again."

Her eyes widened. The picture Miss Danvers presented was one of artless loveliness. The deep blue silken ball gown clung alluringly to her petite frame, hugging her curves. She was small-boned, curvy, with a tiny waist, and heart-stoppingly lovely. A thick band of rose silk encircled her waist, and the low neckline of her gown was embroidered with flowers in delicate seed pearls. The creamy expanse of her shoulders drew his eyes to her décolletage.

But it was her face that encouraged study. Her cheekbones were elegantly slanted, with classic delicate bones and a faintly haughty nose. She was the possessor of the blackest wavy hair he'd ever seen, supple, flawless skin, full mouth. Miss Danvers caught her soft lower lip between her very white teeth. She had a small overbite. Her lips were too full and pouting.

Alexander couldn't say she was beautiful in the

conventional sense, but she was arresting.

He'd not lied when he mentioned the powerful force of curiosity that had compelled him to travel to London. Each newspaper mention had been a taunt, a beckoning lure, an artfully worded invitation, a curse, and Alexander had almost driven himself mad with the need to confront the charlatan impudently using his name and arousing his long-dead soul in such a manner.

Yet here he was, and his curiosity had not abated. It had multiplied, infinitely, with no possibility of it ever ending, with so many confounding needs and wants desperately seeking to be assuaged.

How terribly droll yet fascinating.

This encounter had already revealed much about Miss Danvers.

She'd never been kissed. No young buck or seasoned rake had ever tried to seduce her, or if they had attempted to, they had abysmally failed.

She seemed to approach life with grace and humor. More than once she'd attempted to introduce levity into their unexpected encounter, despite the frantic fluttering of her pulse at the base of her throat.

And the most astonishing revelation: He'd truly expected a hardened lady used to deceiving the world to get ahead. Yet Miss Danvers glowered with a unique innocence and appeared too soft and sweet to be real.

Alexander caught a glimpse of vulnerability in Miss Danvers's unguarded expression before she lowered her eyes. And his admiration for her mettle soared. Few ladies would deal with his appearance without descending into hysterics. But then her outrageous exploits as his supposed fiancée had already informed him of her daring nature and spine of steel for someone so young.

She was gentle and proud, and in her eyes, he saw shame she'd had to lower herself to such deceptive manners to support her family. But a stubbornness borne from adversity let him know she would do it all over again.

Though Alexander's body remained unmoved, she aroused his mind. He wanted to know more… everything about her until this perplexing hunger was sated. And suddenly he needed to possess her more than his next breath.

Foolish, of course, as he had nothing to offer her, certainly not pleasures of the flesh. His title, perhaps, but nothing more. There would never be a babe to fill her arms, he would never see her soft and replete with pleasure, and eventually, the cold loneliness would chain her—as it had imprisoned him for so long.

Her gaze flicked behind him, then settled once more on his face. She lifted her chin, clearly attempting to be brave. "I believe it is time for me to return to the ballroom, Your Grace."

"Then go," he murmured.

Her lids lowered, shadowing her expressive eyes. She dipped into a curtsy. "I bid you good evening… Alexander."

How soft and curious and achingly tender she sounded.

And that bit of sweetly offered intimacy when she had been so reluctant before sealed her fate.

"I believe I shall enjoy the duration of our attachment, Miss Danvers. I shall call upon you tomorrow at Portman Square by noon. I will be received with all cordiality."

She stumbled slightly, her hand darting out to grip the padded armrest of a chair for balance. "Your Grace...I..."

"We will discuss the terms of our engagement then."

Miss Danvers gave him an agitated look and seemingly could make no reply.

He lifted her hand and brushed his lips across her knuckles. What a pity she had replaced her gloves. Alexander turned around and opened the door to his waiting servant and bath chair. With a silent groan of relief, he settled into the chair and was pushed away.

The travel hadn't been easy, for he had spent days alternating between being in the carriage and on horseback traveling from Perthshire to London. The few times he had stayed overnights at inns, his sleep had been restless and pain filled.

"To the carriage, Your Grace?" his manservant Hoyt asked, clearly sensing his master's need for privacy.

"Yes." Alexander would send a note to Sanderson in the morning. The man had been a friend in the past, and it was he who had closed himself from Sanderson while Alexander healed in Scotland.

"Was the meeting all that you expected, Your Grace?"

Alexander swore his servants were too interested in his private life. Their excitement as he'd packed for the journey had been appalling, and they had made no effort to contain their hopes of a duchess at last. He'd even discovered the damn butler in the servants' parlor, reading the scandal sheets to all fifty servants of his castle, who had appeared to be listening with rapt attention and bated breath.

Curse them, he thought with amusement.

"It went better than I expected," he allowed, blaming himself for their impudence, which he'd permitted to go unchecked over the years.

He felt his manservant's satisfaction as he replied, "Very well, Your Grace."

As his man pushed his chair along the hallway, he could feel Miss Danvers's stare boring into them. Alexander had no earthly idea why the visceral need to be in her presence had flourished and bloomed through his heart. Nothing good could come of it. She could be neither his mistress nor his duchess. The notion of friendship had sprung from a well of confusion over the feelings she roused. No doubt he had frightened her immensely, and she had no notion of what to make of his demands.

That makes two of us, Miss Danvers…

• • •

The next morning, Kitty reposed by the windows facing the small side garden of their town house, waiting for the arrival of the Duke of Thornton with admirable equanimity. And upon a new plush rose-colored armchair, Kitty sat, the small notebook with the sum of all she owed the duke opened on her lap.

Almost a thousand pounds. A fortune she had no

hope of repaying soon.

A careful economy and a well-situated post as a governess should allow her to repay him half in several years. With a scowl, she slammed the notebook closed. How foolish she had been to allow that solicitor to convince her to let the town house, have it furnished, and to hire more staff than her family had been accustomed to. She'd feared her refusal would be suspicious, but all that careful plotting, and the duke had still come for her.

And had alarmingly declared, in a no-nonsense fashion, that they would be friends. How preposterous. How frightening…and how thrilling. Surely a friendship of sorts would be quite beneficial to her family. The tentative connections they'd been slowly forming would strengthen, and the future for her sisters seemed infinitely brighter.

Yet Kitty was beside herself.

That was an understatement. She felt ridiculously vulnerable and out of sorts and hadn't gotten a wink of sleep since returning from the ball. News would circulate of the duke in town for the first time in years, and his arrival portended only trouble.

Her mother had accompanied Judith and Henrietta to the park on a picnic, and Anna had taken a ride with the baron in his Landeau with their lady's maid as chaperone. Kitty had not informed anyone the duke was to call, sensing all plans for the day would have been canceled. It had taken some finessing on her part, but Anna had promised to keep her confidence about the duke's arrival at the ball. Of course, by the time her mother and sisters returned home, they would be fully aware, for the news was certainly already about town.

Kitty hadn't wanted her family to meet the duke until she was much more confident of their arrangement. Friends indeed. *Kissing friends?* As if she were a light-skirts or someone easily persuaded to act wantonly.

Kitty scowled. Her ruse might have been outrageous, but she would disabuse the notion that he was allowed any sort of liberties for his silence and participation.

In anticipation of his call, she had dressed in her prettiest day gown and had artfully arranged her hair in a style of fashion. The best of refreshments had been ordered, the already spotless drawing room had been aired, and fresh flowers—roses and tulips—graced the room. When the butler came to announce His Grace, the Duke of Thornton had come to call, she almost cried her relief.

She surged to her feet when he strolled in, the epitome of masculine grace and confidence. The duke did not walk with a cane of assistance, and for someone who had been missing from society for so long, he appeared a man of fashion immaculately garbed in fawn-colored breeches and waistcoat, knee-high walking boots, a dark blue jacket, and an exquisitely tied cravat.

He stopped, almost in the arch entrance, and their gazes met across the expanse of the room. There was no mask, and the severity of his scars in the daylight were more pronounced and hinted at a painful past and perhaps a lonely road to healing.

What had happened? The questions tumbled in her mind, desperate to be voiced, but she held them back. According to the rules of etiquette, it would be distasteful to intrude upon his privacy in such a brash manner when they had no familiarity between them.

He had a presence that was both intimidating and devilish. Kitty's breath hitched at the flash of emotions in his eyes, a hint of a shadow, perhaps uncertainty. She stared at him, quite astonished.

Was it that he, too, was nervous?

It seemed so improbable, yet…

She inhaled softly to steady her nerves, then dipped into a deep curtsy before rising. Kitty thought it prudent to keep her gaze discreetly lowered. "Your Grace, how delightful to see you again."

"I do not believe it for a moment."

"Believe what, Your Grace?" she asked without removing her eyes from the elegance of his tied cravat.

"This sweet, contrite, submissive act, my impudent minx."

That shocking, outrageous description had her snapping her gaze to his in undisguised alarm. The dictates of civility forbade her from uttering a scathing retort, and she did not know the manner of this man. They assessed each other in a silent duel of sorts, and it befuddled her to see the crafty humor in his gaze.

The duke strolled farther into the room. "So, we are delighted, then, and not apprehensive to see me?"

Clearly the duke wasn't one for polite subterfuge. "Of course not. Are we not to be friends of sorts?" She forced out the words as if such a thing could ever be a reasonable proposition.

"I can fairly see that you are biting your tongue, Miss Danvers. I've roused your ire."

"A lady should never be uncivil, you know," Kitty said with a small, self-conscious laugh.

His eyes were sharp and assessing upon her person. "I wonder, can one be crafty and delightfully wicked and still pretend quaint gentility and a soft heart, which define ladylike qualities?"

She gasped softly at this effrontery and could only gaze at him open-mouthed. "You've visited to cross wits with me, Your Grace? Or to discuss the terms of our…attachment?"

He smiled, and her heart trembled.

She looked at him with misgiving and said, "Please, won't you be seated? I will ring for refreshments."

He lowered himself to the single sofa opposite her. The housekeeper, who'd been on alert of his arrival and possibly just as anxious as Kitty, bustled in with a tea service.

"Thank you, Mrs. Hedgepole," Kitty murmured, preparing tea for the duke.

She felt the weight of his stare, the way his gaze seemed to trace every visible inch of her.

Kitty handed him a cup with a saucer, which seemed to be swallowed between his large yet surprisingly elegant hands. Fine networks of scars slashed ragged over the back of his left hand. Her gaze lingered a moment there before snapping up to his face.

He regarded her over the rim of his cup as he took several sips. The cup was then lowered to the small walnut table between them. "I passed an overly enthusiastic journalist lingering by your front door. He tried to engage me in a conversation, but I did not oblige the man."

She cleared her throat. "Your resurrection is noteworthy and will add fuel to the flames that had already been dancing around me. You...you have been away for years. I am still in disbelief you are actually sitting before me."

A brief smile touched his lips, but he made no reply, seemingly content with staring at her. Surely he knew such an unabashed regard was rude and provoking.

"Miss Danvers—"

"Your Grace—"

She detected laughter in his steady gaze and was disconcerted by it.

"It seems we are both eager to get to the heart of our compromise."

Kitty laughed, a trifle nervously. "I do admit I have been baffled as to how a...friendship with me is beneficial to you, Your Grace."

There it was again, a flash of haunting shadows in his eyes.

"I haven't found much to fascinate me in recent years. When I do find such a treasure, I explore it thoroughly until I am satisfied."

Dear God. And she was that treasure? "And then?"

"Then I move on to the next interesting one," he said with mild surprise, as if that thought should be evident.

An odd chill of warning kissed down her spine.

Whatever transaction she entered into with this man, she would have to be infinitely careful, lest her heart become tangled only to be casually discarded later.

"I see," she said softly, taking a delicate sip of her tea. "Firstly, I would like to point out that no one encouraged me in this folly. My family is ignorant of the matter, entirely blameless, and I would like to keep it that way."

"Very well."

"And to be clear…you will not reveal to anyone within society that our engagement is a farce?"

"For a price, of course," he smoothly replied with such arrogant self-assurance, it set her teeth on edge.

It seemed he would exact his pound of flesh for her audacity. "The price of friendship," she reiterated carefully.

"Hmm."

"What will you require of me?" she murmured.

"We shall spend time together." His manner was very much that of a man accustomed to command. "I've never had a friend of the opposite sex…or one as frightfully interesting as yourself, Miss Danvers."

She stared at him, thinking surely that could not be it. The benefits of this arrangement were far greater for her. Why would he want to be friends with her, someone who had shamelessly used his title and connections?

Her breath hitched softly as an improbable idea caught at the edges of her thoughts.

He is lonely.

The awareness pierced her, and she stared at him helplessly.

Who are you? An inexplicable need to know

what his life had been like for the past several years filled her. "How will we be friends, Your Grace? Surely you see how odd such a notion is."

"Ah…let that be my concern."

She wondered if now was the time to point out that they would never be kissing friends. "There will be no impropriety." She dared to sniff derisively.

A faint glint of humor appeared in his eyes. "You'll attend Lady Carnforth's ball tomorrow. We'll start from there. Then perhaps the theater. I haven't seen the stage in years." There was a hint of surprised yearning in his tone. "Perhaps an outing to the museum. It shall be whatever interests me, and I'll require your company for it."

A peculiar jolt darted through her, with an unknown sensation that disappeared too fast for her to give it name. "You've been away from society," she said. "Lady Carnforth is a fearsome dragon and is known for her sarcastic wit and outrageous, cutting tongue. Her yearly summer ball is legendary among society. Only the who's who were invited. I assure you I am not on that list despite my recent popularity."

He made a noncommittal sound, as if thoroughly unsure of how to relate to that bit of information.

"You'll receive an invitation." How confident he sounded.

She realized for him to be aware of the ball, after just newly returned to town, he would have gotten a belated invitation. Kitty supposed every hostess would be clamoring to have the elusive duke at their balls, literary saloons, and drawing rooms. Had he missed the elegancies of life the *ton* had to offer?

"The ball is tomorrow. If I receive an invitation, I would attend with my sister and mamma."

The duke smiled, which made his forbidding countenance appear very much more pleasing. It also tugged her gaze to the rope of scars marring his face. Why had he worn a mask last night but not today?

"You honor me, Miss Danvers," he said with a smooth charm that belied the cool watchfulness of his gaze.

It was as if he wanted to court her. Preposterous, of course. They were to simply act as if they had an attachment with all the intimacies and expectations of a real engagement.

The notion was frightening and exquisite all at once. Anna's chance of securing a well-connected match was even more possible.

But after such public outings, the end of their engagement would ruin all chances for Kitty of any respectable alliance. Society would remember for years that the Duke of Thornton had jilted her, and questions of her virtue and faults would linger in their minds. This was a deeper ruination than she'd imagined, but she was willing to pay whatever price, within respectable reason.

Kitty owned that the advantages of such an alliance would outweigh the drawbacks. If they could have a six-month engagement, that would be perfect. Perhaps even Judith could be engaged by the end of the season. In one fell swoop both her sisters could have their futures secured.

Oh, it would be worth it in every way. For when it would come time for Henrietta to have her season,

Kitty's scandal would be old, and Anna and Judith would be perfectly positioned to sponsor her.

She smiled at him tentatively.

He then said, "And your presence at my estate in Scotland for a week or two is required. *Without* chaperone."

She was for the moment unable to find words to express her bewilderment. "I beg your pardon!" she finally cried, quite taken aback.

"You heard me, Miss Danvers."

"But surely I could not have, Your Grace."

"I value my privacy, and while you are a guest in my home, I will not have a keen-eyed gossiper reporting anything of my life to the press or society. Curiosity and conjecture I will not tolerate. I trust this will be no hardship for you."

"I fear I cannot visit you in Scotland. That is an outrageous suggestion, and I must not undertake to do so," she said, perturbed at his unapologetic audacity.

"I've not allowed any room for negotiations."

His brilliant blue eyes chilled, and that loss of warmth sent a warning down her spine.

"I cannot traipse around the countryside without a chaperone. My reputation might come under the severest of scrutiny."

Another sip of his tea, an artful, calculating pause. "How surprising you think of matters such as your reputation. After this elaborate ruse, I cannot believe you are as delicate as you protest to be."

A mocking brow arched, and she flushed. That low tightening in her stomach and the slow drum of her heart when their gazes collided was a decidedly odd sensation.

The teacup and saucer were lowered carefully to the walnut table. He leaned back against the cushions in a relaxed pose, crossing his long, muscular legs at the ankles. "A lady of your daring should have no reservations."

"I will not be goaded into acting without propriety. I am not the rash sort, though I daresay it may appear so, Your Grace," she retorted.

Tension crackled in the air between them.

"Ah, so your deception to pose as my fiancée was methodically planned and craftily executed."

Kitty blinked, at a loss for words for precious seconds. "Let me ardently assure Your Grace, I did not enjoy the disagreeable necessity of the charade I orchestrated for society."

That oddly admiring smile once again curved his lips. "How old are you, Miss Danvers?"

She considered refusing the unexpected question, then said, "Three and twenty, Your Grace."

"You are not a debutante who requires constant supervision. You are ingenious enough to surrender to my plans without a prick to your reputation. I trust you will see it done, hmm?"

He remained entirely unmoved.

"Your Grace—"

"You will agree to all my terms or end the engagement today."

His voice was so low and well-modulated, it took precious seconds to absorb the ruthless intent laced within its soft tones. Her entire body trembled, and her heart fluttered like a captive bird. It was a minute or two before she could trust herself to speak, and the dratted man simply waited.

"The season is a gauntlet that needs the most delicate of guidance. My sisters cannot do without me. Everything I've sacrificed is for them. To leave them when they need me…" She paused and took a deep breath.

His closed expression suggested her pleas were futile.

"You'll be gone for a week or two at most; they'll survive," the duke said drily.

"I owe you much, Your Grace, but surely there is a different manner in which I might make amends."

He favored her with another of his measuring glances. "I will have my godmother—the Countess of Darling—take your sisters under her wing. Lady Darling's stamp of approval will surpass your hovering presence as they navigate the marriage mart."

Kitty's breath exploded on a gasp. The countess was one of the most influential ladies of society, and her patronage was more than Kitty ever dreamed of for her sisters. Emotions clogged her throat as she stared at him. "You are willing to do that?"

"Yes. And if this is any consolation, my sister, Penny, will be our shadow. She'll be a very interfering chaperone," he said with mild amusement and a good deal of fondness. How startling to see the softening of his severe features.

"Your sister resides with you in Scotland?"

"Yes," he murmured, an odd look of calculation in his eyes. "I believe Penny has read all the newssheet mentions of your particular bravery and is keen on meeting you."

Perhaps there was still hope she could turn this

situation to her advantage. "I am very much obliged to you, Your Grace," she said softly. "May I propose how long our engagement should stand while we explore the bonds of a possible friendship?"

His lips twitched. "No."

His absolute denial sent a strange shock through her. "Your Grace—"

"The duration will not be bounded by time but by my…interest."

She snapped her spine straight. In other words, if he found her company to be boring, he would not endure it for six days, much less six months. Kitty realized then he did not care why she had taken on such a deception; it mattered only that he had found something new and shiny to play with. And she was in no position to negotiate. The situation was becoming intolerable.

Then an unexpected warmth unfurled through her. This man was the elusive and powerful Duke of Thornton. Kitty quite believed he could have any number of ladies, both respectable and tarnished, by his side in whatever manner he desired. Yet it was something about her, a wallflower to the *ton*, that had captivated his regard.

Her foolish, foolish heart unexpectedly started to beat faster in sheer fascination. "I will make myself available, Your Grace."

His eyes gleamed with satisfaction. "Then our negotiation is completed." He lifted his teacup in some sort of salute before swallowing the contents.

They heard the sound of the front door opening, and anxious footsteps danced a hurried beat on the marble tiled floor. Kitty suppressed a groan as the excited tones of her mother and sisters filtered through the hallway. She stood, smoothing the wrinkles in her day gown, and took a steadying breath.

The duke obligingly followed suit and slowly stood, facing the open door, his hands clasped behind his back, his bearing one of command and power.

Discomfort curled through her, and she worked to banish it.

"Katherine, I've heard the most astonishing news—"

Her mother faltered upon seeing the duke, her hand fluttering to her chest. She appeared to be quite overcome as her gaze snapped from her daughter to the duke.

"Mamma…" Kitty cleared her throat, feeling unaccountably nervous. "Your Grace, may I present my mother, Viscountess Marlow, and my younger sisters, Miss Judith Danvers and Miss Henrietta Danvers."

Her mother and sisters dipped into deep and elegant curtsies. Upon rising, her sisters made a valiant effort to not look directly at the duke's scars, but her mother stared at him without any revulsion. In truth, Mamma's eyes were soft with compassion and respect.

"It is a privilege to make your acquaintanceship, Your Grace," Mamma said with a smile.

The duke stepped forward and surprised Kitty by offering them a most charming bow in return.

"Lady Marlow, how delightful to make your acquaintance at last. Misses Danvers, I've heard many good things about you; I'm charmed."

Kitty watched in muted amazement as her

mother and sisters flushed, and as the duke transformed himself into a most amiable gentleman, being very subtle but eloquently persuasive with his compliments. He politely declined the offer for more refreshments and made a promise to call with his godmother in a few days. Her mother almost swooned with rapture at that piece of news.

Soon the duke departed with a speaking glance in her direction, and her sisters were shooed to the smaller sitting room by their parent.

Now that they were alone, Kitty almost fidgeted under the penetrating stare of her mother.

"When you told us the duke was your fiancé, I grappled to believe it. And despite the announcement in the papers, I thought the engagement was not real," she said softly, her eyes searching every nuance of Kitty's expression. "You have always been too daring and irrepressible, and I wondered…"

"How astonishing you should think that, Mamma." Kitty kept her face serene despite the awful jerking in her heart and lowered herself onto the sofa. "Shall I ring for more tea?"

"No," her mother murmured, strolling over to sit beside her. "The duke's arrival in town was all anyone could speak of. I ran into Lady Goodall and Lady Weston, and I had to pretend knowledge of his appearance at last night's ball and the shocking news you disappeared alone with him for several minutes."

She clasped her mother's hand. "Forgive me, Mamma— I should have informed you this morning. Last night the duke's appearance was unexpected. He wanted to surprise me. And we did have a private audience."

Her mamma squeezed her fingers reassuringly. "And did the private meeting accomplish what you desired?"

Kitty hesitated, the need to fling herself onto her mother's bosom welling in her heart. It had been so long since Kitty had sought comfort and direction from her parent. In truth, it felt as if Kitty herself had been the directional force in the household since Papa died, and it was she who supplied reassurance and handled all the troubles they faced. For more than five years, they had depended on her for food, household management, stability, and a sense of safety. Not once had she crumbled, but now her lips trembled, and her throat burned with the need to unburden. If only for a few minutes.

Her mother was staring at her, clearly waiting for her to say something. It was a tactic that had worked alarmingly well from when she was a small child. That piercing and unflinching stare from their mother always had her children revealing all their secrets and shenanigans.

Kitty felt her cheeks grow warm with a guilty blush. "The duke…the duke has invited me to his Scotland estate for several days."

It was tempting to lie and pretend, but she was heartily sick of misleading the woman she loved. Now that everyone would surely believe her engagement with the duke was beyond reproach, she could be more transparent with her mother. For, especially now, Kitty hungered for some sort of guidance. "He has stipulated no chaperone, Mamma."

"Well!" her mother gasped, releasing Kitty's

hands, a thoughtful frown splitting her lovely face.

"I do not think the duke means any harm but that he wishes to know me better without being scrupulously watched. He has a sister in residence, and she has a governess. I'm sure it will all be proper."

If only her voice did not lack conviction, and if only her heart did not pound with such shocking anticipation. *Goodness, what is wrong with me?*

Her mother smiled warmly and wrapped an arm around Kitty's shoulders. "Sometimes a gentleman needs the encouragement of a lack of chaperone to be bold. That was how it was with Artie and me. A few stolen moments here and there cemented our love," her mother said, her cheeks pinking. "The duke may require such moments with you, my dear, and I must say I agree with the man. You are three and twenty, and by all accounts the duke is thirty. You are both sensible adults with a public attachment."

Kitty's throat closed in shock. Her mother was giving her leave to be improper. The viscountess had always been such a stickler for propriety. It was Papa who'd been more lenient and understanding of Kitty's and her sisters' antics. It was inconceivable that her mother would make such an unorthodox suggestion. "Mamma—"

"I will discreetly allow with certain friends that you will visit your aunt Effie in Derbyshire for a week or two, as she is feeling poorly."

"Mamma!"

Her mother stood and peered down at her. "I daresay if the duke should be given the chance to know your sincere heart and wonderful nature,

nothing would prevent him from making you his
duchess," she said softly, her eyes growing watery.

Kitty stood, searching her mother's expression.
"Mamma—"

The viscountess lifted her chin. "I want that for
you. Not because a connection with the duke will be
beneficial for our family, but because you deserve
to secure your place in this world, and I will not be
ashamed to ardently wish it for you with a man of
rank and wealth. My dear, fortune favors the bold. I
need not say more."

Her mother swirled and sauntered from the
room, leaving Kitty quite astonished with excitement
and trepidation filling her heart.

Fortune favors the bold?

Well, surely she needed no more encouragement
than that to lead her heart to possible ruin and pain.

Not that she would ever be so foolish to set her
cap for a duke, and certainly not one as enigmatic
and odd as the Duke of Thornton. Certainly not one
who could ruin her if he whimsically decided she was
no longer interesting.

Yet the memory of his lips ghosted over hers. She
could still feel his arms enclosing her, as if his touch
had been imprinted on her skin. The subtle taste of
his passion, the wonderful scent of his masculinity,
and the yearning in his eyes just now when he'd
called her a treasure.

Her! A treasure he wanted to explore. *Utterly
ridiculous.*

She closed her eyes, pressing her palm flat against
her thumping heart as she whispered, "And yet also
so very wonderful."

CHAPTER SEVEN

Alexander lingered within the shadows of the high balcony of Lady Carnforth's luxurious and opulent town house ballroom, watching as the crowd milled about. A few well-connected and familiar members from the press mingled within the crowd, chatting with the prime minister, the Duke of Bancroft, and the vivacious hostess. At times, their hungry gazes settled on him, their eager attention assessing his half mask and the ebony cane gripped in his hand.

Fashionable London was positively addicted to gossiping and the newspapers that fed their habits, and tomorrow all would read and speculate about the Duke of Thornton's visit to London in ever greater detail.

An odd sort of amusement arrowed through him. Even odder, a sense of nostalgia filled his heart. There had been a time he'd loved being about town, the frivolities of the season a thing to look forward to with keen want. How strange to think he might have missed it while he'd been healing in Scotland.

The fashionably dressed society surged around him, the scent of various perfumes, the facile chatters and loud laughter assaulting his senses. Many faltered, avid stares lingering on him where he reposed against a Corinthian column. Their curiosity about the man behind the mask was palpable, but no one had the audacity to approach.

His title floated in the air in hushed whispers, and

more than once he wondered what in damnation he was truly doing. He'd never fancied himself a man ruled by impulse or passion. Not even when he had been a part of the social scene years ago, the sobriquet of "mad, bad, and dangerous" haunting his name, had he acted rashly. Everything had always been methodically planned and executed, and it had been that strategist in him that had admired Miss Danvers's ingenuity.

Yet since his discovery of the delightful minx, impulse was his name. The ungovernable cravings she roused in him demanded study and exploration, and he was recklessly surrendering to all urges.

Was his life truly so empty that his sole occupation was now the unraveling of Kitty Danvers?

It seemed to be, for he could not convince himself with logical arguments to crush her ruse and walk away. She was an imposter and certainly deserved to be unmasked, but that cold thought had melted, and only the burning curiosity to understand her complexities and peel back this peculiar creature's layers remained.

"Viscountess Marlow, Miss Kitty Danvers, and Miss Anna Danvers."

His attention was entirely arrested by the butler's announcement. Then she appeared atop the opposite landing and completely stole his breath.

How and why, perhaps he would never understand. The reporters who covered these events so tomorrow's scandal and fashion sheets could report all the *on-dits* snapped their gazes from her up to the high balcony where he lingered within its shadows. Once again, Miss Danvers would be the centerpiece of their articles, and surely they would paint him as the besotted fool who had stood frozen and stared at her arresting presence.

Alexander was uncertain how to feel about the adoration the *ton* claimed he owned for her. He was not the kind of man given to softer sentiments. Not that he did not believe in the higher power of love. He did. In the past there simply had never been any lady in his life to inspire feelings beyond mild affections and fleeting lust. Even his fiancée of the time had been about power and connection, the brightest diamond of society paired with the coveted rising star of politics and the heir to a dukedom.

The paper hadn't dared then to mention the words "love match." Yet now the cartoons painted him slavishly in love and spoke about his adoration of the delightful Kitty in mocking tones. Another sin to punish Miss Danvers for, surely—he should not be remiss in that.

Miss Danvers wore a brilliant dark green gown, a provokingly stunning jewel in the midst of pastel and warm colors of the other gowns. He allowed his gaze to unabashedly travel over her. Through the elegant drape of her dress, he could see the lines of her hips, round and lush, the slender curve of her waist, the beguiling weight of her breasts. A few young bucks, and even one or two more stately gentlemen, sent her quick, covetous stares.

Miss Danvers seemed unaware of her own desirability, for she did not blush or preen, merely assessed the atmosphere as she made her way down the stairs. She was petite, sleek, lushly curved, and the raw sensuality of how she moved held him momentarily spellbound. His fiancée was remarkably pretty, with an inviting mouth which was unmistakably provocative. Alexander could only marvel at the dim-witted idiocy of the men of the *ton* for not marrying such a delight.

Another young lady descended behind her, and she was garbed in a pale pink gown that also clung to her willowy frame. The two women spoke briefly, then made their way through the crowd toward the sidelines. The whispers floating about revealed her to be Miss Danvers's sister.

They were lovely ladies. It was a pity the men of the *ton* decided to judge their worth based only on their family's purse strings and connections.

Lady Carnforth approached him in a swirl of golden ruffles and glittering diamonds. "My dear boy, how wonderful to see you; it has been years!" she gasped dramatically. "Though I do hope it is you under that mask, Alexander. How I missed you. Quite dreadfully."

He leaned in and dutifully kissed the cheek she lifted to him. "It is I, Cousin Miranda. I missed you as well." Alexander was mildly surprised to feel the truth of his response. He had missed Miranda's eccentric, flamboyant manners and opinions.

Alexander straightened as Kitty's gaze unerringly found him atop the balcony. She went remarkably still before lifting her chin in acknowledgment. There went that unusual warmth pouring through his heart again.

Perhaps he needed to see one of his doctors.

The curious brown eyes of his cousin settled on Miss Danvers, then swept the crowd below. Miranda cast him a curious sidelong glance. No doubt she anticipated his reaction to the *ton*'s inquisitiveness. Many matrons of society and several debutantes blatantly ogled him. He could feel society's rabid stares and ceaseless speculations like poisonous ants crawling over his neck and back.

"Our society can be a tad bit ridiculous," she said with a sniff. "I've ordered the most lavish food for refreshment, decorated the room in an Egyptian theme. They are all the rage, you know. And invited everyone who has some secret attachment or scandal swirling around their name. But they are too busy watching you and Miss Danvers. You've quite upstaged me, dear boy."

"It was not deliberate, I assure you."

"Hmm, I gathered after your order to send her an invitation, you would actually attend. Why was it so important for Miss Danvers to be here tonight?"

"It simply was."

She harrumphed, no doubt irritated he would not divulge anything noteworthy for her to gossip about.

"She is a trifle…loud, my boy; I'm surprised at your choice," Lady Carnforth said, sidling closer to him. "I confess I knew nothing about Miss Danvers or her family until a few weeks ago. I was shocked the girl already had *four* seasons. Truly some people ought to know when to give up, though I must declare she should be ecstatic at snagging you."

His cousin had missed the mark entirely. "*You* are loud and flamboyant, Cousin Miranda. Miss Danvers is something altogether different. A rare hothouse flower in the midst of hardened diamonds."

Another sniff. "You sound as if you admire

her. Clearly the newspapers were right about your adoration!"

He made no answer, content to watch Miss Danvers's interactions within society. Stares of stern disapproval and envy followed her stroll across the expanse of the ballroom. It was in the bold way she stepped, the daring green of her exquisite gown, the proud angle of her head. He sensed she hadn't worn such colors before her transformation to Kitty Danvers. What had she been like before? The same? Different? A timid mouse or the tigress before him now?

He truly liked the exuberant way she sashayed to the edge of the ballroom. There was a haughty lift to her chin, and it was bravado, as if she dared anyone to remark on her presence. It was a defense, and he wondered if she had a difficult upbringing to be this prickly…to be this *different*.

And it seemed an injustice to use such an inane word to describe the woman below.

She wasn't the sensible, proper sort of lady he'd been told lovingly by his mother years ago would make him the perfect duchess. Odd that had been her recommendation, for his mother hadn't been the well-behaved sort.

Miss Danvers was the opposite of anyone who'd ever held his attention. She appeared to be a woman who could be as brilliant as a flame and as fickle as the wind.

Would my mother have liked you, Katherine Danvers? Would you have appalled her…or would you have fascinated her, as you've seemingly bewitched me?

Alexander caught himself studying the way her hands moved, the turn of her head, and the sweet, oftentimes earnest expression on her face as she spoke with her sister. "My fiancée is fine as she is, Cousin Miranda," he replied to her silent glare.

"My dear boy—"

"And I will not take kindly to anyone who implies otherwise," he murmured coolly. "She is to be treated with all cordiality and respect."

A waltz was announced. Both Miss Danverses were asked to dance, and with wide smiles they allowed themselves to be escorted onto the dance floor. The orchestra swelled around him, the most powerful and eloquent notes filtering through the air, music he had missed more than he realized, and not once did Alexander remove his regard from the dancing figure of Kitty Danvers.

It was in his arms she should be; the inane thought ran through his mind on a loop.

"You are staring at your fiancée, quite shamelessly I might add." Cousin Miranda sniffed.

"That I am."

And he would not apologize for it or pretend gentlemanly contrition. He had the urge to be the one dancing with her, holding her close, perhaps directing her away through one of the terrace doors to steal a kiss.

Odd, that. This was the second time in as little as a day he'd thought about kissing her. For the first time in years, Alexander felt as if he did not know himself.

What am I to really do with you, Miss Danvers?

• • •

Kitty stood on the fringes of Lady Carnforth's ballroom away from the fashionable crowd, content with rejecting her third offer to dance. One waltz had been enough. Chandeliers sparkled with hundreds of candles shedding rich light on handsome men and gorgeously gowned women, strolling about in silks and satins as they laughed and twirled around the expanse of the ballroom.

The fashionable elites were in their element, and Kitty had never felt more out of place.

She was in attendance only because the duke had used his influence, and it was this morning an invitation had been delivered to Portman Square with a personal note apologizing for the oversight from Lady Carnforth herself. Her mother and Anna had been beside themselves with glee, and the house had been filled with peals of laughter and excited chattering. Hours later, dressed in their best ball gowns, with hair styled into the artful chignons with tendrils kissing their shoulders, Kitty and Anna had made their way to the ball with their mother.

She had lost her mother in the crowd, but Anna she could see, her radiant smile seeming to light the entire ballroom, wearing her admiration of the baron openly for all the world to observe and speculate. If she were not careful, the rumors could turn sly, considering he'd not yet declared himself in any promising fashion. Even though Kitty admitted the baron as he stared at her sister appeared equally besotted—if not more.

With a heavy sigh, she snagged a glass of champagne from a passing footman.

"The newssheets tomorrow will speak of your droll boredom and marvel that you could be aloof at such a remarkable event, which boasts a twenty-piece orchestra and the king himself, who is yet to arrive."

Kitty whirled around, grinning. "Dear Ophelia, how glad I am to see you."

Her friend was exquisitely gowned in a dark yellow ball gown, her wild beauty appearing more delicate and ethereal than ever. She had been the only friend out of their set likely to be invited to Lady Carnforth's illustrious ball.

"I'm incredibly pleased to see you as well, Kitty. I dare say my night will not be so tedious anymore, for I have your delightful company," Ophelia said with a pleased grin.

Kitty laughed. "I, too, am glad for your company."

"You do appear out of sorts. Is all well with Thornton?"

At the mention of the duke, her stomach flipped alarmingly, and she did everything in her power to not glance toward the shadowed balcony. Quickly she recounted to Ophelia all that had happened.

Ophelia shot her an astonished glance. "I should mention within the next few days to our friends that you'll be visiting your aunt in Derbyshire for a couple of weeks, but you'll not be visiting Aunt Effie but with the duke in Scotland?"

A flush worked over Kitty's face. "Yes," she said, meeting her friend's eyes unflinchingly. "I want everyone to think that is where I am. I'll confess all once I've returned and there are no rumors, of course."

"Oh dear," Ophelia said. "That is quite scandalous indeed. Are you by chance developing feelings for him?"

"Of course not!" But the denial sounded hollow to her ears. "I've only just met the man, and he is decidedly peculiar and unlike anyone I've ever met. I like his oddities and I truly think we could be friends. It is unusual, is it not, that none of us is friends with someone of the opposite sex? It promises to be quite interesting."

"Yet, my dear Katherine, you seem perturbed."

She lowered her head conspiratorially, and Ophelia obligingly dipped hers in turn. "He has demanded I visit him without the benefit of a chaperone. I'm to travel *alone* to Scotland with the duke."

"How terribly exciting!" Ophelia gasped, her eyes twinkling.

"It is outrageous, that's what it is," Kitty cried, unable to still the flutters in her stomach. "However disagreeable the thought of being with the duke in such an unusual situation may be, I am determined to bear it."

"Perhaps it is an opportunity."

She glared at her friend. "Have you gone daft? The only opportunity is one for ruin!" And she had to do it or risk the dratted man calling off the engagement publicly. Kitty did not want to believe his promise to do so a bluff and regret it later.

"Or to become his duchess in truth," Ophelia murmured.

"Do hold your tongue!" Kitty cried, not wanting

the foolish hope to lodge in her heart.

"I daresay this is the chance to beguile the duke with your natural charm."

Kitty suppressed her groan, then faltered into complete stillness when the duke suddenly pushed from the shadows. Whispers erupted and churned in the air. And the *ton* ogled him shamelessly as he moved through the throng, yet the duke bore such attentions as though they hardly concerned him.

He seemed immune to it all as he descended the wide staircase. His body moved with easy grace, and a surge of surprised concern went through her as she noted the absence of a cane. His face, however... once again a mask covered the scarred half side, though this time its color was black with striking filigree of gold and blue. The effect was stunning and provocative.

The duke carried himself with such a command-ing air of self-confidence, one would hardly remark on his mask or the slight limp in his gait if he were observed closely. And Kitty felt the regard of their society was entirely upon him.

"Do you know why he is here?" Ophelia asked, shifting protectively closer to her.

"No," Kitty said, unable to wrest her eyes from him. "But it was the duke who arranged for Lady Carnforth to bestow an invitation to me."

Ophelia bumped into her shoulder quite indelicately. "Oh, Kitty, please do look away; you are being fast and scandalous!"

Heat rising in her face, Kitty tried her best to comply. Several prominent lords and even the prime minister, and the minister for foreign affairs, made their way over to him. She discreetly watched as he conversed with apparent ease, showing no reaction to the avid staring at his mask. At times his lips curved in amusement, other times he laughed, and she fancied she heard mocking disdain in his tone. Either way, the lords and ladies currently gathered in his circle seemed enraptured with whatever he said, yet there was an air of isolation around him, as if he were detached from it all.

The half side of his expression not hidden by that beautiful mask was one of worldly cynicism, his mien one of exquisite boredom and apathy. So why had he come?

Unexpectedly, his head swiveled, and their gazes collided. She tilted her head in greeting, a peculiar warmth flooding her lower belly. Without further acknowledgment of his compatriots, he made his way over to her. Kitty wanted to fidget as the dozens of eyes suddenly were upon them.

"Lift your chin; be arrogant and beautiful. Remember you are Kitty Danvers," Ophelia whispered beside her before discreetly melting away.

Kitty sank into a curtsy when the duke stopped before her. His responding bow charmed her, the tender warmth in his eyes seduced her, and she glanced away, peering above his shoulder lest she make a fool of herself.

Remember I am simply a toy, a pawn in a game where he is the only player and the rule maker.

He held out one of his arms. "If you would honor me with a dance, Miss Danvers. I have it on good authority another waltz is to be announced."

Rather bewildered, she gave him her hand,

curtsying slightly. They made their way onto the floor as the orchestra struck up a waltz. His hand slid slowly about her waist, drawing her close. With a slight shift of his palm, he guided them into the waltz.

Dear God, we fit.

That was the inane thought blaring through her mind as he rested his hand atop her shoulders, and she lightly touched his as they twirled into the beat of the elegant dance.

"I thank you, Miss Danvers. I haven't had this pleasure in years."

"The pleasure is entirely mine, Your Grace."

Another fleeting smile touched his lips. Several questions tumbled through her thoughts, but she held them back lest she offend him. Kitty couldn't help wondering how he could command her movement with such effortless grace when only a few days ago, he'd arrived at another ball in a wheeled chair.

"What do you like to do?"

Kitty frowned. "Why?"

"I am trying to ascertain the kind of woman you are, Miss Danvers. I watched you earlier, and I do not feel as if balls are that exciting for you."

She stared at him with a mixture of dread and fascination. In all the seasons she'd had, and the few gentlemen who'd danced with her or paid a call upon her, none had ever asked her what she liked to do.

How very odd she hadn't realized before. "Your Grace, I—"

He stumbled, his fingers tightening on her shoulder and hip to the point of likely bruising her. She swallowed the cry of discomfort and met his eyes. They were shadowed with pain and fierce pride.

And Kitty knew in that moment she should not question the lapse in his movements or dare suggest they stop.

He twirled her with lithe grace, his tight grip never relenting, his lips flat, his words silenced, the command of his pain absolute. And she flowed with him, ignoring the tight clasp that he seemed unaware of, and danced with him in silence.

The last notes of the waltz died away. He released her, bowed, and then straightened. His gaze was inscrutable, and her heart trembled. Then, without speaking, the duke turned and walked away. He disappeared quickly into the crowd. Several curious whispers buzzed through the air, and she strained to watch him above their heads until she saw him no more.

She hesitated for only a few seconds before making her way through the throng. Something was wrong, and she could not ignore it in good conscience.

Glancing discreetly about, she slipped through the open terrace door. Several ladies and gentlemen were about, but they seemed more to mind their own business than to assess hers. Kitty remained on the terrace for a few seconds before accepting that he had continued. She hurried down the small steps that led along a cobbled garden path. There a few people lingered in darkened alcoves, and giggles and husky murmurs reached her ears.

She kept going, glancing about to see if she could find the duke. Kitty almost missed the stone bench near the entrance of the conservatory, hidden by shadows and overgrown plants. There the duke sat in a shocking display of disarray. His jacket and cravat had been discarded, and his fingers dug into the harsh stone bench. Surely he would rip the nails of his fingers to shreds. There was a sheen of sweat about his brow; the corded neck of his throat was stiff with tension. Yet he was absolutely still, his breathing deep and even.

Then a rough, tortured sound rode the air. Kitty pressed a hand across her heart, her eyes closing briefly at his pained groan. Her throat went tight, then a soft, stupid smile curved her lips.

He had willingly endured this pain…to dance with her. *Why?*

He shifted, and the shadows obscured his features wholly, yet she knew the moment he saw her. Kitty's body suddenly felt weightless; her heart trembled, and her awareness of the duke heightened with shocking intensity.

Though he did not speak, the demand for an explanation was palpable. In the dark shadows of the gardens, he stared at her, no gentlemanly consideration of her sensibilities as his eyes skimmed over each swell and dip of her body. Something unknown crawled through her body, heating her from the inside.

Kitty glanced back at the pathway, feeling discomfited at their isolation. She returned her regard to him, and he was still considering her in that piercing manner. She became increasingly uneasy under his silent scrutiny, and it forced her into speech.

"You escaped as if the devil were at your heels, Your Grace." She pushed tendrils of hair behind her ears. "I…I wanted to inquire if you are well."

Damn her curiosity. She had been conscious,

almost from the start of their acquaintance, of a compelling attraction between them. It wasn't wise to be with him alone, in such an isolated area of the garden. Kitty wondered whether it was the rebellious streak in her, so frequently deplored even by her mother, that had drawn her irresistibly to the duke.

Silence lingered. The stillness of the night enfolded them.

"Come sit with me, Miss Danvers." With a dip of his head, he motioned her to the iron chair in front of his, under the warm splash of light from the nearby gas lamp. Where he would be able to observe every nuance of her face and demeanor while he remained shadowed.

A thrill of frightened anticipation touched her spine, and an oddly primitive warning sounded in her thoughts—*run, run, run as fast as you can.*

He was an exotic creature she felt ill equipped to understand. A fire that burned cold, one she could admit she was undoubtedly, dangerously attracted to. Still she made her way over and lowered herself into the iron chair. Shadows closed around them, the scent of jasmine and lilies redolent in the air.

"May I assist you in any way, Your Grace?"

He turned his head, regarding her with faint amusement. "Is that an invitation to sin, Miss Danvers?"

"Of course not," she murmured with a small smile. "I can tell that you are in terrible pain."

His face closed, as if guarding a secret or maybe his pride. "Leave me!"

The cold command cracked through the air. How mercurial. Instead of obeying, she stood, made her way to his stone bench, and lowered herself beside him. He was too broad shouldered, his legs too long, to share the space comfortably.

Her thighs pressed against the hand clenched on the edge of the stone bench, and a flush worked through her body, but she would not run away like a silly, hysterical miss. This unfathomable agony he endured was because he'd wanted to dance with her. Possibly to help cement her position within the *ton*, perhaps because he wanted to feel what it was like to take a twirl across the room after so many years secluded away.

His reasons seemed as if they would forever be incomprehensible to her, and Kitty only knew she would feel wretched if she walked away and left him alone with his pain.

They sat silently for a long time, or was it mere moments? His fingers flexed, and she glanced down. His knuckles strained from the death grip he had on the bench. A low groan slipped from him before it was ruthlessly contained.

He released the bench to clasp his thigh, where he dug in his fingers and kneaded. It did not seem to help; the low curses spilling from under his breath attested to that. She snuck a sideward glance at him. The pale splash of light clearly showed the grooves of pain bracketing his mouth.

Her heart ached, unable to imagine what he felt. His control was admirable and spoke of how much he suffered in silence. The moment seemed private, and she felt the worst sort of intruder, yet her mind would not allow her to shuffle away silently.

Nervousness coursed through Kitty, but she took

a deep, steadying breath. *I can do this.*

She reached out, slowly, in the same manner she'd used to approach a wild dog once in the country when she'd offered it some scraps from the kitchen. The duke's gaze fell on her outstretched hand. She felt the searing heat of his regard, could sense the disbelief winding through him. Yet Kitty ignored all of that and gently rested her hand on his lower thigh.

A blush engulfed her entire body at her terrible impropriety. She felt burned and struggled not to snatch her hand away. The muscles beneath her palm bunched and knotted, impervious to the dig of his fingers to release the tension from the cramps.

Kitty lifted her gaze to his, hating that she was blushing so fiercely. She shifted closer, slanting her body so she could better grip his thigh, careful to not let her fingers touch his. She could feel his muscles flex a little beneath her fingertips, and the sensation made her redden. The duke faltered into remarkable stillness, his hand slipping from his thigh, and even his breath had hitched, though he had yet to exhale.

The silence felt thick, charged.

She pressed deep with her fingers, massaging the twisted muscles. No sound passed his lips; in truth, Kitty believed he still held his breath. It was clear the sheer intimacy of her touch, the presumption of her action, rendered him speechless.

"You are the most brazen, shameless, impudent..." The low words exploded from him on a sharp exhale.

Her movements faltered, and she snapped her head up to peer at him. They sat together for a moment, frozen, staring at each other. His head dipped forward, his features spilling into sharp relief. The mask had been removed, his lips were flattened in a harsh line, and his eyes were chilled. Distressingly, their faces were so close that with just the slightest shift from either, their lips would meet. Her stomach clenched tight at the awareness, and a peculiar longing swelled inside her.

"How do you dare?"

The biting words sliced through the stillness of the night. An alarming distance cloaked his demeanor. Something unknown trembled inside her. But she managed to shrug and say, "Are you not in pain? Perhaps my touch will help. When my papa was alive, we had horses. Many times, I assisted with rubbing them down and massaging their flanks. I daresay this is similar and may provide some relief."

"Your continued impudence staggers me." His voice sounded strange, unusually rough.

Kitty flushed in acute embarrassment. She was unable to explain that she cared. That somehow it hurt to think of another in pain and ignore their need when she could possibly help. *And I am silly. Why should I care about him?*

She was, after all, only a curiosity to him. A cure for his boredom, a passing interest of which he would soon tire. "Do you wish for me to stop?"

He drew back into the shadows but did not proffer a reply. The muscles jumped beneath her fingertips, twisting into hard cramps. She felt his entire body stiffen against the pain, and Kitty simply shifted, placing both hands on his thighs, and started to massage.

Seconds, then minutes passed, until the tension

eased from his body and the muscles beneath her touch became more pliant. He made no effort to break the odd tension, and she truly had no words. The duke placed his hand atop hers, halting her massage.

Kitty glanced up at his hidden mien.

"Thank you, Miss Danvers. The pain has eased considerably." Now his tone was soft, questioning, with another indefinable undertone.

She slowly pulled her hands from beneath his, hating how her heart jerked. "You are welcome, Your Grace. I'm relieved my impudence helped."

His lips curved in a semblance of a smile.

Then more silence. And she wondered if there would ever be a time she would be comfortable within his presence. They were simply worlds apart in their connections and personalities. With a silent sigh, she shifted her attention to the fountain in the distance, not liking that he could see every facet of her expression when his was still so carefully hidden. "Why did you dance with me?"

Another seemingly contemplative silence, then he said, "I wanted to."

She tipped her head to the night sky, gazing up at its vast beauty. "Was it worth it?"

"Look at me."

Everything inside her tensed, but Kitty turned to him. "Come into the light."

Another dip of his head, and their lips were once again improperly close and the cast of his face revealed. He reached up and smoothed her hair away from her brow. A terrible weak-kneed feeling assailed Kitty. She swallowed her gasp of surprise and simply stared at him. Suddenly it seemed important to say something, but her tongue would not obey.

Oh, why had she followed him?

"It was worth it," he finally murmured. "Thank you for the honor."

A soft gasp escaped her. The dratted man could be charming when he wanted. Her emotions were running amok, and she could not understand any of them. It was imperative for her to flee this darkened piece of their world, but she wanted to stay, to know more about him if he would allow it. Wasn't that how friendship was formed? Through honest conversation?

"Why did you stay away…from society?"

He glanced at her, visibly struck.

Would he answer? She felt adrift in this strange, fraught tension.

"A faint sensation would rush to my head whenever I thought about stepping about in society. The walls seemed to close in, making it difficult to breathe. For months, the memory of falling in the House of Lords haunted me. The pity and derision on the faces of men I'd called friends. Men whom I'd drank with and even raced with. The idea of facing them made my heart pound, the cravat around my neck feel like a noose, every scar feels like a failure, though I know how ridiculous the notion was."

Kitty was still, unafraid to move lest his low murmur halt. He spoke without shame or embarrassment, only a rueful reflection.

"By the time I realized I truly did not care for

society's opinion, I was no longer intrigued by the frivolities of the *ton*. There was no need for me to seek a duchess. There was no need for me to speak in the House of Lords when my letters have proven to be just as powerful. And my sister needed me; that became my source…of everything."

Until now lingered unspoken in the air. But there was an inescapable implied awareness of it.

Until now.

Her lips curved. "Thank you for sharing with me, Your Grace."

He stared at her. "You have a beautiful smile, Miss Danvers."

A breath caught in her chest at the husky timbre of his voice. "I…thank you."

"Are Kitty and Katherine the same, I wonder? Have you always been this bold and determined?"

"Yes," she whispered.

"Then why has society missed you all these years? It is impossible to hide fire."

Her throat worked on a swallow. "To be your fiancée and entice the *ton*, I chose to stop hiding. As young ladies, we are taught to suppress our sincere hearts lest we offend."

"Ahh."

His soft exhalation of satisfaction had an odd ripple of delight coursing through her.

"So you do not regret riding astride…*twice*, daring to attend Lady Appleby's ball without a corset, and rescuing a cat in a tree for a little lady?"

Shock parted her lips. "So you've read all the scandal sheets."

He reached for her, skimming the back of his

fingers over the soft swell of her cheek, lingering at the curve of her jaw, his thumb smoothing against her lips.

A startled laugh escaped before she choked back the sound. Her heart pounded, and her mouth went dry. "Your Grace?"

For the briefest moment, he, too, looked startled. As if he'd not planned to touch her. As if he'd been compelled to lay his hand against her skin. Her entire body warmed.

She turned her face into his palm and brushed her lips briefly over his wrist. *Oh dear. No, no, no.* They froze, and mortification burned through her. She had acted without thought, driven by a need she hardly understood.

Their eyes met. Again, that shock of want and need long denied welled inside her heart. For no apparent reason, she suddenly recalled the brief press of his lips against hers when they'd first met. He'd tasted like coffee, whiskey, and desire.

Birds took flight in her stomach and a slow, languorous ache rolled through Kitty, scaring her with its intensity.

Not wanting to face the consequences of her impulsive actions, she lurched to her feet and hurried away, conscious of his gaze burning a hole in her back. At the edge of the iron gate, he spoke.

"Miss Danvers?"

She froze. *One…two…three…four…five…* That was a useless exercise. Her heart pounded more instead of lessening. "Your Grace?" she said in a shaky, breathless voice.

He waited…and waited. Kitty stepped forward.

"We leave for Scotland in a few days," he murmured, yet his voice reached her, arresting her movements.

It was an extraordinary sensation. This mix of fear and anticipation.

"Very well, Your Grace. We leave for Scotland."

CHAPTER EIGHT

A week after Lady Carnforth's ball, Kitty and the duke set out for Scotland, and now they had been traveling for three days. Before they left town, she had attended the Theatre Royal, Drury Lane with the duke to the rabid curiosity of the *ton*.

The black and gold half mask of the duke had rendered him aloof and unapproachable as he sat beside Kitty in the plush private box situated above the rest of the auditorium. He had seemed immersed in the rousing tale of unrequited love and revenge and had paid her little regard, and she had been too uncertain to attempt any conversation. They had been the recipients of many quizzing glasses, as the lords and ladies of society had presumably thought her and the duke a better performance to observe. It had taken several minutes before Kitty had ignored it all and relaxed into a world of greasepaint and artifice.

The entire affair had been decidedly odd, for he had escorted her home with little conversation beyond the polite pleasantries. Kitty found that she wanted to ask him about his experience after being away from such entertainments for so long. When she had asked the duke if he wished to attend the museum before departing for Scotland, his response had been an unreadable "no."

With a sigh, she peered out of the carriage, mightily tired of being enclosed. The duke had elected to ride on a massive stallion ahead of her equipage. At times when she drew back the curtains and peeked out, she would see him cantering ahead. Other times, he traveled in the second carriage rambling behind her coach.

Kitty found it curious he did not wish to be enclosed with her. It was almost as if he avoided her presence. Even at the two inns they stayed overnight, she'd dined and broken her fast alone. He'd ensure the best rooms at the inns were assigned to her, and a stout and friendly widow had traveled as her chaperone. That lady, a Mrs. Williams, rode in the second coach with a few other servants, their luggage, and sometimes the duke.

The man kept a very careful distance, though she was grateful for the space. Every day she thought about their encounter in the garden at Lady Carnforth's ball, wishing she had not stayed, other times wishing she'd been brave enough to press her lips to his. As if controlled by another, her fingers fluttered to her lips. It infuriated her that his kiss the night they met, though quite chaste, haunted her, when Thornton probably did not spare her a thought beyond how to use her for his amusement.

She was not some foolish girl who dreamed of love, was she? Surely she was more practical than that. *Then why do I think about the dratted man so often?*

Glancing through the carriage windows, she observed him ahead on his stallion. The duke was shouting something at the coachman and pointing upward. Kitty peered above the tree lines in the distance. The skies had darkened, and it appeared that rain would be imminent.

She had heard Scotland was frightfully wet, even in the summer months.

The carriage lurched ahead, the pace increasing considerably. With a sigh, she lowered the curtains and leaned back against the well-padded squabs. It was impossible to envision what their week or two would be like at his home. Would he ignore her there, too? Would dinner be as silent as the theater? Would her presence be a mere ornament? Or worse, what if he demanded she stay longer? *That* she would refuse and would bargain fiercely for another outcome.

With another huff, she reached for the small valise underneath the seat, opened it, and withdrew a book—*Castle of Wolfenbach*. Opening the pages, she resumed her read from where she'd stopped, burying the anxiety filling her heart. She needn't fret about that brief kiss, or how intimate their encounter had been in the garden, or the duke's aloofness now. The duke had no intention of marrying—she would not follow Ophelia's or Mamma's advice and hope that this outrageous stay at his castle might turn into something more.

Kitty's mission was clear and simple. Be his friend, whatever that entailed. Ensure that he did not call off the engagement before the necessary time. *Not kissing friends*. And just maybe she would survive the experience, and all would be well with her family and sisters.

That was all she should care about. And so she would.

• • •

Alexander rode ahead, urging the horses to keep a brisk pace. The wind had risen, scuttling dark clouds across the sun. It felt as if he raced against the doubts filling him. He wasn't a man prone to indecisive thoughts, yet the closer they were to his castle, the more he was certain he had made a blasted mistake. To take a young lady from her home and into the wild moors of Scotland was truly foolhardy. And without a proper chaperone.

If a hint of this escapade was revealed to society, surely her reputation could never recover. One moment's indiscretion could unleash a scandal. And he did not want that for her. That daring spirit should be gently encouraged to bloom vividly, not crushed and misunderstood.

He'd spent a good part of his journey home thinking about the gamble she had taken for the sake of her family and what it said about the lady herself. Miss Danvers was courageous, loyal, witty, and a woman with unusual humor and tenacity. And kind…even at the cost of her reputation.

In other words, a woman unlike any he'd ever known.

He pulled on the reins of the massive stallion, forcing it to halt. The carriages rumbled closer, the beat of the horses' hooves almost a taunt to his earlier ruthless confidence. Alexander scowled at the black sky. A storm such as this in May.

Perhaps it was an omen.

A fat drop of rain splashed on his cheek and he cursed. They were at least an hour's ride from home, but the roads tended to become mud-logged during and after a deluge. And this promised to be quite a squall. The trees were bending under the force of the wind. His top hat tugged from his head and soared away before he could react.

Stifling another curse, he urged the horses ahead. Despite the biting cold penetrating his jacket, he would not ride inside the carriage with Miss Danvers. The second coach within which he traveled sometimes had already gone ahead hours ago and should be at the castle already. He'd ordered his wheeled chair and canes to be put away in defiance of his manservant's protest. Alexander had determined, despite the twinges of pain in his back and lower extremities, he would return home under his own steam.

After a few more minutes of traveling, the rain sleeted down, and with a curse, he bid the coachman to stop the carriage. He carefully dismounted, ignoring the shock of pain that traveled up his back. After a few bracing breaths and ruthlessly beating back the fiery swarm of pain, he took the first steps toward the equipage. "Hitch Hercules behind the coach. The rain is too fierce to continue that way. I will ride with Miss Danvers for the rest of the journey."

His coachman, George, a spry man despite his advanced age, moved with alacrity to do Alexander's command. The man had the audacity to smile slyly and wink. The impudence. He should fire him as he'd threatened to do these last ten years.

George had been hinting throughout the journey that he should keep the ravishing Miss Danvers's company. He'd fallen silent this morning only when Alexander had promised to remove his tongue from his head. Though he'd said it with a modicum of affection, it seemed George had believed his irritable vow.

The steps to the carriage were knocked down, and Alexander clambered up and into the warm confines of the carriage. Miss Danvers's lips parted on a silent gasp and she lowered the book she read.

"Your Grace…" She glanced out the small window into the rain.

"Miss Danvers. I hope you will permit me the pleasure of your company for the rest of the journey."

She smiled, and his heart ached. How in God's name did she do that…with only a damn smile?

"I see you were forced to join me."

He grunted, and her grin widened. Her boldness knew no bounds, and he had yet to decide if he liked it. Except for his sister, he was quite used to ladies operating within the confines society and their family placed them in, and he had no notion of what to make of Katherine Danvers.

Alexander was still haunted by her actions in the garden. Never would he have expected such daring from any young lady. Even at the theater, she had displayed a strength of character in the face of his silence and the blatant ogling of society. She had been so unflinching, so certain, so unafraid. He'd wanted to kiss her more than he wanted the pain to stop.

Even now it was there, a fester, a clawing need that would not abate. Alexander had the fierce urge to gather her to him, to kiss her face and throat, to taste the sweetness of her lips, inhale her scent, and make it a part of him.

The attraction he felt confounded him. Katherine

Danvers was not the type of lady he would have pursued in the days he'd been "mad, bad, and dangerous." The diamonds of the *ton*, women who could match him in wealth and beauty and connections, were whom he'd pursued. He and his eventual fiancée had been declared the match of the season, and all of society had praised their alliance. Yet Lady Daphne had been quite sweet and docile, her likes and wants a secret to him, and he'd never made the effort to unearth them.

Still, this burning desire to know all of Miss Danvers would not leave him be. Surely this could not be a simple reflection of his boredom with life? Though Alexander must admit the empty well inside felt like it had been given a drop of something precious. Something was different. The jagged emptiness had not tormented him these last few days. How long would it last?

Her throat cleared delicately, and a delightfully pink blush ran along her cheek. "You are staring, Your Grace."

Her cheeks grew redder under his slow, careful appraisal.

He gave her a faint, mocking smile. "Surely you know how beautiful you are," he returned smoothly.

The woman rolled her eyes, pulling a smile to his lips.

"You do not believe it to be true?" he asked, mildly surprised.

"I'm pretty," she said softly. "And I've been told my eyes are lovely. 'Beautiful' is perhaps a stretch, hmm?"

His heart stumbled in his chest. "I agree, they are

remarkably fine eyes, particularly so when sparkling with indignation or when they begged for a kiss. But you are also unquestionably more than pretty, Miss Danvers."

She was unique in her boldness and beauty.

She gasped, staring at him with those wide, impossibly lovely eyes. "My eyes did not beg you to kiss me," she whispered furiously, looking as if she wanted to hit him with the warming pan.

Alexander chuckled. "Was it the word 'beg' that appalled you?"

She growled low in her throat, cocking her head in a decidedly impatient and annoyed gesture. He smiled, and she narrowed her eyes, doing an excellent job of appearing threatening. Her posture did not paint a picture of a woman who accepted defeat easily.

He liked teasing her. Seeing the myriad expressions chasing across her face. They were all beautiful in their complexities. How unforgivably idiotic he was being.

The carriage lurched jarringly, throwing her forward. He grabbed her, steadying her as they came to a shuddering stop. The carriage door swung open, and they peered down into George's worried face.

"A mountain of a tree fell 'cross the road, Yer Grace. 'Tis impassable."

Alexander cursed under his breath. They were too far from civilization to turn around, and there was no inn close by. "What are the options?"

"We could go 'round, Yer Grace, and use the bridge. Might take a few minutes more."

That bridge was a rickety old thing that was slated for repairs. It was a risk, and one he wasn't sure it made sense to take. "When last did you travel upon it, George?"

"Only last week, Yer Grace."

"If the river is swollen, we must find alternate means," Alexander replied.

George nodded and closed the carriage door. A few moments later, they rumbled away again. Miss Danvers once more peered into the sleeting rain.

"We are soon to arrive, then?"

"Yes. Less than an hour."

A soft sigh slipped from her. "I do not know what to expect," she confessed.

"Neither do I."

She slanted him a quick, searching glance. "It warms my heart to know you are similarly uncertain."

"Does it?"

"Hmm, that tells me you have no nefarious plans to do away with me."

"I was uncertain about what I shall do with you *outside* of my dastardly plans, Miss Danvers. Wickedness can take up only so much time."

"You tease me, Your Grace?" She laughed lightly, and the cold retreated and warmth filled his bones. *How fascinating*.

The carriage suddenly careened wildly.

"What the devil—?"

An ominous groan was the only warning before they became weightless, the bridge caving and dumping them into the raging waters of the river.

• • •

Kitty suppressed her panic as the duke shoved at the carriage door. The equipage was rapidly sinking, and the pressure of the water made it difficult to pry the door open. She scrabbled to his side, lending him her strength. They pushed, the door blessedly sprang open, and they spilled into the swollen waters.

The icy cold shocked the breath from her body and she wheezed. She grabbed onto a piece of the coach, very aware that it was submerging, and it was the only thing keeping her above water. The sleeting rain stung her eyes, and Kitty futilely swiped the rivulets from her face. The coachman was shouting something and pointing toward the banking, but Kitty could not discern his words over the roaring water and the intermittent thunder.

"Can you swim?" the duke demanded, coming to her side.

Fear iced through her heart. "No," she gasped. "Can you?"

His reply was lost in the wind. With grace and speed, he spun in the water, wrapping his arms across her waist from behind. The banking of the river was close by, but it felt like it took forever as he pulled against the churning waters to get her to safety.

Wanting to help him, she kicked her legs.

"For God's sake, do not move," he roared.

They sank briefly, and everything muted as water rushed over her head and the weight of her dress and petticoats pulled her down. Yet panic did not rush in, for Kitty sensed he would not let her drown. Another surge and they were once more above water, and thank God, the banking was there.

She giggled, possibly from hysteria, when he

planted his firm hands on her buttocks and pushed her up the slippery slope. She gripped the lush, thick moss that grew along the embankment, hauling herself up. Once she was safe from the churning waters, she turned around to help him. But he was swimming back toward the carriage that was almost submerged.

"Alexander!"

He did not turn at her cry. George, still in the water, was busily unhooking the animals, and the duke headed for his stallion hitched to the back. The animals were screaming, their cries lost in the ripping wind. A trembling seized her limbs, and she could only watch helplessly as they unhitched the horses from the rapidly sinking carriage. The duke slapped their rumps and the horses instinctively, thank God, lunged and swam toward the banking, then mounted the riverbank to safety.

The carriage sank, and the exhausted coachman slipped beneath the rushing waters.

Oh dear God!

The man did not surface, and the duke went under, disappearing for several moments. Kitty's heart was a drum in her ears, and she trembled violently as she prayed for the duke and the coachman to reappear. Helplessness surged through her, and she watched the frothing waters, furiously wiping the rivulets from her face.

A sob of relief tore from her when she saw him with George clasped in his hand. The duke tried to swim over, but she could see that he struggled. Her heart pounded with fear, and grabbing at a nearby tree branch, she held onto it and slipped it into the churning water. The cold once again shocked her, and her breath exploded on a gasp. But her feet touched the bed of the river, and that mattered more than anything. With her death grip on the branch, which bent as if it would break at any moment, she inched her way toward the duke.

He glanced back as if to assess the shores and spied her. He shouted something to her, but the wind ripped it away. The duke seemed to double his effort. Kitty kept inching closer, carefully bracing against the waters and ensuring her feet could touch the ground. She paused when the water finally reached her chin, and she held out a hand. The duke reached her, and she grasped one of the shoulders of the coachman.

With a groan, the duke slipped from beneath him and stood in the river, supporting the man under his arms. Kitty helped him by lifting George's face above the water, and they painstakingly made it to the banking. Then she rested the weight of the coachman on the duke and, using the branch, hauled them from the waters. It took several attempts amid much sliding and grunting, but she made it. Kitty turned around, panting, reached down, and helped drag the man out of the river while the duke pushed. With a grunt, Thornton heaved himself from the churning waters.

He lay back on the muddied grass, breathing heavily. With a deep groan that spoke of agony, the duke pushed to his feet, staring at her.

"Thank you," he said, his eyes intent, a grove of pain bracketing his mouth. "Not many people who cannot swim would dare to brave these waters to help rescue a servant."

"It is a kindness I would do for anyone," she whispered. Then she lifted a hand to his brow. "You are in pain. I can see torment in your eyes."

"It is nothing," he said gruffly, his expression shuttering.

She lowered her hand and shockingly, he leaned forward and pressed a kiss to her forehead. Unexpectedly, a beguiling jolt of ice and fire lanced through her. Kitty had no time to respond before the duke turned away and looked at his man lying on the muddied earth.

"We need to get him out of the rain," he said, dipping and then hoisting the old man over his shoulder.

Kitty hurried after him as they made their way toward the dense section of the woods, away from the shattered makeshift bridge and the swollen waters. As they entered the tree line, a few large oaks provided some relief from the rain. The alcove was thick with sheltering trees, the scent of oak moss and pine redolent in the air. The grass was verdant and soft, and the duke lowered himself to his knees, slinging the coachman to the forest floor. The duke remained on his knees and pressed an ear to the coachman's chest.

The duke pushed himself up and glanced at her. His eyes were ravaged with pain and grief. "One foolish decision and now a good man has died."

Shock tore through her. "He's dead?"

The duke lowered himself again, pressing his ear close to the man's chest and then his mouth. With a grimace, he straightened. "I cannot hear his heartbeat or feel the heat of his breath. I fear he is truly dead."

For a moment the two stared at each other without further sound or movement.

Kitty looked at the duke in ill-concealed fright. "Surely it cannot be so. How dreadful!"

Her heart ached at the naked agony in Thornton's gaze. "He has a wife…children and grandchildren."

"I…" Her throat went tight at the senseless loss. "I'm so sorry."

He scrubbed a hand over his face. "Why did I risk going over the bridge?"

The hollowness in his voice tore at Kitty. Uncaring that the muddied ground would damage what was left of her dress, she lowered herself to her knees and touched his shoulder in gentle support.

"I'm so terribly sorry, Your Grace." It had all been so sudden and violent. She couldn't believe the grumpy coachman who had seemed overly familiar with the duke could have just died so. "I am so sorry," she whispered again.

"God damn you," the duke roared, slapping the man's chest.

The sacrilege, beating a dead man's chest. He repeated the motion, this time his sound of fury and denial muted. Just as she was about to order him to stop, one of the man's fingers twitched. She screamed and then slapped a hand over her mouth.

"What is it?" the duke demanded, his eyes scanning behind her, sharp and calculating.

"I…I thought he moved." Every foolish gothic book she'd ever read in the late evening blared through her mind. It did not help that the sky had the ominous darkness of a fiercely brewing storm or that the wooded glen was so empty.

His eyes cut to the man on the ground, and he bent over, pressing his ear to the man's chest for several seconds. The duke's eyes closed, regret lining his handsome features. "He did not; he's dead," he said flatly. Yet his eyes spoke of pain and grief.

"Are you certain?"

"Yes," he said, bowing his head as if in prayer.

Several moments passed in taut silence. Kitty had no notion of how to comfort him. "Your Grace, I believe we should—"

A groan came from the body on the ground, and he twitched. Kitty gasped, grabbed onto the duke's shoulder, and tried to haul herself up. She tumbled into the mud and rolled down the gentle slope. Somehow, she came to a sprawling stop on her back. She hurriedly turned over, still sliding in the muddy grass, pushed herself up, and stared at the body. "Did you see that he moved?" she yelled.

The duke's face was a mask of astonishment as he stared at her, then back at his coachman. The man jerked and then turned over to his side, coughing up mouthfuls of water. When he was done, he sat up, his bleary gaze scanning the woods, a fierce scowl on his weathered face. The man who'd presumed to be dead was muttering under his breath, rubbing at his chest as if the spot was sore, and glaring at the duke.

"Ye had to thump so hard, Yer Grace?"

"Yes," he said gruffly. "I'm glad you're well, George."

The duke glanced back at her. His lips parted, his eyes crinkled at the corners, and the dratted man started to laugh. Rolling belly laughter that sounded like thunder itself, and at the heart of it, she heard the relief. "Did...did you perchance think George was the living dead, Miss Danvers?"

Kitty scowled, humiliation heating the tips of her ears. She was vexed to feel herself coloring. She had reacted like a silly, hysterical miss. "Oh, for heaven's sake!" she finally burst out. "I do not believe it is humor that is required in this situation, Your Grace!"

There was an amused expression in his eyes as he said, with perfect gravity, "Miss Danvers, how you've brightened my day. I shall not forget today anytime soon."

Pulling her tattered dignity around her, she struggled to her feet. Tendrils of hair clung damply across her forehead. Mud slurped at her half boots, and her hem was muck-encrusted. Kitty had never felt more bedraggled, while the duke was still flat on his arse in the mud, shoulders shaking with silent laughter.

After a few moments of rest and recovery, the coachman pushed to his feet and glanced from the duke to her. Then he, too, grinned, and Kitty scowled.

"We're close to Emmet's cottage, Yer Grace," he said with a trembling cough, holding out his hand and assisting the duke to his feet.

Then surprisingly the duke pulled his coachman into a hug. She faltered, staring at them in mute amazement. Kitty had never witnessed such familiarity between servant and master before. The kindness radiating in the duke's eyes and the affection in his embrace brought a lump to Kitty's throat. That the cold and aloof duke had such an attachment revealed much about the man's character. An altogether new sensation unfurled through her belly. Unidentifiable but pleasant.

George muttered something, and with a low chuckle, the duke released him after slapping his back.

"That we are. Let's make our way, then." He held out his hand to her. "Come, Miss Danvers. We must get out of the rain and to a shelter."

Grateful that shelter was nearby, she hurried over to his side.

He shrugged from his wet jacket and threw it over her head. She tried her best not to gawk at the outline of his chest beneath the waistcoat and shirt. The rain plastered his clothes to his lithe, elegant frame.

"Thank you," she murmured, fancying she could smell his unique scent in the waterlogged garment.

She stumbled, and with lightning-quick reflexes, he grabbed her.

"It is very slippery, is it not?" she breathed, shocked at the strange feeling low in her stomach at his touch.

He laced their fingers together, and for precious seconds she stared at their clasped hands. Then he tugged her forward. Each step felt as if she were headed into something new and terrifying. It was her silly imagination, of course, but she could not escape the sensation that something about her life had altered. And it hadn't happened when she met the duke, or when she agreed to accompany him to his remote castle in Scotland…but now, in this moment, their hands fused palm to palm as they silently made their way, heads dipped low to brace against the wind and rain.

CHAPTER NINE

Kitty had never been to Scotland before. She hadn't paid much attention to the landscape in the carriage, content with reading to pass the journey. In truth, she was not even sure when they had crossed the border into the lowlands. It must have been some time ago if they were now close to the duke's castle. Her impression of Scotland was rain and verdant beauty with rolling hillsides and valleys. The wildflowers dotting the lowlands were breathtaking in their vibrant colors.

After trekking for about fifteen minutes on the rain-and-mud-logged path, they broke through a wide clearing to find a cottage with a heavy stone chimney and thatched roof. A sigh of relief slipped from Kitty. She needed desperate relief from these wet, muddied clothes and boots. The coachman clambered up the few steps before them and opened the door.

Alexander paused for several moments, then slowly ascended the steps and went inside. Kitty followed, glancing around warily. The hallway was small and clean, and she stooped and untied the laces of her half boots.

At the duke's pointed stare, she replied, "I would hate to track mud all over the place."

The corner of his mouth twitched. "I will have the cottage cleaned when we depart. The parlor is this way, if you'll follow me, Miss Danvers."

The duke preceded her, his gait slow and slightly uneven. Concern blossomed through her, but she held her tongue. They arrived at a simply furnished parlor with two armchairs by the hearth, a small table with four spindly chairs positioned near a small window, and a dark blue rug in the center of the space. Or perhaps a sitting room? Either way the clean elegance of it surprised her.

George, who had lit a fire, stood and nodded to the duke as if he'd asked a question. Kitty hurried over to the fire and held her hands above the flames. She couldn't prevent the soft groan of pleasure as the heat of the fire warmed her chilled fingers.

The duke made his way beside her, removed his sodden gloves, placed them on the mantel, and pushed his hands close to the wonderful warmth. "The cottage is clean. The firewood is stocked. And there is food in the larder. The roof was recently rethatched, so we should be fairly safe from the wind and rain."

She snuck a sideways glance at him. He was staring at the fire, his expression carefully neutral.

"Do you think we are in for more of the storm, then?"

"Yes."

She swallowed, not liking to remember the frightful ordeal a few minutes past. "And where exactly are we?"

"This is my groundsman's cottage."

She glanced around at the clean, neat space. "It has the touch of a lady," she said.

"He is recently married."

Look at me, she silently implored. "I gather they

are not here?" There was an echoing emptiness to the home.

"They're gone on their honeymoon."

She blinked, never hearing of a groundsman taking his bride on a wedding trip before. "I see."

Finally, he shifted his regard to her. There was a bleakness in his eyes she'd not expected. He stepped back, encasing himself further in the shadows of the small room, and she wondered if the bleakness had been her imagination.

"There is a path from here to my estate. It is a long walk. A couple hours at a brisk pace. George will make the journey soon and come back to us."

"I'll go now, Your Grace," the coachman said.

"It is still raining," the duke pointed out.

"And it shall rain the night. Best I be going now." The old man gave her a sly glance. "I'll be back with help soon, Yer Grace."

Kitty frowned, suspecting the man lied, but couldn't credit he would not heed his master's command. It was as if they were friends. The notion was odd and entirely possible as evident by the fact the duke rolled his eyes.

Who is this man?

"With all alacrity, George, return with all alacrity," the duke said with dry fondness. "Alert only the necessary staff. We must be protective of Miss Danvers's reputation, and I do not wish to hear even a whisper of this incident."

The man dipped into a quick bow and hurried away on legs that moved rather quickly despite their shortness. A strange sensation unfurled through her stomach when she sensed the intensity

STACY REID   153

of the duke's stare.

"Will he be back soon, do you think? And with the proper help?"

He grunted.

She sent him a scowl. "Was that an answer?"

He smiled. "I suspect he will be back when the roads are passable."

"And when will that be, do you think?"

"A few days."

Alarm jolted through her. "*Days?* Surely you jest!"

His eyes narrowed, shrewd and probing. "Perhaps two or three."

She glanced around the cottage. To be alone with the duke for days? In this small cottage? The thrill of something unexpected and wicked tingled along her spine, but she quickly suppressed it. This situation was intolerable, and very different from being alone with him in a castle with dozens of servants, plus his sister and her governess. "And are you to promise marriage after?"

His expression became impenetrable. "Of course not."

She folded her arms across her middle in a protective gesture, disliking the slight unease wafting through her. "Then you know *that* situation cannot happen. I cannot stay with you in this cottage for a few hours, much less days. It's…it's too improper, Your Grace!"

He hobbled over to the front door and held it open. A frigid wind blew through the door with misty rain. "I'm sure if you hurry you will catch up to George. He'll gentle his pace, so you can keep up with him. There you can tidy up and reassure my sister I will return as soon as the roads are clear enough for a carriage to come for me."

Shame burned through Kitty that she hadn't thought to truly consider why they, too, were not trekking back to his estate if they were within walking distance. She made her way over to him. "How selfish I've been; you're hurting. Please forgive me, Your Grace."

"Think nothing of it," he murmured after sending her a side-eyed assessing glance. "Do you wish to leave?"

She gripped her hands very tightly at her waist, indecision beating at her. He was in pain, and she did not want to leave him alone. She swallowed with difficulty. "No," she finally breathed.

He closed the door and the latch with a soft *snick*. Immediately the sense of intimacy increased, even as the howling wind and beat of the rain muted. A soft grunt escaped him as he made his way back toward the fire. She'd never seen him limp so, and she felt wretched with shame. He had done everything to save her, the horses, and his coachman. At the cost of himself, and from the deep grooves bracketing his mouth, he was in agony.

"Let me help you, please," she whispered fiercely.

"I am well, Miss Danvers," he said, moving stiffly over to one of the armchairs. "The rain will pass soon, and then we will make our way to the estate."

And what was he to do then? Suffer horribly in silence? Her throat went tight. "I can see you are on the verge of collapsing; please let me offer assistance. Did my touch not help before in the gardens?"

The raw flash of anger that seared from his eyes had doubt clawing at her. Dear God, had she offended his pride? "Your Grace—"

"I wonder, Miss Danvers, how industrious are you?"

"I beg your pardon?"

"George will not return tonight with help, not with these wicked rains and winds."

She glanced at the window at the sleeting rain, recalling that sly expression on George's face. Kitty quite agreed; the man had no intention of returning, even if he could.

"We will have to serve each other."

The truth of this observation struck her most forcibly. The words settled between them in the small space. The duke was without his valet and manservant, and he was a sodden, muddied mess. This would go beyond a shameless massage of his damaged muscles. His boots would have to be removed. His clothes. Her breath panted harshly. *Dear God.* And so would hers, and without a lady's maid.

Good heavens.

"I see," she murmured, thoroughly vexed with the heat flushing through her body and up to her cheeks. She couldn't have stopped her blush if her life depended on it.

"Are you up to the task, then?" he asked, his tone coolly mocking, his eyes watchful.

The bonds of probity and all that was proper shattered and dissolved at her feet like fragile chinaware.

"Ah, your expressive face reveals your worry."

She folded her arms across her waist and glared at him.

His slow smile made her heart beat suddenly faster.

"Do not fear— wretched, drowned cats are not to my taste," the duke said with mock sympathy. "A tigress would be another matter entirely."

The wretched tease! She released a breath she hadn't been aware she held. "Of course I am up to the task," she said with calm practicality. And she would find some way to cease the infernal blushes!

"I will accept your aid, Miss Danvers, but only after I have assisted you from those sodden garments and dried your hair. My conscience could not bear your death."

"I beg your pardon?"

He pressed a hand against his heart and bowed. "It would be my honor to be your lady's maid."

There was no help for it. Taking a deep breath, she tried to find equanimity. Her flesh crawled with the desperate need to be out of her wet, muddied garments. She glanced around the cottage and made her way down a small hallway to another room. Right before it, there appeared to be a linen closet. There she found two small towels, a blanket, two sheets, and no more. They would have to do.

Then she went to the bedchamber, over to the armoire, and opened it. Only two dark plain dresses and a nightgown lingered within its confines, and at a glance she deduced the groundsman's wife was a large lady. The garments would swallow Kitty. There was a fawn-colored shirt, a blue one, a jacket, and trousers also neatly folded.

With trembling fingers, she closed the door to the armoire.

"We'll make do," the duke murmured.

She stiffened at the closeness of his voice. She hadn't heard his approach. Taking a soft, bracing breath, Kitty faced him. "I suppose we shall."

Something unreadable touched his gaze for a fleeting moment. "Our situation is unusual, isn't it?" he asked.

"It is." And the dreadful anxiety coursing through her was intolerable. Worse, there was a strange but pleasant thrill thrumming through her veins. Kitty could not decide if she liked the sensation. It felt hungry and chaotic, and the secret heart of her liked being alone with the duke.

His midnight gaze bore into her, a searchlight, as it caressed over her face. "We'll have to rely on each other until George returns with help."

"Which could be days," she pointed out, still disbelieving of that.

"Hmm, days."

"Do you not think that deliberate, Your Grace?"

He gently turned her around. "I daresay it is time you call me Alexander…Katherine."

She remained motionless for a moment. "Kitty," she finally whispered. "My friends and family call me Kitty."

He dipped behind her, his lips perilously close to her ear. She could feel the warmth of his breath, the heated press of his body scandalously close to hers. The devil insisted on teasing her so!

"Kitty," he finally said.

There was a hint of bemusement in his tone. A

touch of curiosity and something unidentifiable. Yet her body reacted shamelessly, that peculiar heat curling from her toes all the way to her throat.

"Allow me to assist with drying your hair."

A subtle tremor flowed through her limbs. "I… My hair is the least of my worries."

As if to mock her words, rivulets of water trailed from her forehead down her cheeks and neck. The icy water still soaking her strands dripped onto her face and throat. And a mortifying sneeze slipped from her.

"I would hate for you to fall ill…or worse, meet death because of a false sense of propriety. We are alone. No one shall ever know how we assisted each other. We'll share a secret, Miss Danvers, and quite a wicked one, too."

"You have my permission."

He removed the pins from her hair, tumbling the wet, heavy coil over her shoulders down to her lower back. A towel was pressed to her strands, and he attempted to dry her thick mass with brisk movements. His economic movements reassured her, and some of the tension eased from her frame.

"Do you need help in undressing?"

It was impossible for her to remove her carriage gown without aid. How would she reach the hooks and small buttons of her various garments? Kitty had never had a reason to attend to her own dressing. Even now, with their finances so dire, their mother allowed for the hiring of a lady's maid, whom all her girls shared. The proper appearances had to be maintained.

No one will know…

"Yes," she said so softly, it was a wonder he heard.

Awareness of her vulnerability seeped into every crevice of her being. In silence he unfastened her gown, and the heavy, sodden garment dropped to the ground. She was suddenly petrified to face him, though she remained in her stays and petticoats. Never had she been in such a state before a man.

"There is another matter that we must discuss."

Her entire body quaked when he slowly, oh so slowly tugged at the laces of her stay. "And that is?"

"There is only one bed."

That was the last thing Kitty expected the duke to say.

Her gaze jerked to the small but seemingly sturdy bed flushed in the far corner of the cottage. *One bed…one bed…oh!* Then she considered the two small padded armchairs by the fire in the parlor. With his leg bothering him, it would be selfish to even think for him to retire in one of them. But might she push the two chairs together and find some sleep atop its lumpy cushions?

"Are you thoroughly wet?"

She snapped her head around to meet his regard. The deep blue of his eyes glinted with wicked knowledge and mirth. For an alarming moment she'd thought he referred to the strange dampness she could feel between her thighs, where that unladylike ache resided.

Fighting another dreaded blush, she turned away from his too-knowing stare and faced the armoire. "Yes, all my garments are dreadfully soaked."

"Should I then remove your stays…and petticoats?"

She was stricken to silence and was aware of nothing but the hammering of her heart. *Dear God.* Kitty closed her eyes. *And there will be no marriage after this.*

She tried to think logically. The air was chilled and the fire in the hearth barely suffused the room with warmth. She was sodden through, and it would be impossible to remain in this clothing. He was being so matter-of-fact about it…except his voice had a low, raspy quality that did utterly odd things to her heart. How it tumbled and flipped with frightful intensity.

How do I dare? The wildest improbabilities darted through Kitty's thoughts. "Yes," she finally said. "I certainly do not wish to catch my death."

He jolted, then faltered into remarkable stillness. Clearly the duke hadn't anticipated her response. They stood silently, breathing together. Her body felt incredibly alive, every sense feeling somehow keener, sharper. A bittersweet longing flooded her. She braced herself against the rioting, foolish needs with a long, steady breath.

His hands tugged at her stays. Her lids fluttered closed, her heart a thundering roar in her ear. *I am three and twenty*, she reminded herself fiercely. *Not a silly miss.*

It did not work. The shivering sensation low in her stomach intensified and felt as if she were falling…endlessly.

With alternately sharp and gentle tugs, he unlaced her stays and petticoats, and within seconds she was down to her chemise and stockings.

"Go behind the screen," he murmured. "I will

take a basin of water to you...and a blanket."

She glanced at the pitiful excuse of a screen, appalled at how little privacy the groundsman's wife would have when she cleaned herself. Was it the way for the lower classes to be freer with their nakedness?

Kitty felt his retreat more than heard him. How did he move so soundlessly when he hurt so? Clutching the towel between her fingers, she hurried behind the small, sheer screen. Turning about, she could easily see him through the material.

And that meant he could see her with similar ease.

A blush engulfed her entire body. How could they bear such intimate familiarity for days?

A basin with water was placed at the edge of the screen. He disappeared in that silent way of his and returned with a second basin of water and a small bar of plain soap.

"Thank you," she whispered, unsure if he heard.

Bending, she tugged it to her and rested it atop a small wooden table. Glancing up, she observed as he hobbled with an uneven gait to the sole armchair in the small bedroom and lowered himself into it. She couldn't discern if he returned her stare through the flimsy screen.

Kitty was in an agony of apprehension. How terribly wicked and improper it all was. Her eyes trained on the shadowed form of the duke, she bent slightly and rolled off the ruined stockings. There was no sound in the cottage save for her soft, ragged breathing and the crackle of the fireplace.

Did he stare at the screen, or were his eyes closed?

She straightened and, taking a steadying breath,

removed the last protective garment. The chemise dropped to the floor, and then she was naked. Her body felt flushed and unfamiliar. Kitty turned away from the shadowed form of the duke. If his eyes were indeed open, and he could discern her shape through the screen, it would be her backside he would see. *For shame!* The thought had her body blushing more fiercely.

Taking up the bar of soap and dipping the washcloth into the cold water, she washed herself as thoroughly as possible. Several minutes later she was trembling but blessedly cleaned. She finished drying the heavy mass of her hair to the best of her ability with the small towel before pinning it haphazardly in a loose chignon. Then she wrapped her body into the blanket, forming a bulky toga around her frame. Taking a bracing breath, she peeked around the screen.

The duke's head was tipped to the cottage's ceiling, and his fingers were dug into the armrest of the chair.

Kitty strolled over to him with the second basin of water, which she had not used. She placed it by the side of the armchair, and without speaking, she lowered herself to her knees and tugged at his knee-high boots. The fingers clenched into the armrest flexed, but he remained silent, his regard on the ceiling.

She removed his boots one after the other with careful consideration of his discomfort. Placing them neatly by the side, she took the washcloth and dipped it into the basin, then gently lathered it with the soap.

Coming onto her knees, she leaned forward and reached up, wiping the caked mud from his cheek and chin. His eyes snapped open, and he stared at her. Swallowing away the nerves, she cleaned away the mud and twigs as economically as possible. She dipped the washcloth into the basin, so very aware that his brilliant, piercing stare watched her every movement.

This time she lifted the washcloth toward the scarred section of his face. A terrible tension wound itself through his body, leaped from him, and twined itself around her. His skin pulled taut over the sharp edges of his cheekbones. The eyes that stared at her were so cold and watchful, it was a miracle her teeth did not chatter.

Holding his stare, Kitty pressed the washcloth to his scarred skin. His jaw clenched under the tip of her finger. Then she wiped away the mud, her stomach knotting at the ridges of scars felt through the cloth.

One of his hands released the armchair, and a finger slipped beneath her chin and lifted her face to his penetrating stare, searching her upturned face.

"How brave you are, Miss Danvers."

Unaccountably, the softly spoken words felt like a threat.

He lowered his hand back to the armrest.

It was impulse that guided her to use her fingers to brush locks of hair from where the wet strands touched his forehead. Cynicism and pain were carved in the ruthless lines of his patrician face. Not allowing herself to be drawn into crossing wits, she lowered the cloth to the basin, pleased with the job she had done.

Then she reached up, unknotted his cravat, and tugged the muslin cloth from around his neck. It slid through her fingers, soft and supple, the slowness of her motions feeling sensually intimate. She dropped the scrap of cloth onto the floor. She undid the top buttons of his shirt one by one, revealing the strong column of his throat. There, too, he had twisting scars. Unable to help herself, she dipped the washcloth once more and brought it to his exposed throat. The flesh there was clean, but she carefully wiped along the ridge of his wounds.

There was a perceptible stiffening of his posture. The duke followed each movement with his eyes, his expression carefully inscrutable, but now…now she could see the beat of his pulse at his throat. He was not as serene or unaffected as he presented to her, for his pulse fluttered like a caged bird seeking escape. And the knowledge acted as oil to kindling. A flame of heat, unexpected in its intensity, blossomed through her.

What would he do if I leaned in and kissed his throat? The wildly improper thought burned shame through her. It was as if the situation had encouraged all her good senses to leave her and to draw forth the wild heart she'd always struggled with.

She stood, gripping the edges of her blanket. "If you will stand, Your Grace."

He obeyed, and she tilted her head slightly to hold his unflinching regard. Her gaze lingered one second too long on the golden skin at the base of his neck. "Am I to act as your valet?" she murmured, a blush crawling over her entire body.

"Alas, I am quite able to undress myself, Miss Danvers. I'll not shock your sensibilities anymore."

There was that provoking amusement again in his tone, and she was glad for it, because now some of the tension that had been thickening the air like smoke had dissipated.

"If you will make us something to eat, I shall tidy myself posthaste."

Make them something to eat? Having never prepared a meal in her life, Kitty's mind blanked for precious seconds. But never the one to shy away from impossible tasks, she made her way toward the small kitchen. Once there, she was grateful to see a few tallow candles had been lit. The counters were neat and tidy, and it did not take her long to discover the cheese. There was little else in the way of food that she could prepare. Still, by the time she returned to the small room, the duke was standing by the fire in clothes that were decidedly not his, yet fitted his lithe frame well, raking the towel through his thick dark hair.

"Cheese and apple?" she asked, placing the plates on the small table in the center of the room.

His gait was very slow and uneven as he made his way over and lowered himself into one of the two chairs. She sat, conscious her sole claim to clothes was a blanket. They ate their simple fare of a few chunks of cheese and apples in silence. Kitty was of a mind to think they might starve for the next few days.

A clap of thunder had her jerking and glancing out the lone window into the darkness. "Do you believe George has made it to your estate?"

"He is clever, adaptable. And used to the terrain. He'll be quite all right."

Then dratted silence again. Sudden exhaustion pulled an indelicate yawn from her. Flushing, she glanced at him. "I believe I shall go to bed."

"There is not much else to do," he replied, an amused twinkle in his brilliant blue eyes.

She nodded, pushed from the chair, and all but marched over to the armoire. The lady of the cottage was in possession of a nightgown. Rummaging through the armoire, she grabbed the voluminous dark cotton garment. It would have to do.

She went behind the screen, pushed off the blanket, and slipped the gown over her head. It hung ridiculously on her smaller frame, the hem dragging several inches on the ground. The front gaped, and she gathered it to her chest, made her way from behind the screen, and scrambled onto the bed.

She lay there for several moments, cursing the fact she'd agreed to his ridiculous command to travel with him here. But could she truly have resisted? And Kitty wondered if she had tried enough to resist his blackmail coined as mutual bargain, or had she too willingly tumbled merrily down the path of ruin? Surely he wouldn't have ruined her...

The silence lingered, and it felt awful and uncertain. With a gusty exhalation, she jumped from the bed and fisted a hand on her hip.

The duke had reclined once more in the armchair, his head tipped to the ceiling.

"Your Grace."

He lowered his regard to her. "Are there ants on the bed, Miss Danvers?"

She scowled and he smiled. Odious, odious man! Still… "Do you plan to spend the night in that chair?"

"I have little wish to further traumatize your sensibilities."

"Your Grace, we are adults. You are honorable, and I am a lady of good sense," she said with a touch of desperation. "Surely we can spend the night together in a bed without any inappropriateness or discomfort in each other's presence."

The intensity of his gaze kissed over her in a heated caress. "And I'll not be met with swooning and hysteria in the morning?" This was demanded with a healthy dose of skepticism.

"I'm not a silly miss!"

"No…you aren't." He stood with pained slowness. "You are quite safe with me. You can rest assured on my honor you will be."

She circled the bed, tapping her chin thoughtfully. "You will rest on this side. And I will take this side."

Then she grabbed one of the two pillows and placed it in the middle. Kitty was nervous. Silly to be, of course, with all the shocking intimacy she just endured with this man.

With a huff, she settled on the bed once more, lying on her side with her back to him. Several moments later, the bed dipped. Fighting the temptation to turn around, she slammed her eyes closed, until they naturally remained that way because of her exhaustion.

CHAPTER TEN

An odd sound roused Kitty from slumber. It took a few seconds to realize she was precariously perched on the edge of the bed. It was little wonder she had not tumbled to the floor. The chamber was dark, the embers from the fireplace were barely lit, and the air was chilled. It was then she observed a blanket had been tucked under her chin and around her body. She snapped her gaze to the duke in bemusement. He lay flat on his back, without the benefit of the covering of blankets, his chest rising raggedly.

A rough groan slipped from him. There! It was that sound that had brought her awake. She noted the terrible tension in his frame and that his fingers clutched the bedsheets.

Another tortured groan echoed in the small chamber.

Tentatively, Kitty slid one of her hands across the bedding and touched his clenched knuckles. She sensed the moment he surged awake. His entire body stilled, and he commanded his breathing so it no longer sounded ragged. Yet he did not pull away from her tentative touch, and she did not withdraw her hand.

"Your audacity should not be able to surprise me any longer."

"I had to rouse you, Your Grace. You were dreaming," she whispered.

He turned his hand in hers so they were palm to palm.

"Always...I dream every night."

His low response hinted of torments she would never understand. But he did not sound ravaged, more accepting.

She stared at their clasped hands, uncertain if she should pull away or stay. "I'm sorry."

"You were not the cause, Miss Danvers."

"I'm still sorry."

A pause. "I like my dreams."

She shifted closer, all but climbing over the pillow that was between them. "I thought they were nightmares."

Something naked and vulnerable flashed across his face before his expression shuttered. "When I dream of that night...I do not dream only of the fire."

Her gaze jumped to the scarred side of his face. She could barely discern those dreadful marks. "I wondered what had caused your pain."

"Hmm."

He made no other reply and she did not probe, though she wished to know all his secrets, the good and the bad. A very silly yearning, but nonetheless it was there. She pulled her hand gently from his clasp and folded it beneath her chin.

"Would you share with me?"

"I've never shared before," came the soft reply.

"Why not?"

"No one has ever asked."

A jerk of her heart. "They were perhaps scared or too intimidated by you to pry," she whispered, sensing it to be true with the force of personality she'd witnessed in the duke. "How would they dare?"

"And you are too impudent to be scared, hmm. Just as how you were not scared earlier to help me save George. I admire your bravery."

Heat burst inside her heart. "I'm glad that you do."

It felt as if the very air shifted, and something unknown but pleasant settled between them.

Several claps of thunder rumbled in the distance, and the rain turned into a heavier downpour. "Perhaps it is safer between strangers already sharing secrets. Upon my honor I would not betray your trust, Alexander."

A slow curve of his lips, yet he remained silent. With a sigh, she closed her eyes, letting the pitter-patter of rain on the roof lull her back to slumber.

"My mother had the loveliest laugh. That morning as I made my way to the breakfast room, it was the first sound that greeted me. My father had shockingly stolen a kiss, and my sister, Penny, all of seven at the time, was equally delighted and appalled to have been a witness. We always broke our fast together in the morning. Penny was never banished to the schoolroom but dined with us adults."

Kitty opened her eyes slowly, not daring to move or breathe.

"Afterward, Mother spent the morning with Penny on the lawns reading, and Father and I discussed estate matters. Then we all took a jaunt to the village in the carriage. That evening, instead of attending a local charity ball, Mother and Father stayed home. And we dined together, Penny included and quite pleased to be at the table with us. We retired to the drawing room, Mother played the pianoforte, and I sang."

Another pregnant pause, and the rain drummed with more insistence on the roof. Kitty shifted closer and, acting on impulse, tugged some of the blanket from her side and tucked it about his waist. He said nothing, but another small smile curved his lips.

"That night, it was Penny's distant cries that woke me. Somehow, Penny had made her way to my chamber. The drapes were already on fire, and it was a wonder we found breath in the stifling heat and smoke. I lifted her in my arms and rushed into the hallway. Fire razed the west wing of the castle, and everything was chaos. The stairs were engulfed, and the way to escape had been blocked. The only means seemed to be back into my room. I waded through the flames…and as you can see, the monster caught me. I shoved open the window…and jumped."

"It must have been horrifying." The fear would have been so overwhelming. The agony when he realized what had been lost…

"Whenever I dream of that day…I see the entire day, from the joy and laughter to the screams and agony, and for that reason…this nightmare I revisit so often is very precious to me."

Something shattered inside her, and the ache in Kitty's chest grew until the pressure threatened to smother her. "Then I shall not wake you the next time."

His lips tipped. "I am not sure how to feel that you believe there will be a next time. But I thank you, Miss Danvers."

She flushed and was grateful for the barely-there light in the chamber.

Kitty had the most ridiculous urge to scuttle closer and hug him. His strength awed and humbled her. They remained unspeaking for several moments, and gradually his breathing evened out. Still, she wondered. "Are you asleep—?"

"Are you asleep—?"

He chuckled, and the low, rich sound heated her from the inside.

"It seems we are like-minded in our questions, Miss Danvers."

She smiled. "Evidently so. Please, you go first."

"I am curious about you, and since knowing of you, all the space in my thoughts has been dominated by you."

She faltered into astonished stillness. She couldn't move, couldn't speak, couldn't think of anything to say. So she simply waited, her heart tripping a sweet beat.

"You seem remarkably adept at taking care of your family. You would sacrifice all for them. I find that admirable."

She snorted. "So admirable, you found it necessary to blackmail me?"

"Oh? I thought our negotiation one of mutual satisfaction."

She huffed out a breath.

He folded his hands behind his head. "I wonder, what do you dream of?"

Well, that was quite easy to answer. "My sisters—"

"For yourself," he murmured. "What do *you* hunger for?"

She stared at him in bemusement. No one had ever asked her that, had they? In truth, Kitty wasn't certain she'd ever asked herself the question. Since the death of Papa, every thought had been about how to make her sisters and mother happy. "I haven't had time to dream."

"Then dream for me now," he murmured.

She gasped softly. "Whatever do you mean, Your Grace?"

"Tell me the secret hungers in your heart. The ones you've suppressed as you put your family and duty even above your reputation and happiness."

"And are you so certain hidden desires of such a kind exist?"

"Every man, woman, and child possesses them. From the whimsy to the grave ambitions. Only a few have the audacity to transform a dream into reality. You are in that category."

A peculiar warmth flowered through her entire body. Had she ever wanted anything for herself?

She rolled onto her stomach and propped her chin in the palms of her hands, very much like she did when conversing with her sisters. "Once I dreamed of acting on the stage, like my aunt Harriet. She shocked the family, you know, and they've all but disowned her."

"But not you," he said musingly.

She laughed lightly. "Not me. I've snuck away to watch her onstage. She is beyond wonderful. Her talent immeasurable. Before Papa died, we visited her often whenever she was on break. She taught me all she knew about being an actress. Mamma was horrified, but Papa was more indulgent."

"Had you any serious pursuits?"

She recalled a time before Papa died, a time she hadn't thought about in years. "I wanted to see the world. We spent most of our lives in Hertfordshire. And I imagined the world to be quite large. Papa bought me a globe for my fifteenth birthday and a fire lit inside me. I wanted to see it all, Egypt, the Americas, China, India. Even when Mamma lamented how unrefined everyone else was, how uncivilized and savage, I wanted to see it for myself. Overnight, Hertfordshire became a grain of sand, and I hungered for the entire ocean. It was all I dreamed about, it was all I spoke of. Mamma wanted to ship me off to school to reform my manners," she said with a ripple of mirth. "Papa would not hear of it, and because she loved him so much… somehow Papa convinced Mamma that my oddities were practical and sensible, and my whimsies were indulged."

"Hmm, as I indulge you *shamelessly*?"

"I declare it to be so," she said softly, not understanding why her heart pounded in this manner. This feeling brewing between them, this feeling of comfort, of…friendship. Was it one-sided? How she wished to ask.

"You miss your father."

An ache built in her chest. "I do."

"How long has he been gone?"

She hesitated slightly. "Almost five years."

The bed dipped as he shifted on his side to face her, his hands still propped behind his head. "You are smiling, Miss Danvers."

"I was thinking how wonderfully odd this all is.

We are sharing stories…as if we are…"

"Friends?" he asked archly.

Kitty silently admitted she'd never experienced anything so wicked and improper, and having such an attachment with the duke promised pleasure, darkly and sweetly. "It *is* strange. I've only ever spoken this way to my other sinful wallflowers."

"Oh? I sense a fascinating story."

"One you've not earned yet," she teased, almost hating the ease at which they bantered. She liked and admired the duke so, yet she was a mere plaything that he would eventually tire of and discard. Worse, she wanted to kiss him. It was a desire she had been denying since their carriage ride from London.

"So you are no longer worried being alone with me, hmm?"

She scowled. *The wretched tease.* "Your reputation had given me pause, but I can see it does not precede you."

He lifted an arrogant brow. "And which reputation do you throw at me, Miss Danvers?"

She hesitated, not sure why she wanted to tease him so in return. "The one that called you mad, bad, and dangerous."

Amusement lit in his eyes, and her heart shivered to see it.

"You've also forgotten the fiendishly sinful bit," he drawled, eyes alight with provoking humor and something so warm, her mouth dried.

"I was about to come to it," she said with a smile. "Mad, bad, dangerous, *and* fiendish. A truly appalling combination." Her heart whispered "ruthless" and "indomitable," qualities she should not admire so.

He touched her face fleetingly, his finger leaving a trail of warmth across her cheek. She felt the pull of his stroke in her belly. It was a rather disconcerting sensation.

"And do you believe everything you read, Miss Danvers?"

His question was a wicked purr of warning, one she had no intention of heeding. Later she would blame it on being locked in a small cottage, with the rain hammering against the slatted roof and windowpane. The fire in the hearth danced merrily, yet the room was cast in intimate shadows. The silence that stretched between them was filled with something dangerous and exciting.

A reckless and wholly improper feeling stirred inside her. *I want to kiss him, and I am a silly wretch to think it!*

"Your scowls are frightening me, Miss Danvers. Pray tell what murder and mayhem do you currently contemplate?"

Each time he teased her, Kitty hungered to clasp his jaw and kiss him with all the brewing passion in her heart. She felt she would slowly expire from the torture of always wanting, not knowing, endlessly desiring him. That frustration and hunger snapped, uncoiling within her. She shifted closer, ignoring his start of surprise, stretched up against him, and pressed her lips quickly to his, entirely without grace.

Kitty fastened her mouth to his—it was awkward yet so wonderfully tender. She paused, holding her breath, waiting for his response…which never came.

Mortification pinched her and she pulled away, a trembling sigh falling from her lips.

The duke was remarkably still, his eyes hooded and unfathomable. A battle flashed across his shadowed features—stark hunger, uncertainty, before aloofness painted a curiously indifferent mask. "What did I do to deserve such attentions?" he drawled.

"I just wanted to get that dreadful anticipation out of the way," she said with a nervous laugh.

"Do explain."

"I knew I would go mad confined with you for two whole days or more in this small cottage." She held up two fingers for emphasis. Her throat worked on a swallow. "I would go mad from wondering what it would be like. Can you imagine the awful anxiety of wondering and not knowing? But now I know."

He stared at her as if he did not know what to make of her, and a flush worked itself through her.

"What do you now know, then?"

"Why…what it felt like to kiss you properly, of course." *Yes!* She sounded perfectly nonchalant and worldly. But how her belly flipped as a million butterflies—or more like eagles—took flight inside.

"What an injustice," he murmured. "It almost borders on criminality."

She frowned. "What is?"

"That you truly believed that bit of slobbering was a kiss."

Kitty gasped her outrage. "Slobbering?"

"Hmm. My dogs greet me in the same manner."

The low growl from her throat shocked her with its ferocity. "How do you *dare*!"

Amusement fired in his eyes. "Forgive me for teasing. I suspect I've injured your pride."

She sniffed derisively, but mortification burned the tips of her ears. "I suppose you believe you could do better? Do not answer that! For I recall our meeting in its entirety, and that nip was hardly worth mentioning."

"Ah…an invitation? I accept, Miss Danvers. I accept." Chuckling, he drew her near and kissed her.

She bit his lip, hard, and with a muttered curse, he released her.

"Impudent hellion!"

She pushed aside the blanket and scrambled from the bed. With an indignant scoff, she flounced toward the armchair. *Slobbering.* If she possessed any wisp of rationality, she would ignore him and try to get some sleep. The man had said he would never marry, and she did not desire ruination, but he'd lit a fire inside her. Or perhaps she relied on that excuse too quickly. But Kitty spun around to see that he, too, had left the bed and was standing.

She marched over to him, grabbed his shoulders, tipped on her toes, and mashed her lips to his. *There.* She would show him. *Slobbering?* Odious man!

A muffled sound of surprise came from him, and then they were tumbling onto the bed. She landed on him with an *oomph.* Their foreheads bumped, and with a cry she reared up, rubbing the bruised spot.

"Your tough head has fairly cracked my skull," he muttered darkly.

"Why, you—"

He caught her lips with his. The second their mouths met, it was as though the hunger, which had been carefully contained, escaped with an intense rush. This time their kiss was slow…indulgent, and oh so wickedly thorough.

"Part these pretty lips for me," he murmured against her mouth.

Kitty gasped, parting her lips and giving him the entry he sought.

Fire blazed through her body, glorious, wanton heat at the first touch of his tongue against hers. A soft bite at her lower lip. A nibble. Then another deep kiss, their tongues mating with carnal enticement.

His moan resonated with longing. Her heart jerked with joy.

Their lips parted, and he spun with her so she was beneath him. Kitty felt faint at this new, provocative, and intimidating position. She knew it would likely break her heart, but she couldn't steel herself against this unknown passion he roused.

I'm being foolish. His reputation and title had been a means to an end, nothing more. And for him she was a dalliance…a mystery that needed to be dissected and then forgotten. *Then why…oh why do I feel so?* Kitty hated that she was falling headlong into something elusive, and she could not stop it.

This man…this *duke*, who was so far removed from her in everything, would break her. She saw the knowledge in the gaze that peered at her. Yet…she was helpless against his pull. She almost hated him in this instance.

"You will break me," she murmured, holding his gaze, wanting him to scoff and deny. Or fall back on the humor that seemed to have saved him when his world had turned to ashes.

A dark knowledge lingered within his brilliant stare. A finger trailed along her cheek, sorrow…and something unfathomable whispering through his stark gaze. "You will recover," he said softly, his tone ruthless and implacable.

Kitty flinched.

No promises lingered, nor were any implied. And the first crack in her silly, reckless heart appeared.

They stared at each other; the darkened chamber clasped them in an intimacy that made her believe all their secrets would be kept safe. All their kisses, improper glances, wicked touches would be only a memory between them and this small cottage. Society need not know, and ruination would be averted.

I'll know, her aching soul cried as she allowed the heart that had dreamed once but had been buried under duty to flicker to life.

As if he sensed the hunger jerking inside her, his head dipped, their noses rubbed briefly, then his sensual mouth claimed hers in a kiss of violent tenderness. She floundered in a blinding sea of sensation, desperate to sink deeper. Her fingers dug into his hair, holding him steady, pushing him away, urging him on all at once.

• • •

Hunger flamed through Alexander's soul, a wicked craving that crawled to burrow deep under his skin. The wonder of Katherine's lips against his felt like his first brush with intimacy. He almost went to his knees, so urgent and desperate was the need to be touched by her and to feel the burn of pleasure. Even when he'd teased her of slobbering earlier to save himself…to save her from this fiery madness, her taste had enslaved him.

Touch me, please, he silently, desperately implored.

The sweet taste of her spilled into his mouth; her soft sighs of pleasure vibrated through his body, burrowing their way down to his heart. It beat. For the first time in years, he felt the shudder of his soul and heard the echo of his heartbeat. It transmuted a halting stutter to a thundering roar within seconds. How long had it been since he had tasted such sweetness? Felt such pleasure? Ten years? *A lifetime.*

He could feel the dull ache of awakening desire in his cock, and he trembled in reaction, shock tearing through him. He was *impotent*. For ten years, doctors had probed and prodded; the Marquess of Argyle had sent Alexander some of the most exotic and wicked Parisian courtesans, and all had failed to rouse his ardor.

While his cock wasn't rushing to attention, he felt something…and that was *everything*.

Miss Danvers's mouth was a sweet silken flame under his as she responded with artless wonder to his ravishing kisses. She made an achingly hungry, demanding, yet soft sound against his mouth. Every muscle in his body tightened, every echoing emptiness in his soul expanded to be filled with a strange sensation akin to wonder. He cupped the back of her head with one hand, cradled her cheek reverently with the other, and slanted his mouth over hers more forcefully, a desperate need burgeoning inside to feel the press of desire.

Alexander sensed the heated quickening inside, and though he felt a throb along his shaft, the phantom pulse of remembered pleasure, his length did not harden. She whimpered into his kiss, and he felt her pulse fluttering wildly against his palm like the wings of a captured bird. He shifted, and pain flashed up his thighs and into his hips.

With a muffled moan, she pushed against his chest. He released her immediately and shifted so that she rolled away from him, taking great gulps of air through her swollen lips. Her body was flushed, the creamy mounds of her breasts quivering through the gaping nightgown. She touched her full lower lip with a fingertip, and her eyes were wounded shadows in the paleness of her face.

He took a deep, deep breath. "I've frightened you," he murmured.

"No…I've frightened myself."

And he understood.

"Come here, Katherine."

Her eyes shot with a defiant spark, and her tongue darted and wetted her bottom lip, a nervous gesture. "Are you making an offer, Your Grace?"

A pounding ache went through his heart. "No."

Indignation brought a flush to her cheeks. "Then you will refrain from taking liberties," she whispered, her voice achingly soft. "Though I was foolish to kiss you just now, I do not wish to be reckless and impetuous with my virtue. I… If I should succumb to your ravishment, I would expect and demand a marriage. Our situation is very…unorthodox, and we must not give in to any temptation our forced intimacy imposes. I must not give in and you must not be the devil's advocate. I've no brother or father to protect my honor, so I must use my good senses."

She looked pale and stricken and heartbreakingly beautiful, yet so very fierce and determined.

His fingers lightly caressed her arm, and he bent his head closer to hers. "Then use your good senses wisely, Miss Danvers."

She was so endearing, so indomitable, so damn sweet. She had a stubborn strength that did not lessen her beguiling femininity. And Alexander wished and hoped for things he hadn't longed for in years. The ability to give…pleasure and joy and his name and protection. It was foolish, it bordered on rank absurdity, but suddenly he wanted Kitty Danvers with all her bold impudence, reckless heart, and vivacious personality…to belong to him.

If only…

He rolled onto his back and stared at the ceiling, hating the empty, hollow feeling once more rising inside. He'd conquered these emotions years ago when he'd wanted to rail at life and become a monster in his grief and despair. He'd accepted the certainty this would never be his, so why was he tempting himself again with things that could not be?

You will break me.

He hadn't forgotten that shocking statement. Her voice had been so quiet, the hint of vulnerability and apprehension in it digging sharp claws of discomfort into his conscience.

You'll recover.

How cold and unfeeling he'd sounded when

everything inside him had been burning with hunger to taste, to smell, to simply touch her. Alexander was damned if he knew how to handle what she made him feel. He had nothing to offer as a broken man. He knew this… It had been imprinted on his soul. He'd accepted years ago that normalcy in a relationship would not be for him, so it would be a waste of his energy and time to pursue anything in that direction. And he was not the kind of man to invest where there would be no gain.

What is it that I hope for?

Instead of launching from the bed as he'd anticipated, she shifted closer to him, her shoulder bumped fleetingly against his shoulder.

"I never knew a kiss could taste like sunshine," she said softly.

"And also of the storm," he murmured.

Alexander swore he felt the smile blooming on her face.

If he didn't breathe, maybe she would touch him.

And she did. A fleeting caress against his knuckles. *Ah yes…Christ.*

"I truly believe, Miss Danvers, there are infinite possibilities for us as kissing friends."

"You mustn't give me encouragement of this sort; I can be frightfully wicked," she teased.

He arched a brow but did not look at her. If he did, he would ruin his honor and trust by hauling her into his arms. "Oh?"

"Yes," she said, at once prim and mischievous. How did she do it?

They stared at each other at the same time, and he smiled at the fancy of it.

"You want to kiss me again," she said with a sigh, her expression hidden in the flickering shadows.

"I do, Miss Danvers."

"I thought we'd agreed on informality."

"When I want to save myself from acting the fool…I must say Miss Danvers."

Her eyes widened. "I quite like your name on my lips, Alexander."

"And I treasure the sound of it."

She turned more toward him, and it was the daring tigress who peered up at him. Then, as if the most natural thing in the world, his wicked hellion kissed him. Her fingers threaded through his hair. Her lips, her mouth, moved over his with scorching carnality. She made the softest, sweetest sounds of pleasure against his lips, and Alexander hoarded them, interring them deep in his heart where the memory would sustain him for years to come.

Something he had thought long dead rose from the silent depths of his soul. It stirred, stretched, and hummed as a blast of pleasure and pain arrowed through his cock.

Sweet mercy…what in God's name is this?

CHAPTER ELEVEN

With a virulent curse, Alexander pulled from Katherine and launched from the bed. Too fast and without form. The muscles of his legs twisted, pain ricocheted up his back, and his leg crumpled. He stumbled back against the bed, and with a cry, she jerked up to catch him. His weight flattened her against the bed, and it was all so ridiculous, he laughed.

"This is not remotely humorous," she muttered, her lips pressing against his shoulder.

With a grunt, he moved, and she scrambled from beneath his weight. He shifted onto the bed, and the pain came, a dark tide that rolled over him, freezing him in place. It spasmed from his calf, the muscles knotting in urgent demand, his heart racing, his body tensing against the agony. He'd thought he defeated the episode earlier when he'd spent almost an hour working through the knots and cramps while she'd slept.

"Let me," she whispered, coming up on her knees and pushing the two pillows beneath his leg.

A groan slipped from between his teeth, and it bothered him that she would see him so weakened.

Worried eyes peered at him. "Where does it hurt most? Alexander...please trust me with your pain as you did with your memories."

The softly whispered entreaty burrowed into his heart. He lifted his chin toward his left thigh. And without hesitation, she gripped his flesh and started a deep press of her fingertips into his muscles. The cramps fought her ministrations, sweat beaded his brows, and he gripped the bedsheets between his fingers.

She muttered soothing nonsense each time he tensed. At times he stilled, and it was the cadence of her voice, and her foolish promises he would be well, that urged him to relax. His mind searched for something to take away the pain. With her touching him, it was quite difficult to transport himself to the varied places he normally willed his mind to in order to escape the pain.

"I could bring you more pleasure than you've ever dreamed of." Truly, his tongue seemed to be disconnected from his mind. Still, he watched her reaction keenly, anticipating the possibilities of her delightful reaction.

Her eyes widened, and the fingers kneading the muscles of his calf paused. "I do not think we should be speaking of pleasures now," she murmured huskily, resuming her wondrous massage of the knotted flesh of his legs.

How intriguing that she was not repulsed by the twisted muscles.

She bit into her bottom lip, a frown furrowing her brows, her lively, intelligent eyes shooting him curious looks.

Ahh. "You are tempted."

A flush ran along her body. "I am human; I daresay it is normal to be curious. I've heard many whispers throughout the season, and, since I've no hope of marrying, I daresay I do not have to be at all proper, do I?"

The notion of Miss Kitty Danvers being more

improper…perhaps even a bit wicked, had his groin responding with a sweet, terrible ache. The sensation of arousal was so visceral, sweat beaded on his forehead, and with hungry desperation, he searched into himself, wanting to keep that feeling with him, wanting to know once more the sensation of lust pounding through his cock and hardening it.

Yet his cock did not respond, remaining flaccid within the confines of his trousers. Until her kneading fingers drifted up to his thighs, until the image of her sprawled on the small bed, eyes wide with desire and apprehension, her dress hiked wantonly to her hips as his eyes feasted on the pale skin of her inner thigh, sent a violent ache through his length, causing it to flex and harden.

The shock of it almost caused him to expire on the spot. A certain long-dead part of his body was stirring.

Impossible. Too many years longing. Too many nights dreaming.

"If you wish to be wicked, take off your clothes and come here."

"You are outrageous, Your Grace," she cried, blushing something fierce.

"Alexander," he teased, distantly wondering what the hell he was doing.

Yet she did not run from him in feminine outrage. No, her beautiful eyes measured him, her lips pursed thoughtfully.

"And how would you pleasure me?"

"Strip naked, come sit on my mouth, and I'll show you," he drawled provocatively.

Her eyes widened until he thought they would

eclipse her face.

"Sit…sit…" This time her entire body blushed red. "I cannot perceive your meaning," she squawked, pushing his legs away without any finesse and jumping to her feet. "I…I…cannot credit you would be so indecent to even s-suggest…" she spluttered, fisting a hand on her hip.

"Sitting on my face so that I can lick your pretty quim?" And he knew it would be pretty, soft and plump, wet and silky. And sweet mercy. Tight.

Alexander couldn't say what possessed him to tease her in such an outrageous and wicked manner. With a squeak, she fled from the bedroom, as if he had grown horns and a tail. He chuckled. An apology for his provoking crudeness must be made at once. And atonement, of course.

He shifted, ignoring the pain whispering through him. Before he could make his way from the bed, Miss Danvers returned, a basin clutched between her hands. Alexander narrowed his eyes as she marched over in quick, determined strides. "Miss Danvers, allow me to offer my sincerest apol—"

Icy water dumped over his head, shocking him.

The impudence! With a scowl, he glanced at her. "You wet our bed."

Her eyes glowed with fire and, if he wasn't mistaken, defiance and amusement. "Has your ardor cooled?"

An unidentifiable emotion swept through him. It hadn't risen. Except…a heat stirred low in his gut, and a ghost of desire caressed over his cock, causing it to twitch. He faltered into complete stillness.

It was not his imagination. *Sweet mercy.*

"Alexander?" she asked with a frown, lowering the basin. "Are you well?"

When he did not reply, she dropped the basin on the floor and hurried over to him. "What is it? Speak to me, please."

Then she touched his shoulder.

Suddenly, nothing else mattered but touching her, holding her.

Acting on the impulse, he tugged her onto his lower thigh, ruthlessly ignoring the shock of agony. He slowly breathed through the pain until it lessened and simply hugged her. And without question, she returned his embrace. The sexual need had vanished, and in its place was something tender, and for some reason that sensation felt more important. He kissed the top of her head, unable to express his appreciation.

"What was that for?" she whispered.

"For being a friend," he replied gruffly.

Slowly her face turned toward him. Her eyes widened; her lips parted on a silent gasp. She pressed a delicate hand to her chest and regarded him without betraying either dismay or astonishment. Then she smiled, and it was the most radiant thing he'd ever witnessed. "I quite like being your friend… Alexander."

The dawn broke right at that moment; the sun crested the horizon, warm glowing light chasing away the dark remnants of the night. Light spilled through the window, splashing bright sun into the small bedroom.

"I need to see the morning," he murmured.

She did not question the odd turn of phrase, and

he fancied she understood this was a routine for him. Each day, at the crest of dawn, before he broke his fast, he met the sun, the skies, the birds.

He stood and slowly made his way from the bedroom and down the small hall. Once he reached the front door, he opened it and breathed in deeply. The scent of last night's rain was still heavy in the air, and he swore he could almost taste the purity of the sunshine.

Katherine came up beside him. "Don't you smile?"

"I do."

She arched a brow. "When? You are all but scowling now."

"When the mood calls for it."

Kitty shrugged. "I smile when I wake."

An odd warmth slowly twisted through his body. "Do you?"

"Mm, the simple joy of greeting the sunshine and the morning."

He squinted toward the sky, and she laughed.

"I smile when I hear the chirping of birds, when I smell the rain, hear the rumble of thunder. I smile before I sleep. I smile…because I am."

"Perhaps you are merely addled," he mused. "I've heard tell lunatics tend to grin a lot."

Kitty spluttered, and she mockingly punched his arm.

He shifted, facing her, head tilted in quiet contemplation. "Perhaps I've been asleep." For years so many feelings and sensations had been dormant, but now, everything pulsed beneath the surface of his skin, raw and primal, thrilling…and oddly enough, uncertain.

Alexander wasn't sure who he was with this woman. And he did not like that. He liked a surety of emotions and the path one should walk in life. He prided himself on his honor and consistency of character, but for the second time since meeting Katherine Danvers, he wondered who he was... around this woman.

Something inside awakened with a trembling force. He wanted to make her his...in a way a man would make a lady his. *If only...*

Something stirred in him deep down, something gentle and tender and long forgotten.

He refused to draw her enticing scent of lavender too deeply into his lungs. He'd want it to stay there forever, and he couldn't be that cruel, for he had the wealth and ruthless will to bend her to his whims.

But she could be mine...if only for a little.

He stared at her, assessing the needs burning through him. "I like you."

"You say that as if it is a grave crime," she said with a teasing smile, though her eyes were curious... scared, almost, as they caressed his face.

Damn his selfish hide. *She invited this*, his ruthless heart whispered. Everything had changed. *Everything*.

"Perhaps it is," he murmured.

Then he faced the breaking dawn, lifting his face to the paltry sunshine as it broke through the swollen clouds. At times like this, he needed no conversation, and he would spend the first hour or two of the day in silence.

He wanted to share his silence...his loneliness.

Except with her breathing in his space, the soft

rasp of her breath lingering in the air…it filled the room with a measure of peace. Odd, to be certain. But there it was. Contentment.

Silence had always been dark, a reflection of past nightmares, a reminder of loneliness, an echo of emptiness. Now this silence seemed intimate, tender, hushed, hesitant, and a question lingered within its confines.

What do I hope for?

• • •

Kitty and the duke were kissing friends.

Such conduct, if it were known by society, would sink Kitty below reproach. It was outrageous and wicked, and she did not regret it.

She took a breath, feeling grumpy at the stiffness of her clothes. They had been barely wet earlier, and she had redressed with the duke's help into the damaged clothing. He, too, had redressed, and they hadn't spoken as she had acted his valet.

No, Kitty had been too busy blushing.

After more than an hour watching the sunrise in silence, hunger forced them to dress and had driven them to the larder, where they had stared, bemused, unsure what to do. Now they were in the small but very neat kitchen, determined to figure out something to eat. That packed larder hadn't been with food already prepared. And Kitty planned several ways on how to gut George when she saw him. The man could have returned to them with help hours ago. But clearly, he wanted her alone with the duke! The sheer gall of it was flummoxing.

The duke took it all with his peculiar dash of humor, even though he swore to reprimand the man if he did not return today.

"I do not think we are getting it right," the duke said dubiously, glancing from Kitty to the worn sheaf of paper in his hands.

"Not at all," she replied cheerfully, "I daresay we are doing fine. We've followed all the instructions written down."

"I've never seen such a lump at my table before. And let me tell you, Mrs. McGinnis works in my kitchen."

Kitty scowled, some of her triumph and pride leeching away. They dipped their heads in unison, looking once more on the recipe. Kitty had been the one to spy the recipe papers and had adventurously declared that they were highly intelligent people and could figure out how to bake a simple cake. Why, she spoke three languages and excelled at watercolors and geography. The duke shockingly spoke nine languages. He was a great orator in the House of Lords and had once been praised and revered for his statesmanship. Surely two crafty and cunning heads could produce a cake eligible for consumption.

Only now, Kitty doubted it.

"I think…I think we forgot the eggs," she muttered, squinting at the paper. "I did not see any eggs in the larder."

"I thought I heard a fowl outside." The duke peeked at her sideways. "I do not jest. Unless my hearing is now impaired."

They glanced down at the half-white lump of batter on the stone counter.

"I do not recall adding sugar, do you?" Alexander asked with a heavy dollop of skepticism.

"That was *your* job. Can you not recall?"

The duke grabbed the large earthenware bowl over to his side of the counter. He bravely pinched off a piece of the dough and popped it into his mouth. His eyes widened before they fluttered closed. He made a rough sound. She clasped her hands and waited, but the dratted man only chewed. "Well! How is it?"

His mien was serious as he replied, "Divine."

"Truly?" She pinched a piece, popped it into her mouth, and choked. *Dear God!* "We are going to starve," she said mournfully.

A flash of a smile. "Rubbish. If it gets bad, we'll simply eat the dough. I've had worse."

"You've had worse than this? I do not believe you for an instant!" To disabuse him of the notion, she hurriedly took it to the wastebasket and dumped it.

His low laugh pulled a smile to her lips.

He grabbed the sole remaining apple. "Let's share."

She nodded, sauntered over, and rested her hip on the counter. The duke held the apple out to her, and she leaned forward and took a generous bite. He scowled, then glanced at the apple and back at her.

"What big teeth you have, Miss Danvers."

Kitty giggled, crunching her generous portion hungrily. He then took a bite before holding it back out to her.

And they ate the apple like that, neither commenting on the fact that a knife rested on the stone counter, and he could easily have cut the fruit in half.

CHAPTER TWELVE

A few minutes after breaking their fast with the apple, George had returned to the small cottage, to Kitty's abject relief. To spend another night with the duke in the same bed had simply been too much to contemplate. She was sure something debauched and regretful would have happened. She would have been ruined and sad and, well…the duke would be himself, none less for the wear.

"Didna I tell ye no' tae worry," the coachman had said in a mocking thick brogue when he had returned. There had been a definite salacious twinkle in the man's light hazel eyes as he'd glanced between her and the duke. Alexander hadn't rebuked the coachman for the impudence. He had only smiled and informed the man it was fortunate he'd returned just now.

Kitty had sent them her fiercest scowl, to the coachman's amusement. Then it had warmed her heart to observe the gruff way the coachman questioned Alexander if he were well, and the genuine love and concern in his eyes.

She'd simply accepted their unorthodox relationship, admired it, even.

The carriage that had collected her now rumbled along a rocky road, and the driver urged the horses with speed, uncaring of her posterior. The duke had elected to ride ahead on his stallion, and once again, Kitty did not mind the privacy his decision afforded her. Unfortunately, it gave her time to dwell on his wonderful kisses—she could still taste and feel him against her lips—the improper manner in which he had teased her, and the wicked desires he roused in her heart. She was still slightly annoyed with herself for letting her guard down with him in the cottage.

I can give you more pleasure than you dream of.

And foolishly, she wanted to explore with him. Reckless!

Still, Kitty closed her eyes, leaned her head against the squabs, and allowed herself to imagine kissing the duke endlessly. If she were thinking clearly or logically, she would have been urging her thoughts in the opposite direction. But it seemed the only place she could be with him so freely and wantonly was in her dreams, and she would shamelessly indulge.

After about thirty minutes of driving along the rough, muddied path, they entered a well-paved road with towering elm and beech trees on each side of the road. The long driveway was stately and well tended, the rolling lawns spied through the trees seeming to spread for miles. She moved aside the curtain covering the carriage window, her breath catching at the magnificent view ahead.

Kitty felt as if she'd entered a fairy tale.

She had expected a dark castle with crumbled walls, thinking the duke's reclusiveness had meant he'd shut himself away from everything. How utterly wrong she'd been. The rolling lands the carriage rumbled past were breathtaking. The looming castle atop a slight incline, surrounded by verdant grass and flowers, was a palace of dreams.

The carriage pulled into the grand courtyard some minutes later, and the steps to the coach were knocked down. The door opened, and the duke was there to assist her from the equipage. Kitty allowed him to help her, and once she was from the carriage, she stared about her in stunned wonder.

The harsh gray of the granite castle was offset by beautiful gardens decorated with classical fountains—sea nymphs frolicked around a statue of Neptune, and a stag worshipped at Diana's feet.

Behind the exquisite castle, a sweeping lawn led down to the picturesque lake. Within the lake were many small islands that were bedecked with weeping willows and abundant greenery.

"This place is magnificent, Alexander. A paradise."

Before he could respond, a squeal of surprise or perhaps excitement tugged Kitty's gaze to the steps leading to the large oak door with a lion head knocker.

A young girl and a gentleman walked toward them, and in their fair coloring, Kitty saw a resemblance. They were both blond and quite beautiful. The girl wore a pale pink dress, her blond ringlets caught in a loose chignon with artful tendrils cascading to kiss against her shoulder. As she drew closer, the shocking blue of her eyes was a perfect reflection of the duke's wicked gaze.

The young man beside her, while they shared the same blond hair and fair complexion, had eyes of a pale green, and they were filled with friendly welcome. Sudden self-consciousness bit at Kitty, and she ran her hand across the front of her wrinkled, deplorable gown.

"You are beautiful, always. I daresay even in a sack you would be ravishing," the duke murmured.

"Outrageous nonsense," she said under her breath. Deep down, though, she was so pleased, she could barely contain it.

He smiled and stepped forward as the couple arrived.

"Alexander, I am so relieved you are home!" the girl cried, her inquisitive gaze darting between him and Kitty.

He bent to drop a kiss on her cheek. Then he shook the hand of the young man, who did nothing to mask his curiosity and stared at her with uncomfortable frankness. Kitty scowled at him, and his gaze widened.

"Miss Danvers, may I introduce you to my sister, Lady Penelope, and my cousin, Mr. Eugene Collins?"

"Oh, Miss Danvers! I've longed to meet you," the girl cried, clasping her hands before her with barely suppressed excitement. "Please do call me Penny; I truly cannot credit that you are here! Miss Danvers is Alexander's fiancée," she added with a ripple of mirth.

The girl's pleasant warmth put Kitty at ease. "How delightful to make your acquaintance, Penny. And Mr. Collins, you, too."

Mr. Collins drew an audible breath. "Fiancée?"

"Oh yes," Penny drawled mischievously with an audacious wink in Kitty's direction.

Mr. Collins looked startled and, at the same time, incredulous. Then he dipped into an elegant bow. "I am charmed, Miss Danvers. Quite charmed to meet my cousin's intended."

His shocked tone implied he was everything but charmed.

Another curious look of Mr. Collins's volleyed from her to the duke. A few minutes of polite chitchat soon revealed he had a cheerful, matter-of-fact manner, while Lady Penny was incorrigible with her manners and quite impatient. She reminded Kitty of her youngest sister, Henrietta, who often needed a firm guiding hand.

"Miss Danvers, I do have so many questions about town and the season. I hope you'll indulge me!"

Kitty smiled at Penny. "I believe I shall, though I am no authority on the town life and its varied frivolities."

Alexander said, "Miss Danvers is weary from travel and will retire for a few hours."

Penny considered this a moment, and then sighed and said, "Very well, please forgive my lack of consideration."

They proceeded inside, the sweeping arch entrances filling Kitty with awe. She went mute with surprise when the duke introduced her to his butler and housekeeper. They in turn beamed at her, and it was quite evident they were happy for her to grace their home. How very unusual. Kitty was flummoxed and amused in equal measure.

Given the state of her *déshabillé*, Alexander promised his sister they would meet in a couple of hours in the drawing room. For now, he and Miss Danvers would tidy themselves to a presentable state. A maid escorted her along the prodigious hallway, and Kitty couldn't help noting she was directed to a different wing from where Alexander had headed, his manservant accompanying him.

"Where does the duke go?"

The maid who had been introduced as Sarah happily replied, "To the west wing, Miss. Only the duke sleeps there."

How fascinatingly curious. "I wonder, does he have enchanted rooms hidden there?"

The maid threw her a bemused look, and Kitty deduced she'd never heard the tale of "Beauty and the Beast." Even with the terrible scars marring his handsome countenance, the duke was still no beast, nor did he seem to possess the disdainful arrogance so ingrained in most members of the aristocracy. Instead he was a wicked charmer.

And the most incredible kisser...

As they climbed the winding stairs, she couldn't help noting that the castle seemed very lived-in, comfortable, and elegantly decorated. The windows on all the floors were framed by sweeping curtains in lavender silk brocade with the ducal shield displayed in gold embroidery on each of the tassel-festooned pelmets. The walls were hung with impressive ancestral portraits and celebrated works of art— She identified Rembrandt, Rubens, and Raphael.

Her assigned chamber was decorated with elegant furniture in Italian marble and carved mahogany. The four-poster bed with its draped pale blue damask curtains, tied back to the posts with tasseled ropes, seemed to dominate the room. Thick carpet patterned in shades of blue complementing the curtains covered stone floors, and the lower half of the walls had been paneled in rich, dark wood. The upper half boasted a pale wallpaper printed with a silvery filigree. The chairs and sofas were upholstered in silk in muted shades of silver and blue, and Kitty instinctively sensed all rooms would be designed with the same care, comfort, and beauty in mind.

"How many rooms does the castle boast?"

"One hundred and ten, miss," the maid said with evident pride. "And the estate sits on more than two thousand acres."

Kitty made her way to the armoire, pleased to see her valise had been unpacked and her dresses hung.

"A bath will be up shortly, miss, and you just ring for me when you're ready."

Kitty smiled her thanks, and Sarah bobbed and departed. The bath was delivered, and soon she was relaxed into the radiant heat of the rose-scented water. Kitty moaned at the decadent feel, and with a sigh, she lowered herself into the cavernous bath until the water stopped at her chin. Kitty willfully reminisced over each moment of her encounter with the duke in the cottage, recalling his delicious weight as he held her beneath him, the unique masculine scent, and kisses that would haunt her for the breadth of her life.

How could she walk away from the tender sensations rousing in her heart for Alexander? How could she ignore them, when she sensed such intensity of admiration and yearning for another happened perhaps once in a lifetime?

She had promised the duke a week at his castle. *A week*. Unexpectedly tears stung her lids, and she closed her eyes tightly. She liked him, so very much. And Kitty knew she would be unable to stop the headlong tumble into affection for this man. And he…he would break her bloody heart.

Unless, if she genuinely lost her heart to him, she could convince him to give her his in return.

Kitty froze, her heart pounding with such force, she felt faint.

Part of her recoiled at the direction of her thoughts, but another part, which had been dormant for far too long, stirred to life. Could she really try to show the duke they could be perfect for each other?

Surely a man who had been without a duchess for so long would not look at her and believe she was ideally suited for that role. Kitty snorted, hating the hunger crawling through her heart. Impossible yearnings she had suppressed the instant Papa had died, for her family had now become her sole responsibility.

A silent, dangerous thrill coursed through her. What if she could have something more with the duke…something real and not the pretend nonsense she had been living? She could undertake a dangerous gamble: putting her heart and emotions at risk. Overnight, she'd become a fool. One who no longer had rational thoughts but dwelled on love and family…and her own happiness with the most unsuitable man. For he had not shown any inclination toward permanency.

I'll never marry, Miss Danvers.

But what if she could dream a little?

And Kitty allowed wicked dreams into her heart while she bathed: of being the duke's friend…and

his lover, and the woman he would fall hopelessly in
love with.

• • •

The mantel clock chimed the half hour. The third
such chime since he'd returned home with Miss
Danvers in tow. Alexander had summoned his team
of doctors to attend him at the estate immediately
and had indulged in a long bath, scrubbing away
all the grime and mud that hadn't been adequately
cleaned with that small basin of water in the cottage.

Dressed and feeling somewhat human again, he
made his way slowly down the winding staircase,
then the lengthy hallway, relying heavily on the cane
gripped in his right hand. The manner in which he
had pushed himself in the last several hours twisted
the muscles of his lower back and leg. The pain
had barely been eased by the long, heated soak in
the large copper tub and the extended rub by his
manservant. It was time for him to take to his bath
chair and remove the pressure from his body.

Alexander entered the library and let the heavy
oak door close behind him, not surprised to see
Eugene perusing a book by the fire or pretending
to read. His cousin's diversions were usually of a
different variety—namely women and racing.

The book was slammed closed with some relief.
"Ah, finally. I wondered if you would come down."

Alexander made his way over to his wheeled
contraption and lowered himself into its arms. He
almost groaned at the relief that pulsed through
his body. When he glanced up, Eugene peered at

him with concern. His cousin's lips tightened as his gaze landed on the iron chair in which Alexander sat. It had been years, and still, his cousin was uncomfortable looking upon his limitations.

"Had a rough time of it, did you? George told me of all that happened. You took a risk going back for him in those damned waters."

"Ah, but it was worth it. He is alive."

And as odd as it would seem, the servants of McMullen Castle were like his family. They had been with him during every hellish step to recovery. They hadn't allowed him to give up or lose himself in the haze and comfort of opium or other deadly pursuits.

It had taken days and the painstaking resilience of a team of the best doctors from Edinburgh and England to save his life. It had been several weeks later before he had been fit to see anyone. Almost a year before he had walked unassisted without a cane or his hovering manservant. And about three years before he'd stopped being a beast to everyone. How he had roared and screamed his loss and anguish, holding on to the physical pain as his wretched companion.

The pain had been better than a heart heavy with grief.

Eugene grunted, raking his fingers through his sandy hair. "*Who* is this Miss Danvers? While I detected a warmth between you, when I saw you three weeks' past, I heard no news of an engagement, and Penny has a permanent mischievous twinkle in her eyes."

With some amusement in his tone, Alexander told the wicked tale of Miss Kitty Danvers, the ruse she played on society, and his fascination. Alexander

ended with, "Somehow I thought the gossips would
have reached you in Bedfordshire."

His cousin turned a shocked countenance toward
him. "Are you funning me?"

"No, that I am not."

"She lied about knowing you!"

Alexander grunted a noncommittal reply.

Eugene scowled. "Miss Danvers is beyond
incorrigible! To think of such a hoax and execute it…
Why, I am still at a loss at her boldness."

He tried to prevent the smile but failed lamenta-
bly.

Surprise widened his cousin's eyes before they
narrowed thoughtfully on Alexander. "You like her,"
he said softly.

"I am more curious." *Liar.*

"And that is why she is here?"

"I am still figuring that out."

An unusual silence fell between them, and
Eugene made his way to the mantel and poured
whiskey into two glasses. He handed one to Alexander.

"Do you still wish to speak on estate matters?"
Eugene asked. "Or would you like to join Miss Danvers and Penny in the rose parlor? I believe Penny is
persuading your fiancée to play cribbage."

Alexander tipped the glass to his mouth and
took a healthy swallow of his drink. "One or two of
my doctors will be attending me in a few hours. I'll
decline."

"And if Miss Danvers should query?"

"You are not at liberty to divulge my business.
Simply let her wonder."

Eugene grunted and made his way from the library, leaving Alexander alone. He wheeled himself behind his desk, fighting the temptations to join them in the smaller parlor. Instead, he took a packet of letters that had been sent by the prime minister.

A knock sounded, and before he could answer, the door cracked open, and Kitty peered in.

"Hullo," she said softly.

"Most people would wait for an answer before intruding."

"You already know I am not most people." She hesitated before entering. Then she closed the door behind her but advanced no farther, standing with her back against it. "Your sister was quite disappointed that you would not join us."

"And you?"

That elicited a small smile from her. Instead of answering, she said, "Would you like some company?"

"It pains me to disillusion you, but I am disastrous at small talk." The press of silence was where he found his greatest comfort. And yet, he wanted her to stay, to talk, to touch him again. Alexander wanted more than just to touch her, to introduce her to pleasure.

He wanted to know her.

"You did rather well in the cottage." She closed the door with a small *snick*.

Her unique boldness made her intoxicating, enchanting. "Shocking, Miss Danvers, a closed door? I thought you would have wanted some semblance of propriety."

A smile quivered on her lips. "I feel quite safe

with you, Your Grace." Her gaze dropped to the letters from Earl Liverpool. Curiosity lit in her eyes. "Our prime minister writes to you?"

"Hmm, this one," he said, plucking up one of the letters, "is to congratulate me on my engagement and my re-emergence within society. He compliments me for securing such a delightful lady."

She blushed profusely, and he smiled.

"This one is to praise my efforts and his, which led to the recently passed Judgment of Death Act."

"I read about it in the papers. I was quite appalled to know that the simplest of crimes carried a sentence of death. Even children were not spared when they stole food to survive. It is admirable what your motions in parliament achieved." She glanced around his office. "And you did all that without visiting town or the House of Lords."

"Is that censure I hear in your tone?"

She shifted, her dark red muslin evening gown sliding over the thick Persian carpet with a soft *swish*. "Of course not. Only admiration."

"My body was here...but my mind has always been with England and its plight." And over the years he'd fought with the best of them through the power and eloquence of his pen. Only a few months ago, there were more than two hundred offenses in England that carried a mandatory sentence of death. The law had been unforgiving, especially to those of the lower class. A maid within his household lost her nephew to the hangman's noose because he had stolen a gold fob watch. The boy had been only thirteen, and Alexander had discovered the law's reaction to his impudence too late.

It had fueled him, dragged him away from the jaws of loneliness, and had given him another purpose to direct the restless emptiness inside. He had written motions upon motions, and Lord Liverpool and several other influential men in the House of Lords had presented his arguments most passionately. The triumph of the passage of the act had been in the newspapers for weeks.

He wheeled his chair from behind the desk around to the crackling fire and very close to her. Alexander realized he had committed an error of judgment. He was driven to distraction by her soft scent of roses. A hunger unlike any he'd ever known clasped him in an unrelenting hold.

She glowed with incandescent sensuality; a woman like her deserved the richest of pleasures. And he wanted to be the one to give them to her, even if he would receive none in return.

He wanted the taste, the scent, and the feel of her to invade him, to shatter the remnants of emptiness that held him in their cruel embrace. He wanted to take his lips on a journey over her lips, to where the pulse fluttered madly at the base of her throat. There he would linger, nibbling on the soft flesh there, and then he would splay her before him and use his tongue to do wicked things between her thighs.

Regret and anger, terrible and raw, exploded in him. He would never have her like that. *Never.*

The realization stabbed through his heart, pained Alexander, and filled him with such desolation, his hands trembled. The abyss of loneliness loomed once more, somehow darker than ever, corrupting the peace he'd just found in her smile.

"Leave me!" he said, his voice harsher than he'd intended.

Her response was a resounding silence. Then without questioning him, she opened the door and left, and it was as if the light and warmth that had permeated the library had been sucked into a black void.

Alexander wheeled his chair to the closed door and pressed his palm flat against the oak.

Damn his foolish heart for beginning to crave what could never be.

CHAPTER THIRTEEN

Dinner that night was a lavish affair his kitchen staff accomplished with little notice. They evidently wanted to impress Miss Danvers, and she did not disappoint their expectations, relishing each course placed before her and sending her compliments to the cook. She ate with obvious delight and appreciation of the dishes.

Alexander recalled the dainty and graceful bites his fiancée and previous female acquaintances had used to consume their meals. At the time he had believed them to be so delicate and refined, but now only a cynical amusement at their ridiculousness invaded his senses. Pleasure filled him that Miss Danvers was not at all perturbed by her enthusiasm as she demolished each dish. She tilted her head, and the elegant slope of her neck begged to be teased with his lips and teeth.

When she noted he stared, she winked before glancing away.

Her daring oddity was vastly appealing to his jaded and lonely senses. In the few hours she'd been at his castle, a subtle transformation had infused his servants. The footmen moved with more pride, their chests pushed out; the maids seemed eager to attend to Miss Danvers, inquiring after her comfort frequently. They beamed at even one kind word from Miss Danvers and seemed far too interested in every glance and uncertain smile that passed between him and his guest. Alexander was amused by it all, but he did not miss how greedily everyone seemed to bask in her presence.

Especially Penny.

"Have you ever ridden astride in London, Miss Danvers?" Penny asked laughingly. "I daresay a lady of your daring and ingenuity would not hesitate to do so."

Katherine laughed, and the sound clutched at his heart.

"I declare the most outrageous thing I have ever done"—she dabbed her lips demurely with the serviette, but her eyes sparkled with such wickedness—"was agree to become your brother's fiancée."

This bit of mockery seemed to delight his impudent sister, who snorted. "I've heard that the Royal Museums are just wonderful. Alexander has told me so much about them."

"Have you never been to town?" Katherine asked with a frown.

A brief shadow crossed Penny's face. "Not as yet, I'm afraid, but I do not long for it in any manner. Just curious sometimes."

There was an echo of need in her tone, though she tried to mask it with a smile in his direction, as if she wanted to comfort him. It occurred to him once more that his sister needed to be out in society, mingling with other young ladies her age and social background. She asked Katherine dozens of questions: about the theater, Vauxhall, the museums, balls, and dances. And Katherine generously answered each query with admirable patience.

A dark feeling of shame washed over him. His

sister needed a life beyond Scotland. The isolation he'd wrapped them in was impenetrable. They did not even allow the high society of Scotland into their home, and the neighbors had learned over the years not to call or send invitations to McMullen Castle.

The matter would be rectified, and very soon.

"Penny will be traveling to town," he murmured. "Eugene will of course accompany his cousin."

A silence fell over the table, and Eugene arched a sharp brow.

"To London!" Penny gasped, lowering her fork. "Are you to come with me?"

"Of course not."

"Then I shall not leave you," Penny said, her eyes flashing with defiance.

"You are not abandoning me," he said with patience. "You are simply heading to town to visit with my godmother, Countess Darling, who will take you under her wing and show you the sights, take you shopping, introduce you to your society."

"I do not care to leave you, Alexander, and you shall not make me!" Penny cried, her eyes wide with a pain he did not understand.

"Penny—"

"No. Not now. *Please*."

He had not seen his sister appear this dejected in years. Not wanting to wound her further, he nodded. Penny squared her slim shoulders and lifted her chin bravely, but her lower lip trembled as his sister directed her attention to Katherine.

"Miss Danvers," Penny said brightly. "Please tell me about your sisters. The newspapers mentioned you have three. Are any my age?"

Katherine cleared her throat, and the compassion in her eyes was a curious thing to witness. With a smile, she launched into amusing anecdotes about her sisters, especially the younger Henrietta, who had a penchant for harboring animals in their home, to their mother's great distress.

"I never heard anything to equal it!" Penny chortled.

Soon the tension left Penny's shoulders, but she still did not glance in his direction, as if she could not bear looking at him. Several moments passed in discourse, and he made no effort to join in, yet he did not leave the table. The animated manner in which they conversed felt peaceful.

Laughter tugged his gaze to Katherine. A broad smile had blossomed at her lips, and her eyes were alight with humor at some amusing anecdote from Eugene. Her head was turned a little away as she listened to whatever Eugene said with such polite raptness. Or was it more than politeness? Did she admire him, perhaps?

Her quick smiles and flushing cheeks, her teasing remarks to Eugene, filled Alexander with a cold, dark feeling. *Is this jealousy?* he wondered, having never endured the emotion before.

His cousin also seemed enthralled with her. He had a flush on his face and the look of a man about to become besotted. A moment of stark despair pierced Alexander at the awareness that they would suit each other well. Eugene would be a duke one day, and he was quite affable and kind. Miss Danvers's wild and bold appeal would captivate him for years to come. Eugene had been blathering lately about finding a wife and settling down, and it seemed Alexander had unwittingly delivered to him a most appealing candidate.

Instead of eating and joining the different conversations—the weather in Scotland, politics, the latest fashion, gossips—he gave in to the compulsion to simply watch Miss Danvers. He observed her covertly with unabashed interest, noting every expression, the way she gave her undivided attention to Penny and Eugene, the furrow of her brows, the way she laughed with her eyes first, the indelicate way in which she devoured food that she enjoyed.

She looked up, noticing his avid regard. Katherine appeared surprised and then, faintly but unmistakably, embarrassed at the intensity of his stare. She glanced down momentarily, her eyelashes long and striking against the paleness of her skin. How had he not noticed how silky and beautiful her skin appeared?

His gaze lingered on the modest neckline of her crimson gown. The skin of her slender shoulders shone white and luminous in the candlelight. A very modest golden cross around her neck was her only decoration.

For a moment, he pictured her wearing the family jewels that had been discovered in the safe after the terrible, tragic fire that had stolen his parents from him. There were so many pieces that had never been worn since that sad day. Alexander considered whether the diamond parure would look best against her velvet dress or whether the simpler ruby necklace would accentuate her beauty to perfection.

His thoughts wandered to those of her wearing

only jewels and spread upon his bed, then he drove such ideas out, sweeping them away like dust upon a floor. He could not allow himself to have such musings about Kitty Danvers.

Penny sent him a few searching glances, but he still made no effort to join in on their conversations. He was content with observation.

Dinner ended, and instead of withdrawing to his treasure room, he joined them in the music room. Penny, a very accomplished player, sat before the pianoforte and delighted them with a lively piece.

"Please join me, Kitty," his sister called with delight.

Katherine accepted the invitation, moving to stand beside the pianoforte, and happily started to sing. She sounded awful. Alexander was nonplussed at the joy and confidence with which she sang, and from the outrageous twinkle in her eyes, the lady was quite aware she could not carry a tune.

The impudent lady had the temerity to wink at him, clearly amused by his undisguised consternation. An odd warmth arrowed through his heart. And he wished then that they were alone, and she sang only for him. Somehow, he would make his ears bear it, and bask in her smiles and evident delight.

He grunted softly at his whimsical musings. Her voice lifted, and he cringed, yet by God, he burned — everywhere.

And it was all for her.

Alexander was stupidly falling in too deep, and he was helpless against the need filling his heart for this woman. Bemused fascination filled him, for he did not fully understand this desire to keep her with him. *This* should not be happening, not when he had nothing to give any woman. Her presence in his life was simply to be a distraction from the tearing emptiness. Logically, he knew she could not fill that void forever, but his heart seemed to be recoiling against the notion.

Alexander thought back to the cabin. How fleeting their moments had been, yet they had been the best time of his life in the past ten years. Or even before the tragedy that had taken so much. Never before had a woman made him feel so many tangled needs that were almost impossible to unravel.

He wasn't certain if the notion should sadden or thrill him.

"Delightful, isn't she?" a voice murmured to his left.

He made no reply to Eugene's observation, just silently agreed that she was, and so much more.

"I was wrong to think her a wicked user. I misjudged her. Miss Danvers will make you an excellent duchess," his cousin said, a touch of envy in his tone. "If you are of a mind to keep her."

Alexander's heart tripped, then he allowed the ice to encase it and buried the warm feelings that dug at its deliberately hardened surface. For years he hadn't allowed himself to hope or dream. Where there was no expectation, there could be no disappointment or despair.

He closed his eyes and took a long, slow breath. "I've not known her long, but a woman like Katherine Danvers deserves much more than to be a duchess. A title alone would not do for a rich, vibrant soul like hers. She deserves to be a wife in more than a name; she deserves children... I daresay she deserves the world."

His cousin sucked in a hard breath. "Are you falling for her?"

"No." *Never that.*

He was not whole enough to ever allow himself to fall too deeply for any woman. That could lead only to heartache, and there was enough pain living in his memories and heart.

"I've seen how she looks at you," Eugene said. "She *likes* you and seems quite frightened by the notion. It is as if she expects you to hurt her in some fashion. What have you done?"

You'll break me.

That haunted whisper stabbed deep, twisting the most peculiar sensations inside—anger and pain. "I've done nothing." Alexander faced him. "I gather you enjoy Miss Danvers's company. You have my permission to pursue her if that is what you are after."

Shock bloomed on Eugene's face, but there was also want and need there. "Good God, man, are you certain?"

No... Yes... "You are my heir, and you'll be a duke one day. You have wealth and status. You evidently admire Miss Danvers's eccentricity. Whatever I feel for her will not go anywhere, for I shan't allow it, so be free of guilt in your pursuit."

Then Alexander walked away.

• • •

The next evening, after a listless night tossing atop his bed and a day spent penning letters to the prime minister and parliament, Alexander looked forward to meeting with his doctors—an unusual state, for he usually felt bothered by the quarterly checks from the team. He met with three of his doctors in his library, quite pleased they had responded to his summons with the appropriate urgency.

He sat in his wheeled chair by the open windows, gathering his thoughts and the matter he wanted to broach. The silence lingered, and as the clock struck the hour, he realized he had been lost in his thoughts for twenty minutes. Alexander worked the wheel of his bath chair and faced his doctors. His two most senior physicians—Appleby and Monroe—glanced at each other, concern masking their creased features.

Dr. Appleby, a man of average height and slender build, with gray-flecked hair and spectacles, sat in a wingback chair by the fireplace. Dr. Monroe, a few years younger than Appleby and tall with surprising bulk to his frame, reposed on the sofa. The third doctor waited by the mantel, peering into the fireplace as if the dancing flames held some secret he desired to unearth.

Monroe cleared his throat. "Your Grace, you seem well. How are you faring since our last visit?"

That was the opening for all notebooks to appear, and his doctors waited on him with keen patience.

"The pain in my lower back is more persistent this week. But I have pushed myself to be active and on my feet more than I normally risk."

"Have you taken any opium?" Dr. Monroe asked.

Alexander's gut tightened, hating to remember the haze he had once lost himself in to bear the constant pain and torment. "No. Nor have I been tempted."

They scribbled in their notebooks.

"What about laudanum?"

"I smoke my cigars," he drawled mockingly, before saying, "There is a particular woman... When I think of her...I feel a hunger, unlike anything I've ever endured." Alexander smiled without humor and said bluntly, "My member becomes hard, even if only fleetingly. That is a first since my accident; it happens only with her, and it has happened twice."

The quiet that enveloped the drawing room was keen.

"That is exceedingly heartening news," Dr. Grant said, the youngest doctor on Alexander's team and the most enlightened. He alone seemed willing to adopt the latest and most controversial treatment methods, and it was one of the reasons Alexander had kept him on the team who attended him regularly.

"Your Grace," Appleby began, "I do not wish to encourage false hope. In the ten years since the unfortunate accident, your manhood has been flaccid. It is unlikely—"

Dr. Grant interrupted Appleby, laying a hand on his arm and saying quickly, "I do not believe it to be false hope, Your Grace. I've long believed that your...lack of reaction to any such stimuli had to do with the terrible pain your body underwent in its fight to heal. You were not interested in anything else. I did not believe, as my colleagues do, that the nerve damage to your back and legs would prevent you from living a normal life. Your mind and brain simply directed their enormous energy into other areas of your body—healing."

Alexander frowned thoughtfully. "It has been several years, Dr. Grant."

"And your body is *still* healing. You have made incredible strides, Your Grace. The strength and tenacity you have shown I have never seen in another, but your journey is continuing. It would be very shortsighted of us to assume Your Grace's body has finished healing or that it is not capable of improving further. Our understanding of human anatomy is still so extremely limited."

Alexander considered the earnest fervor of Dr. Grant, seeing the validity of his statement. The diagnosis of impotence had been given in those difficult early times.

"You will never walk again, Your Grace, nor will you be able to sire issue." That had been the pronouncement by one of Edinburgh's finest doctors, and another team from England had reaffirmed it. Yet Alexander had defied their expectations and had painstakingly pushed himself past the crippling agony to walk again.

Whenever he had crumpled to the floor, he had been a beast, snarling at his servants to leave him be. And he had crawled, digging grooves and cuts into his elbows and palms as he had pushed himself to make it from the floor by his own strength. Remembered despair and helplessness swamped his senses.

"Eight years ago, Dr. Monroe, you told me in no uncertain terms I would never leave this bath chair. Yet I do so daily, for hours," he murmured.

Sympathy lit in the doctor's light green eyes. "And

the cost must be terrible, Your Grace. Your back and legs were shattered in several places from your fall from a three-story window. I am a man of science, but I still believe it a miracle you are alive—and that you can walk today. As for other functions, the treatment we recommended then did not work at all, so I am not sure what to make of this."

The man glanced at his colleagues, appearing flustered.

Several remedies had been suggested at the time, and some of the most outlandish, such as eating alligator testicles battered in butter, Alexander still recalled. He had not been interested in women, still cut too raw from pain and grief. And over the years, nothing had roused him. His friend George had certainly sent beauties to his castle to entice him to live as mad, bad, and dangerous once more. Alexander had been bored, their high-pitched giggles and lush attractions incapable of touching the empty well inside him.

"I ignored most of the treatment advised then. Eating goat and alligator balls made no sense, and the few poultices made by you, Appleby, simply irritated *my* balls," Alexander said drily.

The good doctor flushed.

Dr. Grant stepped forward. "I must ask…how long have you been able to sustain an erection with…ah, this particular lady?"

The memory of the raw desire he'd felt a few nights ago wafted through him with visceral strength. "It was fleeting, but it happened." And almost every moment when he thought of kissing her, the ache low in his gut grew until he felt mad from want.

The doctor cleared his throat and, prudently refusing to meet his eye, said, "Might I encourage you, Your Grace, to attempt, ah...another connection with this lady, a sustained connection?"

Alexander considered the man. "She is not a doxy but a *lady*."

Dr. Grant tilted his head. "I understand, Your Grace. I would urge you to consider self-ministrations for a few nights. I've never believed your nerves there to be completely damaged, simply that your mind...was uninterested. And if the mind is locked away from thoughts of pleasure, the body will remain unresponsive."

Dr. Monroe surged to his feet, a fierce scowl on his ruddy face. "What nonsense! Self-ministration is harmful to the body and mind!"

Grant scowled and, in an unlikely fashion, rolled his eyes.

Alexander was aware of the different theories in society on self-pleasure. Dr. Grant had brought the matter to him a few years ago, and he hadn't dwelled on it, simply because the emptiness had been spreading, taking all that was light and painting his world in dull shades of gray. But now he could see... and feel himself lying atop the cool crispness of his sheets, taking his manhood in hand, and stroking it...with visions of her, smiling, flashing an ankle, touching him, kissing him. The elegance of her spine, which had been revealed when he'd undressed her in the cabin. How desperately he'd wanted to run his tongue along her curves.

The memory of her sweet mouth and purrs of pleasure had heat rolling through him like a violent wave. Uttering a low curse beneath his breath, Alexander pushed such thoughts from his mind. With an annoyance unlike him, he dismissed the doctors after issuing his customary invitation to dinner, which they accepted.

What am I to do about you, Katherine Danvers?

CHAPTER FOURTEEN

Alexander wheeled himself from the library down the hall to his room of solace. With a pained grunt, he eased from the confines of the chair, stood, and opened the door. He lowered himself back into the bath chair and wheeled himself into the room.

A faint sound had him gently closing the door and propelling toward the back of the room where the shelves stretched toward the high ceiling. He faltered at the presence of Katherine on her knees before one of his wooden boxes. Plucking an item from the box recently shipped from Egypt, she stood and held it up to the light pouring in from the window. It was a necklace with a scarab amulet. She studied it for a while, running delicate fingers over the back of the scarab. With an evident thrill, she placed it back in the box with care and withdrew another item.

He couldn't help smiling at the large ivory-shaped phallus in her delicate hands. Moving with desperate stealth, he eased from the chair without making a sound. Then carefully, he placed one foot before the other, ignoring the slight pinch in his lower back, and made his way over to her.

"What is it?" she muttered to herself, running her fingers along the surprisingly veined ridge.

Softly at her ear, he said, "I'm not sure if I should distress your sensibilities and tell you."

With a gasp, she spun around, pressing a hand

over her heart. A pulse was beating visibly at her throat. "Oh, you abominable creature! To sneak up on me in such a wicked manner!"

"Ah," he said, gently tapping one of his fingers on her nose. "You deserve to be frightened. This room is forbidden to guests, which I am sure you were aware of. Your impudence is unchecked."

She thought for a moment and then said, with a gleam of mischief, "Oh, don't be tiresome; this impudence you keep mentioning is clearly a part of my charm, and I daresay you like it."

Katherine was irresistibly fascinating. Slowly, deliberately, he dipped his head to her arched neck and pressed his lips to the fluttering pulse at her throat. "I do like your bold, willful, *inquisitive* nature," he murmured against the softness of her skin, and to his utter astonishment, his voice cracked.

"Alexander?" How breathless and shocked she sounded.

Common sense reasserted itself, and he stepped back. She stared at him with wide, questioning eyes, the ivory phallus clenched in her hands.

"Why are you in here, Katherine?"

"I thought you might have had an enchanted room here," she uttered in a stifled voice.

"Ah…the beast and the beauty," he said, fleetingly touching the ridges of the scar on his lower chin.

Her eyes dropped to the ravaged side of his face for several seconds. "You're not a beast, far from it. Nor am I a beauty."

"You are the most exquisite woman I've ever met. And I've all but kidnapped you with no plans to release you. Is there not a parallel with that story, hmm?"

Her lips parted in a whisper of a sigh, and the gaze that peered up at him held a thousand questions. They would remain unanswered, for he did not understand the forces driving him.

With only the faintest tremor in her voice, Katherine replied gravely, "Am I to be placed in a tower, then, and let out only when I am to dine with you?"

"No."

They stared at each other, and the silence felt fraught with an unknown peril. Her throat worked on a swallow. "Each moment in your presence threatens ruin, Alexander."

"It does."

Her lashes swept down across her cheekbones, but not before he witnessed the spark of ire in her eyes.

She lifted her chin and stared at him. "When do I return to London?"

"When you no longer interest me."

Her features froze in momentary surprise. And suddenly he felt a villain. But it was simply the truth, and he would not allow either of them to shy away from the knowledge.

An odd expression flickered for a moment in her eyes. "And what if I interest you forever, Alexander?"

He jerked as if he'd been punched; then he schooled his expression into an impassivity he was far from feeling. His heart was beating rather more rapidly than necessary.

The little minx stepped alarmingly close, lifted her hand, and cupped the scarred side of his face, rubbing her thumb over those ugly scars. That light caress was like butterfly wings, and with a defeated groan, he closed his eyes and leaned into her palm. There was a hidden part of him that quite liked the sound of forever. It filled all the empty crevices of his soul with endless possibilities…especially the kissing kind.

Alexander stepped away from Katherine, feeling cold at the loss of her touch. She moved back and lowered her lashes demurely, and he almost rolled his eyes. Katherine would not understand demureness if it bit her in the ass daily. "Would you like a tour?" he asked gruffly.

Delight lit in her eyes. "I thought no guests were allowed."

"I make exceptions for my kidnap victims."

She scowled, and he smiled.

"Ah, Katherine, you are a flame that has no end, and it would be such a damn pity to see your spark dim." He wasn't sure who he amazed more, Katherine or himself.

She leaned her head back and gazed into his eyes. "Why did you say that?"

He permitted himself to touch her cheek. "I do not know, but it is the truth."

She wriggled her nose, clearly irritated. "Only those afflicted with some sort of madness speak without thinking and then have no notion of their meaning!"

"I daresay I can reiterate the same about those ladies whose mouths have no filter."

She chuckled, the sound sweet and stirring, her eyes alight with something far too warm.

And not for the first time, he wondered what had happened in her life to shape such unflinching boldness of spirit. Was it when she had lost her father and had to be strong for her family? Or had her rebellious nature been buried under strictures and dictates of propriety until she'd had no choice but to draw from that inner strength with which she glowed?

Alexander had never experienced such melting tenderness. "Delightful," he murmured.

Katherine lifted a saucy brow and fisted a hand on her hips. "I suppose you have no notion of what you speak again?"

"I referred to your laugh."

Surprise widened her gaze. "I believe you are falling into like with me," she provocatively drawled.

"I daresay I am." And it was foolish.

Katherine faltered, and her gaze met his, demanding, fierce, compelling, yet she made no reply for several seconds.

"I like you, too, very much so," she said simply, her eyes warm with gentle amusement.

He opened his mouth, then realized he had no idea what to say. Without answering, he made his way to his chair with shuffling movements, lowered himself, and wheeled toward a crate. Her inquisitive nature, of course, prompted her to follow him, and he suppressed his smile. Alexander had never shared the contents of the room before with anyone except Penny.

"And what do you think of my treasure room?"

"It is beyond exquisite," Katherine said gaily. "It would take me years to examine each item. They are so beautiful and unknown." She darted from behind him, reached upon a shelf, and lifted a sapphire and turquoise necklace that glittered with resplendent light in her hands. The collar heavy with golden beads was truly a piece of exquisite workmanship, although it was probably not as old as it appeared.

"The description on the plaque says this is an item from Cleopatra's jewels."

"That is what I have been told. Though I believe she would have been buried with her jewels, and a tomb has not yet been found for Cleopatra, or at least no one has admitted to finding it," he said, observing her expression of fascination.

Katherine nodded. "Still, this must be worth a fortune! And you simply have it here on a shelf?" With a smile, she rested it against her throat, and suddenly he wanted her to have the necklace.

"Consider it my gift to you."

She sent him a bewildered frown. "What is your gift?"

"The Cleopatra necklace."

"This is a fortune, Alexander!" she exclaimed, looking considerably astonished.

"It does not signify. Please accept it."

"No." She tipped on her toes slightly and placed it back on the glass pedestal where it had rested. "This is an outrageous and improper gift, and you know it."

"How alarming that you find anything improper."

She giggled, and he hoarded the sweet yet throaty sound like the dragon he was.

They spent the next hour touring his treasure room. Her questions were unending, and he answered each one patiently, not wishing to be anywhere else. She lingered over burial masks, rare gems and stones, a coin with Alexander the Great's image, and silks from India. Now she stood beside a brown bowl that had a hairline crack. Her lithe form as she strolled at his side made his chair-bound state a reminder of what he had lost.

"And this is from Iraq?"

He wheeled toward a large desk, which held a globe, and she followed. Then he spun the globe, allowing his finger to stop at the correct place. "Yes, in Mesopotamia. Right here."

She was silent for a moment. "You have been to Italy, Greece, Vienna, Paris, Egypt, Iraq, Spain, and so many more places." Her elegant fingers danced lightly over the smooth surface of the globe. "Did I ever tell you the story of us sinful wallflowers?"

A rich pleasure arrowed through him. "I've earned it now?"

Her mouth curved into a small smile, and a hint of mischief glowed in her eyes. "Yes."

"Tell me," he said quietly. It was almost shocking how much he wished to know everything about her.

An odd vulnerability showed in her gaze, but she lifted her chin. "There are five other ladies, and they are my dearest friends. Society branded us wallflowers because despite our families' most ardent wish to see us marry, the men of the *ton* are decidedly not interested."

Her lips pursed, the gesture one of clear annoyance. "Why should we live our lives on the hopes that someone might marry us? We've all vowed recently to pursue the desires in our hearts, even if they are the wicked kind. My first sinful act was to pretend to be your fiancée." She sighed. "Perhaps one day I shall see the wonders of Egypt and many other countries as well. Travel the world as freely as any gentleman would. How extraordinary and *sinful* that would be."

The wistful hunger in her voice dug deep into his heart. "I know you shall." Her will and fierceness for life were too vibrant for him to believe in any other outcome.

She sent him a bright smile. "And you will be my knowledgeable companion, perhaps? Do you not long to travel again? As you showed me each piece impregnated with the past, it was as if I could feel your hunger. It was quite beautiful to see."

Alexander stared at her for a long moment, and she did not blush or look away but returned his regard in that impudent way of hers. "I've not traveled in years," he finally said, the old need twisting inside him once more. And perplexingly, he could imagine her by his side, and the delight she would take in discovering a new culture and meeting new peoples.

"Should we make a vow to do so together?" she asked, the laughter still dancing in her eyes.

But there was something beyond the humor in her gaze, a longing so profound it made his damn throat ache to lay the world at her feet. Alexander took a deep breath, trying hard not to picture them laughing together in the shadow of the Sphinx and bathing in the warm waters of the Aegean. Was it so wrong to indulge such fantasies when they danced in her eyes so excitedly?

He chuckled, and the sound was a little sad. "My Katherine, you will not want to drag a cripple around with you; you need a healthy young buck at your side…and in your bed."

Her eyes flew to his in astonishment, a startled question in them. He surmised it was the allusion to taking her to his bed. Unexpectedly, the air tightened with tension, a flush mounted her cheeks, and her eyes darkened. Katherine wanted him with the same intensity with which he desired her. The awareness brought a violent surge of heat to his loins. Alexander gripped the edge of his wheeled chair and slowly counted to ten…backward.

It did nothing to halt the lascivious images flickering to his jaded mind—demanding that she be unclothed and standing before him naked. Ordering her to wrap bolts of sheer silk around her voluptuous body and dance for him as he played the pipe. He could take what her heated gaze so innocently offered, and she would be irrevocably ruined with no chance of an offer from him.

He had the will and these hungers quaking through him, demanding he bend her to the raw, sexual hunger beating through his body. What his cock would not do, Alexander would take with his mouth and fingers.

"I am not a man you should want," he murmured.

"What astounding arrogance to presume to order my desires, Your Grace," she retorted just as quietly. Yet her regard spoke a different message— there was a challenge in the depths of her golden-brown eyes.

Take me if you dare.

And he sensed it wasn't a tryst she tempted him to reach for—but forever.

"I want to see you naked. Take off your clothes for me."

With each word, her eyes grew wider and wider, one of her hands fluttering to settle above her heart.

"You are trying to shock me," she said faintly.

"I've not seen the naked female form in ten years. It is a hunger of mine."

"I am sure there are many who would stand nude before you…without an offer of marriage."

He rolled closer to her and stroked his finger over the curve of her hips and up to her side. She did not pull away but swayed into him, and his heart became a roaring pounding of need.

"Yet it is you I want to see." Alexander was being wickedly provoking, but it was a truth that had been haunting him for the last few days. His thumb slid over the sensitive skin of her inner wrist. "Shall I command you, Katherine?"

She uttered a slightly shocked protest. "You are laboring under a misapprehension to presume I would simply obey."

"You are my captive, and you are wholly at my mercy."

Awareness of her vulnerability shone in her beautiful eyes, along with a flash of such soul-searing yearning, his hands trembled, before he curved them over the arms of his chair, now the one desperate to find a balance. "Why, Miss Danvers, I do believe you *want* to be wicked with me."

Her lips curved into a sweetly sensual smile, and dark lashes shielded the expression in her eyes. His gaze lowered to her mouth, as if some unseen force controlled them. Her lips were pink, lush, sweetly curved, and perfect, and Alexander wanted to kiss her without consequences.

A long breath burst from him as she slowly lifted her day dress above her slippers and bared a stocking-clad ankle to his eyes. So innocent, yet charmingly provocative.

He snapped his gaze to her, and the minx winked at him before laughing, inviting him to share in the sensual humor.

He wheeled his chair toward the door, and right before he opened it, Alexander paused. Then he turned abruptly away and said harshly, "I am the villain of this piece, Miss Danvers. You should do well to remember it."

CHAPTER FIFTEEN

Kitty had been at the Castle McMullen for four days. In that time, she'd hardly seen the duke.

Each day, Alexander disappeared behind the beautifully carved door of his treasure room for hours. It had been one of the most exquisite rooms she had ever seen. Three floors of books, ancient artifacts and relics, paintings, sculptures, and scrolls. When not in his treasure room, he retired to his study. In there, Kitty assumed he did whatever dukes did in overseeing their vast estates.

The constant rains had kept her indoors, and that was entirely unsuited for her disposition. Kitty loved the outdoors, riding, taking long walks, inhaling the various fragrant flowers redolent in the air, and just basking in the beauty of nature. She, however, tried to endure the restrictions with some cheer, and most of her time had been spent reading *Sense and Sensibility*, which she had found in the castle's original library.

She had discovered another splendid room in the castle and one of the reasons she would wish to stay there forever if she were the silly, romantic sort. Three stories high, the library was resplendent with shelves lining all the walls, and every one of them filled with fascinating books. Beautiful books, lavishly bound in the finest gilded, embossed leather. A wheeled ladder hung on runners, which could be moved back and forth to reach the books on the highest shelves.

Kitty also enjoyed chatting and playing parlor games with Penny, who was a charming girl, even if rather garrulous. It was through her that Kitty learned that Mr. Eugene Collins was first cousin to Alexander, their fathers having been brothers. Mr. Collins's father had gone to his final rest only a year after his brother had died in the fire at this castle, so he was now Alexander's heir.

Penny's eyes had been wide and wounded as she reflected on their tragedy, though she had tried to sound unaffected. Kitty had gently shifted the conversation toward the history of the castle. That had been a few hours ago, and the young girl had disappeared for the rest of the day with her governess and tutors, while Kitty had retired to her chambers with a novel.

Today dragged on most unsatisfactorily, and unexpectedly Kitty felt bored with reading. The book was unable to turn her mind away from the duke and why she was still at his castle. After dreading this possible visit and what the duke would do with her, the absence of anything happening puzzled her immensely.

What if I interest you forever, Alexander?

How hungry he'd looked at her question. How frightened, as if she offered him a hope that could be ripped away.

Thunder rumbled in the distance, and the sky took on a darker cast. It was barely noon yet it appeared to be late evening. Kitty placed the book on the bed, then selected a shawl from the armoire and made her way from the chamber. Perhaps she needed a more diverting novel to engage her thoughts. She passed a few servants in the hallway, who bobbed and smiled at her. The longcase clock on the landing chimed. She entered the library and let the heavy oak door close behind her. It took a while to understand the sight before her.

"Your Grace?" Kitty questioned sharply.

He was sprawled on his back on the floor, his legs spread open, his hands behind his head. Kitty couldn't determine if his repose on the carpeted floor had been chosen on purpose or if he had taken a fall. His chair was several feet away by the fire, and he was in the center of the room, with four thick leather-bound books scattered around him.

"Shall I summon your manservant?" she asked tentatively.

He grunted a reply that she missed. Worried that he might be hurt, she spun around and gripped the doorknob. A book slammed into the door above the handle. She whirled toward him. "Alexander!"

"Summon no one," he growled irritably. "I shall be able to move soon."

She marched over to him. "You threw a book at me, Your Grace."

"At the door, Miss Danvers. At the door. I was quite confident it would not hit you or else I would not have risked it. Now stop shooting daggers at me with your eyes."

This was said with wry amusement, but in the gaze that peered at her, she spied discomfort and a simmering anger. That slow brew of emotions she could hardly understand had her stomach fluttering in nervousness.

The duke was not pleased she'd come upon him

in this vulnerable state.

She removed the shawl and let it drop onto the sofa, then glanced around the library. "I came to borrow a book."

"Did you now?"

How cutting his tone sounded.

She paused, hesitating for a moment or two, and then said, "I was dreadfully bored holed up in my room. The constant rain is ghastly, and I daresay you are a poor host. I am not at all surprised you receive little to no visitors."

His lips twisted in a cynical smile. "You are not my guest."

She folded her arms and scowled. "I'm not?"

"You are my captive," he said repressively.

"You are the most provoking creature I've ever encountered!"

Kitty lay down on the carpet beside him. She mimicked his posture by lacing her fingers together and placing them behind her head. They did not speak for several moments, and Kitty was acutely conscious that if she shifted ever so slightly, her shoes might brush his.

Acting on the impulse, she inched her booted feet over and nudged his shin. "So, you fell," she finally murmured.

"So, I fell."

Her heart squeezed at the dry flatness in his tone.

"How long have you been lying here?"

"You ask too many questions."

"You are boorish whenever you are embarrassed."

He grunted, and her lips twitched. "Would you

like me to summon Hoyt or one of the other servants now?"

"No."

"Whyever not?"

"The reason is irrelevant. Simply know that is my wish and you will obey."

She turned her head on the carpet and stared at the starkness of his profile, which spoke of an ageless strength. An unexpected admiration for him swelled within her heart. "Would you like me to leave?" Her stomach went tight at his quiet contemplation.

"No, it would please me for you to stay."

It was hard to explain the happiness that swarmed through her veins. "But you do not wish my help, either," she murmured.

"You are getting to know me, Miss Danvers."

Kitty scoffed. "I doubt that. I've barely scratched at your surface, though I daresay I would like to."

"To scratch me? How unusual."

She was maddeningly conscious of his body next to hers. "To get to know you."

As if sensing the weight of her curiosity, he slowly turned to look at her, his gaze flickering over her in a thorough appraisal. His eyes glittered with such intensity, Kitty was almost discomfited. She became flushed and breathless but filled with a strange sense of anticipation. With a muttered, indiscernible curse, he glanced away. *What are you afraid of, Alexander?*

"Ask me any question and I shall answer."

"Truly?"

"Of course."

"Do you think of our time in the cabin?" And Kitty had not realized those words had escaped. Her cheeks grew hot, and she instinctively pressed her hands to them. Why had she asked that?

His seemingly bemused silence encouraged her mortification.

"I do," he finally answered.

Kitty waited a few beats before saying, "That is all you have to say on the matter?"

"Yes."

"You are a maddening creature!"

"You still like me," he said with rough amusement. "It is a part of my charm."

He had a rare gift for rattling her nerves and causing her to blush. Kitty swore that before the duke, she had never blushed more than once per year. "I... One of the old rumors when I announced our engagement was that you had been poised to marry the Countess Lynwood."

"Lady Daphne, a lady of exaggerated sensibilities and a propensity for crying pretty tears."

"Did you love her?"

"I enjoyed her company, but it was not love. It was a match encouraged by our parents. Our joint holdings would have been one of the most powerful in England. I agreed with my father's suggestion of Lady Daphne as my bride, and she was content to marry for the sake of a great position."

Kitty shifted slightly on the carpet so she could observe his expression better. "Do you regret not marrying her?"

"No."

The swift reply and surety soothed the unexplained ache that had risen inside her.

"The lady cried off after seeing my scars and

broken body. The memory is hazy because of the laudanum, but I still recall her fainting at least three times and wailing to her father that she would not marry a monster."

"But you are such a charming monster," she murmured.

His lips twitched; he tugged one of his hands from behind his head and ran a finger over his scarred cheek. "Besides Penny, you may be the only woman of my acquaintance who looks upon me and does not flinch from my ugliness. Quite admirable."

"I believe people look away because it is uncomfortable to gaze upon another's pain when it is bare for the world to see. How do they relate? Or offer words of compassion when they truly cannot understand your pain? It would seem pretentious to say the least, and they are aware of it, and thus become flummoxed and perhaps act like fools. You are one of the most handsome men of my acquaintance."

"I can easily believe it is your eyesight that is sorely compromised."

With a grunt, he pushed himself to his elbows and closed his eyes. His jaw clenched against the pain he must be feeling, but he did not ask for her help. Frustration bit at her, and she wanted to shout that she did not pity him but quite admired his fortitude, yet she knew he would reject such assurances.

Kitty swung herself into an elegant sitting pose and watched as he grunted and heaved himself into the same. She stood, walked over to the wheelchair, and rolled it over to him. She expected to see anger in the gaze staring up at her, but instead there was warm amusement. It flustered her, and she walked around the chair and held out her hand.

"You are determined to help me, hmm?"

"I daresay it equals your desire to not ask for it."

She held out her hand; he grasped it and tugged her to him so she tumbled onto the floor into his lap. With a pained groan, he fell back and she sprawled over him, quite inelegantly. Her face was pressed to his chest, one of her legs draped across his thighs. Kitty was practically lying on top of the duke, and the shock of the position froze her for several moments.

A choked noise, which suspiciously sounded like laughter, came from his chest.

"I cannot find anything humorous in the situation," she gasped, trying to scramble off him, pressing her palms flat against his chest and rearing upward.

An exaggerated moan of agony slipped from him. "Dear God, Miss Danvers, pray do not move."

"Good heavens! I am hurting you," Kitty cried and remained still atop him. "I'll be gentler," she breathed, trying to reassure him. Except with each minute shift atop him, another overly long groan came from him, and Kitty found herself unable to move for fear of hurting him. "I am going to ease toward your left side; please remain still and—"

A perfunctory knock sounded, and with a gasp, she turned her head to the door. It opened and the housekeeper bustled inside. "Your Grace, I—"

She gaped at them, and then to Kitty's astonishment the most delighted smile creased the woman's face and she clapped her hands together twice in her excitement, for it was certainly not alarm at a witnessed impropriety. Without another word, the housekeeper turned and hurried away, closing the door behind her.

"Why, I cannot credit it!" Kitty gasped.

She snapped her gaze to the man beneath her and stilled. His eyes were glowing with something wicked. "You wretched tease, you are in no pain! And your servants are in serious need of correction!"

Ignoring his laughter, she pushed herself off his body, uncaring her knees went perilously close to his man's part. Kitty stood, fisted a hand on her hip, and sent him a glare that promised retribution, before storming away and out of the library.

She did not make it far before she paused and pressed a hand over her mouth, stifling her laugh.

The odious man.

She hurried back and gently eased the door open. He was in the wheeled chair, clasping the edges in a white-knuckled grip, bracing against whatever pain ravaged his body.

Understanding dawned, and her throat burned. Alexander had not wanted her to witness this pain… that he possibly saw as weakness.

His head was tipped back against the headrest, and his chest rose and fell rapidly as he conquered the pain. She made her way over to him, uncaring he would want her gone, desperate to offer some comfort.

She stepped behind him, and the eyes that had been shut and lifted to the ceiling snapped open.

"You came back," he grunted, his lips tightening.

She brushed a damp tendril of hair from his forehead with acute tenderness. "I came back."

He stared at her, and she wished he would voice

the questions in his gaze. Perhaps then clarity would come to her heart and she would understand the feelings growing for him. She leaned down. "I forgot my book."

Appreciation lit in his eyes, but the pain lingered.

"I'll sing for you," she offered.

"Dear God, no, I am already in enough agony."

Kitty gasped in outrage and started to sing. He shrugged in mock resignation, as if he would just have to bear it. But upon his lips a smile curved, the hand that had gripped the chair loosened, and the frown that had split his brows disappeared.

An odd sense of happiness and belonging burst inside her when he started to laugh, realizing the song was about a young lady who ended up strangling a duke while he slept.

A short while later, Kitty left the duke nursing a whiskey and reading a book, a small smile seeming to be permanently affixed to his lips. She grinned, knowing she had put it there.

She settled into a chaise longue beneath one of the wide windows in the parlor, peering out into the rainy landscape.

"Ahem," a voice said, dragging her from her whimsical musings.

She glanced at the butler, startled to see him with a bouquet of flowers in his hands.

"These are for you, milady. And is there anything special you would like for supper?" he asked, his voice hoarse with emotion.

Behind him, the housekeeper lingered, beaming at Kitty. She flushed, recalling the compromising position the woman had seen them in earlier. Surely, they would think her a doxy. Yet all the servants seemed to stare at her with a bewildering degree of pride and hopeful excitement.

A couple of the servants were hastily dabbing at their eyes and noses with handkerchiefs. It occurred to her that her presence meant something profound to them. A blanket of hope had settled over the castle, infusing the servants with fresh smiles and far more solicitous natures than she'd ever witnessed. Kitty had even heard a maid singing while she dusted.

Do not be so silly in your hopes, she warned the servants silently, accepting the flowers.

Though if she admitted it, the warning was more for herself.

Kitty tethered on the edge of a most dangerous precipice—falling in love with a man who had no lasting interest in her.

CHAPTER SIXTEEN

Alexander held the binoculars firmly in front of his eyes, all thoughts of examining the estate ledgers his steward had sent him from his manor in Kent forgotten. A rueful chuckle escaped him.

Ladies did not climb trees. Though clearly she was a different sort, he still did not expect such an unconventionally audacious nature. Nothing Miss Danvers did would ever surprise him again. With her, he would learn to anticipate the unexpected. He studied her as if she were an exotic creature that had fallen from the sky and landed in a perch high in the gnarled branches of an elm tree near his favorite grotto, the hem of her blue day gown whipping in the wind. She was without her half boots, and her stocking-clad feet dug into the branch with firm purchase.

Evidently, she was an experienced tree climber.

Several feet from the ground, Miss Danvers balanced perfectly on the branch, her forearm resting on another that was in line with her chest. He watched her for several moments, and from the movement of her lips and the delight on her face, he surmised the woman was singing.

Perhaps the reason she traveled so far from the main house was to spare the household.

At the bottom of the tree, a basket leaned against the trunk; a blanket was spread on the soft, verdant grass; and a book rested atop the blanket.

Swinging the binoculars back to her, he noted with some surprise how alone she appeared, gazing out at the distant horizon. He watched her face for several minutes, observing every tiny shift in her expression. One of delicate yearning settled on her face, and his heart jolted painfully when his name shaped her lips.

Alexander...

The curious detachment he'd built around his heart shuddered as if it had been dealt a terrible blow. She sighed his name, longing swept across her lovely features, and she pressed a hand between the cradle of her breast. Heat tugged at his groin, and his heart clenched.

An array of shocking, yet undeniably wickedly carnal images of making love with Katherine danced through his head, causing it to ache. Alexander desperately wanted to kiss her, over and over until she cried her pleasure into his mouth. With such dangerous needs storming through his heart, the last thing he should want was to be with her. Cursing savagely, he rang the bell and summoned his manservant.

Several minutes after Hoyt appeared, they rumbled over the vast lawns of his estate toward Miss Danvers.

"I took the liberty of collecting a book of poetry from the library, Your Grace, when you made it known you would join Miss Danvers," Hoyt murmured expectantly.

Alexander grunted but made no reply. A mistake, for his manservant took that as an invitation to continue his impropriety.

"Cook also sent a bottle of wine and a French cake soaked in rum. Miss Danvers has expressed a delight for the treat, and Cook has been preparing them for her."

Wine and cake. Good God. Still, his curiosity stirred. "Miss Danvers likes cakes?"

"Oh yes, Your Grace. She came down to the kitchen and chatted with the cook about her secret recipes yesterday. The cook…well, everyone is quite delighted. It is our hope Miss Danvers's stay will be a permanent one."

Hoyt audibly held his breath, no doubt waiting for Alexander's confirmation of the young, unwedded miss's status in his life.

Alexander made no answer, and his manservant huffed an irritated breath. The wheels crunched noisily over the grass and fallen leaves as they made their way closer to Katherine. When they were only a few feet from her, Alexander said, "Leave me here. I'll continue with my stick."

"As you wish, Your Grace."

"You may take the bath chair and return within the hour."

"And the cake and wine?" Hoyt asked so hopefully, Alexander smiled.

"I'll take them."

"And the book of poetry?"

"Put that in the basket, too," he said, mildly surprised he was indulging his servants' ridiculous meddling in a situation that was none of their business.

Hoyt came around to Alexander's front and pressed his walking stick into one hand and the small basket in the other. He pushed from his chair and, with a silent nod, encouraged Hoyt to grant them privacy. His manservant visibly battled with a pleased smile before departing.

Alexander swallowed away the irritable grunt. His servants' ceaseless speculations needed to be taken care of.

Alexander made his way over to Katherine's tree and placed the basket beside a copy of *The Murderous Monk*. He glanced up in the tree to see Kitty peering down at him, her mouth a moue of astonished pleasure.

"I shall be right down, Your Grace," she called out.

Ignoring that assurance, he dropped his walking stick on the blanket, reached for the closest branch, and hauled himself up. A curse escaped at the savage pain that tore through his lower back, but he gritted his teeth and pushed onward.

He *wanted* to be up there with her, and by God he would do it.

Several moments later, he was standing beside her, their heads above the branches and the valley below them a stunning splendor.

Her eyes shone with rich pleasure. "You did not have to come up. I would have come down to you."

"I wanted to stand beside you."

"We could have done that down there."

Unexpectedly, she stroked his brow, her fingers tenderly sifting through his hair curling above his forehead. How he wanted to lean into her touch. He reached up and gently plucked a blade of grass from her hair. "Were you rolling in the grass, by chance, Miss Danvers?"

"I was," she said on a light laugh. "I was making

a snow angel but without the snow," she said with an irresistible smile before glancing out in the distance.

Alexander's heart skipped a beat…then another.

"It is so wild and beautiful. And windy." She patted her bonnet to ensure it was still in place.

He didn't have the heart to point out that it sat askew atop her head, and a wild array of curls had tumbled to her shoulder, and lovely wisps caressed her cheeks. She looked delightfully mussed and improper.

"I can understand why you prefer this wide-open space to London. Oh, look at the birds," she gasped, pointing to a flock of starlings that seemed to dance in perfect harmony against the skyline painted in shades of lavender and gray.

"So, we are bird watching," he mused.

She laughed, and the infectious sound wreaked havoc with his heart. "And also land watching. And the sky. Look at the clouds. I swore I saw a monk just now playing the harp."

He glanced up. A gust of wind scattered the clouds and reshaped them. "I see clouds."

"Alexander," she cried in mock horror. "Where is your imagination? Look now, do you see the man and woman dancing? I daresay it is the waltz, too."

He peered up and made a noncommittal sound.

"Did you not create entire stories watching the clouds as a child?" she asked wistfully. "I did that with Papa often. He taught me the beauty of imagination and to see possibilities of an adventure in almost every situation."

"He sounds admirable. My mother would have liked him."

"She would have?"

"My mother also saw adventure in the clouds and the stars. My father once told me he fell in love with her because of her spirit for the whimsy," he said gruffly.

Kitty grinned, apparently delighted by that tidbit. "It was a love match?"

Alexander looked out across the valley. "He said he saw her at a ball, stepped on her toes in the crush, and she laughed. He said he knew then he would marry her."

"How lovely," she said with a soft sigh. "My mamma and papa were childhood friends, their estates abutting each other. Papa said he knew at the age of twelve that Mamma would be his wife. Mamma, who was ten years at the time, said she also knew—and she wonders why her daughters are incurable romantics."

A large bird swooped low and perched on the branch right above their heads. Katherine grabbed his arm excitedly. "Oh, look at those glorious feathers!"

They watched the bird in silence until, with a flap of its wings, it flew away, soaring toward the clouds.

"I've been thinking," she murmured.

"What beautiful mischief is churning in that mind of yours?"

She bounced him with her shoulder playfully, then delicately cleared her throat. "Our charade cannot be forever…your interest ensnared endlessly."

He wanted to refute her claim, truly unable to imagine a moment where she would not captivate him. She was clever, resourceful, impudent, and just so damn lovely.

"I owe you an astronomical sum of money, and I—"

"You owe me nothing," he said gruffly. "The amount to let the town house is a pittance."

"Still, once our engagement ends, I cannot importune on your generosity further."

"And do you suppose it shall end soon, Miss Danvers?"

She sent him a sidelong glance. "I would ask the same of you, Your Grace. My expectations have been upended. I am not locked away in a tower like a heroine in a gothic novel despairing for my virtue while hatching desperate plans to escape the wicked, wicked man who whisked me away from the comforts of my family."

She was laughing at him.

He grazed the softness of her cheek with the back of his hand. "Do you want me to act the ravaging beast, Katherine?"

Her pulse visibly leaped at her throat.

"You do know I cannot stay here much longer," she whispered. "I was thinking you could come to London. We could go to the theater. The gardens. Even the museum. Wouldn't that be fun? And we *are* engaged, so there should be little to no speculation."

Her eyes sparkled with unspoken promises, and he did not have it in him to be cynical. Instead, he drifted closer to her on the branch, surrounding her with his bulk and thinking for a moment that such promises could be real.

"Do you imagine you could live here and be happy?"

There lingered a teasing pout to her lush lips.

"An extremely dangerous question, Your Grace. It implies you plan to keep me captive forever."

Before he could answer, she tipped onto her toes, leaned in, and kissed his brow. Truly her impudence could startle him no longer. She continued her ministrations by tenderly kissing the bridge of his nose and finally, his mouth. The softest of brushes, yet it reached down into his cold, lonely heart and filled it with astonishing warmth and a lightness he had never felt before.

Refusing to deny himself in this moment, he cupped her cheek with his free hand, dipped his head, and took her mouth, softly and tenderly at first, then wild and rough. Her mouth was a living flame beneath his—passionate, sweet, and irresistible.

Then it was over before it truly began. He pulled away slightly and waited for her to say something, anything, but she only stared across the wild beauty of the land. Yet her lips remained curved in a secretive smile. Awestruck by the beauty and power of her smile, he simply stared, but at her, not at the scenery before them.

They did not mention the kiss, but she watched the clouds alive with the birds and the lands that he owned. Disembarking had been tricky, but he made it down without much mishap, though he had barely resisted the urge to groan aloud as his muscles absorbed the shock of his descent. Once on the ground, they had reposed on the blanket and drunk the entire bottle of wine and ate the delicious rum cake. Alexander had even suspected his Katherine might have been a bit foxed. He had stupidly made snow angels without snow at her delighted insistence, and grass was everywhere on his body and in his hair.

They had argued more over the shapes in the clouds and had debated the merits of a headless horseman being real and how he could be a champion of the underclass of London. After a while he had wondered if he, too, was foxed, since their conversations were unlike any he'd ever had before. They had spoken at length of the orphans of England and the motions he would have his supporters take to parliament in its next session.

More than an hour had passed. A chill permeated the air, and a lavender cast blanketed the sky as twilight approached. Yet they did not make any effort to retreat inside the castle walls. Nor was Alexander startled when Hoyt appeared with two very warm blankets, cushions, and a lit lantern. The man had set them down without a word and melted away discreetly. Katherine had laughed in happy bemusement and had hurriedly swaddled herself in a blanket after wrapping one about his shoulders.

Now he sat with his back against the tree's trunk, one leg drawn up and the other stretched out, his thigh acting as a pillow for Katherine. Upon his leg, her head rested as she read the gothic and surprisingly engaging story of *The Murderous Monk*.

His heart started beating again, if unevenly. And for the first time in a long time, he allowed the dreams to burrow a little deeper under the hardened icy surface.

CHAPTER SEVENTEEN

The day after Kitty's magical adventure in the tree with the duke, she wrote to her mamma, informing her of plans to extend her fictitious visit to her aunt in Derbyshire for another week.

Outrageous, absurd even, but she had followed the impulse and requested her letter to be delivered posthaste. Since then, another few days passed charmingly yet had been fraught with an unknown peril. An odd sort of tension existed between her and the duke whenever they crossed paths or dined with his family. He'd rarely allowed them to be alone, and she had not noticed before, too uncertain of the strange feelings he inspired.

Kitty laughed at the idiocy of it all, though she sobered immediately.

Why won't you be alone with me, Alexander? And why am I not finding every reasonable excuse to run far away from you and this situation?

She knew she should be in London with her sisters. That old refrain only made her sigh with impatience. Kitty was both baffled and intrigued by the manner in which her mind and heart regularly turned to the dratted man. All the buried hopes had been stirred up, and Kitty was never one to shy away from her impossible and daring dreams or escapades.

With a sigh, she closed the book she'd been reading, lowered it to the small writing desk, and made her way across to the wide windows of her room. She stepped closer, pressing her palm against the cool glass as she spied Alexander seated in a rowing boat, gently floating atop the lake. As she stood watching the duke, a most astonishing truth became evident to Kitty. The duke was indeed *afraid* to be alone with her. *Is it because you like me, too, Alexander?* For she had not tried harder to leave his castle simply because she felt with her entire heart a connection of unprecedented proportions lingered between them.

A flash of green caught her attention, and she shifted her regard from the duke. Mr. Collins ambled across the lawns with a posy of flowers in his grip. He would bring them to her as he did each day, and they would take a walk along the lake, where he would make her laugh with amusing anecdotes of his travels. No anticipation shivered through her at the prospect of taking a stroll with Mr. Collins, though he was so very amiable and attentive.

Was Mr. Collins courting her? *Merciful heavens.* The idea seemed too outlandish. The man thought her to be Alexander's fiancée.

Unless he knew the truth?

Yesterday, on a short stroll through the gardens, he had suggested calling upon her in town to meet her mother and sisters. She hadn't had the chance to answer, sensing someone watched them. It had been Alexander, on top of the hill overlooking the gardens. When she noticed him, he'd merely turned his chair away and wheeled himself from her sight. She had made a cake of herself by grabbing the folds of her skirts and hurrying up the slight incline in his direction. By the time she'd arrived at the summit,

Alexander had disappeared from view, leaving her to wonder where he'd gone.

Mr. Collins had seemed decidedly disgruntled by her actions, but he'd made no comment. Kitty moved from the windows, plucked the book from the writing desk, and slipped it into the deep pocket of her day gown. She made her way from the chamber down the long hallway and winding staircase. Mr. Collins smiled upon seeing her.

"Miss Danvers, good afternoon. Might you accompany me on a stroll?"

"Mr. Collins," she said warmly, accepting the flowers he held to her. "Thank you for the invitation, but regrettably I have other plans. Perhaps after dinner, we could take a turn through the gardens? With Penny accompanying us, of course."

He masked his disappointment quite gallantly and even made a charming bow. Kitty excused herself, placed the flowers in a vase, and rested them on the walnut table in the smaller drawing room. Then she made her way outside, walking along the path that led to the lake in the distance.

"Miss Danvers!"

The call had her turning around. "Mr. Collins, is all well?"

He reached her, panting slightly, his hair no longer impeccably styled, as if he had repeatedly raked his fingers through it. "It is," he said with a smile. "I suspect you will visit Alexander, and I thought I might accompany you on the stroll to the lake."

She hesitated, then replied, "I would like that, Mr. Collins."

Kitty ambled beside him for a few paces and shot

him a curious glance when his steps slowed before halting. As she'd suspected, there was more in this than merely keeping her company. "Do you wish to speak with me, Mr. Collins?"

He grimaced, staring off in the distance before settling his regards on her face.

"I suspect you are in love with the duke. On our long walks, I could feel that your mind was with him…and yesterday, the way you ran after him…"

Kitty flushed in abject mortification. "I admire and *like* him, yet I believe there is a difference," Kitty said softly, glancing at him with a proud tilt to her chin.

He was silent for a moment, staring into her eyes. "He's the loneliest man I've ever known. He needs love to ward off that loneliness. Yet he does not accept comfort willingly or readily. I suspect, though, he would give away his entire wealth if you were the person to offer it."

"How absurd you should think so!" Yet her heart pounded with desperate hope, and from the smile on Mr. Collins's face, he might have seen it in her eyes.

"I suspect you are aware of the terrible tragedy that took so much from Alexander years ago. For a time, he was an angry beast, snarling and hating the world for the loss of his parents and his inability to be the man he once was. Society did not call him mad, bad, and dangerous for sport. I daresay he was reckless and intemperate, young, and foolish in his pursuits: gambling, racing, I assume you know there were Cyprians. Alexander was well loved and respected. He has lived with pain, horrible pain as he fought to recover."

Mr. Collins shifted his attention to the lake. "Years later and he is still not physically able to do many of the things he once did, and I suspect part of him relives that loss every day. It is hard for me… for Penny, for all those who care for him to touch that loss and offer comfort because, for all intents and purposes, we are still perfectly fashioned. And the most interesting thing about my cousin, Miss Danvers, is that he does not *require* that comfort from us."

"What do you want him to share?"

Mr. Collins raked his fingers through his hair, mussing the once neat style. "Anything! He does not tell us he is lonely or unhappy, but we see it. He has eschewed all form of female companionship, and…" He blew out a frustrated breath. "Pardon my indelicacy, Miss Danvers. I will see you at dinner."

Then he walked away, and she watched him until he disappeared from sight. What did Mr. Collins want from her? And not only him but Penny as well. Even the staff seemed to watch Kitty with an unexplained air of expectancy.

She continued her walk to the lake, and once there, she lingered by the bank, watching the duke rowing lazily atop the waters. Kitty was afforded an opportunity to study him at her leisure and couldn't help noting how alone he seemed. Surely there must be some connection, she mused, for he paused, seemingly took a steadying breath, and then shifted his regard to her.

She lifted her hand in a wave, and from where Kitty stood, she saw a small curve to his lips.

Relief darted through her when he used the oars

and turned the boat toward her. He stopped only a few feet from her, the muscles of his arms working as he angled the boat so the bow gently tapped the banking. Then he released the oars, resting his arms casually atop his thighs, and stared at her.

His cerulean blue eyes were so empty and distant, her heart ached. Kitty did not flinch from his regard but held it with a lift to her chin. "Have you been ignoring me, Your Grace?"

"Good afternoon, Katherine," he finally said.

"Ah…so no walls up today. I anticipated 'Miss Danvers' from your lips."

His eyes lost their cold, rather cynical expression, warming with humor…and desire.

She was surely too practical, and had too much common sense, to be beguiled by a smile, yet her heart fluttered madly at the sensual curve of his mouth. A sweet twisting ache stirred in her belly, and her heart quickened. "Would you like some company in your boat? I have a book," she offered impulsively.

"Yes."

Kitty would have been considerably disappointed if he'd refused.

Alexander stood, rocking the boat, and held out his hand. With caution, she stepped forward and reached for him.

"Jump," he said, his eyes alight with amusement.

Kitty glanced at the space between the boat and the embankment with a scowl. "And if I should fall in?"

"I'll not allow it."

And without hesitation, she jumped, trusting him to help her safely into the boat, which rocked far too

precariously when she landed. With a soft grunt, he
steadied her, then assisted her in sitting down on the
thwart. His touch muddied her thoughts and made
her warm all over. "Do you row often?" she asked, a
bit too breathlessly.

"There are times the walls of the castle feel…cold
and oppressing, when the memories torment," he
said mildly.

"And you come here…" She glanced around at
the wide-open waters, the graceful weeping willow
trees in the distance.

"And I come here."

He sat directly in front of her, collected the oars,
and started to row. They stayed like that, in this
silence that felt so peaceful. Kitty lifted her face
to where the rays of the sun valiantly attempted
to peek through swollen clouds. After a while, she
withdrew the small leather book from her pocket
and decided to start from the beginning, in the event
he'd not read *The Legend of Sleepy Hollow* before.

She started reading, changing her voice at times
to reflect the different characters who appeared in
the story. Several minutes passed before she paused,
glancing up. The duke was staring at her. A ripple of
warmth shivered through Kitty's heart at the tender
regard in his gaze.

"You read beautifully," he murmured.

"Thank you. I do so often for my sisters and
mother. And Papa, too, when…when he was alive."
She cleared her throat. "Shall I continue?"

"Please," he murmured, pushing the oars forward,
then clawing them back with powerful grace. The
muscles rippling under his shirt quickened her pulse

alarmingly, and she looked away, hating the blush rising in her cheeks.

She read, and he rowed, his face slightly tipped to the warmth and beauty of the sun.

Kitty peeked at him over the pages at times, wanting to be a part of the peace he seemed to exude. The scarred section of his face seemed to pull taut over the elegant ridge of his cheekbone, and in the midst of it, an icy radiance appeared to emit from the duke. How odd that he found such enjoyment in loneliness. Or was it that he was too enmeshed with the state?

A surreal sensation gripped her, and she wondered if she would ever completely know the man before her. Even now, there was a terrible air of isolation about him.

Closing the book gently, she rested it on a small basket on the floor of the boat. She noted the apples and sandwiches tucked neatly in. "Does it matter to you at all that I am here…in this boat with you?" she asked softly.

He stopped rowing. The eyes that peered at her were unfathomable. He reached for her, his fingers tracing the lines of her cheekbones and jaw.

"You are the only person I've ever wanted to share my silence."

She did not understand, though she hungered to. "Alexander—"

"The beauty of silence is that it simply is. In the stillness and tranquility, I find peace. Instead of being afraid of the void, I embrace it."

Kitty thought of her mother and sisters and how quickly they rushed to fill any quiet moment with more laughter and conversation. How strange and complex they would find the duke.

"Do you hear your heartbeat?"

"No," she whispered, her mouth drying when he slid his hand from her face and rested it against her chest. Kitty flushed, and millions of birds took flight in her stomach.

"In silence, the senses are heightened. I hear your heartbeat...and mine; I hear and feel the gentle rushing of the wind, the fishes swimming below us in the water, your sweet, soft sighs. There is such beauty in silence before the breaking dawn, after the violence of a storm, in the snow that blankets the land in winter. There is peace, and in the presence of silence, we find the answers to difficult questions."

"Are you not lonely within the silence?"

"Infinitely so, echoing, endless loneliness."

Kitty's heart shattered at the icy acceptance in his voice.

She leaned lightly into him, tilting her face to his. "Why do you stay in this remote place, Alexander? Why not come to London, be a part of the season?"

"It is not the frivolity of the season, empty, aimless chatter, and hypocrisy that fills the void in me."

"What does?"

An uncomfortable beat, then he said, "You."

She searched his face, her heart pounding. "Then, why have you been avoiding me since our day in the tree?"

His expression stilled; he made no response. They stared at each other for a while, then Kitty said, "I can now hear your heartbeat, though I am not touching you. How it pounds...and that is because I am sitting so close to you, isn't it? Do I dare think you are falling for me?" she taunted with a slow smile.

"You impud—"

"Impudent minx," she finished for him with a low laugh.

The beginning of a smile raised the corners of his mouth. "You must learn to swim, Miss Danvers."

The change in conversation startled her for a moment. "I daresay one day I shall. I've always thought sea-bathing such a risk—"

Kitty barely had time to gasp when the duke released the oars, grabbed her, and tumbled with her over the side.

"You beast!" she shrieked, spluttering and grabbing onto the side of the boat.

"I thought you were adventurous, Katherine."

"You…you odious man," she said with a choked cry.

"You are not sinking," he said, his voice low and reassuring behind her. "And I am right here." He was pressing into her, and the feel of his hard body against her made something wicked and delightful stretch deep inside her. A light touch against her hip and it was as if the sun burned her so bright.

The sensation was so electrifying. The chill of the water had no impact, for she was heated from the inside.

"You dumped us in the water to distract me from my purpose," she accused.

"And what was your purpose?"

Ignoring his low question, she asked, "You are afraid of what I make you feel… *Why?*"

In reaction, he gripped her hips so tightly, she couldn't breathe, but for a moment, she didn't care, just savored the feeling of being surrounded by him.

"Your mouth has no filter, does it?"

A prickle of uncertainty moved down her spine. "Do you want me to be circumspect?"

"No, I quite like when you are bold and fearless. I want you... I know that I shouldn't, but how I do crave you, Miss Danvers."

She didn't respond immediately. She couldn't. All she could think of was the way he'd tormented her with pleasure in the cabin. A low throb moved through her abdomen, and an unbearably keen awareness scythed through her. Kitty touched him, gliding her fingers over his clenched fist, slowly straightening them so they were palm to palm, then she interlaced her fingers with his. Kitty felt her heartbeat, erratic and uncertain as his own under the tip of her fingers.

She turned in the cage of his arms, her back pressed against the gently bobbing boat, but it was he who held her above water.

"Wrap your legs around my waist; it will be easier to keep you afloat that way."

The wicked suggestion of such intimacy stole her breath. Kitty stared at him in mute shock, then glanced behind him at the castle and rolling lawns in the distance.

"Most of our bodies are under the water... No one can see."

He took her by the waist, pulling her away from the boat. The only support she had now was his body, and she willingly wrapped her legs around his hips.

They stood, practically in an embrace, with the raw power and vitality of him surrounding her. She could feel the grace and strength in the legs that kicked below the water keeping them from sinking into the murky depths.

Strange bewilderment filled her, and she felt unmoored and conflicted. *We will have to be wicked and improper to get the things we want.* Since the night in the cabin, Kitty couldn't stop her headlong slide into attraction to the duke any more than she could make water flow uphill. Her complicated feelings could little withstand the force of reason. "Have you ever felt like this before, Alexander? With anyone?"

The brilliant blue of his gaze became suddenly intent, searching her face. His silence made her heart beat still more violently.

He seemed exasperated, even a bit amused. Then he leaned in close, pressing his mouth against her temple. "No."

The admission disarmed her. She blew out a breath to dispel it, and immediate relief swelled through her body. She wanted to press her face into his throat and breathe in his scent. Instead, she turned her face so that her cheek rested against his. "Neither have I." She heard herself laugh, all breathless, incredulous delight at her daring admission.

Lightning streaked and forked above, followed by the ominous boom of thunder, yet neither moved. Her hands shifted of their own volition, sliding up along his back. "Do you fancy you could feel like this again?"

At his silence, she leaned back so she could

observe his expression. There was a peculiar look on his face.

"No, I do not believe it to be possible."

"I dare not believe it to be possible, either." A flush warmed her face. "Then, what are you going to do about it, Your Grace?"

He shook his head, a rueful gleam in his eyes. "You are not at all like other ladies, are you?"

Her heart gave a lonely throb. "Do you want me to be?"

He brushed a thumb over her cheek. And that caress was a source of cold fire that burned everywhere that he had lingered on her body.

"Never," he murmured. And then he kissed her.

CHAPTER EIGHTEEN

The moment Alexander's lips touched hers, Kitty was consumed—by fire, happiness, and an all-encompassing desire.

He kissed her with a passionate urgency, and she responded with flaming wonder. A wild impulse unraveled in her, and with a sweet sigh of surrender, she parted her lips and allowed him to sweep his tongue along them. The taste of him spilled through Kitty like sunshine, darkness, and temptation.

This kiss was harsher, more delicious, and more ravishing than any before. Pleasure coursed through the heated nerve endings, and she shivered in his embrace. Then the sky opened, and with a gasp, they broke apart.

"Come, we must return at once," he said, drifting with her toward the gently rocking boat.

He helped her in and then hauled himself into the boat. Alexander grabbed the oars and, with powerful moves, clawed through the water toward the shore. Kitty glanced behind her. "We are not heading to the main house?" she asked huskily, rubbing her arms to keep the invading chill at bay.

"No."

"Well, that sounded appropriately ominous," she said with a scowl.

"I'm directing us to the southeast side of the estate, to the conservatory, which is much closer than the castle."

The sky rumbled, and the drops became more insistent. Thankfully, within a few minutes, they were able to disembark the boat and hurried along a cobbled path toward a large half-brick, half-glass enclosure that loomed in the distance.

They entered the conservatory, and the lush, sultry scent of moisture and fragrant blooms beckoned her deeper into the room. A wide stone path led into the shadowed greenery deep inside the conservatory, and she could see that it opened into an extensive, lavish garden.

"It is wonderfully warm," she said on a pleased sigh.

The boiler there was lit, the air redolent with the many blossoms. A wrought-iron bench was pushed against a corner, and a large oblong table was in the center of the room with pruning shears atop its surface.

A soft noise had her turning around. He held up a blanket. "Will you permit me once again to be your lady's maid?"

There was that provoking humor in his eyes again, but there was something else there, too: need and an awakening hunger. An undeniable awareness filled Kitty, and a languorous feeling spread through her limbs. *We must be wicked and improper…*

She moved closer to him, and he wrapped the blanket around her sodden clothes, warming her even more. Kitty spread her hands over his chest, feeling the warmth of his skin under her fingers. It was then she realized the duke closed his eyes whenever she touched him. A slight caress. A bold brush of her fingers along his chin. Each moment was as if he savored her.

Kiss me again, Alexander. The words were so close to emerging that she could feel the desperate weight on her tongue. But the idea of voicing such a wanton thought mortified her.

"I can feel your heart racing," he murmured, his expression one of passionate need.

She suddenly could not hold his eyes. *Would you always look at me so? Please, God*, her irrepressible heart prayed. *Let Alexander look at me in this manner—with hunger, tender desire, and admiration—always.*

Her forehead fell to his shoulder, and he cupped the back of her neck firmly, as if encouraging her to stay there forever.

"I am so tempted," she whispered into the crook of his neck. "So very tempted." The words emerged like a desperate sob, and she closed her eyes against the aching needs within them.

A finger slipped under her chin and lifted her face to his. "To do what?" His gaze held hers, and his voice was tender and rough.

"To be wicked…and free…and to take something for myself without worrying about consequences, and I want to do it with *you*."

Something hot and hungry flared in his expression. It tightened, his cheekbones becoming more pronounced as his lashes lowered over his eyes. Lifting his regard to her, he brushed a lock of damp hair gently behind her ears.

"What consequences do you worry about?"

She laughed lightly. "As indelicate as it seemed, my mother warned her girls about wicked, licentious rakes leaving unwanted babies in our bellies, and I assure you, we are suitably filled with fears of ruin and disgrace."

His eyes went dark with indefinable emotions. "I am impotent, Kitty."

Her heart lurched at his serious tone. "I know you said—"

"I see you do not perceive its meaning. I am unable to make love with a woman properly. My licentious raking days are long gone. I am unable to father children. If I could...I believe I would make you my duchess."

The world fell away from beneath her feet, and it was only he who anchored her.

"You're mad," she whispered. She felt shaken. Hopeful. Delighted. Aroused.

"Perhaps. I want to strip you, lay your heart and mind bare before me, and make your secrets my own."

"A terrifying proposition," she murmured, scanning the nuances of his expression. She pushed past the shocking revelation he would make her his duchess if he could. And... "Your impotence, this is the result of your fall?"

"Yes."

"I am so sorry, Alexander." An ache rose in her throat as she tried to imagine the desire of having children being taken away from her. What woman did not dream of a husband, children, a happy home?

Even though Kitty had other dreams in her heart, there still lingered that plan that said at the end of it all, perhaps she would have to settle with a man who was only a companion, but she would be surrounded by smart and rowdy children until it was her time to leave the world.

"There is no need to be sorry," he said. "I've had ten long years to accept it. My heart does not ache for the loss of something I no longer have. Nor do I hunger for it."

She stared at him in mute shock. No hunger for a family or children. Could anyone truly ever be contented with being alone? "Do you not hunger for a family? A large one with much laughter?"

"Why would I crave the nuisance of noise?"

She narrowed her gaze on him, truly wondering if he were being honest with her. "And this is why you've made no plans to marry?"

"A part of it."

Then silence.

"Must you make me impolite enough to ask?"

He chuckled, and the rough sound rolled through her like fire, warming her chilled skin.

"I've not met a woman interesting enough to tempt me to the state."

Her breasts were swelling beneath his gaze as if he were stroking her. How exquisite were the sensations tightening around her heart. She felt weak, undone, hopeful, and afraid. "Until me?"

"Do I find you interesting, Kitty Danvers?"

There was an invitation in the brilliant depth of his gaze. "I suspect so," she whispered, "or I would still be in London, you would be here, and we would have never met."

A smile curved his lips. "I might feel a touch of something unusual." Then he sobered, his eyes serious. "I am addicted to you, Miss Danvers. And I know all about drugs."

"Do you?" she asked archly, though her heart was a quivering mess.

"I do. For some time, opium was my best friend. Hashish my lover. Laudanum my brother, and we got together often in my despair."

Her heart gave a sudden, sharp thud. "And now… are they still your companions?"

He smiled, barely. "Not for the last six years."

"Why not?"

"Penny needed me…so I became present."

And that indomitable will peeked out from the brilliant beauty of his eyes once again. He dipped his head and leaned in close so their lips almost touched, their noses brushing. "I want just one small, infinitesimal piece of your affection to carry with me always. At first, I thought your smile would be enough. Then maybe your laughter. How wrong I've been, Miss Danvers. Foolishly…quite foolishly, I am desperate for *more*."

"I am falling for you," she said softly, and with every honest emotion in her heart. "I want a piece of you as well. Memories that will live with me for this lifetime and the next." *But I would much prefer if you never let me go, Alexander.*

He captured her mouth in a searing kiss. She allowed the fire of lust to consume her world, willingly burning away the doubts. His embrace was fierce, unyielding, and she shivered at the sensations rioting through her. Each kiss went deeper, lingered longer. Everything in her yearned for this, craved him.

It had been so long since she'd done something for herself.

Passion blazed between them, sweeping the last remnants of cold from her body. Kitty burned everywhere, and her needs were so chaotic and terrible, she sobbed against his lips. And he swallowed it all, every moan, every inarticulate cry of wonder and desire.

Kitty gasped when he lifted her and, in a few steps, had her seated atop the large table, the duke standing between her thighs, which she had instinctively widened to accommodate him. And through it all, he continued kissing her with ravishing tenderness.

"I am going to be *very* wicked with you, Katherine," he murmured against her lips, in a voice that had gone hoarse. "If you have any objections, please voice them now while I am still sensible."

His words set a path of fire down her throat and into her stomach. "Yes," she said, unable to resist the needs in her heart and body for him.

He made a murmur of approval and slid his hand around her nape, then kissed her lips with such tenderness, a lump formed in her throat. Rain muttered dimly against the roof of the conservatory, but the air within felt hushed and full, heavy with expectation. As his kisses gentled, the sensations within her body exploded with pulsing heat. Then he broke away to kiss her chin, her throat, the crook of her shoulder.

Her nipples became so hard, so tight, they were a near-violent ache. "Alexander," she moaned, low and husky.

His thumb made a slow stroke across her inner elbow, a soothing, sensual caress. The high waist of her gown was tugged down, and his mouth brushed the top of her breasts; then his lips closed over a nipple.

A wild cry tore from her throat as aching, desperate sensations began to pulse through her. "Alexander!"

His mouth pulled, and the tug was felt low and hot in her belly. She held his head to her, her fingers gripping perhaps too tightly in his hair. The strokes of his tongue sent heated delight flushing through her.

He dragged the heavy, sodden skirts of her dress up, his fingers tangling into the material, inching it upward little by little. His touch lingered against her calves, her knees, her thighs, then skating past her garter along her thigh, and then he was at the wet, warm center of her sex. He was touching her *there*.

And it was *glorious*.

She cried out brokenly, her breath coming in ragged gasps. They both froze at the wicked, wicked act of intimacy. She felt the weight of his touch, the shocking pleasure, and the impropriety of it. Before she could process it all, his hand disappeared, and he urged her to recline. Kitty complied and braced on her elbows, staring at him in dazed arousal. She wanted to protest when he lowered himself, as surely his back and hips would suffer for it. She made to rise up, and one of his hands pressed against her stomach, the casual, dominant touch spiking lust through her veins.

She felt his smile of pleasure against her wet, aching folds…and then he kissed her even more carnally, taking her nub between his teeth and devastating her senses. She cried out sharply, unable to contain the sound. The urge to whisper to him beat at her, but what to say? If there were words that would encourage more of his diabolical debauchery, they eluded her.

Only incoherent sobs tore from Kitty. And pleasure—the exquisite pleasure was overwhelming.

Kitty arched into him, sobbing with the terrible need working through her system. She needed more to reach that unimagined pinnacle that hovered with such intensity. "Alexander, more," she demanded huskily.

He licked her drenched sex, forcing a piercing pleasure through her swollen nub every time he caught it with his tongue in a sweet, carnal glide. He released her from the diabolical torment of his tongue and rose up so he could peer into her eyes. His features were savage, a grimace of male ecstasy.

"I want to see you, touch you," she said shakily.

Without waiting for a reply, she removed his waistcoat and started to unbutton his shirt. Her duke went still, the expression in his eyes stark and wary, but she also spied his indomitable strength.

"You are scared," she said softly, pressing a tender kiss to his lips.

"Only my doctors have seen me…" He leaned in and placed his forehead against hers. "I want you to…"

"My darling…thank you for trusting me." She leaned back and held his eyes as she removed his shirt. The pain and agony painted on his body burned her throat with tears. There were so many scar tissues on his left side, from his chin down to his neck, chest, and stomach, disappearing into his pants. Kitty could not imagine enduring and surviving such pain. She glanced up from the scars on his stomach and met his eyes. With boldness and wickedness she had never dreamed herself capable of, she opened the buttons of his trousers. Even there he had scars on his hips....

She reached into his pants for that bulge that testified he wanted her with a similar need.

"Katherine," he began warningly, his throat working in deep, almost nervous swallows.

She caught the thick, warm length and stroked him, at first clumsily and then with more boldness. He trembled in her embrace, his face a grimace of awe and lustful greed.

"This should not be possible," he groaned, cupping her cheeks and kissing her with an almost violent passion.

Their lips pulled apart, only a scant inch between them. "Why not?"

"I...I..." He pressed his forehead against hers, his words missing. Cupping her chin, he stared into her face, his eyes searching, for what she did not understand, but she submitted to his need.

He was silent, watching her. But it was more than that. He had disappeared somewhere, inside that emptiness that had saved him. But she saw it now, peeking at her like a live entity. She could almost touch the wall of terrible isolation that surrounded him. She leaned into him and kissed his chin. "I am here, in this moment with you." *And forever...I want to be here with you forever.* "You are so beautiful, Alexander."

A small smile curved his lips. "You are still lovely even when you say such foolish things."

Kitty kissed him, at first with gentle tenderness but then with all the passion and growing love in her heart.

"Open your legs for me," he murmured against her mouth.

She complied immediately, snared by the command in his tone and the lust in his eyes. He pressed closer to her body, a hard, muscled thigh pushed between hers, spreading her legs even wider. Without breaking her gaze, he slipped one of his hands between them and down to her wet sex. In his eyes, she saw a hunger deep, wild, and so urgent, it scared her.

A very strange but sweet twisting ache stirred in her belly, and her heart quickened. He slid a finger inside her, a slow penetration that arrowed a thousand darts of fire to burn her from the inside. Another finger entered her, a pinch of pain that melted quickly, and then he began to move in and out while his thumb pressed and rotated against her nub of pleasure.

Kitty cried out and arched upward as an unbelievable sensation spasmed through her. Her body bowed, her breath catching on a near sob, as lust rose and splintered inside. He held her as desire made her body tremble, destroying everything she thought about herself.

Oh God. What have I done, and why do I want more…everything?

Yet she could not move from the warm shelter of his arms or the soothing touches against her back.

CHAPTER NINETEEN

The agony in Alexander's cock was…exquisite.

It was the most beautiful, most painful pleasure he had known in his life. The feel of her lips against his neck, his hands on her bare flesh, her tentative touch against his hardened length. With a groan, he stuffed himself inside his trousers. He tasted Kitty in his mouth now as he never had before—sweet, so damn sweet—and her subtle lavender scent infused his lungs. Her thighs had trembled beneath his carnal kisses, and he wanted to take his cock and sink it into her welcoming heat.

Merciful Christ.

Alexander wanted her forever; the need was so visceral, he almost fell to his knees. She had the potential to be his heart, his soul, the happiness he had always believed he would never find. He trailed his fingers up the length of her leg and over her silken stockings. Then he explored farther, letting his hand drift up the sensitive skin of her inner thigh. Soothing her. Wanting her.

His member, which he'd thought dead, got even harder, and the muted pain in his back and left leg began to shout louder, but he ignored it.

"Why did you stop?" Her voice was tentative and roughened with burgeoning passion. Admittedly, she did not understand what it was she asked. It was the desire clouding her judgment.

Lowering his head to press his forehead against

her trembling shoulder, he swallowed tightly, fighting with every iota of self-control he possessed. She did not deserve ruination. He was not a villainous seducer. So he would not slake his newly awaking lust on her body…even if she seemed so wet and wantonly willing.

How could he compromise her virtue more than he'd done already and trap her into marriage when he could never guarantee her a family or a normal life? He'd accepted the loneliness—to consign her to a similar fate was cruel indeed.

There was a chaise longue farther into the conservatory, and he would take her there. He lifted her into his arms, grunting at the fire that sliced through his back. She leaned into him as he carried her, resting her head on his shoulder. His heartbeat seemed far steadier than hers. His legs felt as if they would buckle at any moment, but he ignored the pain, hating that he would never be whole enough to experience certain joys with her. He was only thirty years of age but felt the weight of every wound and scar he'd suffered.

They reached the chaise, and he lowered himself in it, taking her into his lap. Her eyes widened as she felt the proof of his arousal. It was more than that— His cock was so painfully hard, it felt it would split through his wet trousers.

Kitty peered at him with that same expression of tender yearnings she'd had in the rowing boat. *If only…*

He did not want to lose her.

The unexpected thought gave Alexander an odd panic. He accepted then that she was totally wrapped around his heart, and there would be nothing left once she was gone. "I would lay the world at your feet if I could, Katherine."

Her eyes crinkled at the corners. He loved that her eyes always smiled first. Then her lips curved, and her whole face changed, glowed, making her even more beautiful.

"I do not need the whole world. Just a little bit of you, Alexander," she said huskily, her gaze searching his expression intently. Then she leaned in, and her lips trembled against his in a soft kiss.

This can mean nothing, he wanted to warn her. But could not bring himself to say the harsh words. She cupped his jaw tenderly, and her touch was like a soft brush of satin.

"I never knew pleasure could be so beautiful. Thank you for sharing it with me."

The impending sense of loss drove him to lean forward and place his lips tenderly on her brow for long moments. His throat burned as he grieved for the thousand small moments they would never be able to share.

She leaned back and peered into his eyes. "What was that for?"

Her words trembled, and in her gaze, he spied fright, as if she sensed the pain of his decision cleaving through him. *Farewell.*

"It is time for you to return to London," he said.

Her eyes flashed with defiance. "Alone?"

"Yes."

Her entire body went rigid, and wounded eyes settled on him. A breath shuddered from her. "And what we just shared?"

"Do not look at me like that, Katherine. I made no promises."

"Then make them now."

Something broke inside him. Odd, that, for he'd genuinely believed he had nothing but emptiness inside.

She kissed the underside of his jaw. "Make them, Alexander…and I'll make mine as well." This was breathed with that fascinating mix of shyness and daring.

I promise I will cherish you forever. Yet he did not utter those words. He said, "Do you not wish for children…a family to dote on? To travel the world, to live life with your unique, inspiring boldness?"

The barest of tension wound through her frame. "I…"

"Honesty, Katherine. That must never be compromised between us. Now answer my question."

She uttered a tiny spurt of laughter. "I believe many, if not all, women have such yearnings. I, too, desire to have a large family, but I do not define my hopes and dreams by it."

Children…a boy, a girl…maybe two more or six. Alexander's heart jerked in pure, startled joy at the visceral images of a boy and girl running through the halls chasing puppies, of Katherine laughing as she chased after the rowdy bunch. She would be just as sweet and informal as his mother had been. Even more so, for she did not seem to be the kind of woman impressed by society's dictates.

His Katherine would be…

His mind blanked. *My Katherine? No…not my Katherine…never mine.*

Suddenly he felt unsteady again, the old needs roaring to the surface.

The anguish of all he had lost and would never regain broke through the hollow grave he'd buried it in so many years ago. Once that ugly loss had haunted him like a specter, cutting daily into his flesh anew with wounds that felt as if they would never heal. He wanted to roar, for he'd defeated this loss of hope, had stomped it into the earth, had triumphed, had seen some small flashes of light in the darkness. He had held on for so long, hiding in the emptiness, but now it was revealed that hard-won peace and contentment with his lot was only a mirage.

"You make me hope," he snarled low and dangerous. "Like a goddamn idiot, you make me pray, you make my throat burn with the need to scream and beg God to give you to me, to treasure, to worship… to love until the end of my days." He had to close his eyes to control his ragged breathing.

"Alexander…."

"I will *not* love you, nor will I ask you to stay," he ground from between clenched teeth.

She had gone very pale.

"Eventually the need for more will eat at your soul, and I could never bear to see you so unhappy and unfulfilled."

He could not allow her to own his soul, for his fragile world would fall apart.

• • •

Pain washed through Kitty in waves, making her breathing choppy, the fight to hold back her tears impossible. God, it was ridiculous to feel this profound sense of…hurt, and desperate, tearing loss. No promises had been made, and she had been the one to allow improbable dreams to fester deep in her heart. Yet every sigh, kiss, and illicit touch had communicated such passion and want. "Do you deny there is something between us?"

His expression closed. "Do not be silly. There cannot be, for I have nothing to give you."

The chilling finality in his tone cut her heart in two. She rested her forehead against his and closed her heart against a buried desire. "I can live without children. Our life can be rich and incredible in so many other ways, my darling."

He jerked as if she had punched him in the gut.

Every muscle of his body appeared rigid and locked in place. "I would never do that to you," he said fiercely, his eyes flashing with dangerous ire and need. "I am not that damnably selfish to confine so bright a treasure as you to my lonely existence. Family means so much to you, Katherine; you placed your reputation and future at risk for them. You came here, not knowing what I would demand from you, for them. I could have been a dastardly villain who would have seen you only to ruin, ravishment, and scandal, yet you came. You are fearless and boundless, and *that* is how you should live your life in every way. None of what you are should be caged or contained, by you, me, or anyone else."

Kitty's heart skipped a beat and then another. "I would not be lonely… You would not be lonely… We…we would have each other, always."

He reached out to brush a strand of hair from

her neck. "It is more than that. I may never be able to make love properly, and certainly not with the frequency a woman of your lush passion deserves. Nor would I even be able to give you the full joys of pleasure that a man can give his woman. You are a flame, Katherine. A burning wonder whom I cannot cruelly hurt with my desires."

"No…no, Alexander. Do not decide for me! Do not try to silence the passion in my heart for you. We will make the best of our situation, and I shall not be unhappy at all," she vowed fiercely.

"Your naïveté is truly remarkable," he murmured icily. "Our…engagement has ended, Katherine."

Her lips opened and then closed soundlessly. A chill trembled through her. "How do you know we cannot be happy together?" she snapped, anger and loss tearing through her, for she could feel his conviction, see that distance growing in his eyes. "You simply decided that we cannot work, without trying. I did not think you a coward!"

"Katherine—"

"Are you afraid of living because you are terrified to face pain and loss again? Are you?"

"Do you dare?" he snarled, his eyes flashing a dangerous warning.

A chill danced over her body, removing the earlier satiety of heated arousal. "Yes! I dare because I see how you look at me, feel how you touch me. And I can also see that you are afraid of reaching for me. But I am meeting you halfway, my darling. I will come in even further if you'll but open your arms."

He flinched, his eyes darkening with shadows and emotions she feared she could not pierce. It scared her that even at this moment, it was as if she did not know him, that there were so many complexities to this man, it would take a lifetime for her to unravel, understand, and accept them. She feared that perhaps she was too limited in her understanding of pain and tragedy to comprehend his demons.

"And when you travel the world, exploring Italy, France, Egypt, the places and distant horizons in your hearts, will you do it with a man in a wheeled chair?"

"Yes!"

"Liar," he snapped.

"Do you doubt the feelings that have grown down to my very soul for you?"

"They will not last."

"Do not presume to judge the strength and honor of my character." Her voice broke, and to her astonishment, her eyes were welling. She had stopped dreaming of children and a husband so very long ago. She had known such things were not meant for her, not when she had her mother and sisters to protect and ensure they had a bright future.

But from the night she'd danced with the duke, something unfathomable had pierced that acceptance. She had hoped again for the dream of love and family, the desire to see the world, or as much of it as she could, which had once been hers. What she hadn't expected but wanted more than anything in the world was the wonder of the man before her. And now it felt as if her heart was being utterly devastated.

"I can make you happy," she breathed out shakily.

"I do not doubt it," he said hoarsely. "Because

you already do, my Katherine. You already do."

She reached between them and pressed the flat of her palm against his chest, right above his heart. She could feel its beat drumming fast and hard beneath her touch, and his chest was moving rapidly.

"Let me love you," she whispered against the pulse fluttering madly at his throat before biting down hard.

The words fell into the space between them. She leaned back and met his stare. He looked helpless, hungry, and before he could protest, she shifted in his lap so her legs spread open over his thighs. The man looked so shocked, she almost laughed, but only a hoarse, choked sob escaped her. He inhaled sharply as she rolled against him.

"What the hell are you doing?" he demanded, gripping her hips as if he would shove her from his lap.

Nothing was clear to her at this moment. It was all an irrational cry in her heart, but with unshakable certainty, she felt that with touches and kisses and whatever it was that men and women did to make babies, she could show him all could be well. "Impudence has many wicked forms, you know," she breathed and took his lips in an open-mouthed kiss.

Kitty poured all the feelings in her soul for him into the embrace, licking and biting on his bottom lip and then soothing the sting. She was so lost in him already. With a moan, his lips parted, the hands gripping her hips slipped around to her buttocks and grasped her. It was her turn to sigh, to shiver, and to slide her tongue against his. The hands gripping her buttocks clenched harder, tugging her close and rocking her onto the hardness beneath her.

Kitty cried into his kiss, feeling all sense of control spiraling, caught in a storm of reckless passion and desperation she could not touch or explain. She was helpless against the sweeping sensations working through her body. She allowed her fingers to coast over the sleek, powerful muscles of his chest.

There was movement. He'd lifted her, and now she was beneath him, spread wide for his ravishment. There was furious rustling as he shaped her sodden gown and petticoats to his will, pushing them to her waist. Yet they never stopped kissing. The air felt charged, throbbing with erotic sounds and scents. They broke apart, panting, and she stared into the beauty of his blue eyes.

Love, affection, respect.

"With you I do not know who I am. I feel so much for you, my Katherine, and I do not want to hide it," he said, holding her gaze with infinite tenderness and that flaming adoration.

She saw it so clearly, and with trembling hands, she touched his lips. He reached between them, his knuckles brushing against her wet sex.

Kitty's moan echoed in the conservatory.

And he did it again, rubbing his knuckles over the aching folds of her sex. Kitty had never dreamed any touch there could feel that wonderful. His fingers glided up to her nub and rubbed. She screamed, hips jerking at the terrible lash of ecstasy. A large bluntness pressed against her entrance, and he pushed. The pressure felt enormous and decidedly unpleasant. Her breath gasped from her at the burning sensation, then the feeling vanished.

Alexander rolled from her, falling to the cold floor of the conservatory, his expression twisted with agony. For one bleak, horrifying moment, she froze. She had never seen such pain, and the very sight of it on his beloved face nearly undid her. He gasped as another twinge of agony shot through him. Kitty pushed to her knees and knelt beside him. Fear iced through her as his body jerked and spasmed with violent force. She held him, afraid to release him, for his head would knock against the hard stone floor.

She grabbed a cushion from the chaise longue and pressed it beneath his head. But his convulsion dislodged it again. He stilled, a groan rumbling from his chest, sheens of sweat on his body.

"My back," he groaned harshly. "Something is wrong."

Kitty was cold and shaking with a frightened knot twisting in the pit of her stomach. "I'll go for help," she said, gently easing away and hurriedly fixing her wet clothes to some semblance of decency.

Then she ran from the conservatory.

CHAPTER TWENTY

"Get that goddamn leech off me," Alexander snarled, his eyes snapping open, an unbearable fire tormenting his lower back. He grabbed the slimy creatures sucking at his chest and flung them away from him. The pain pummeling his body was a ravaging force and reminded him of the agony in the early days of his healing.

"Your Grace!" Dr. Monroe cried, quickly pulling away the rest of the slimy, blood-sucking creatures from his chest. "I believe there is an infection in the blood, and they are needed to assist your recovery! You are feverish and not yourself at the moment."

A hiss slipped from Alexander as pain crowded his thoughts. Sweat coated his skin, and an odd weakness quivered through him. Despising any form of fragility, he pushed to his elbows and shoved the sheets from his body. The billowing dark blue curtains hanging from the four-poster bed served only to increase the heat. With a grunt, he made to move from the bed, and a cold knot of fear iced through his veins. "Why am I not feeling my legs?"

Dr. Grant came forward, his eyes serious and worried. He pushed his spectacles up his nose before answering. "The spasms this time were bad, Your Grace. We fear the constant movement over the last few weeks did more damage than good. The inflammation seems extreme, and...and..."

"And what? Come, man, do not quibble," he snapped.

It was Dr. Monroe who stepped forward. "There is a possibility you may never walk again."

A flash of horror pierced his soul before he buried it under layers and layers of ice, suppressing all emotions. The darkness that had slowly hovered slipped around him, and in its embrace, he found the cold comfort of silence.

For several moments, the only sound in the room was the crackling fireplace and his harsh breathing, before even that faded away as he exerted his will over the raw emotions that could tear him apart if he allowed them to. They watched him, anticipating his reaction perhaps, but he had nothing to give. "I have been told that before," he said flatly. "Provide another prognosis at once."

"Your Grace...your many fractures healing would have always taken years. Inflammation is a recurring problem, and there are theories that when the ligaments and muscles are overly inflamed, it can lead to an infection and irreversible damage to the bones and structures, which have struggled to heal themselves over the years. We... I will summon Dr. Perrott from Edinburgh right away. But I am not hopeful a life out of the bath chair is possible."

"Do not say that," a fierce voice whispered from halfway across the room; then the door was gently closed.

A ripple of awareness pierced through him. *Katherine.* He'd not heard her entrance.

Footsteps echoed, and she appeared in his line of vision, striking in her loveliness. He tried to swing his foot from the bed to stand, but his body did not respond, and it took every ounce of willpower he had built over the years not to bellow his rage, frustration…and fear.

She glared at the doctor, a righteous yet frightened lady given the paleness of her face and the redness of her eyes.

She had been crying. For him.

"Surely you are aware of the manner of man Alexander is," she said. "He *will* walk again. If your words will not be positive, you will leave this chamber!" Her voice cracked, but she lifted her chin in that familiar defiant way of hers.

The doctors stared at her as if she were an unusual creature.

"I beg your pardon," Dr. Monroe said with a stiff upper lip. "And who might you be?"

"Leave me," Alexander commanded, staring at his doctors. "I wish to speak with the lady for a few minutes."

"Your Grace, you are fevered, and we must—"

A wave of anger burned through him. "I will not repeat my request for privacy with Miss Danvers!"

They complied immediately, leaving him alone with Katherine, who watched their departure with an air of anxiety. She whirled to face him. "We will fight this, and I believe with all my heart in your full recovery," she said, her eyes alight with fear and pity. "Please allow me to summon back the doctors to tend—"

The pity sent fury surging though his heart, and the awareness he would have to permanently let her go sliced through him like a poison-tipped blade.

"We?" he said with such lethal softness, she flinched.

She searched his face and firmed her trembling lips. Her chin lifted once more, and her beautiful eyes flashed their defiance. His brave, foolish Katherine then leaned in and brushed the softest comforting kiss along his jaw, scattering tender kisses up and down its rigid curve. "Yes, my darling, *we*."

Her assurance was a hot lance through his heart. He disentangled himself from her soothing embrace and reclined against the headboard. "There is no *we*. My problems, whatever they might be, are my own."

"Do not be a stubborn, boorish—"

"You bore me, Miss Danvers," he said, softly but with cutting precision. "As agreed, the instant my interest wanes, our agreement has ended. Whatever happened in the conservatory was an aberration that is unlikely to ever happen again, for I would never allow it."

He cleared his throat and gripped the bedsheets, bracing against the pain he would cause them both. "Now I will ask you to leave my chambers and prepare to return to London. The rent on the town house there is paid up for a year, and the carriages and horses are yours. I will leave it to you to decide when to inform society the farce of our engagement has ended. But understand me clearly, for I shall not repeat myself. Whatever madness pushed me to blackmail you to stay here has ended."

A raw breath hitched in her throat, and the vulnerability that lined her face shredded through his soul. She held his gaze, her eyes huge and heart-stoppingly delicate, and they filled with tears.

"Come now, what nonsense is this? Tears, Miss

Danvers? We hardly know each other."

The words felt like glass scraping at the inside of his throat.

And he knew if she cried…dear God, if she cried, he would pull her into his arms and consign her to share his damnable fate.

She pressed two fingers to her badly trembling lips. The dark depths of her eyes were reflecting so many emotions, they took his breath. "Alexander… you do not mean what you say. I—"

"I am perfectly lucid, Miss Danvers. This show of emotion is entirely unnecessary and unwelcome," he said in deliberate accents of withering scorn. His voice sounded rough, foreign to his ears.

Katherine stared at him wordlessly. The look of rejection in her eyes was unbearable to witness. That pain unmoored him, made him want to bow his back and scream. But his burdens were never anyone else's to bear, just his alone. That had been his will for more than ten years, and it would continue so.

He wanted to lay the world at her feet; he wanted to know her dreams so they could also be his, and to cage such a wonderful spirit as hers would be a grave sin that he couldn't condone because he loved her, utterly and completely.

Sweet Christ. The awareness was like a honeyed blade, painfully cutting but wonderfully sweet. The agony that stabbed at his chest felt as if a physical knife had pierced him. "You are no longer my captive… Now go!"

She dipped into a mocking curtsy. "Of course. As…as you wish, Your Grace."

Her lips trembled, but a fierce and unwavering

pride shone from eyes washed with tears. She turned away from him and moved brusquely toward the door. But he saw the stiffness in her frame. He almost called her back, begged her to share the darkness that would once again come for him. Alexander could always feel it crashing against his senses, taking the pinprick of light that had been inside him these past few weeks. The door opened soundlessly, and she slipped through like a waif without looking back.

I love you, Katherine. God, I love you.

He bit into his lip until he tasted blood, as he fought the need to shout for her to come back, please. A profound welling of desolation swamped his senses. He allowed it to drown him, taking away the light Katherine had placed in his heart in the form of hope.

. . .

Alexander felt weak and depleted, but blessedly the ravaging heat had lessened, and only a slight throb remained in his lower back. A cool finger brushed against his forehead. "The fever has broken," Penny said softly. A gentle kiss against his cheek elicited a vexed snort from him, and it felt good to hear her laugh.

"Rest. Do not be your stubborn self and move from this bed," she encouraged, and then her presence vanished.

He closed his eyes, taking stock of the various pains and aches within his body.

"He might not walk again."

"We shall perhaps need to operate on him."

"He might need opium for the pain. The diluted bit in laudanum will not do."

The whispers of his doctors echoed while he had thrashed as fever rattled around his head. Alexander grabbed the sheets covering his lower limbs and tossed them aside. He stared at his feet, trying to take stock of the varied sensations running through his body.

An unexplained sense of urgency did not have him tarrying long on that matter. With a groan, Alexander pushed onto his elbows and up, bracing his back against the headboard, and then scanned the room. He tried to remember all that had happened, recalling only the terrible pain that had burned its fiery path along his back, the spasming, and Katherine's cries of alarm.

Katherine.

He sensed a presence in the room but knew it was not her. If it had been Katherine, every part of him would have surged to life. "How long have you been here?"

"More than an hour," his cousin murmured. Indecipherable emotions twisted in his voice and scraped at Alexander.

"I need no expression of pity or remonstrance. I've had enough for the last ten years." His voice cracked like a whip through the room.

For several moments, Eugene made no answer. Then he replied, "I have never pitied you, Alexander. A stronger man I've not had the privilege to know. My only desire is to inform you that you are never alone."

Alexander glanced around the room, a shadow

of discomfort lurking in his mind. Unexpectedly, his heart ached, and a feeling akin to fear settled in his bones. "Where is Miss Danvers?"

A shadow detached itself from the wall, and Eugene stepped from the window where he'd been overlooking the lawns of the northern side of the estate, then made his way over to the bed.

He made no reply, and unease wafted through Alexander. "Where is she?" he demanded.

"A couple of hours ago, she left this room with such haste, it was as if the devil chased her. There were many tears on her face. And in her eyes, I have never witnessed such heartbreak."

You now bore me... Go.

The memory washed over him in an unrelenting wave of unexpected pain. He ruthlessly suppressed the tangled emotions, trying to accept that it was for the best. "I see," he murmured, dropping back against the headboard and lifting his head to stare at the painted ceiling of his chamber.

The cold insouciance that had normally cloaked his emotions seemed impossible to find. His heart pounded a desperate, furious rhythm, and he held the sheets in a tight fist which gripped, struggling against the feelings hammering at his heart. Silence. Loneliness. The empty spaces where he could always find solace were filled with jangled, complex sensations he did not understand for having never endured them before.

"I have only one question, then I shall take myself to the library, where I will drink and read while trying to pretend you have not foolishly given up on your only chance of happiness."

Eugene sounded angry, and Alexander lowered his head and considered him through hooded eyes. "Ask your question and then leave me be!"

"Do you love her?"

More than I thought possible.

Yet he could not bear to say it aloud lest the loss became unbearable. "I like her," he said gruffly, scrubbing a hand over his face. "I hold her in considerable affection."

"*I* like her," Eugene snapped. "I do not stare at her like a hungry wolf desperate for a taste."

Alexander tried to sit up farther to relieve the uncomfortable ache in his back. He dragged himself weakly toward the mound of pillows and cushions in the center of the overly large bed. With a savage curse, he tumbled back onto the bed, hating how he felt so weakened. It had taken so much to be self-sufficient, and to be reduced so piteously again filled him with a fury unlike any other he had known.

Yet there was no piercing sense of loss or pain at his misfortune.

Alexander could not afford to repeat the dark days of his past. The echoing despair tried to creep up on him. He closed his eyes. Fought against it. *Never that*, he vowed. He would never be that man again. Even if it meant he had lost the use of his legs forever.

But there was an awful pain eating at his chest. All that was reserved for Katherine.

"I've answered you, Eugene; now leave me be."

His cousin scowled. "It has been a couple of hours since you callously ordered her away from your life. The last time I checked, the carriage was being prepared for the four-day journey to London."

Those words propelled Alexander from the bed with a strength he'd not thought he possessed. He grabbed his stick resting by the headboard and tried to stand, but his legs would not cooperate with his desperate intentions. A fire rippled along his back, and a hoarse groan escaped Alexander. *Sweet mercy*. Sweat popped along his forehead, and for a moment he wondered if the fever had returned.

He stepped forward and toppled. Eugene lunged, caught him, and assisted him into his wheeled chair.

"I must find her, Eugene." What he would say, he had no notion. Alexander couldn't explain the sensations sweeping through him, knowing only he must go to her. They could not part with such hurt between them. "I cannot let her leave with bitterness between us. We must remain friends at least." That way he would still have a part of her always.

"What did you do to place such heartbreak in her eyes?"

Alexander turned the wheel of his chair toward the door. "She is a flame I will not out," he said, unable to render any more explanation.

Eugene seemed to understand, for the man sighed after closing his eyes briefly. "You are very disheveled. Let me summon your valet and—"

"No. Take me to her." Without waiting for his cousin's assistance, he spun the wheel of his bath chair and pushed himself toward the door and out into the hallway. At the top of the stairs, he grabbed the railing and, with a grunt, hauled himself to his feet. He took one step, then another, and another before he crumpled.

His manservant was hurrying up the stairs, his face creased in worry. Once he reached him, Hoyt assisted him up and back in the chair. Then the man deftly maneuvered him down the broad staircase with thumps and grunts.

"Take me to Miss Danvers," he ordered.

Hoyt's face lit with approval, and Alexander did not have the care to inform him that he meddled and assumed wrong. The man pushed him with impressive speed down the large hallway toward the front door. The butler wrenched it open, and Alexander wheeled himself over the threshold, staring at the departing carriage that had nearly reached the end of the mile-long driveway.

"Should I summon another carriage for you to follow, Your Grace?" Hoyt asked, his tone hopeful and anxious.

Alexander made no reply, staring at the coach until it disappeared from view down the rough roads that would take her back to London. Probably once back in town, Katherine would find that she went on quite happily without him. Perhaps she would discover her feelings for him were not love but merely a passing fancy, an infatuation. Then the pain he'd seen in her eyes would lessen, and she would smile that winsome smile of hers again.

Yet such justifications did not dull the hunger and desperate love that had grown in his heart by the minute for Katherine Danvers.

I cannot let her go.

He closed his eyes in defeat, knowing he had even less to offer her now than he had a few weeks ago. Then, he could be on his feet for a few hours.

Now…he glanced down at his bare toes, a silent snarl covering the edges of his lips.

"Take me to my room." The moment of madness had passed, and rationality had returned.

Farewell, Miss Danvers.

• • •

The evening sun burned low in the sky, slowly slipping behind the mountains in the distance. The cool breeze sweeping across the land, the twinkle of sunset glistening atop the lake, the fresh, crisp scent of the air did not bring the joy to which Alexander had been accustomed. A painful, aching tightness lingered inside him, and at the crest of each dawn, that lingering torment only increased its intensity.

It was a little more than a week since Kitty Danvers had left Scotland and his life. The bleakness he endured had nothing to do with the fact that he had not left his wheeled chair in the wretched nine days she had been gone or because it would take weeks, possibly months to regain his ability of leaving it for even a short time without severe discomfort. He had pushed himself for too long because he had desired the sense of normalcy he had dreamed of in her presence.

But his body would heal, his strength was returning, and eventually he would find himself out of the chair again, even if it was only an hour or two each day.

This emptiness was all because of his stupidity in pushing her away.

Nothing stirred within his gut any longer. No

burst of heat, no fleeting flash of pleasure. He had consulted a few days' past with the more open-minded Dr. Grant, who believed the re-inflammation of the bone might have had a deleterious impact on his awakening manhood. The man had once again suggested self-ministration, but Alexander had not attempted to try.

The soft crunch of footfalls echoed, and Penny came up beside him. Dressed in a red carriage dress with a matching bonnet, she looked the epitome of an elegant young lady. The picture was ruined by the small piglet clutched lovingly in her arms.

There had been a strain between them, for he had arranged for her to travel to London. The season was quickly drawing to an end, but there were enough weeks for her to take to society and charm them with her lovely manners. He was confident of her grace, poise, and wit. He trusted his godmother to take care of his sister. Her inheritance of sixty thousand pounds and her dark beauty would see many gentlemen flocking to court her, and Alexander expected the man she decided on would be understanding of her quaintness and sometimes unchecked opinion.

"There are those who will think you are eccentric if you take…piggy with you," he said, staring out at the lake.

Penny sniffed. "I do not care what others think; you've taught me that." She shook her head, wiping moisture from her eyes. "I do not want to go, Alexander."

"You cannot remain buried here in Scotland. You are seventeen. It is time to meet other young ladies of your society. Expand your wings and mind."

"And dancing at balls will do that?" she demanded scathingly. "I doubt it!"

"What are you afraid of?"

Her breath hitched, and her calm facade crumpled. "Leaving you here...to be alone."

His heart cracked. "I am never alone. The memories are always with me."

She shook her head, her eyes fixed anxiously on his face. "Memories are fleeting and insubstantial."

"They are real enough."

"I can barely recall Mamma's face or her scent or her laughter. I remember through you. The stories you tell me are how I keep them alive. Sometimes...I fear if I leave here, I will forget them entirely." She cast him a sideways glance, her eyes large and wounded. "Do you fear that, too...that if you leave, all memories of our parents will vanish as ashes do in the wind?"

"I do not," he said gruffly. "Leaving here and living your life is not a disservice to their memory. That is what Mother and Father would want. For you to have a season or two. Marry well, have a family of your own."

Her chin lifted stubbornly. "And if I have other dreams?"

Alexander smiled. "Such as?"

She tucked a loose wisp of hair behind her ears. "What...what if I want to travel the world, too? Visit the great sights?"

"Then I'll support you, always."

"I'm the daughter of a duke. Society will have different expectations of me."

Her earlier confidence had dimmed, and she now sounded young and uncertain.

"Hang society. You are the sister of a duke, and I will support you in any endeavor. Within reason, of course."

Penny chuckled. "I'll not do anything to embarrass you."

"That I believe is impossible. You are planning to carry the pig to town." They remained silent for several moments and stared at the beauty of the lake and the lowering sun. "I'll visit you in London," he murmured.

She hurried to stand in front of him, blocking his view of the starlings gliding over the lake and dipping low with such swift grace to fish.

"Do you promise it?" she whispered fiercely.

"When I am strong enough. I will need to be there to warn any rakes and libertines away with the point of my rapier."

She smiled, relief glowing in her eyes. There was the slightest hesitation before she asked, "And what of Miss Danvers?"

"I am certain you will be guaranteed to encounter her."

"And the engagement?"

"It is over."

Penny searched his face. "Will you make an announcement that she is no longer your affianced?"

Why did his heart twist in such a violent manner? "If I do, Miss Danvers's reputation will be tarnished. It is perhaps better to allow the lady to do the jilting."

She sighed, then leaned in and kissed his cheek.

"I love you."

When she made to straighten, he grasped her by the shoulder and hugged her close. "I love you, too. Now go and finish your packing. All shall be well."

He released her, and she nodded but did not attempt to leave.

"Do you love her?" she whispered. "Miss Danvers…do you love her?"

A pounding ache darted through his chest and seemed to split him open from the inside. The feeling was so unexpected and visceral, he rubbed at his chest. "What do you know of love?"

She thought on this for a moment and then replied, "I believe I saw it when you smiled at Miss Danvers. And you did, quite a lot. In unguarded moments when you thought no one observed you, or perhaps it was as if you could not help yourself. She would be walking in the hallway, and you would falter, as if arrested…more like spellbound…and you would stare and then smile. You did this several times a day, as if seeing her was the only thing you needed to brighten your mood. I do hope that is love."

Christ. He scrubbed a hand over his face. "Penny…"

"I am filled with vanity of self, I think," she continued as if he had not spoken. "Oftentimes I wonder if I had been hurt as you had, broken bones and dreams, scarred with no hope of a normal life, could I have borne it? There was a time when you wanted to give up, Alexander. I recall slipping into your rooms against express orders to stay away. There was a sweet, awful scent in the smoke that surrounded you. Opium…the servants would whisper. The air would reek of it, and at times I would stray from my room and hear your bellows of anguish and loss. Then one day I crawled onto your bed, slipped my hands into yours, and told you I needed you."

She swiped at the tears running down her cheeks. "Do you remember, brother?"

"I do, Penny." That had been the first ray of light to pierce his darkness and pain.

"I want you to be *happy*. I want you to love and be loved in return. I might not know much about romantic attachments, but Kitty...whenever she looked at you, I felt almost embarrassed at the yearning in her eyes. Her sentiments were wholly returned, and you would be a damn fool if you let her go." She flushed. "I'll not apologize for cursing. The brother I know and love does not feel fear or act foolishly. Please do not do so now...not when I can tell she is so very precious to you."

Then she stood and walked away.

Alexander turned the wheel of his chair and watched her go. How much she had grown up over those ten years, maturing into a perceptive and intelligent young lady.

Katherine was precious to him, and he'd had to stop denying it the first night he slept in the castle knowing she was no longer resting herself in the east wing. That night he hadn't slept. Or the next night. Exhaustion had claimed his mind and body on the fourth night of prowling the corridors of the west wing, wheeling his chair over and over down the hallway, unable to stop the strange tempest brewing in his gut.

The crunch of boots had him shifting toward the

direction of the lake. He spied Eugene, and the man had an expression of someone tormented.

"You heard the conversation with Penny," Alexander murmured.

His cousin glanced toward the mountains and skyline for several moments. "I'd planned when in town to call upon Miss Danvers in the hopes she might consider me. But now... You *love* her. I saw your face when Penny spoke just now, Alexander, and I've never seen such hunger and need on another before. I entreat you. Share with me."

The silence stretched, and then he spoke. "To have Miss Danvers's uncompromising trust and friendship, to see her smile every day for the rest of my miserable life would be worth anything," he snarled, slapping a hand over his forehead, hating that tears pricked at his eyes. He was a goddamn duke. A man who had endured hell and had been reshaped with an iron will that had never failed him. Tears were not for the likes of him, yet his throat burned.

"I have often wondered what it would be like to be not quite so alone in the nights, to have a wife, a friend...a lover to confide my sorrows, expectations, and joys. I've struggled against falling in love with her, for the unsuitability of our match was quite evident to me. Yet the feelings she has roused in my heart are unalterable. Sometimes fear clutches at my heart when I think how unlikely our meeting was. What if Miss Danvers had chosen another man to pretend to be her fiancé? What if she had taken a different path?" Alexander murmured roughly. "I would have missed her, Eugene. I would have missed knowing her laughter, her brightness, the taste and feel of her. I would have missed knowing that happiness is still possible."

"Then for Christ's sake, man, *how* do you bear letting her go?"

"I do not bear it," he said gruffly. "The world feels dark without her. And I hurt her…when she is so precious to me."

An overwhelming panic crawled through Alexander's senses, jerking his heart in a manner never before experienced. *What a damn fool I am.* She was something rare and unbelievable, and he had thoughtlessly lost her.

For so many years, he had been alone. Those who had tried to connect with him, he'd declined their help, seeing it as a lowering weakness. He'd refused to bow to his infirmities and had shrouded himself in cold distance from it all—empathy, curiosity, love, and understanding. All the things Katherine offered. And more: her smiles, her kindness, and her breathtaking acceptance of all he was.

Alexander wasn't a beast, but nor was he a beauty.

And she seemed to like him despite all of it.

But where to start when he had been so foolish… where to start when he could not give her more than his title?

Anything but silence…a deep stillness inside him whispered.

And Alexander hoped he could start with a letter and a prayer.

CHAPTER TWENTY-ONE

Kitty's return to town a few days after she had departed Alexander's estate was unremarkable. Other than a few newssheet articles speculating if she had run off to marry the duke in secret, there had been little other mention of her almost three weeks' absence. Her family appeared to have been very well without her, and her sisters happily spent hours that evening informing her of their generous reception within society. They'd received more invitations to balls, picnics, and routs over the last few weeks than during the three years Kitty had been out in the *ton*.

A Miss Laura Powell, a very charming young lady of six and twenty with brisk common sense, was now employed as a governess for Henrietta. Miss Powell and her charge got on rather famously, and Henrietta seemed to take to her lessons with pleasure, a feat Kitty had never been able to accomplish. Normally Henrietta tolerated her lessons in Latin, geography, and literature with a stoicism reserved for a more mature child. Now she hummed with eagerness to begin her daily lessons with Miss Powell.

Another sum to add to the growing bill she would eventually owe the duke. A painful breath sawed from Kitty at the thought of Alexander. She felt so cold and empty, her heart destroyed. His words tormented her and cut daily into her like a poison-tipped knife.

Kitty was aware of a strange numbness somewhere deep inside. In the nights as she lay in the dark thinking of him, that numbness would thaw, and she'd rage, resenting him with such passion, she trembled. Then that rage would switch so fast to deep yearning, tears would come to her eyes. Kitty hated the conflicting emotions, for she knew the duke did not spare her a thought. For the sake of her family, she had to put on a serene countenance and try to exist as if all were well.

Alexander's godmother, Lady Darling, had enveloped Kitty's sisters under her bosom with encouraging glee, and after spending the better part of the afternoon taking tea with Lady Darling and her mamma in the drawing room, Kitty suspected the countess had relished the challenge of making society fall in love with the poorly received Danvers girls. Kitty also believed the entire mission had enlivened the countess's boredom.

"So tell us, my dear, how is my godson?" Countess Darling asked, taking a sip of tea and peering over the rim at Kitty with a searching stare.

Her mouth dried, and she shot her mother a disconcerted glance. "Mamma?"

Fortifying herself with a deep breath, her mother replied, "Lady Darling...Sophia and I have become dear friends, Kitty. I told her the truth. That you were in Scotland with the duke and not in Derbyshire. You've been home several days now, and I can see the pain in your eyes. We want to help in any way that we can."

Kitty bit back her groan and tried to affect an unconcerned mien, but nonetheless she flushed.

Gripping the delicate china teapot, she poured more tea into a cup, frantically gathering her thoughts on what ought to be a proper response.

Lady Darling smiled. "You may rest assured of my confidences, dear. My heart was awfully glad to hear you were with Alexander in that ghastly remote place of his. I have despaired for him for so many years. When news of the engagement swept through society, I was perturbed and believed it another baseless rumor. There have been so many over the years, you know. Your mother reassured me greatly on the legitimacy of the attachment. Please do not take her to task for telling me."

The countess set down her teacup, arranged the skirts of her dress in a more conformable fashion, and pinned Kitty with an assessing stare. "Now, Katherine, why are you here?"

Because he sent me away, with cruel words and emotionless eyes. Because I was simply a plaything to him and an utter fool to my own heart.

Because he does not love me.

The memory of it all churned her stomach. She had reacted like a silly miss, rushing from his chamber with tears blinding her vision. What had she really expected from a man who had never promised any tender sentiments?

She had packed hastily and had said her good-byes to Mr. Collins and an upset Penny, who had tried to convince Kitty to stay. The servants had been somber, the housekeeper's eyes had been suspiciously bright, and a few of the maids had sniffled. The butler had bravely asked if she would return. Kitty had made no promise, her heart an aching mess as he'd loaded her two valises and small portmanteau into the carriage and departed from the duke.

You bore me… Now go.

"Well, my dear?" the countess prompted.

"I beg your pardon, my lady, but this is my home." *Temporarily*. She had to find other accommodations very soon. They could no longer live off the duke's generosity, not when the sum she owed was already so very astronomical. Not when the hopes he would fall in love with her silly self had been dashed so painfully. "And the duke requested I return to town."

Her mother and the countess both looked utterly aghast.

"Is…" The countess cleared her throat, her pale blue eyes glowing with worry. "Is the engagement off? Is that why you have returned?"

Another silence fell, broken only by the ticking of the large clock on the mantelpiece.

"The duke and I had no conversation regarding our…affianced state before I left McMullen Castle," she answered with great discomfort, and not for the first time wondering if she should have stayed and fought more. But for what? To be slapped with a more humiliating truth, that she had been the only one to lose her heart to the reckless passion that had burned between them?

"Was it that you were compromised?" Lady Darling asked archly, anger flashing in her eyes.

It was as if the countess resented Kitty for leaving the duke. Her heart quaked as wicked memories seared her. She could still taste his kiss on her lips, still feel the unfamiliar ache between her thighs. Kitty's composure began to desert her, and her entire body blushed red.

The countess's eyes widened, and her mother appeared faint.

"Katherine!" Mamma cried in reproach, fanning herself vigorously with a delicate blue and silver hand-painted fan. Yet she shared a slyly triumphant glance with the countess before a facade of motherly concern settled on her face.

"My godson took liberties? I didn't think he had it in him," Lady Darling mused softly.

"I declared nothing of the sort," Kitty retorted, lifting her chin. "My presence at McMullen Castle was improper and scandalous. I am home now, thankfully without society knowing where I have been unchaperoned. If you require any more information as to the state of my attachment to Alex… to His Grace, please confer with him, Lady Darling." Her chin wobbled and she fought the impossible tears that smarted her eyes. "If you will excuse me, I have a headache. I shall retire to my chambers."

Kitty stood, dipped into a slight curtsy, and hurried from the drawing room, up the stairs, and into her chamber. Once there, she flung herself on the bed and buried her face into the softness of the pillow. A cozy fire crackled on the hearth, warming the spacious bedchamber, yet there was a chill in her bones that she felt would never depart.

She curled into the thick blankets and tried to rest. Her lids closed and her breathing evened out. Kitty soon found herself plagued by another malady—dreams of the duke, or more like a collage of every tender and wicked moment they had shared.

"Why must you torment me when you are

indifferent!" she cried into the pillow. With a raw sob, she pushed from the bed and sat at the very edge of it, gripping the sheets between her fingers.

A knock sounded on the door, and before Kitty answered, it was pushed open, and Anna barreled into the room. She appeared frazzled, almost frightened. Her bonnet was squashed between her two hands, and grass stains lined the hem of her dress.

Kitty lurched to her feet, her heart pounding. "Anna, what has happened?"

"Oh, Kitty," she said, her eyes glistening. "I…I…" Then she laughed and burst into tears.

"Do not torment me so with your silence. Are you hurt?"

"No, far from it." Anna tossed the bonnet onto the chaise longue by the fire and clasped her hands, a radiant smile curving her lips. "William asked me… to marry him!"

William? For a moment Kitty did not understand; then she gasped. "You are engaged to Lord Lynton?"

Anna nodded happily, her corkscrew curls bouncing on her cheek. "He asked me just now on our walk through the park. He will speak to his father tonight and then visit Mamma tomorrow morning. Oh, Kitty, I am a nervous wreck. What if his father should forbid the match because—?"

She hurried over and hugged her sister to her. "Because you are wonderful, charming, exceedingly kind and selfless, and so very pretty with the most amiable manners. You may not have a dowry, Anna, but that does not define the quality of wife you would be. The baron has seen that, and I daresay he fell in love with your incurable romantic nature."

They broke apart laughing.

"Wouldn't Papa have been so proud? You to marry a duke and me to marry a baron, a man whom I love with my whole heart. I daresay if there is a heaven, he is strutting around with his chest puffed with pride."

"I am sure of it," Kitty murmured, then appalled herself by bursting into tears. "Oh, Anna, forgive me!"

Concern darkened her sister's eyes, and she gently led her over to the chaise, where they sat. "No, forgive me for thinking only of my happiness. I noticed last night there was a sadness in your eyes, but I thought to leave it alone until you were ready to confide in me."

"Oh, it is nothing. My nerves are simply over-wrought from all that ghastly traveling. With more rest, I shall be quite fine."

Anna held her hand between hers. "Are we not as close as we once were?" she asked with a worried frown.

Kitty's lips parted, and suddenly she could not bear to utter another falsehood to her sister. "The duke and I are not engaged," she confessed on a rush, closing her eyes.

"No wonder you appear so wretched, after such a public—"

"We were never engaged," she said hoarsely, fresh tears springing to her eyes. "I made it up, and then I went and stupidly fell in love with the man. For you see, I was with him in Scotland and not Derbyshire, and now everything is ruined. But we might be saved because you are engaged, and it might not be so awful once society knows there is no longer an attachment." Then she spent a few minutes telling her sister of the scheme in its entirety.

"I...I...I'm astonished you would sacrifice so much for us," Anna whispered. "I am certain without this mad scheme of yours, William and I would never have met."

And Kitty's heart was glad for it, even if the cost now felt exceedingly heavy. But she could never regret it; she would do it all over again for her family.

"I love you, and Mamma, Henrietta, and Judith," Kitty said softly. "I'm not ashamed for what I did."

"And I daresay you should not be," Anna said with a wobbly smile. "This calls for me to sneak some port from the kitchens or a bottle of wine. For you must tell me everything that happened in Scotland."

And they did just that. Drank a bottle of fine wine, becoming tipsy together as Kitty shared everything with her sister, who listened without condemnation.

• • •

Another week passed since Kitty's return to London, and she had waited in dread for an announcement from the duke to appear in the papers. "*The engagement of Miss Katherine Danvers and His Grace, the Duke of Thornton is invalid.*" That was what she'd expected to read about and she had vowed fiercely to face the scandal with courage.

The only announcement had been the engagement of one Miss Annabelle Danvers and Baron William Lynton in the *Times*, *Gazette*, and *Morning Chronicles*. Of course the more sordid papers had

also run their headlines, speculating on the sudden-
ness of the engagement with lurid and outrageous
suggestions. But nothing had been able to dim the
happiness of her sisters and their mother, and that
was all that mattered to Kitty.

Wedding plans were made with swift economy,
and Anna would marry her love only three weeks
from today at St. George's Hanover Square. Her
gown had already been commissioned, and the mo-
diste worked tirelessly with her team of seamstresses
so it would be ready in time.

Mamma and the girls excitedly chatted about the
type of flowers Anna required for the day and where
she and the baron would honeymoon. The majority
vote was for Italy, and Kitty could not help the ache
that bloomed in her heart whenever she looked upon
her sister's radiance. Then she felt entirely wretched
for even feeling a moment of envy for her happiness.

Excusing herself from the breakfast room and
their lively rowdiness, Kitty headed toward her room
to collect her bonnet and shawl. A long walk to clear
her head and a visit to her friends were well in order
and were sure to help with the awful sadness that
had been plaguing her. In the hallway she paused,
momentarily startled at the exquisite arrangement of
flowers in the footman's hand.

"These arrived for you, Miss Katherine," he said,
walking toward her.

Kitty frowned. "For me and not Anna?"

"Yes, miss. The delivery boy said Miss Katherine
Danvers."

She approached it cautiously, as if expecting one
of the beautiful arrays of yellow roses with one white

in the center to come alive and attack her. Kitty had never received flowers before, and she was entirely uncertain how to feel about the matter. A note was attached, and she plucked it from among the stems with trembling fingers.

Miss Danvers,
I regret I did not ask you of your favorite flowers. I have a particular fondness for the primrose.
Alexander.

Kitty stared at it, astonished. Her heart pounded with uncertainty, for she could not decipher his intentions. The note was decidedly unromantic. There were no expressions of apology or remorse for his hurtful words that had deeply wounded her heart and pride. Why had he sent her flowers? She pressed them to her face and inhaled the fragrance deep into her lungs.

She smiled at the footman. "Thank you, Morton."

With a short bow, he made his way to the servants' staircase. Heading toward the smaller parlor, Kitty placed the flowers on the walnut table by the window. She walked over to the writing desk, withdrew a sheaf of paper, dipped the quill into the inkpot, and scrawled:

Dear Alexander,
I like bluebells and lilacs.
Kitty.

There, it was just as flat and uninspired as his note. Polite, even. Yet she was quite aware she shared a small bit of her that he had not known.

Kitty desperately wanted to ask after his health and recovery, but he had not mentioned it, even knowing she might worry. She sensed he did not want to be defined by his injury or be inundated with sympathy, and she would respect that, though she desperately wanted to know how he fared. Surely Penny or Eugene would have written had Alexander's prognosis worsened.

Kitty added the wafer and summoned a maid to instruct the butler to ensure her letter was posted immediately. And without dwelling for long on the matter, she vowed to visit her friends and not think of the duke at all.

A few days later, three to be precise, another beautiful bouquet of flowers and a small leather-wrapped book arrived for Kitty. Grateful her mother and sisters were at the gardens with Lady Darling, she took them from the butler with a tight smile and hurried to her room. Hating that her fingers trembled and her heart raced with such terrible uncertainty and anticipation, she closed the door behind her and leaned against it for several seconds.

Kitty ambled over to the padded window seat and opened the note.

Dear Katherine,
I enjoy the rain, and I oftentimes stand at the edge of the cliff that abuts my estate and allow its fierceness to pound against my skin. I hope you enjoy this volume of poetry by John Donne.
Alexander.

"You wretched man!" she cried. Kitty hardly knew what to make of it, but anger started to brew in her heart. Why did he toy with her emotions so cruelly? Nothing was resolved between them, yet he sent her flowers and ridiculous notes…ones that she read over and over until their papers were a wrinkled mess.

A most wonderful bouquet of flowers, this time bluebells and lilacs, arrived with another of his infuriating letters.

Dear Katherine,
I enjoy the color blue. It feels warm. It sounds warm. And reminds me of your smile.
Alexander.

Several days passed, and then at least eight letters came in a packet, as if he had written one daily but sent them together. She couldn't help realizing that she had claimed to the *ton* when she had spun her falsehood that he had wooed her through letters and poems.

Are you wooing me, Alexander? she silently demanded.

Slowly, with shaking fingers and a pounding heart, she untied the blue ribbon holding them together and read the first letter.

Dear Katherine,
I miss our friendship, and I find myself wheeling out to our tree to simply sit and remember our foolish antics. I've been cloud watching, and I am astonished to say I noticed a twenty-set orchestra playing in the skies recently. I find that I miss your laughter and

your smile. I daresay I even miss your impudence.
    Alexander.

She read it twice before folding it closed and then opening another.

Dear Katherine,
    Last night I dreamed of you. We danced and danced under the glittering candlelight in a large ballroom. We were the only people there, and you were resplendent. My heart wept when I woke and realized it was but a dream.
    Alexander.

Dearest Katherine,

Her breath hitched at the change in his salutations. Somehow the duke now greeting her with a "dearest" felt sweeter…gentler, as if he had said "my beloved."

She lowered her gaze to the body of the letter.

Last night I wished upon a star that streaked through the cold night air. Only my friendship with you could have inspired such foolhardiness.
    Alexander.

Dearest Katherine,
    Penny gifted me with a piglet today. I am not entirely sure why she believed this to be an appropriate gift, but my piglet, so adorably named "Hattie," reminds me of you.
    Alexander.

That letter had made her splutter with outrage and laughter; then she had wept. Other times he wrote her lengthy letters that made no promises and revealed nothing, but she read the words several times.

Then she had replied:

Dearest Alexander,
I pondered this for a bit, and I am at a loss as to how Hattie brings me to mind.
Katherine.

Her response was quite succinct, but she could not bear the notion of showing her heart any more when he did not speak of love. His reply had come so swiftly, she imagined he had several footmen waiting with horses, always prepared to send his response. The very idea made her heart ache but brought a smile to her lips.

Dearest Katherine,
You share a similar impudence. Hattie does not realize she is a piglet and insists on sleeping in my bed.
Alexander.

Then the shortest one, which had robbed her of breath for the longest time.

Dearest Katherine,
I am so sorry.
Alexander.

She tried to occupy her days by attending a few

routs, the museums, and art galleries with her mother
and Lady Darling, but Kitty grew more wretched
and despondent. Her family noted her liveliness
was dimmed and wondered too often to her if she
were ill. Kitty tried to rally her spirits and had even
attended a ball on the previous night.

She missed him so much that it was like a physical ache. Ridiculous, of course, for surely he did not
endure a similar yearning. She had been a fleeting interest, one that bored him in too quick a time. Kitty
had simply been silly enough to fall so deeply in
love with his cynical charm and wickedness.

Except…why had he sent her flowers and letters
if he thought of her no more? Crossly she prayed
she haunted his dreams and every waking moment,
for he surely vexed her spirit in all her sweet, heated
memories.

The yearning to be with him sometimes felt
as if it would tear her apart from the inside out
until there was nothing left to give. Kitty could not
understand it. Was this really love? This aching
need to see, touch, and kiss him? To her shame and
frustration, she sobbed into her pillows at night,
hating that he had given up on the possibility of their
being together so easily.

*Why do you send me flowers and those madden-
ing notes?* She would not demand an explanation.
And Kitty knew it was her pride that prevented her
inquiry, but he had wounded her heart and dignity in
a manner she had not forgiven, even if she loved him
still.

She could not explain the savage pain tearing
through her heart, though she did her best to be

cheerful for her mother and sisters. Kitty skillfully deflected each query about the duke and when he would appear again within society.

A few days later, Kitty stood in a sea of people at Lady Hadleigh's midnight ball, feeling quite determined to have some fun. She had dressed in one of her best gowns, a dark yellow satin one draped with an overskirt of ivory lace with matching kid elbow gloves. Her hair had been caught in a simple but quite elegant chignon with tendrils artfully arranged to brush against her cheeks. Kitty had received several admiring glances from some of the most sought-after bachelors of the season, but no excitement had filled her at the attention.

To her alarm, the Marquess of Sands requested her hand in a dance. To be asked to dance by a man of his rank and fortune added to any female's consequence, and his attentions would convince society further that her family was not to be overlooked. Yet Kitty could not imagine herself in his arms, even fleetingly, when it was Alexander she dreamed of every day.

"I thank you for the honor, my lord, but it is not my desire to dance this evening."

His expression was inscrutable, and for a moment he said nothing. The marquess was a terribly handsome man with his raven-black hair and eyes as dark as the night itself. That uncomfortable penetrating gaze cut to Charlotte, who stood on the sidelines tapping her feet with a wistful look on her face as she observed the current dancers. For a moment his mask slipped, and the wild, haunting hunger that settled over his face like a second skin rendered Kitty's mouth dry.

It took a few moments before she was able to regain some measure of composure. Lord Sands held a similar regard for Charlotte as she had for him.

"Perhaps you might show your favor to Miss Nelson instead," she urged softly, not sure if her friend would be grateful or angry for Kitty's meddling.

Those obsidian eyes clashed with hers once more, and a peculiar smile curved his lips. "A pity you will not dance, Miss Danvers. I bid you good night." Then, after offering a clipped bow, the man melted into the crowd.

Charlotte watched his departure, her affection evident for the world to mock and speculate on.

Devil take it all.

Kitty wanted to curse love and the burden it had on the heart. Charlotte's father had passed with a cloud of debt hanging over both her and her dear mamma's head. She needed to make a well-connected match, but no gentleman of rank or fortune would consider a poor wallflower when so many heiresses peppered the *ton*. Charlotte's mamma had spent the last of her juncture this season, in hopes her daughter would make a match that would save them.

Kitty snagged a glass of champagne from a passing footman and made her way over to Charlotte. A smile lit her entire features, her blue eyes sparkled with welcome, and her unique prettiness struck Kitty. Charlotte's alabaster skin mottled easily under the rays of the sun, and she had the blackest hair Kitty had ever seen on another. Many times they had laughingly called her Snow White, drawing an undeserved comparison to the Grimm brothers' fairy tale.

"Oh, Kitty, I am frightfully bored," Charlotte said by way of greeting.

"Perhaps we are getting old," Kitty teased.

Her friend rolled her eyes in an unladylike fashion. "Why yes, we are decrepit at three and twenty."

They shared a laugh.

"I have decided on a path for my future," Charlotte murmured unexpectedly.

Kitty looped their hands together and directed them toward the upper bower's balcony for privacy. Though with the crush and loud laughter and facile chattering, there was little chance of being overheard as it was.

"I… The marquess is seeking a mistress, and I mean to apply for the position."

"Charlotte!"

She looked a little conscience-stricken. "I have few choices remaining open to me now," she said after a moment's reflection. "I've no offers but indecent proposals."

"This is far wickeder than even what I conceived to rescue my family!" Kitty said, considerably intrigued.

That set her incorrigible friend's eyes dancing devilishly. "He wants me desperately, you know… and seems willing to grant me whatever boon I want to allow him to be my protector."

This was said with such wistful yearning, Kitty's heart ached for her friend. "If he desires you so ardently, why does he not offer marriage?"

Charlotte hesitated, coloring a little, and then

said, meeting Kitty's look of inquiry, "It is frightfully complicated, I fear."

Kitty touched her shoulder lightly, knowing of Charlotte's stubbornness once she had decided on a path of action. "I would be remiss if I did not caution you about the scandal and ruin you may find in the marquess's arms."

Kitty saw the stricken look on Charlotte's face, the color ebbing from her cheeks.

She twisted her fingers together and said with ill-concealed difficulty, "There is even worse ruin in poverty."

Kitty found herself unable to utter a word.

"Now, let's speak of other matters," Charlotte said with a small smile.

They chatted amicably for a few minutes before Charlotte pled a headache from the stifling heat of the crush and promised to call upon Kitty in the upcoming week.

She spied her sister coming toward her and waved. Judith ambled over, and not for the first time Kitty admired Judith's peach ball gown with its modest neckline trimmed with delicate and elegant lace. Her blond hair was caught in an array of charming ringlets, and the entwined ribbons did not lend the air of maturity for which she had hoped. While Kitty was in Scotland, their mother, with encouragement from Lady Darling, had allowed Judith to be out, in the hope of improving her matrimonial appeal with the eligible beaux. And tonight Judith appeared just as she was—a young, innocent debutante not yet jaded by dashed expectations and a treacherous heart.

"Oh, isn't the ball simply wonderful! I've had so

many dances, my feet are sore," Judith said with a rueful yet mischievous smile.

"I daresay it is fun," Kitty obligingly replied.

"It is more than that!" Judith cried dramatically, her brown eyes kindling with indignation. "You and Anna never told me balls and soirees were just so splendid." She looked about her with bright-eyed appreciation. "I was asked by my new friend Lady Jane if we are to attend Lady Beadle's masquerade party next week. Jane said it promises to be the most convivial of the season. Wouldn't it be infamous of us not to attend? Oh, please convince Mamma we must go, Kitty!"

"I shall speak with Mamma and Anna," Kitty promised with a light laugh.

"Capital! I shall inform Jane there is a chance I might attend!" her sister cried, delighted, hurrying back to her friend.

The rest of the ball passed in an uninspiring blur for Kitty. She tried her best to smile and laugh when appropriate, but there was a fog clouding every moment of each encounter. Kitty felt breathless with shock to realize it was an awareness that she was inexplicably lonely.

It cleaved at her daily, loneliness, as intense and frustrating as it was unexplainable. Yet she had been for some time, even before she met the duke, and had buried the unwanted frustration behind duty, filling that empty space with a sense of purpose and responsibility for her sisters and mamma.

She did not want to bear it anymore. And so something must be done.

Kitty felt such sorrow to realize Alexander had

felt this aching emptiness for years. He had been lost in loneliness, doubt, and a loss of hope long before she knew him. She recalled the bleakness in his eyes as he had stared at her, no doubt feeling the icy loss of more freedom if he should never walk again.

Do you think me so shallow I can love you only if you are perfect?

Yet that assessment of his character felt wrong. Was he afraid she would be unable to share that hollowness that he said was unending? Her conviction fought with the burning memory of his dismissal.

You bore me, Miss Danvers.

His tone had been flat, but his eyes had been wild and bright with pain...and fear...and perhaps, just perhaps, there had been love.

Oh, what am I to do?

CHAPTER TWENTY-TWO

Dressed in a lime-green day gown, Kitty glided down a curving flight of steps to the main floor. Her friends were all gathered in the drawing room, after insisting on having this month's intrepid meeting at her town house, simply because she had never hosted the Sinful Wallflowers before. Her previous humble abode's location had not been ideal. And Kitty was glad for today's meeting, for she needed their advice and comforting presence.

She entered the drawing room, and lightness entered her heart to see the heads of Ophelia, Maryann, and Fanny bent together as they giggled over pictures in some book.

"I do hope that is not another naughty book snatched from your brother's collection, Maryann," Kitty greeted, closing the door behind her to afford them privacy. She was pleased to see tea, sandwiches, and cakes had already been sent up.

"Charlotte may not make it; her mother has forced her to take a carriage ride with the odious Viscount Mauler," Fanny said crossly, closing the book. "He attempted to take liberties with her on their last outing, and she smacked him with her parasol. I am surprised he is still pursuing her."

"He wants his heir," Ophelia said with a snort of disgust. "The man has been married twice and has seven daughters! I cannot believe Charlotte's mamma is even entertaining the man's pursuit."

"And the viscount is older than her father," Maryann said with a scowl.

"She must be devastated," Kitty said, moving to sit between the girls on the sofa. "I believe she truly admires Lord Sands, and to be forced to marry where her heart does not lie is so cruel! We must help her escape his clutches."

Her passionate outburst had her friends examining her rather closely.

"I can sense we are about to hatch a plan to save dear Charlotte," Maryann said, fixing her glasses firmly on her nose. "But first we need to fix you."

"Me?" She glanced around the room. "And where is Emma?"

"Yes, you," Maryann retorted. "Emma is in Cornwall visiting her aunt who is ill."

"We have seen your despondency," Fanny said archly, artfully passing around tea for everyone. "We would be poor friends if we had not observed the strain in your smile at last night's ball. Now, tell us what happened in Scotland. Ophelia of course told us where you went."

Kitty scowled at her friend, and Ophelia merely gave an inelegant shrug.

"Did you mean to keep it from us?" Maryann asked gently, a vein of hurt in her tone.

A lump formed in Kitty's throat. "Of course not. You are all my dear friends, and I trust you to keep my confidences. I have simply been so wretched!" She took a deep breath and spilled the entire story with the duke, even including details she had not shared with Anna. Such as the fact that Kitty had kissed the duke several times.

"Well, upon my soul, you love him," Fanny gasped, her eyes wide.

"I do, and I hate that I do, for he does not care for me. I have been away from him for a month, and all the odious man does is torment me with notes and flowers but say nothing more!"

"*Love!* You hardly know him, Kitty," Ophelia objected, sounding considerably surprised.

Kitty surged to her feet and started pacing by the windows. "How long does it take to fall endlessly into passion and feel tender sentiments for another? No other has ever held such power to sway my emotions from one extreme manner to the next as the duke. I ache for him, and then I feel such anger, then I cry, and then I laugh when I remember the incredible moments we spent together." She paused and stared at her friends, who returned her regard with an air of astonishment.

"There is something wonderful between us, and it sparks to life from a mere glance and transcends into something so profound at times that I am breathless, unable to believe such feelings for this person could be real. I am certain, so certain that the duke feels it, too! That wretched, odious man!"

Ophelia's eyes widened, and she lowered her teacup and saucer to the table before their sofa. "Your nerves are overset."

Kitty snorted inelegantly and resumed her pacing, wearing the carpet into the floor. A stark emptiness rose inside her like a great swell, threatening to drown her. "With Alexander, I saw…" She choked on the words, tears welling in her eyes.

Maryann stood, ambling over, and touched

Kitty's hands fleetingly, her eyes warm with compassion. "What did you see?"

"Happiness." She closed her eyes, and a tear rolled down her cheek. Kitty swiped it away with anger. "I cannot explain it. I *am* happy with Mamma and my sisters, doing everything I can to help them find their place within society. But since I met the duke, I saw…I saw happiness for *me*—and for him. This hope is unlike any I've ever felt and I daresay will ever experience again. It feels raw, powerful, and fills every part of my heart with a certainty that Alexander is an important part of my life. He is not my life…but he completes it so fully, I know now how empty I've been. I suspect I am his happiness, too, but he will not reach for me. He sends me notes and flowers yet no words of love or commitment. He mocks every emotion I feel in my soul for him by remaining silent!"

"What do the notes say?" Maryann asked.

"They are all simple letters… He misses me… He thinks of me," she said with a note of wonderment. "Things we had not shared in our time at McMullen Castle. But if he wants me to know these things, why is he telling me in this wretched manner with little directions to his regards?"

Fanny also stood and drifted closer. "Perhaps he is afraid."

"Afraid?" Kitty cried, her heart incensed beyond measure. "He is Alexander Masters, Duke of Thornton. What about me can he fear?"

"Of disappointing you, hurting you with his limitations, loving you so much, he would rather set you free than be a burden," Ophelia murmured.

"How absurd. A man as self-assured and

indomitable as Alexander could never think he would be a burden," Kitty said softly.

But then her thoughts drifted to their moments on the lake. *With you I want to share my silence.*

Alexander was a man who had chosen to exile himself from society. And had done so for ten years. Yet he had stepped from his cold, lonely world and braved the scandal sheets and society's overly lurid speculation to meet her. The first such person to interest him…touch him…kiss him in years.

She pressed the tips of her fingers to her lips, remembering the incredible taste and feel of him, the powerful press of his body against hers.

Yet it wasn't those memories that made her throat ache with longing. It was the way he'd teased her, charmed her, brought laughter and happiness to her heart. And it was the way he had made her feel comfortable to speak about her dreams and to be natural without fear of being lambasted for being willful or overly passionate.

He liked her impudence.

And she…she loved him.

"He believes his limitations will be a burden to my happiness when it is so far from the truth. He said…he said he may never be able to love me as a man loves a woman; he may never be able to grant me children. We had an intimate moment, and he got hurt during…during…" She ended on a huff, blushing furiously. "After that, he rejected every offer of comfort and my love. Since then I have been so despondent and unlike myself!"

Her friends were silent at this passionate confession.

"And you want him still?" Fanny asked, searching her expression.

"Yes." That truth she could not hide from, nor did she want to pretend about the affections she felt for Alexander.

Ophelia smiled. "If he'll not come to you, you must go to him."

"And do what?"

"Convince him that you are meant to be together," Maryann said with conviction. "You are fierce and brave and quite inventive. I've never known you to wilt away from any challenge."

Kitty stared at her friend. "He should be the one convincing me! I do not know if I *wish* to sway him. He is the one who sent me away."

"That is foolish pride and fear speaking, Kitty," Fanny whispered. "You are already so certain you and the duke are meant to be. You need no convincing on that matter."

Those softly spoken words pierced her heart deeply. She pressed a hand over her lips. "I would not know what to say."

Ophelia pursed her lips. "Seduce him."

"Seduce him?" Kitty gasped.

"Yes. You said there were intimate moments before he got hurt. Perhaps it is still possible. Charm the duke with kisses and improper touches and show him that there can be normalcy between you two."

Maryann gasped, while Fanny laughed with delighted wickedness. Kitty could only stare at her friends. "What do I know of seduction? And I hardly think *that* might sway Alexander."

Ophelia took a demure sip of her tea, the slow

movement quite at odds with the terribly devilish glint in her eyes. "Men have a reputation of being weak…desperately weak to our kisses, you know. And if the duke truly wants you as much as you want him…I daresay kisses are bound to work."

Maryann flushed and asked, "I gather you speak from some experience?"

Ophelia tossed her dark head. "I have a friend… you may have heard of her—Cosima Wagner."

Kitty eyed Ophelia with new appreciation. Those who had been acquainted with her father knew that he was dotingly fond of her, perhaps to Lady Ophelia's determent. Kitty had no notion her friend was being this naughty. To be friends with a lady rumored to be a courtesan?

"The Prussian princess who is in exile? There is a rumor she is the mistress of that vile gaming hell owner. The one who is always in the paper for his wickedness," Maryann gasped.

To Kitty's shock, a flush ran along Ophelia's cheek.

"Devlin Byrne," she murmured.

"A very made-up name if I ever heard one." Fanny sniffed. "But yes, *that* is the man, and everyone believes the princess and Mr.—"

"They are not lovers!" Ophelia said, a peculiar vulnerability flashing in her eyes before she lowered her lids. "We are friends of sort, Cosima and I. And she is very knowledgeable about men…and what is needed to seduce a gentleman to our way of thinking. She says there are many arts to rousing a man's body. I daresay a woman should know more about it than stuffy old doctors!" She looked away, a full blush engulfing her body at her friends' stare.

Kitty hesitated, at a rare loss for words. Finally, she asked, "You have inquired of this lady how to seduce a man?"

She nodded guiltily, her color deepening. "Yes."

"Ophelia, what have you been doing?" Maryann cried.

Shock blasted through Kitty anew. "For what purpose?" she asked in a dramatically low voice. An indecipherable emotion flashed in her friend's eyes before it was shuttered, and Kitty realized with a good deal of alarm that she was not the only one acting in a wicked and ruinous manner.

"Did we not all promise to be wicked, bold, and unflinching in our desire to secure our happiness?" Ophelia demanded. Yet her voice cracked, and in her eyes, Kitty saw an uncertainty she would not have thought possible in the most daring of her friends.

"We did," Kitty said softly, taking Ophelia's gloved hands between her own.

How marvelous if we should all be guilty of doing something wicked, just for once? It felt like she had asked this question of her friends a lifetime ago. And yet here she was giving up on the promise of a forever kind of love, the kind she had to show Alexander was worth any risk.

"Do you believe she would teach me?"

Ophelia smiled and said obligingly, "If you have the courage to ask, my dear Cosima will tell you whatever you wish to know."

"And am I assured of her discretion?"

"I have been meeting with her for more than two months. No one is aware of our friendship."

Kitty took a steadying breath. "Please introduce me to her. I shall be excessively thankful if you would."

• • •

Alexander closed the book he'd been reading and exited his library. He called for Hoyt, who assisted him to his chamber, another loss of dignity he now accepted he must suffer. Years ago, he had converted a room downstairs to a chamber, finding it arduous to get a bath chair up those stairs, finding it humiliating to be lifted about by his manservant. That had been one of the reasons that had driven him to leave the chair, and he had learned to conquer those damnable stairs on his own terms and had ordered his chamber to be set back upstairs. Once again, now he could not make the stairs without help.

"I am here, Your Grace," Hoyt murmured, appearing by his side. "Let me carry you up." A suggestion he made each time Alexander would ascend.

"No." A reply he would always make.

With a grunt, he heaved himself from the chair. Hoyt hooked one of his shoulders under his arm, and they slowly made the climb. A footman lifted the bath chair and plodded patiently behind them until they reached the landing of the upper floor. Once there, he settled into the chair, glanced at them, and nodded his thanks. Very much used to the ritual and his peculiarities, the footman bowed and returned belowstairs.

Hoyt wheeled Alexander to his room without

speaking. A fireplace crackled merrily in the spacious room, and though Katherine had never entered his private chambers, he scented her lovely and alluring fragrance in the air. His manservant assisted him from the chair and removed his boots, trousers, waistcoat, jacket, and unmentionables before aiding him to slip on a dark blue silk banyan.

He stood by the windows, staring across the vast lands. The sun was down now, and deep purple twilight blanketed the mountains and valleys in stunning splendor.

"Shall I escort you to the bed or the chaise, Your Grace?"

Alexander shifted and faced his manservant. "Leave me with my stick, and I shall make it there tonight."

Hoyt hesitated briefly, then complied. Alexander grasped the walking stick, placing most of his weight on it, and propped his left shoulder on the wall by the windows.

"Shall I ring for a bath?"

"I had one only a few hours past," he murmured drily.

"A brandy, then? Or whiskey?"

Alexander considered his manservant critically. "What are you worried about that you must hover so like a nanny?"

Hoyt's craggy face creased into a scowl. "A nanny, Your Grace?"

"Yes."

His manservant took a steadying breath. "You seem different tonight. You did not eat supper again, and Cook is a mite worried. Shall I tell her to send up a tray?"

"I'll eat a hearty breakfast."

Hoyt nodded, glancing around the space before resting his gaze back to Alexander. "The room smells pleasant."

Alexander arched an incredulous brow. "I am aware you ordered the maids to spray my room with lavender. And the drawing rooms. Music room. And the hallway. Now leave me be!"

The man had the grace to flush, but he made no reply to Alexander's annoyance at their incessant meddling. Hoyt bowed and left the room silently, closing the door behind him, and Alexander released an irritable grunt before smiling.

They hovered around him as if he were a babe, and while it irked him, a peculiar warmth also filled his chest. They did more than just serve him—they cared for him, and for the first time in a long while, he acknowledged his relationship with his staff was more than a master servant exchange.

They, as much as Penny, were his family.

They hadn't given up on him; they had cried when he cried and felt anguish when he did.

Now they felt the loss of his Katherine and did everything within the bounds of propriety to urge him to think of her, and he knew for what they hungered. A mistress of McMullen Castle, a duchess, the pitter-patter of little lords and ladies in the nursery.

Alexander tugged the heavy drapes open even wider and nudged the window up. A biting chill slipped into the room, but he did not tug the pane back down. The sky was overcast, with all the stars hidden, and the weather dreary although they were now slipping into the high point of the summer season.

Katherine was gone, and Eugene and Penny would depart in the morning. Only the memories of family, passion, love, and laughter would linger within Alexander, and he cursed himself a thousand times for not chasing after her, even if he had barely been able to walk.

Most days, he couldn't bear to think of the manner in which he had hurt her. And yet he could think of nothing else. It had been weeks since he had ordered flowers delivered to her daily. Only a simple note had accompanied the blooms, for he had not known what to say, how to express his regret and his uncertainties. A man once lauded as an orator in parliament for his speeches championing the indigent found himself bereft of words.

I am so damn sorry, my darling Katherine seemed inadequate to express the pain and embarrassment he had caused. Her replies were even more succinct than his and bereft of any warmth or sentiments or an inkling of where he stood with her.

And he deserved her insouciance.

He jerked away from the windows and ambled carefully over to his bed. Resting the cane on top of the plush comforter, he climbed onto the bed with a soft groan of relief. He thought of what the doctor had advised and what it might mean if he successfully roused his cock to life.

He might be able to give Katherine a life that was not so empty.

Alexander stared at the Renaissance-painted ceiling for several minutes, clearing his mind from all the doubts that lingered within. He filled his mind with Katherine. Her warm scent, the sweet shyness of her smile that could so easily bloom to that of a wicked vixen. The way she tossed her head when she laughed, that soft, hungry moan she'd made when he had touched his tongue to hers that very first time.

A kiss of heat coasted over him, and he closed his eyes, allowing only Katherine in his mind. He imagined tracing her spine downward to that delicious curve of her buttocks, then upward again, caressing the delicate softness of her bare shoulders, trailing his fingers along her collarbone and over her rosy nipples. His heart jerked, and desire warmed his body.

Alexander gripped his flaccid cock in his palm and slowly rubbed his hand over the length. With each stroke, he pictured Katherine flushed with passion, remembered the hot, sweet taste of her quim on his tongue, felt the tight clasp of her cunny as she had squeezed his fingers. His gut clenched, his heart raced, and a hiss escaped him as urgent need coiled through him. Yet, as expected, his cock remained limp.

He shifted closer to the edge of the bed and reached for the jar of lavender-scented oil on the bedside chest. Bringing it just below his nose, he inhaled deeply, stirring his senses by recalling Katherine's subtle and arousing smell. Alexander pried the lid open and dipped three of his fingers in the oil before stretching to place the open jar on his chest. He allowed the oil to trail between his knuckles down to his palm. Using his oil-slicked hand, he reclaimed his cock once more and began a slow massage.

Alexander stroked from the base of his manhood up to the tip several times to no avail. He tugged and even jerked harshly a few times before he released his manhood, placing his hand across his forehead with a groan of frustration. There was no pain to distract him, yet he could not rouse his body.

His breath puffed harshly in the stillness of the room, and it shocked him utterly to feel tears sting his eyes. With a snarl of frustration and determination, he freed his mind once more and clasped his cock, and after several minutes of trying to rouse himself with chaotic thoughts and images of a well-pleasured Katherine crowding his senses, he accepted defeat.

Alexander acknowledged then that this was the very reason he had waited almost two weeks after Dr. Grant's suggestion of self-ministration to tempt his cock to rise. Fear of failure.

Alexander ached, quite desperately, to bring into existence the future he envisioned with Katherine—traveling the world, making love with her, but most of all, the laughter...the sweet way she smiled, her bold vivacity for life...that would sweep away the emptiness he had lived with for so long.

But more than anything else, he wanted to fulfill her happiness and dreams.

His heart was lost to Katherine Danvers, and every prudent consideration as to why their match would be ill judged scattered like ashes to the winds.

He would go for her...and explain that while she

had his heart, his love—everything else he could give her as a man…as a husband had been lost. The promise of pleasure that had been rekindled had vanished, and it might never be regained. His heart, his title, and his wealth would be hers, but her body would never know the fulfillment of pleasure, and she would not have a child to cradle against her bosom.

You are a flame that has no end, and it would be such a damn pity to see your spark dim…

Words he meant with his entire being. And damn his selfish soul, he could not let her go. He loved her too much. Hungered for her too much.

But once he took her, it was inevitable that burning passion and sweet flame would eventually die. And even knowing that, he closed his eyes, damning himself *and* Katherine, for tomorrow he would prepare to travel to London for her and, if she would have him, never would he let her go.

CHAPTER TWENTY-THREE

Kitty had not supposed a well-rumored courtesan and wicked lady of society would live in one of the newer and far more elegant townhomes in Mayfair. Perhaps Soho or a less respectable part of town she had assumed, to her shame. Nor would she have thought Princess Cosima Wagner to be so beautiful, charming, kind, and just lovely. Ophelia and Kitty had called upon the princess at her invitation that morning and had been escorted by a chirpy young maid to an attached sitting room in her private boudoir, which was lavishly and charmingly decorated in peach and with artful touches of pink.

The petite and lushly curved princess hadn't batted one of her perfect lashes when she had heard the explanation for Kitty's visit. Ophelia had left, granting them privacy, but thankfully the princess hadn't launched into lessons right away, perhaps sensing Kitty's nerves. For the last hour, they sat and spoke of the amusing trivialities of the *ton*. The tension that had held Kitty rigid had passed, and she found herself relaxing and even laughing gaily at Cosima's—as she insisted on being called—amusing recollections of court life in Prussia and how that life compared with England's *ton*. Though many supposed her to be indecent and lascivious, she and her father, a grand duke, were invited to most drawing rooms.

We could be friends, she realized with a sense of

shock, and she fancied Cosima had the same thought at the warm smile they shared.

"I am so very pleased Ophelia has introduced us," said Cosima. "Often she has spoken of her other friends, and I admit my heart has been hungry for more friendship so far away from home."

"I am very glad we could meet as well," Kitty said with a smile. "I've enjoyed our talk." And it saddened her that should society know of this visit, they would seek to cast Kitty and her sisters in a scandalous light, and possibly they would be cut by the very people who had been recently embracing them.

Pushing a strand of her vibrant dark red hair behind her ear, she asked, "Are you ready to tell me what you want to know about making love with a man?"

"That was rather blunt," Kitty said faintly, blushing.

"Seduction often is," the princess murmured. "Though it is the nature of the man that determines how forward we should be. Some men like…even hunger for us ladies to be the seducer…then for others we must be the tasty morsel they entice with kisses and barely-there touches."

In her eyes, there was no judgment, only compassion…and an odd glint of wickedness. Kitty realized Cosima was quite comfortable with her sensuality and perhaps reveled in her rebellious nature.

"You must tell me of this man so I might advise you," she said in her purring accent.

"Not just any man," Kitty murmured, her belly fluttering with anxiety and anticipation. "He is…" And she stopped, lacking the words to describe the complexities of Alexander Masters.

"The Duke of Thornton, society's most enigmatic
recluse," Cosima filled in. "The newssheets speculate
frequently on his life, and there is no one to help
society separate the truth from the lies. I do not
have enough information to inform you of how to
approach him."

Of course the princess would correctly assume it
was the duke. With a heavy sigh, Kitty leaned against
the padded back of the comfortable sofa and tipped
her head to the ceiling. "He had a terrible accident
years ago."

"What manner of accident?"

"I'll not divulge it," Kitty said, quite aware society
was not entirely certain what caused Alexander his
greatest pain. "But it has made him believe he…he
cannot give me the pleasure a man would give his
woman."

There was a speculative pause in which she
shifted her head to stare at the princess, who was observing her rather keenly.

"And you believe otherwise? A man in charge of
his faculties would know more than anyone else if he
can achieve a cockstand."

Kitty's eyes widened. "A cockstand."

The princess seemed to consider just how improper she could be, then answered, "When that part
of him that is in his trousers becomes hard…very
hard. It is called a cockstand or an erection. And
from your terrible blushes, I will guess that you are
familiar with the duke's manhood."

Kitty bit back a groan and bravely said, "To an
extent."

"And was it hard?"

Searing heat burned through her veins when she recalled the thick hardness she had clasped in the conservatory.

"I can see that it was," the princess said with an airy laugh.

"It was not for long," she confessed. "And...and I was not entirely sure about the details of what should have happened between us. One moment I felt such pleasure I believed I would die, and the next my arms were empty and a most awful, unfulfilled ache lingered in my belly. He got hurt and...and our moment was interrupted; I fear we may never get it back."

The princess nodded. "I will impart all that I know...but in good conscience, I must confess I have never been intimate with a man myself. Shocking, I know," she murmured, her eyes twinkling. "At a young age, one of my father's paramours befriended me, and over the years my views have been scandalously enlightened. I am pleased to share all I have heard and seen. But I would be a poor friend to promise it would allow you to achieve what you want from the duke."

She leaned forward and clasped her hands between hers. "Thank you, Cosima. I believe a chance is all I need."

•••

Three days after meeting with Cosima, and with the gleeful aid of Lady Darling, Kitty crossed the border into the lowlands, toward Alexander and the possibility of an even greater heartache.

Early that morning, as she and her lady's maid had left the inn where they had stayed overnight, the day had seemed bright, clear, and without threat of rain. Now the sky was painted in shades of gray, and thunder rumbled quite ominously in the distance. Possibly a portent of how the day would unfold.

Alexander hadn't indicated he was willing to fight for a life together, and here she was traveling once more to his home, without an invitation…

To seduce him.

It all seemed so frightfully silly and scary to her. Touching the mind, body, and heart of a man who seemed to love her but was afraid to allow her into his life presented an impossible task. The easy solution would be to walk away, to take no more risks with her heart, for it was still so horribly bruised and now beat with an uncertain rhythm.

But it went against her nature to give up anything, and this…this was a forever kind of love.

And it is worth fighting for.

The carriage jolted once again over the rocky, uneven ground, and she shifted the curtain and peeked outside. The castle on the horizon seemed an eternity away, but then in a few short minutes, they were rounding the long driveway. The sounds of the steps knocking down reached her, and she took an even breath, struggling for equanimity, before the carriage door opened. She allowed the coachman to assist her down, and as her booted feet touched the graveled driveway, she swayed under the enormity of what she had committed to.

"Are you well, milady?" the man asked with a

concerned crease to his brow.

"I am quite well. You may take the horses to the stables for a rubdown and oats and apples. If you were to go to the kitchens, I am sure you'll be given a meal," she said to the coachman, her lady's maid, and the other two tigers who had journeyed with them.

She breathed deeply of the clean, cool air and gathered her nerves, which shivered with such alarm, it was a wonder she was standing. Kitty had missed the castle, and she envisioned it would be quite easy to call here home when not in London. Her heart pounded, and she clasped her hands tightly together to prevent their trembling. She marched to the front door and lifted the large iron knocker a few times. In the other hand she held onto her small valise, with its scandalous garments, as if her life depended on it.

Kitty waited a few beats and knocked once more. If no one answered, she would make her way to the side entrance to the kitchens, where the servants should be up, stirring the fires and preparing breakfast for His Grace.

The door opened, and the butler stood, impeccably dressed and ready to serve his household for the day.

The man sucked in a surprised breath. "Miss Danvers! Please come inside."

Kitty entered, handing over her shawl, hat, and gloves as she strolled with affected serenity into the castle. She glanced around, a surge of longing piercing her chest. The butler cleared his throat and she glanced up, astonished to see that his eyes were misty.

"How are you, Albert?" she asked warmly, some

of her nerves dissipating.

"Quite well, Miss Danvers."

She peered down the large hallway and then up the winding stairs leading to the west wing.

"His Grace is in the breakfast room."

"I do not wish him to know I am here," she said softly. "Please inform as few servants as possible of my presence."

The butler blinked. "I see."

She glanced about the hallway, then lowered her voice. "How is he, Albert?"

The butler's countenance turned grave. "His Grace hardly sleeps or eats. However, I believe your presence will rectify that."

A raw ache bloomed in her heart. "I have a frightfully bold plan that requires your utmost discretion."

"Anything, Miss Danvers," he said with a small bow. "I am at your disposal."

"If you could take me to a chamber…in the west wing without the duke knowing."

"The west wing?"

She wanted complete privacy from the rest of the household for her scandalous plans, and she blushed when the butler's eyes sharpened with interest.

"I assume there are other chambers ready there and not only the duke's?"

"There are," he murmured.

"Then one of those shall do fine. I require a bath, as I am dusty from travel. An hour from now, I would urge you to create a situation that would allow for the duke to enter my chamber," she said, aware of the furious heat flushing along her entire body.

Yet the butler did not appear censorious but as if he wanted to shout with relief—or glee.

"If you'll come this way with me, Miss Danvers. All that you requested will be provided with *utmost* discretion."

"I knew I might depend on you," said Kitty, swallowing her nerves.

A few minutes later, they made their way down the long hallway of the west wing. The butler opened a door and allowed Kitty to precede him inside. She gasped, staring at one of the most beautifully decorated chambers she had ever seen.

"The duchess's apartments," the butler said from behind. "There is a dressing room, a small sitting room, and an antechamber leading to a larger drawing room."

She whirled around. "I do not think this is the most…appropriate room." Her voice sounded so hoarse to her ears. But she could not escape the feeling she should be in this room only with Alexander's acceptance of her into his life.

Her gaze swung to the connecting door. She walked slowly over to it and grasped the doorknob.

"Does this lead to Alexander's chamber?"

"Yes."

She rested her forehead on the cool surface of the oak door. "Does he have any reason to return here within the hour?"

"No, milady. After breaking his fast, he will retire to his treasure room for an hour. Or perhaps to his study to attend to business and estate correspondence."

There was an odd note in his voice, and she

suspected he withheld information from her. She lifted her head from the door and glanced around at him. "Do you believe you could get the duke to his chamber without arousing his suspicions?"

The butler bowed. "I'll see it done."

"Thank you," she murmured, then opened the door and stepped into the cool, partially darkened room of the duke.

Kitty inhaled deeply, breathing in the subtle masculine scent that seemed infused into the fabric of the room. Bright sunshine peeked from between the slits of dark blue drapes, and she ambled over and drew them open, allowing light into the room. Dropping the small valise on the chaise longue by the window, she stared at the bed, recalling the last time she had been in this room, the pain and fear that had been wrapped tightly around her heart.

She walked to the large four-poster bed, with the dark blue and silver curtains billowing around it. Once there, she ran her hand over the softness of the bedsheet, imagining Alexander lying there. Her fingers trembled as she lifted and pressed them to her cheek.

The princess had been explicit with so many instructions, and the most terrifying one was that Kitty would have to take command in a matter she had never experienced before. She would have to present her naked form without blushes or anxiety, rouse his body with touches, entice his mind with artful flirtation.

The bath was prepared, and with the aid of a maid, Kitty was soon freshly scrubbed, her hair brushed in tumbling waves to her mid-back. The maid made no comment as she helped her slip on the sheer peach silk banyan, which clung to her curves shamefully.

"You look right beautiful, miss!" the maid exclaimed, her eyes dancing.

Kitty sensed belowstairs would soon get an earful on her fast and scandalous attire and intentions.

The maid slipped away, and Kitty sauntered over to the cheval mirror in the duke's dressing room. She stared at her reflection and the provocative picture she presented. Glancing away, she went back into the bedroom and made her way to the bed, where she sat on the edge.

The anticipation was almost unbearable, and so was the anxiety churning low in her stomach. Her curiosity, trepidation, desire to hold him in her arms were aroused to a staggering degree.

Will you allow me to kiss and hold you, Alexander? Or will you push me away once again?

• • •

Alexander wheeled his bath chair from the breakfast parlor into the main hallway and was startled to almost crash into his flushed manservant. He frowned, noting the glitter in the man's eyes, the choppy breathing, and a general sense of excitability.

"Are you fevered?"

Oddly, the man smiled. "No, Your Grace. I am quite well, quite well indeed."

Alexander considered him for a few seconds, absently noting the housekeeper was humming a tune happily beneath her breath as she walked toward the servants' staircase, searching through a heavy jangle of keys. He could only assume his manservant told everyone he was headed to London and that he had sent word to have the town house made ready for his occupancy. The first such orders in almost seven years.

When he had visited a few weeks ago to claim his Katherine, he had stayed at his good friend George's home. Opening the town house would send waves of shock and intense speculation through the busybodies of society. It had certainly invigorated his staff, who had been overly morose since Katherine's departure.

"Are all the arrangements made for travel?"

"Yes, Your Grace. The carriage is ready to depart. And all the luggage has been added to the second coach. Notice has also been sent to Lady Penny and Mr. Collins of your imminent arrival."

"Good." He made to wheel around him, and the man stepped into his path. Alexander sent him an inquiring glance.

"Ah…Your Grace. A message arrived earlier from Miss Danvers."

The earth fell from beneath his feet, and he held the handle of his wheelchair in a white-knuckle grip. They'd had no correspondence in almost two weeks, and he resented the way his heart jerked with uncertainty and desperate hope. "Where is it?"

"I've had it delivered to your room."

Alexander glanced up the winding staircase, which led to the west wing of the castle, before leveling his gaze on his manservant. "Why?"

The man looked bemused for a few minutes, then

replied, "Miss Danvers had insisted her message be viewed alone. I assumed you would want to…read it in the privacy of your chamber and not in any of the lower rooms where a servant might barge in at an inopportune moment. Forgive me if I overstepped, Your Grace."

He made to order Hoyt to retrieve her note but hesitated, glancing abovestairs once more. What could the content be if she wanted him to read it in privacy? "Assist me to my apartments."

Relief lit in the man's eyes, and he moved with swift efficiency to obey Alexander's command. Several moments later, he wheeled himself down the hall and to his room. Hoyt hovered behind him, his air of anxiety baffling.

"Your Grace, I…"

"Yes?"

Instead of replying, his manservant bowed, turned, and walked away. The man was behaving oddly even by Alexander's standards. He opened the door, wheeled into his room, and closed the door with a *snick* behind him.

A ripple of awareness danced over his skin as he inhaled the subtle scent of lavender…and then the woman herself. He scanned the room, searching for the impossibility of Katherine being here in his chamber.

She lay prone across his bed, on her stomach, her chin propped up by her hands. Dark, mysterious eyes stared at him. The emotions raging within him were too complex and fierce to be understood and shaped into any semblance of coherence or rationality. She shifted on the bed, the movement so slow and sinuous. Alexander wanted to speak, but his tongue felt stuck, his throat tight, and his heart jerked in a furious beat.

He felt off-balance, as if he were dreaming.

He wheeled toward the chaise longue closest to the bed and gripped the cane resting atop the surface. Her gaze felt like fire on his skin, and he ruthlessly bit back the questions pummeling at him. What was she doing? It seemed obvious yet also hidden.

Alexander gripped the cane and slowly pushed to his feet. The effort was not easy, and he moved with care to lower himself onto the chaise. Finally he dredged up the nerve to ask, "Are you truly here, my Katherine?"

She made no reply but stared at him with large eyes that held remnants of pain and unfathomable emotions. He needed to find the courage to inform her that her efforts would be wasted. This was a seduction; it was as clear as the bright stream of sunlight caressing her hair and body, bathing her in an entrancing glow of warmth. Then he would have to inform her that even though she braved coming to his castle, she might never leave it again, even when her every expectation would soon be at her feet in tattered remnants.

"I was an idiot, Katherine," he murmured, regret slicing deep in his heart and staying there.

Her lashes swooped down, hiding the beauty of her eyes from him, before she met his regard once more, her expression carefully contained. And they stared at each other for several moments. The memories seeped between them like an invisible thread of connection, tugging from her heart to his.

"I hurt you with my fears and cruel words," he continued, "and I will regret it always. I beg of you to forgive me."

A slow blink, and her throat worked on a visible swallow, yet she remained silent.

"Before I knew you, I was captivated by you. Your adventurous and improper spirit bewitched me, and I had...*had* to know you. Since then, every moment with you has been a dream I despair of waking from."

He stared at her for several seconds before adding gruffly, "I had been looking at you...me...*us* through the lens of the impossibility, when I should have looked at what was possible. I see laughter, us lying on the floor in the library having discourses covering the trivialities of the *ton* to my motions for parliament. I see us climbing trees when I am able, making angels in grass and in snow, traveling together. I see you in my arms in the night when I sleep; I envision kissing you endlessly. I see us sharing dreams and hopes and uncertainties and always finding comfort in each other. Those fall in the possibilities of us. But I am also damn afraid. So afraid, my Katherine, because there are so many things I'll never be able to offer you, and there is nothing I want more than to always see joy in your eyes and a smile on your mouth. I want you happy... always."

Her lips parted on a silent sigh, but several beats passed while she made no answer, and for the first time in years, he resented the silence, hated it, even. Her sweet voice and atrocious singing had haunted his dreams, pitching him between loss and despair, love and hope, and more than anything, he wanted to hear her speak.

The ormolu clock on the mantel ticked away several more tense minutes, yet she did not speak. He was desperate to hear her voice, when he did not merit it.

"I am afraid one day I'll look in your eyes and see despair. See sadness because I cannot give you more. Lovemaking…children. There will always be those missing elements, and I could not bear to see such unhappiness on your face. I am not a man to give in to fear. But my heart trembles with it when I think of losing you forever…when I think there may be a day that I open my arms and you do not walk into them. I have never in my life wanted anything more than I want you for my own—to love, to cherish, and to protect. Forgive me for being a damn fool, my Katherine."

The corner of her mouth curved upward in an oddly seductive and secretive smile.

With a supple elegance, she slid from the bed and stood. A silk banyan clung to her alluring curves, and he could see the shadowed valley of her breasts and belly, where the front of the silk was slightly parted. Her beautiful hair tumbled over her shoulders in a riot of becoming waves and curls. Sensuality breathed life into every line of her body. Unexpectedly, he also saw shyness—sweet, wonderful shyness. Her pulse visibly pounded in the hollow of her throat and the delicate line of her collarbone.

"I fell in love with you in that cabin, Alexander."

The words came spearing through his consciousness, breaking the silence, suppressing the hollow emptiness that had started to beat inside his heart. The cane dropped from his hand, and he leaned forward. She sauntered closer until she was only a few feet from him. The nearness of her gave him great comfort. It took some effort, but he stood, ignoring the pain in his lower back.

She placed her open palm flat on his chest and tilted her lovely face up to his. "I fell in love with you, Alexander, and each day away from you was a torture. And then despite everything, I continued falling for you."

A hot ache grew in his throat. Reaching out, he gripped her shoulder gently and tugged her in even closer. His arms closed tightly around her. "I love you," he said hoarsely. "So damn much."

He slowly became aware that his heart was pounding beneath the palm she had placed on his chest.

"I'll never doubt it again," she whispered into his chest; then she tipped and brushed a soft kiss against his chin.

"Marry me," he groaned. "Be my friend…be my wife…my duchess. I promise to love you with every breath in my body and every emotion in my heart until the end of my days, Katherine. I vow it."

She stepped back and stared at him with eyes swirling with emotion. "You want to marry me even though you believe we might never make love or have children?"

"Yes." And he braced himself against the pain the admission elicited.

Yet she smiled—and it was glorious.

She leaned in, and her kiss touched his lips like a whisper, one he greedily drank in the sweetness of. "I love you, Alexander, and it would be my honor to be your friend, your wife, your duchess...and your lover."

Katherine stepped back and shrugged from the sheer peignoir as if such actions were everyday occurrences. The splendor of her naked form exercised a powerful effect upon him. Maybe too powerful, for Alexander was certain he'd forgotten how to breathe. "Miss Danvers," he started. "I—"

"Ah, I've rattled you."

He stumbled, dropping back onto the chaise longue, and stared up at her in aroused shock.

"Miss Danvers... Katherine... I... I..." Sweet Christ, he had no notion of what he wanted to say.

She dropped to her knees before him, and Alexander gripped the cushioned edges of the chaise. An ache pounded through his cock, and though there was a hot, urgent ache in his belly, his length had not hardened.

"Are you in pain, my love?"

"No."

"Do not move. I will be in control...and you'll follow my lead," she said with a saucy wink.

She tugged off his boots, one after the other. Then she leaned up and loosened his cravat and pulled it off. His Katherine slowly undid his jacket, waistcoat, and shirt. When it came to his trousers, she merely opened his flap, darted her delicate hand inside, and withdrew his cock.

Alexander almost expired.

The feel of her hands on his flesh had him

gripping the cushions even harder.

Her color heightened considerably. "I've learned this is your manroot...your manhood...your cock."

"Christ," he muttered hoarsely, shocked and intrigued at her carnal knowledge.

"I've learned I can...kiss you here...and the pleasure for you would be immense...as it would be for me to know I have roused you so. Do you have knowledge of this?"

Unable to speak, he nodded, and she smiled. The sexual energy she exuded was palpable; the dance of her fingers over his cock provoked a response in him that was downright atrocious and beguiling. Alexander's mouth went dry, his gut tightened, and pleasure speared down his cock in a wickedly painful rush, hardening his length in her hand.

"You respond to me," she murmured, sounding awed.

"Always, my Katherine, always."

She rose and came over to him, bracketing her thighs on each side of his, her straddled position opening her quim directly over his throbbing cock. He released the cushions and grasped her hips, his breathing harsh and ragged.

She gripped his shoulders. "I was obliged to face the necessity of learning about making love from a courtesan," she murmured, kissing his lips softly. "It has taken so much courage to stand before you naked."

"You are beautiful," he assured her gruffly. "So brave and lovely, my darling."

"You were making love with me in the conservatory...until you got hurt. I daresay we will be able to make love again…maybe not as often, but we can have normalcy." She stared into his eyes. "Will you try with me?"

"Yes."

Her lips trembled on her smile, and her eyes glistened. "And if we fail this time?"

"We'll try again…"

Her satisfaction was expressed in the moan that whispered over his cheek. Her face flushed a delicate, rosy hue and became a study in sweet carnal pleasure. Her forehead dropped to his, and they stayed like that for several moments. And it was telling for Alexander that his cock had not softened—in fact, the damn thing strained toward her like it had a mind of its own, and the ache in his belly had become a fiery throb of raw need.

He couldn't speak, for every one of his senses was focused on the woman in his arms, desperate to give her everything she hoped for.

Spearing his hands through her thick mass of hair, he tugged her head up and then down to meet his kiss.

CHAPTER TWENTY-FOUR

A fire of need and desire swirled through Katherine's veins. All her senses centered around the featherlight pressure of his mouth. It was as if he savored her, slowly and sweetly. Her throat ached, and her heart swelled with happiness that rivaled anything she'd ever felt before. His large hands cupped her cheeks, his touch almost unbearable in its tenderness.

"I love you, my Katherine," he murmured against her mouth as his covered hers hungrily. Alexander ravished her lips with unchecked sensuality, and she responded, wantonly, eagerly, with soft moans of desire spilling from her lips to his. The hands that cupped her cheeks began to shake, and they broke apart, their foreheads pressed together.

She pushed her knees into the soft cushions bracketing his hips, and she twined her hands around his neck. His hardness nudged her at the swollen mound of her sex, and she trembled at the sensations that shot through her belly. Kitty raised trembling fingers to touch his mouth. "It physically hurts, the way I crave you."

He brushed the lightest of kisses across her mouth. "I want to be gentle with you," he whispered gravely. His face was drawn into hard lines of hunger and hope—stark and agonizing. "I want to bring you pleasure."

She felt the trembling in his arms, the pounding of his heart against her chest, sensed the hope in his soul that they could consummate their union. "And I you," she whispered, achingly pressing a kiss to his scarred jawline. "Let me love you, my darling."

"We can wait," he said, tightening his hand in her hair. "Until our wedding night…we can wait."

"No."

He brushed a gentle kiss against her forehead. "Katherine, my darling—"

She captured his words with her mouth, enticing him with deep, carnal kisses that went on endlessly. With a ragged moan, he surrendered to the wild passion beating between them. He trailed his fingers down her jaw, over to her collarbone, down to the underside of her breast. His palms cupped her breasts, his fingers tweaking at her nipples, plumping them. A jolt of exquisite pleasure lanced through Kitty, and she gasped. Alexander released her mouth to press kisses against her shoulder, her chin, down to the sensitive hollow of her throat.

Then he leaned in and sucked a pebbled nipple into his mouth. His lips closed over her sensitive nipple, his teeth rasping, tongue licking. She caught her breath and then couldn't exhale, so exquisite was the sensation that pierced her most intimate part. "Alexander," she moaned raggedly, aware of sweat slicking her skin.

Desire burned away all uncertainty and filled her with a ravaging hunger that desperately needed to be assuaged. She was terrified of what to expect and yet remarkably breathless. One of his hands slid around to her back and down to her backside, which he gripped tightly in his large hands…and squeezed. The other hand slipped between them, and she dazedly felt his fingers stroke along her inner thighs to the wet, aching center of her.

His thumb dragged against the inside of her thighs, creating little sparks of sensations that shot directly to the throbbing flesh between her legs. He dragged his fingers back down and then up again, never touching that empty place where she desperately needed him. All of Kitty's awareness focused on the delicate, excruciatingly light stroking, as his fingers drawing along the sensitive flesh of her inner thighs had the sweetest pressure building between her legs.

Finally, he was there, and a moan of need poured from her.

With a soft glide of his fingertip, he stroked over her wet folds with delicacy. She jolted at the wicked contact, and his fingers slipped over her aching nub with even more firmness, and then he pinched down.

"Alexander!"

"Kitty," he murmured tenderly, pressing a kiss to her lips even as his diabolical fingers worked at her nub, rubbing and circling, his questing fingers driving her mad with want. She trembled with powerful quakes, and her breathing became fast and urgent. Then he slid two fingers deep inside her narrow slit. Her core flamed at the sensual pain, and despite the sharp bite of discomfort, sensations peaked in her belly, and on a wordless cry, she shattered as bliss seared her.

"Look at me," he said softly.

Their eyes met, and he reached between them and notched something hot and thick at her aching entrance. A dark flush accentuated the harsh sensuality of his face. "I'll not be able to move," he said hoarsely. "You'll have to ride me."

She placed her hands on his chest and slid them over the powerful muscles there, lingering with tenderness at the scarred side. "I know," she said breathlessly.

"There'll be some pain…but I promise there will also be pleasure. So much pleasure you will scream from the exquisite torment."

He gripped her hips and rocked her down onto his cock. Kitty's back arched, and a cry exploded from her as he sank past her resistance, burying his length to the hilt. Her muscles strained and quivered around him, struggling to accept the broad length suddenly filling her snug channel, her breaths puffing in sharp bursts.

She slipped her hands around his neck and held his gaze. There was an expression of awe and shock in the eyes that lowered to where they were connected so intimately.

"Katherine—" His throat worked on a swallow, and he abandoned speech to hug her tightly to him.

They stayed like that, kissing lightly, then deeply, until she jerked, wanting to sate the growing ache. Alexander groaned; his expression was a tight grimace of pleasure. He gripped her hips and slid her up and then down with excruciating slowness. Several times he repeated his sensual motions. She cried out at the overwhelming sensations.

He bit her bottom lip and then sucked at the erotic sting. Then he murmured, "Ride me, my Katherine. Slow and deep, or easy, or fast. However you want."

"Slow and deep," she whispered against his lips as she slid up and then down onto his throbbing length.

They groaned together at the incredible feeling. Then he pulled her into him and slanted his lips over hers in a deep, tender kiss. Without any urging from him, she rode him, rolling her hips in a rhythm that was instinctively sensual and decadent. Within a few strokes, she lost her slowness, and she rode her love with carnal greed. Alexander gripped her hips, encouraging her wicked motions with murmured praises against her lips, moans, and guttural groans.

Kitty sobbed his name, undulated her hips, whispers and hoarse cries ripping from her throat. The exquisite sensations built steadily, overwhelming her senses. Sweat slicked her body as his skin slid against hers, her fingers tangled in his hair, and her breath trembled from her lips to his as they moved together in the raw, beautiful, and primal rhythm.

A wave of breathtaking heat consumed Kitty, and she convulsed in his arms, screaming her pleasure into the crook of his neck.

He gripped her hips and rocked her onto his cock deep and hard. He kissed her fiercely, capturing her cries, and thrust her onto his thick length with deep, measured strokes. It was agony and ecstasy all rolled into one, and she didn't want it ever to end. The pressure built inside, and far too soon pleasure rolled over her in hot, devastating waves. With a harsh groan, he tumbled with her, emptying deep inside her still-shivering body.

The happiness felt like a burst of sunshine that would never leave. "That was incredible, Alexander," Kitty murmured with a wide smile.

He pressed a kiss to her temple before gently easing her from off his length, and she gasped at the tender ache, flushing. He reached for his discarded jacket, fished for a handkerchief, and cleaned her and himself. Alexander reached for her banyan, and she slipped it on. Then he tugged her onto his lap. They stayed like that, holding each other, for several moments. Her tremors subsided, and he tightened his arms around her, stroking her hair.

"Will you marry me tomorrow?"

She laughed lightly. "Is that even possible?"

He pushed some of her curls behind her ears. "I was coming to London for you, and I'd made arrangements for a special license. Unless you want a grand wedding?"

"I want you," she murmured, snuggling even closer to his chest.

She felt his smile against her hair.

"I wonder if you'll be able to lift me to the bed. I cannot allow Hoyt to see me in this ravished state," he muttered.

Kitty straightened. "Alexander?"

His eyes danced with wicked mirth.

"You wretched tease!" she cried, laughing. "How I love you."

"You have my heart, Katherine, always." The words were soft, spoken almost at a whisper.

And with that promise, she drifted to sleep in his arms with a smile on her lips and an unmatched happiness in her heart.

EPILOGUE

Eight months later…
The River Nile

The private yacht Kitty and Alexander traveled on rocked lazily on the River Nile. She smiled, shifting on the bed as her husband's lips kissed along her hips. She had the happiest news to share with him, but for now she hugged her secret close to her heart.

Kitty suspected she was with child, for all the signs her mother had told her about were present. Her breasts were tender to touch, her cravings for odd foods had increased, and this was the third time she had missed her monthly courses. Still, there would be no way for her to be certain until they returned to Scotland and had the doctors confirm it.

For the last four and a half months, they had been on a sea journey, taking them to several wonderful and exotic places. They'd first visited Paris, where Kitty had acquired a new wardrobe in the latest fashion modes and had toured the wonderful city with her love for three weeks. Then they had sailed on to Lisbon, then Venice. They had stayed another month in Istanbul, and now they would journey on the Nile without docking. After exploring the river, they would return to London, and it would be just in time for Kitty to help Penny and Judith select a new wardrobe for the upcoming season.

Kitty purred a contented sigh as her husband

kissed along her spine. He effectively distracted her from future thoughts with his suggestive touches and slow kisses over her hips, and back and then down again. Soon she was wet and aching, trembling with a fever of need.

"Alexander," she gasped when he bit into the soft globe of her buttocks.

Then his tongue traveled down to the shadowed valley of her thighs, where he nudged her legs wide and licked along her wet, aching sex. His touch disappeared briefly, then he gripped her hips and slipped a cushion beneath her. Her cheeks flamed as her legs were nudged even wider. The bed dipped, and her belly went hot with anticipation.

Kitty moaned with helpless delight as Alexander licked her folds, parting them, and then he covered her nub with his lips, sucking it delicately. The soft lash of his tongue as it circled her bundle of pleasure was too much and not enough. For blissful seconds, she lost all rational ability to think…to breathe. She could only cry out her pleasure for endless moments.

Since their marriage eight months before, he'd often loved and worshipped her body with his tongue and mouth, often reclining while she rode his tongue and then his body. It was naughty…decadent…and wicked sinfulness in one remarkable package.

Ripples of ecstasy danced over her skin, burning her from the outside in. Before she could speak, his warm, powerful body slid over hers and he blanketed her from behind. She turned her head on the silken sheets. "My darling," she gasped, recalling that yesterday they'd spent the day on the deck resting and reposing on padded reclined chairs because of the twinges of pain in his lower back. "Let me—"

"No, I'll be in control," he murmured before easing a hand between their bodies. "I hunger for you like this."

Suddenly his fingers caressed along her thighs, brushing and tugging at her folds and nub of pleasure. Then the hard, thick pressure of his cock pressed against her entrance. Her entire body quaked in response, and her hips arched into him almost involuntarily.

They usually came together with sweet, fiery passion at least once, sometimes twice per week, more frequently than she had anticipated. Kitty, however, always rode her love in exciting and inventive ways. There were nights and days where she peered into his eyes and took them on a slow, sweet glide, and there were days when, though she was on top of him, it was his hands that controlled her movements, slamming her onto his cock with ravaging bliss and directing the outcome of their pleasure.

It was beyond wonderful, and Kitty and the duke couldn't have been happier.

Still, there were a few rare times when Alexander took control, by placing her on her back and coming over her. Or sometimes shifting both on their sides with him curved into her to make love. Never had he taken her like this, where he placed Kitty on her stomach and his wonderful strength covered her from behind.

He kissed her shoulder before nipping along her neck gently. To feel the strength and mass of him behind her made her feel small and vulnerable yet sensual and empowered. She could feel the tremble of his breath, sense the beat of his heart against her back, see the corded muscle of the forearm by her head.

He wanted her, desperately.

"Take me, Alexander," she groaned against the lips that kissed along her mouth. The provocative urge was dragged from her heart, breathed into his mouth.

With his knee, he moved her thighs wider. With a steady push of his cock against her sex, he parted her. His hips flexed, and she couldn't prevent her sharp intake of breath at the thick fullness that invaded her slick channel until he was seated to the hilt inside her.

"Alexander!"

He pressed a soothing kiss along her nape. Kitty gloried in the burn, in the possession.

Then he started to stroke inside her. Pleasure and a bite of pain scorched along her nerve endings, and she gripped the sheets in a fist, whimpering at the overwhelming assault on her senses. He wrenched low moans from her with each excruciating inward plunge, and the heavy pressure blended with the sweetest pleasure, and exquisite tension twisted in her belly.

"Katherine."

Her name was a rough, sensual whisper in her ear.

"You are so hot and tight," he growled against her nape. "So wet for me, my Katherine. I need more of you."

"Yes," she gasped, arching her hips and gripping the sheets.

And her love increased his strokes with piercing depth and strength. Sharp fists of pleasure pounded at Kitty, consuming her. Sweat slicked their skin, and the rich scent of his masculinity engulfed her, spicy and evocative. Just when she thought she couldn't take any more, the tension broke, and she convulsed, screaming her delight. Seconds later, a guttural sound burst from his throat as he was spent inside her.

They stayed like that, their harsh breaths mingling together. His body lifted from hers, and then she felt the press of a cloth between her legs, cleaning her. Strong but gentle hands turned her over, and the most beautiful blue eyes ensnared hers.

He brushed a thumb across her bottom lip with such gentleness, her throat ached.

"Have I told you how much I love you, my duchess?" he murmured against her lips before pressing a tender kiss there.

"Every day, several times, and I love to hear you tell me, because I love you so very much," she said shakily, still unmoored from the bliss shivering through her body. He made her feel beautiful, desirable, treasured. He made her feel so much. "I believe I might be with child," she blurted, and held her breath.

For a timeless moment, he froze; then the tension eased from his muscles, and a harsh breath sawed from his throat.

Her whole being seemed to fill with waiting. He dropped his forehead to hers and closed his eyes; then the most beautiful smile curved his lips.

"How you complete me, Katherine. Thank you

for this future gift."

Happiness burst inside like sunshine. She slipped her hands around his neck and held him tight to her. "We'll know for certain when we return home," she whispered, tears smarting her eyes.

He kissed along her lashes. "Are they tears of joy, my love?" he murmured huskily.

"They are," she said with a soft laugh. "I love you so very much."

"I love you, my Katherine, now and always."

Then he kissed her and, to Katherine's shocked delight, proceeded to make love to her again.

ACKNOWLEDGMENTS

I thank God every day for loving me with such depth and breadth. Nothing can take his love from me. To my husband, Dusean, you are so damn wonderful. Your feedback and support are invaluable. I could not do this without you.

Thank you to my wonderful friend and critique partner Gina Fišerová. Without you I would be lost!

Thank you to Stacy Abrams for being an amazing, wonderful, and super stupendous editor.

To my wonderful readers, thank you for picking up my book and giving me a chance! Thank you. Special THANK YOU to everyone who leaves a review—bloggers, fans, friends. I have always said reviews to authors are like a pot of gold to leprechauns. Thank you all for adding to my rainbow one review at a time.

Turn the page to start reading

It'll take a
shrew to tame
this beast...

THE
BEAST
OF
BESWICK

"A smart, sexy, deliciously feminist romance
that I couldn't put down."
—NYT bestselling author Sarah MacLean

AMALIE HOWARD

CHAPTER ONE

England, 1819

Her pulse drumming at a fierce clip, Lady Astrid Everleigh burst through the front doors of her uncle's country estate in Southend. The flashy coach in the drive was as unmistakable as its owner—the arrogant and deeply persistent Earl of Beaumont. A sickening feeling leached into her as she scanned the foyer. No one would meet her eyes, not the butler, not the footmen, not even her uncle Reginald whose pallid cheekbones had gone an ugly shade of puce.

"You were s-supposed to be at the market," he sputtered in surprise.

"What have you done, Uncle?" she demanded, flinging off her cloak. "Did you arrange this without my knowledge or consent?"

Her uncle's color heightened. "Now, see here," he blustered, "it's demmed high time your sister marry, and you know it—"

Not to *him*. Never to him.

The pit of sickness in Astrid's stomach deepened at the thought of sweet, innocent Isobel in the clutches of such a man. The Earl of Beaumont was scraping the bottom of the barrel as far as Astrid was concerned, even if he was now a peer of the realm.

Throttling the ugly memories his name alone conjured, Astrid turned away from her uncle to her ashen lady's maid, who had appeared upon hearing her voice. "Where are they, Agatha?"

"In the morning salon, my lady. With the viscountess."

Astrid's heart plummeted at the sight of the closed doors. Aunt Mildred's chaperonage would be questionable to say the least. "How long have they been in there?"

"Not five minutes, my lady."

A blink of an eye and yet enough time for her sweet sister to be thoroughly compromised. Isobel was barely sixteen. She'd been an unexpected and much welcomed surprise to their parents, and Astrid had always been protective. To her, Isobel was still a child, no matter their uncle's declaration of her being ready to wed. She hadn't even had a proper Season yet, and already he wanted to marry her off to the highest bidder.

To a liar and a lecher, no less.

Edmund Cain had inherited the earldom from his uncle a handful of years ago. Though a title made him eligible to most, he was still the heartless brute who'd destroyed Astrid's reputation without a qualm during her first—and only—Season, when she'd had the *audacity* to turn down his suit. He'd retaliated with a horrible lie about her lack of virtue, and her entire future had crumbled.

When their parents were taken by illness a year later, she and Isobel had gone into the care of their only living relatives in England. After the year of mourning, Astrid had decided any money left to her would be better saved for Isobel's coming out. She was the daughter of a viscount, and when the time came, Isobel deserved her due.

But that was before her uncle had gotten his hands on their inheritance. Most of it was gone, except for specific, unreleased funds, which would come to them only upon marriage or the age of twenty-six. Astrid was one year away, and Isobel was a decade away, unless a marriage came first, which clearly was the goal here. But now, eight years after her parents' deaths, the girls were nearly destitute, or so her uncle claimed.

Destitute enough to seek a connection with an utterly unsuitable earl? If money was in question, it was a certainty. Uncle Reginald would sell his own soul if he could get a farthing for it.

"Lord Beaumont is a peer now," her uncle said, drawing her attention. "He's not the man you knew."

"A leopard cannot change its spots."

"Now see here, Astrid," he said, blocking her path. "It is done. Lord Beaumont has pledged—"

"You will stay a far step from me, Uncle. And I don't care what that man has promised; he will never—" Astrid broke off, the threat as empty as the power she held...which was none.

Without a husband of her own, the truth was that as their guardian, if her uncle wished to marry Isobel off to a pox-marked pauper, he could, and there would be nothing either of them could do about it. Such was the place of a woman in their world.

Astrid switched tactics, turning toward him, her voice softening. "Uncle Reggie, be reasonable. Isobel hasn't even had a Season yet. Perhaps she can make an even better match, one with greater reward." She let the suggestion hang in the air, knowing the promise of coin would make her uncle salivate.

The viscount thinned his lips. "Better an egg today than a hen tomorrow."

"Spoken by the rooster who has nothing to lose," Astrid said under her breath, though her stomach churned. Had he already made a settlement with Beaumont?

Reasonable discussion was clearly getting her nowhere.

Shooting a look of pure loathing at her uncle, she darted around him to the salon doors and shoved them open, searching for her sister.

Isobel's face was pinched and her spine rigid. With fear or shock, Astrid did not know. Thankfully, her sister sat on the sofa, hands clasped in her lap while Beaumont stood a short distance away. Not far enough away in Astrid's opinion. No one else was in the room. Gracious, where on earth was her aunt?

"I thought I told you I wished to be alone, Everleigh," Beaumont said over his shoulder, annoyance flashing in his eyes for a second before he realized that it wasn't her uncle who had barged in. "Ah, it's the spinster. Have you come to congratulate us?" he drawled, satisfaction creeping over his deceptively handsome features. "I assume you've heard that I intend to court your sister."

She let out a breath, but before she could form a reply, her aunt emerged from the far end of the room, her face pulling tight with vexation. Astrid frowned. Good Lord but Aunt Mildred's designs were transparent. Even though they weren't in London, her aunt well knew the rules of the aristocracy...especially with respect to chaperoning unmarried young ladies.

Astrid swallowed the spurt of anger when she thought of how easily Isobel could have been compromised. Her eyes narrowed with sudden understanding.

Is that what my fortune-hunting relatives intended?

Astrid's frustration pricked as her eyes touched on the smug face of the Earl of Beaumont. She bit her lip, fingers clenching at her sides, her stomach threatening to upend itself. If she hadn't forgotten her market day list, she would never have returned in time…and who knew what else might have happened. Right now, however, Isobel was safe and that was all that mattered. She *was* safe, right? Swallowing a rise of dread, her gaze shifted to her sister.

"Isobel, are you well?" she asked.

Her sister nodded, though her rosy skin was ashen. "Yes, but I do feel a bit of a megrim coming on."

"Perhaps you should rest."

With a grateful look, Isobel nodded and stood, bobbing a hasty curtsy in the earl's direction, and fled the room with Aunt Mildred on her heels.

Beaumont gave a careless wave as she left. "I'll be seeing you soon, dearest."

"You will not," Astrid said.

His stare raked her from head to toe, making her feel as if she were wearing far less than the sturdy gray woolen dress with matching pelisse, buttoned up to her neck. "Tell me, Lady Astrid, what can *you* do to stop me?"

"She's sixteen," she said.

He nodded. "Indeed. Marriageable age."

Astrid swallowed the rise of anger. The same age *she'd* been when he had first set eyes on her in London. His interest, intent, and timing were no mistake. The newly minted earl was back to settle a score.

"Isobel is to have a Season in London," Astrid said.

"Not if your uncle accepts an offer beforehand. She will make a lovely countess, don't you think?"

Astrid scowled, her heart thudding. "Why are you so fixated on her for a wife? She's not part of your set."

"Perhaps because I was denied nine years ago."

And there it was as plain as day—the heart of the matter—the *score*.

A calculated stare met hers as Beaumont approached where she stood, her posture rigid with a sick combination of fear and fury. His victorious smile made Astrid's blood run cold. He'd already wrecked her future. She could not...*would not* let him threaten her sister's.

"No, I won't allow it," she said. "I am her guardian."

"Ah, but Viscount Everleigh is *your* guardian, is he not? And *his* approval has already been granted, or at least it will be once we come to terms. You, my dear, have no say in the matter, and as much as you think you can sway me, you will find that what you desire is of no import. You had your chance, as they say." His grin was slow and mocking. "I told you that you would regret it."

Stifling the retort that she absolutely did *not* regret refusing him, Astrid sucked in a calming breath. "Isobel is barely out of the schoolroom. You are four and thirty, Edmund. Surely you can find a more appropriate wife closer to your own age."

His eyes narrowed at her use of his given name. "It's Lord Beaumont now. Are you proposing yourself as a substitute? Though, for a woman in your situation, marriage would be out of the question now, of course." He canvassed her figure with a lewd glance that made her want to cover herself with a blanket. "However, I could be moved to reconsider with the right incentive."

"I'd rather be mauled by rabid dogs."

"Ah yes, there's that barbed tongue of yours," the earl replied. "You're like a fine-aged whiskey with a bite that has only sharpened with time. Lady Isobel seems much more well-behaved, though it will be my greatest pleasure once we're wedded to discover if she has a stubborn streak like you."

Astrid stiffened. "You will marry my sister when hell freezes over, *Lord Beaumont*. Count on that." With as much effort as she could muster, she tamped down her mounting temper and swept from the room.

Shaking with outrage, Astrid attempted to compose herself in the corridor. Regardless of Beaumont's looks, title, or fortune, she would not wish such a heartless man on her worst enemy, much less her sweet, innocent sister. Given a proper Season, a jewel like Isobel would have her choice of husbands.

Her uncle knew it, and Beaumont knew it, too.

Once the earl had taken his leave, she sought out her uncle, who had retreated to his study, giving her tongue free rein. "How could you? She's only sixteen, for God's sake." She turned to her aunt standing quietly near the desk. "Aunt Mildred, have you nothing to say? What about Isobel's feelings on the matter?"

Her aunt's mouth thinned. "Her future husband will tell her what to think."

"Said no woman with half a spine ever."

"Would you rather her end up like you, then?" her uncle said. "Unmarried, ruined, and a bloody burden to your aunt and me?"

She sucked in a gasp. Her father, the previous viscount, had made sure that his daughters would live comfortably, with the hope that his brother would do his duty by his nieces. Her sister and she had learned early on that that would not be the case. Their father's old family solicitor, Mr. Jenkins, who checked in on them once a year, had advocated for their father's wishes, including a Season for Isobel once she came of age, but Mr. Jenkins had passed away a year ago. His firm oversaw the estate, but there was no one left to keep the greedy Everleighs in line.

"Papa made sure we would not be," Astrid said, striving for patience. "We did not come to you cap in hand."

"That blunt is gone."

Riled beyond belief, she threw caution to the wind. "Where, Uncle? Where did all of it go? Papa bequeathed us a fortune by any standards."

His nostrils flared, eyes bulging as he rose behind his desk. "How *dare* you, you insolent chit! After your aunt and I took you in, this is how you repay us? With mistrust and suspicion? That demmed money went to gowns, shoes, food, and finishing school." He snorted. "To those books of yours. Your sister's dancing and pianoforte instructors. Do you think it's inexpensive to raise two demanding chits? And what about your horses?"

The horses he spoke of were *his* thoroughbreds bought with his dead brother's money, but Astrid didn't point that out. She glued her lips together, stifling her anger. If Uncle Reginald decided to throw her out on her ear, she would be destitute and homeless. She would not come into her own portion until she was six and twenty, months away, and until then, she had to guard her tongue. Without her, Isobel would be on her own and vulnerable.

"And what about *you*?" he went on, eyeballing her. "You were supposed to make an advantageous marriage. Instead, you've brought ruin upon the Everleigh name." He sneered at her, his eyes cold. "What? You thought your sins would not leach to your poor sister?"

A sound of pain escaped Astrid's lips. Her *sins*. She'd done nothing wrong, and yet she had been the one punished. Excoriated and summarily dropped by the *ton* upon the faithless account of a scorned liar.

"You know what he did," Astrid whispered, hand clutched to her chest and eyes burning with unshed tears. "What he did to *me*, and yet you still welcome his presence. How could you be so cruel?"

Her craven uncle would not meet her eyes. "He is an earl. And perhaps he wants to make it right."

Her uncle was wrong. Beaumont didn't want to *make it right*. He wanted to make Astrid pay.

"Please, Uncle Reggie," she tried, resorting to begging. "Even if that is so, surely you see how poor of a match it is. Beaumont is twice her age. He isn't fit for someone as tender as Isobel. Can't you see that?"

Uncle Reginald's mouth thinned as he stood and indicated the opened study door. "Nonetheless, he is an earl. A rich earl. And you're forgetting that reformed rakes make the best husbands. He intends to join our estates and revive them. Isobel will be a countess and want for nothing. Now begone and leave me be."

What he really meant was that he and Aunt Mildred would want for nothing. Astrid's heart sank as she obeyed the rough dismissal.

Upstairs, she found her sister in the bedroom they shared. Isobel's eyes were red-rimmed as though she'd been weeping, and Astrid went to her immediately.

"What will we do? I don't wish to marry him." Isobel sniffled. "But Aunt Mildred says I must do my duty to our family."

Astrid took her sister's hands into her own. "You won't have to, I promise."

"But how?" Her pale eyes watered. "He's an earl. And since Uncle approves the match, I have no choice."

"Don't worry, Izzy—fortune favors those best prepared." She hugged her sister tight, her resolve hardening. "I will find a way to see us out of this."

Their options were limited. It was clear what her uncle intended—to sell Isobel's virtue to someone willing to pay for the privilege, in this case, Lord

Beaumont. It was unconscionable and it sickened her, but there wasn't a thing she could do about it. Not without help.

Astrid blew out a frustrated breath.

If only her father were still alive or she had a husband of her own…

She blinked, an outrageous idea blossoming.

It would solve everything. It was a dreadful, desperate plan, but it was something. It was a *chance*.

At five and twenty, she was well on the shelf, but she wasn't dead. She might be ruined in the eyes of the *ton*, but she had a sound brain, she'd been raised to run an aristocratic household, and she was the daughter of a viscount. It could work. *It could work.*

She would just have to marry a different kind of beast than the earl to save her sister.

And she knew just the man.

THE
BEAST
OF
BESWICK

Available now wherever books are sold!

A humorous, sexy Victorian romance by Golden
Heart finalist and Maggie Award winner
Kimberly Bell

A Scandal
by Any Other Name

A TALE OF TWO SISTERS

Julia Bishop has led a very sheltered life. Protected by her family from those who might ridicule her for her secrets, she stays hidden away in the country. But she longs for more, if only for an evening. To kiss a rake in full view of the stable boy. Unchaperoned picnics. Romance. But she knows she'll never experience any of those things.

That is, until a handsome duke with a mysterious past of his own arrives...

Duke Jasper DeVere left London to grieve his grandfather's death privately, away from the prying eyes and gossips of the ton. Seeking solitude at a friend's country manor, he's surprised he finds himself drawn to the company of the shy beauty determined to present the epitome of proper behavior.

That is, until the mysterious woman makes an indecent proposal...

Julia can't believe what she's suggested to the duke. Nor that he agrees a distraction is what they both need. But what will happen when Jasper must return to his duties and leave Julia behind? Will the memories of their time together be enough for a lifetime of solitude for either of them?

Because Julia can never leave her country haven and a duke can never stay...

AMARA
an imprint of Entangled Publishing LLC